EVERY FALL

ANGELA DOUGLAS

Text copyright © 2024 by **Angela Douglas**
Cover Illustration © **Nat Mack**
Distributed by **Simon & Schuster**

Line Edit by Tina Beier
Copy Edit by Dylan Garity
Proofread by Sally O'Keef.

ISBN: 978-1-998076-81-9
Ebook: 978-1-998076-82-6

FIC031010 FICTION / Thrillers / Crime
FIC031100 FICTION / Thrillers / Domestic
FIC031000 FICTION / Thrillers / General

#EveryFall

Follow Rising Action on our socials!
Twitter: @RAPubCollective
Instagram: @risingactionpublishingco
Tiktok: @risingactionpublishingco

Our greatest glory is not in never falling, but in rising every time we fall.

—Confucius

For my husband and kids. Without you, there would be no stories.

This book is also written for first responders like my husband who run towards danger, no matter the personal costs, and their families who also carry it. You are all heroes.

EVERY FALL

FILE# 34-2120

My loves,

I never thought it was possible to love anyone this much until I had you. Loving a child is both beautiful and terrifying. The responsibility of protecting you and your lives is too great, and I have already committed the ultimate failure.

I am so sorry it has come to this. I have no other choice. I can no longer survive this way. Your father has hurt us and is leaving us for that trollop he has been running around with.

I have no money or means to provide a life for us outside of these walls, so my story ends here. I can't go on with you, and I can't go on without you. I was so blessed with you both. Your existence in my meagre life has meant everything to me, and I will take that into eternity. Please forgive me, and

1

maybe I will get to hold you on the other side.

Be brave; you won't feel pain for too long.

Always, Mother

PS - And to my dreadful husband, I hope she is worth it.

1

BREE

MAY 12, 2012

I didn't mean to start a family while living in this cesspool, but that was what happened. The neighbourhood jogging track was the safest place in all East Bernheim, affectionately known to locals as Burner. Despite the seedy deals happening down the road and the sex workers waiting on the adjacent corners, this little park was almost as clean and safe as any middle-class neighbourhood, thanks to its security patrol.

It was sunny and unseasonably warm outside, so this was our second walk of the day. As I waited in line at a café, Riley dozed in his stroller, and my pug, Lottie, waited patiently by my side. The barista at the Bad Habits Café did a double take when he placed my order for my second latte of the day. When I was pregnant with Riley, I didn't miss deli meats or sushi. I didn't even miss my old friend, vodka—but boy, did I miss coffee.

I glanced outside and spotted Crystal standing on a nearby corner. "Can I get a large black coffee, too?" I asked. I cared about Crystal. She was in her early thirties like me, though she looked much older. We'd become friendly over the last few years. She was always excited to see Lottie and me.

I left the café with both coffees, and she smiled when she saw me coming.

She bent toward Lottie. "Can I pet her?"

I wasn't sure if she'd forgotten who I was or was just polite enough to ask every time. "Of course." I handed her the black coffee. "How are you doing?"

"Great." She rolled her eyes and let out a hoarse cackle. "How's my lipstick?"

"It's perfect."

She used to approach me with pink wax from lip to chin, and I never knew what to say, so I bought her a compact mirror. Her lipstick *was* perfect today.

Riley had started to wake from his nap. I pointed to him and said, "Better go."

"No worries, doll. Thanks for the coffee." She waved as we strode off.

I used to love living here when I was single—and before I married a cop. It was better to be oblivious to the crime around me than know every little thing that went on. Jake didn't like me walking around here, but I couldn't stay trapped in our six-hundred-square-foot condo all day.

After four laps of the park, black clouds started to roll in. I downed my latte and headed toward the supermarket. Lottie had given up two laps ago and was panting in the bottom compartment of the stroller.

"A quick stop, guys. Just one." I wanted to surprise Jake with a home-cooked dinner—no frozen Hungry Man meals tonight.

I hadn't cooked a proper meal since before I had Riley, nine months ago. This would be a treat for him after a long day at work.

I was a few feet away from the store's entrance when the energy was sucked from the air around me. Some people walked faster or even ran;

others moved more slowly. I didn't know what was happening until I followed the terrified gaze of a teenage boy, standing petrified beside me. A sweaty middle-aged man ran out of the store with a bottle of pills in his hand and no shirt on, a clerk hot on his heels.

"Stop him! He just stole from us!" the clerk shouted, pointing after him. A man in his mid-thirties obliged, stepping up beside me, right in front of the thief, attempting to block his escape.

The distraught man panicked, raising an X-ACTO knife and driving it straight into his own neck, which sent the other man and the teenager running. He pulled it down inside his flesh without flinching. Blood spurted from his neck like water from a timed sprinkler. The ground, my stroller, and my shoes were covered in splatter. It was only seconds before the thief took off—with the box cutter still in his neck.

I stood there frozen, my mouth open, until Riley's screaming brought me back to the moment. I peeked under the soiled stroller hood to ensure he wasn't soaked. Aside from a few drops on the leg of his favourite sleeper, he was clean. My shock and horror quickly turned into disgust and rage, and I stepped a few feet away from the store entrance.

"Has anyone phoned 911 yet?" I pulled Riley out of the stroller, perched him on my hip, and dug around in the diaper bag for my phone. Lottie peeked out from the bottom compartment, unscathed.

"Yes," said a forty-something woman in a business suit who was pacing nearby. "The police are on their way."

I could already hear the sirens. It was one benefit of living in a bad neighbourhood: the police were never far away.

I finally located my phone and texted Jake, knowing he wouldn't answer a phone call while working. My hand shook so hard I could barely type one out.

Some lunatic stabbed himself at the grocery store right in front of me! Are you coming to this one?

2

JAKE

As a beat cop in the worst city in our province, I had already attended several priority-one files that day. I'd just pulled an unconscious five-year-old out of a backyard kiddie pool. His parents were so strung out on crack they hadn't even noticed the kid was missing, until the neighbour called it in. I'd responded to another call where a professional young woman around my wife's age was raped in broad daylight by a cab driver high on amphetamines. This was all before lunch.

I was in my car when the radio crackled with a request to attend a non-priority file. A few other members were already on scene, but there were a lot of witnesses who needed processing. I let dispatch know I'd be there, then turned on my personal phone, which I had turned off at the last scene. I tried to keep my personal life separate from work for my sanity. That last file had been so gutting I couldn't bear to hear about my baby boy while I was telling someone else theirs had just drowned.

The harder files were easier to stomach before I got married and had Riley. Now, I saw my family in these situations; I had so much more to lose. I tried to check in with Bree as often as possible on shift. I knew it was hard for her to hear sirens all day and wonder if I was okay.

I glanced at my phone and saw her text. I sent a quick reply—*On my way*—and sped over.

I didn't want to live in Burner, nor did Bree, but we were stuck here and doing what we could to make the best of it. She had bought her condo before we'd met at the height of the market. Great investment, blah blah. After years of being single, she had no idea that less than a year later, she'd be married with a child.

As I pulled up to the grocery store, I spotted several colleagues interviewing witnesses.

"Bree!" I shouted across the parking lot.

My wife was beautiful, with her huge blue eyes and light-brown hair that had been prematurely streaked with grey since she was twenty. She always smiled, even during a difficult pregnancy and a bad case of the baby blues.

But she wasn't smiling today. Deep, dark circles of exhaustion and mascara surrounded her eyes. She had aged a decade since I'd left the house that morning.

She moved my way, with Riley in her arms.

"Are you okay?" I gave her a quick side hug while checking to make sure no one was watching. We weren't really supposed to hug anyone in public, wife or not, while wearing the uniform and carrying a gun.

"I'm okay," she said, and then teared up.

I wanted more than anything not to be wearing this stupid uniform today. We walked back toward the stroller, which I could now see was speckled with blood. It was drizzling, and the blood ran off her shoes and the stroller, swirling into the puddle we stood in. Riley had calmed down, and Lottie lay still in the bottom of the stroller.

"I gave my statement already, so I can go," Bree said. "But I don't really know what to do about the stroller. And this." Her lip trembled again when she pointed to the bloodstain on my son's favourite fuzzy sleeper.

"I'll take care of it. I hate that this happened to you."

"Me too." She sniffed.

As I wrapped my arms around her, my eyes wandered the scene. A Caucasian male, age unclear from this distance, stood on the nearest street corner looking my way. He wore a ball cap, a red T-shirt, and the kind of jeans that were so dark you could see the bright-white stitching for miles. He looked familiar—maybe I'd arrested him before? *Who haven't I hooked up on this block?*

He smirked, then walked away.

I wanted to stay and comfort Bree, but I wasn't sure how. Seeing her eyes well up at the sight of blood on our baby boy was almost enough to crack my shell. I always worked hard to tamp down my emotions so I could function while on duty, but ever since Riley had arrived, I'd gotten softer. Victim services was already on-site, so I called one of them over. They mostly supported domestic disturbance cases, but in this situation, several of the witnesses were rattled.

"Bree, I want you to talk to"—I glanced at her name tag—"Sarah from victim services. She'll take care of you," I said in my work tone.

Bree looked at me like I was a robot. "Where are you going?"

"I'll be right back!" I shouted on my way to the cruiser.

On my two-minute drive to the detachment, my radio went off again. "White male, fifty to sixty years old, approximately six feet tall, 280 pounds, found in bushes off Route 109. Doesn't appear to be breathing. There's a weapon lodged in his jugular. An ambulance is on the way. Need a car."

Oh good, they found him. Someone else can handle it.

I was often the first on scene, but I wasn't responding to this one. Bree needed me. When I arrived at the detachment, I went straight to the control room to find the commanding officer. He wasn't my direct supervisor, but he was the only one in. I barged through the open door to his office, and he looked up from his paperwork, flinching when he noticed me.

"Hey Sarge, I have to go. My wife was hit with waste at the grocery store stabbing, and she's pretty shook up. I need to drive her and the baby home and dispose of the soiled material." Normally it would have been an "ask," but my shift was almost over, and the night crew was already there suiting up.

He grimaced and looked from the clock to my determined face before waving his hand. "Fine." He wasn't happy about it but couldn't really complain about a one-hour leave after all the breaks I'd missed and voluntary overtime I had worked.

I got changed and cleaned up as quickly as I could, hopped into our family car, and ripped back to the scene. Bree and Riley were sitting under the supermarket awning to get out of the rain.

She looked surprised to see me. "They let you leave work?"

"I didn't give them much choice."

Riley wasn't crying anymore, and he smiled when he saw me.

"Hey little guy." I nearly crumbled. Some stranger's blood had ruined my baby's pajamas. That just wasn't right. This was no place to raise a family.

Bree changed Riley into a clean sleeper in the back seat of the car. Then I strapped him into his car seat as she coaxed Lottie out of the stroller and into the back. That was when I realized Bree had taken off her shoes and was standing in the rain in bare feet. She had goosebumps but wasn't shivering. I tilted her chin up so I could look into her eyes.

"Are you sure you're okay?" I pulled her in for a proper hug and she let it all out, snot-crying into my civilian duds.

"I'm so sorry you had to see that." I tended to forget what it was like to be shocked by anything anymore; I saw so much violence on a daily basis I was numb to it. "Let's get out of here."

"What about the stroller?" She smeared her tears down her face in one motion.

Right. It was garbage now. "Leave it here for them to dispose of. I'll figure out the rest."

She looked like she wanted to protest but said nothing as we got into the vehicle and drove away.

"Jake?" she asked quietly. "Do you think we'll ever move out of Burner?"

"Absolutely. One day." *Not soon enough.*

I was bothered by the blood and the drowned kid and whatever new disaster I would walk into tomorrow or the next day. But underneath it all, I couldn't shake the image of that punk on the corner smirking at me as I stood beside my wife.

3

JAKE

MAY 17, 2012

When I arrived at the detachment a week later, someone called my name as I crossed the parking lot. It was early morning and getting close to shift change, so some members were already safety-checking their vehicles, while others were bolting out of there to go home and get some sleep.

"Stone, wait up."

I turned to spot my best friend and partner Corporal Arlen Matthews coming off the night shift. We worked solo in our patrol cars in this jurisdiction but often rode to files with a partner depending on the staffing situation. The joys of being stretched for resources.

Matthews was a cool, laid-back guy, which helped him on the job big time. The world could be literally blowing up around us and he was the one who stayed calm and present. I would have lost my mind ages ago if I hadn't had a partner like him. He kept me grounded. He was around six feet tall but smart and fast, always thinking ten steps ahead of the perps. He was the best guy to have as backup. We teased him because he used to be an actor, so yeah, he was good looking and blond, and the badge bunnies loved him. I always chuckled while they threw themselves at him; they had no idea he was beyond disinterested and happily married to his husband, Brody.

"Hey, what's up?" Matthews said as he approached.

"You think I could get a transfer out of Burner? What are the odds?"

"Get in line, buddy." He laughed. "A lot of us have tried. They'll tell you to move and commute and then suggest another rathole neighbourhood not far from this one."

Right. We had to live nearby for when we were on call.

"You'd just be trading one shitty hood for another," he said. "Anywhere that's actually better is too far in the force's eyes."

"Fuck."

"Yep."

"You ever think of transferring to a rural post, one of those small towns in butt-fuck nowhere?" I asked.

"Nope. Brody won't go for it. He was raised here, has friends and family here. There's also no way he'd put up with the bigoted crap that comes along with those isolated posts. And have you seen what force housing looks like out there?" He made a face, and I laughed. "You can try, though—it might be your only option."

I wasn't sure if Bree would agree to that. She definitely hadn't seemed keen on the idea when she was pregnant. The nearest hospitals tended to be hours away. "How was the shift?"

"Same shit, different night—10 p.m. stabbing in the drive-thru, gangs having their usual bloody battles, and some high-as-fuck, naked, drunk guy trying to make friends with cars in the middle of the highway." He shrugged and trudged toward his civilian car.

I'd promised Bree I would look into a transfer, but Matthews hadn't given me the positive response I'd hoped for. I went inside to speak to the sergeant anyway, to take my chances, but he was too busy. I sighed but was also a bit relieved to avoid that conversation. I already knew how long I had to stay at this posting before I could leave, so any suggestion of a transfer would meet with a hard no. It was something I'd never mentioned to Bree.

I focused on the vehicle and equipment checklist, making sure my beat-up Crown Victoria was good to go. Most of these cars should have been retired ages ago.

"You ready to rumble, Stone?" Constable Amber Doyle said, pulling up beside me. She winked as she pulsed her lights at me and hung her head out the window. "I'll see you at the morning briefing. We're sharing a car next week, and *I* will do the driving. I've heard stories about you."

She drove away before I had a chance to respond.

I'd met Doyle before in passing, though I'd never worked with her directly—but I'd heard stories about her too. Negative things about her policing skills. Cops gossiped just as much as their spouses, which was why I kept my personal and work lives as separate as possible. I couldn't have Bree hanging out with the harpy spouses and hearing about all the crap that went around about me—my colourful dating history, for one.

The rumor about Constable Doyle was that she'd failed her training more than once, and her law enforcement career was dangling by a thread. She'd just been moved to this detachment. I had noticed on the schedule that I had a shift coming up for scene security where two officers would be in a vehicle together, but I hadn't realized it was *her* I'd be working with. I just hoped I wouldn't get stuck as her new babysitter.

I still had a few minutes before the shift started. The lights and siren were good, the equipment worked, and the car was running, so check, check, check: time to drive straight into the pits of hell. But first, coffee.

#

I spotted Sydney sitting on the sidewalk next to the coffee shop parking lot. She was a harmless drunk who'd been living in her car—and now, on the street. We'd had to hook her up before for prostitution and more than once put her in a cell just to keep her warm.

"Hey, Sydney," I called from the car.

She looked up as though trying to figure out where the voice was coming from. "Am I in trouble, Mr. Officer?" She walked toward the car and leaned in.

"You hungry?"

"Whaddaya got?" Her tone was undeniably flirty.

This was going sideways. I popped open my glove box. "Vanilla or chocolate?" I always had protein bars with me. Food breaks were rare, and the bars helped keep some informants friendly. Cigarettes worked too, but this was different. I had a soft spot for Sydney, and her face was so gaunt it was clear she didn't eat much. She was a good person who didn't belong where her habits kept her.

"Take one of each." I handed her the bars. "You okay? Anyone roughing you up lately?"

"S'all good, Stone. No trouble." She bit a big chunk off the top of the protein bar.

I'd forgotten about her limited teeth and instantly felt bad. Next time I'd buy her a hot meal. "You call us if anyone bothers you, okay?" I held my card out the window to her.

"You know I won't. But thanks, honey." She winked and made her way back to her place on the sidewalk, ignoring my outstretched arm. They never called us. Street rules.

As I drove up to the order screen at the drive-thru, my radio went off. "Two-Charlie-seven?"

"Go for two-Charlie-seven," I answered, hoping I could get my coffee before I had to take off.

"Can I take your order?" a tinny voice rattled through the speaker.

"We have an assault in progress at 1405 Broadway," my radio blared. "Your car is closest. File sent to your mobile workstation. Two white male suspects, one may be armed."

"Two-Charlie-seven, on my way in two," I said before yelling into the drive-thru speaker, "No thanks!"

I tried to get out of there but was blocked by the car ahead of me. I checked my computer to find out if any guns were known to be in the house, and if anyone had priors.

Someone hollered from across the parking lot. "Hey pig! I thought distracted driving was illegal."

Just another day in paradise.

"Two-Charlie-five here. I'm closer and en route."

The file opened. Turned out the house was a treasure trove for criminals. It had everything—drugs, guns, convicts, disease, and children—and was registered to a woman with the legal first name Cherry. The car ahead of me finally got his order and left, and I sped past the window.

"Ten-seventeen, I'm on my way." I flicked on the sirens and lights and pushed the internal button that killed all feeling, preparing to do the job.

As I rounded the corner onto Broadway, I spotted an officer with his gun drawn, yelling at a male suspect lying prone on the front lawn of the house I was heading towards. Constable Abbott was running after a second suspect. I floored it and raced after them until they darted down an alley. My door was already open as I slammed the Crown into park and rolled out of the car, drawing my gun.

"Stop! Police!" I shouted, even though it was useless. Abbott would have already done the same.

They were far ahead of me, so I holstered my gun and picked up the pace. Working out for two hours a day and training in Krav Maga for the last few years had paid off. Plus, we knew these alleys intimately. I'd never understood why criminals thought the alleys were a good getaway plan. We spent more time chasing shit rats down these passages than anywhere else in Burner.

"Stone here," I said into my radio. "Foot pursuit, following Abbott and one fast suspect. Not sure about weapons yet."

My gun and radio secured, I sprinted toward a fence, hoping to intercept both the perp and Abbott. I grabbed the top of the fence with both hands and launched my stocky body over the top like a gorilla. They didn't call me Silverback for nothing. I landed well but split my pants. I arrived just in time to take him down. I lunged at him, my arms encircling his legs, knocking the rat on the cement and watching his ugly face bounce off the curb. I pinned him down a couple of feet away from what looked like a puddle of human piss. No alley in Burner was complete without some rancid mystery liquid.

Abbott was a millisecond behind me, out of breath but looking relieved. "Jesus, Stone, you came outta nowhere." He bent over, coughing. He was in great shape, but it would have been a long run from the house.

My knee was deep into the perp's back as we cuffed him and sat him up.

"Your name is Stone, eh?" The scumbag spit out a tooth as he spoke. I'd have to include that in the report to cover my ass.

Abbott radioed into dispatch, "One in custody."

"Yeah, Vince," I said. "I know your name too. Seems like your little brother on the lawn over there already squealed on you. He told us everything." I had no idea if that was true, but the Scaggs brothers were known to us. I recognized this one from prior interactions. There weren't many sets of wannabe gangbangers who dressed like twins with Ed Hardy jeans and matching cases of meth mouth. Willy was hatless, but Vince wore a ball cap that read *Eat a Dick*. He was a class act.

"Bullshit!" he yelled.

"You sure are cocky for a guy in cuffs. Got any rigs? What's in your pocket? We found a ton of crack on Willy." Again, spitballing.

"I ain't got nothin', pig."

"That isn't true, and it's just not nice."

These dime-bag pukes were all the same. I had relived this scenario hundreds of times in my career. Arrest, seize, lock up, court, release, repeat. Some dealers were less intelligent than others. These guys in particular were so stupid they'd called us once, wanting us to arrest someone for stealing their crack.

"I do know you." He nodded his chin at me. "I know where you live, Stone."

Right. If I had a dollar for every time a perp pretended to know me and where I lived, I'd leave the force a rich man. We searched him and seized a dirty pipe to add to the bag of rock we still had to collect from the trail where we'd seen him ditch it while running. We were hoisting him up to walk back to Abbott's car, since Abbott was the lead on this file, when Vince said, "I seen you."

"It's 'I've seen.'" I fucking hated it when people said that.

"Whatever. *I've seen* you with your pretty little wife and kid."

I was great at poker and didn't let on that his comment had affected me. He was probably full of crap anyway. It was an easy assumption that someone my age would have a wife and at least one kid by now.

We turfed him into the backseat of the car, forgetting to help him bend on the way in.

"By the way, you had a lot of rock on you," I said. "You're going away for a long time this time."

"No, I ain't. You lyin'."

"Oh, I *am* telling the truth. Your brother told the other officers you're in charge of this operation. It's all you. They sent cars to your place with a warrant and found everything. Your house, your name, your crack, your fate. He also said you were the one assaulting the lady back on Broadway." I turned to my colleague. "Hey, Abbott, how long you reckon this guy is going away for?"

"If he doesn't rot in pretrial?" Abbot cocked his head as if thinking about it. "I'd say a few years. *If* he gets a good lawyer."

"I ain't no crack dealer, and this ain't my crack. He lyin'." He was sweating and fidgeting, growing more desperate by the minute.

"Well, Mr. Scaggs, I have a crack meter here," I said, pretending I had a device in my hand. "And *beep boop beep,* it says you're high and full of shit."

I closed the car door so that I didn't have to listen to him anymore. Abbott opened the window a few inches as per policy on a warm day. We stepped away from the car to discuss the report.

Scaggs put his sick mouth closer to the window, and a smile spread across his face. "You guys live on Huxley."

Every hair on the back of my neck rose. *How does he know that?* I recognized that smirk now. He *had* seen me with Riley and Bree outside the grocery store. Fuck.

"Hey, Shit Teeth, why the hell would I live in this neighbourhood?"

"You do. And I'm gonna get you. When I get out of here, I'm gonna go see that pretty wife of yours and make her forget all about her pig husband. You won't want her back when I'm done."

Before I could do anything stupid, Abbott hit the window with his baton. "That's enough. You want to add uttering threats to your rap sheet as well?" He looked at me. "He's full of it, don't worry. I might need to swerve to miss a black dog on the drive back to the station."

That was code for slamming on your brakes with a cuffed suspect in the back. I was staring at Shit Teeth, ready to break some protocols, when the radio went off. "Two-Charlie-seven? We have a B&E at the Burner Transit Station. They're stealing copper again. What's your twenty?"

"Seventeen, on my way." I hustled back to my car, which was still running on someone's lawn a few blocks away.

"I mean it, po-po!" Scaggs shouted. "I'm coming for you, your wife, and yer kid. Better watch your back."

I pretended not to hear him and got into my car, gripping the steering wheel to stop my hands from trembling. Huxley was a long road. He couldn't know the exact building or unit number, could he?

4

BREE

MAY 25, 2012

After the incident at the grocery store, Riley and I spent a lot more time at home. Being a mom was equal parts boring and hard. I loved him to pieces, but I missed my friends, my nights out, and the corporate marketing job I used to complain about. It was a demanding job that required a lot of overtime, but at least I'd been good at it. Motherhood was a different story. No matter how hard I tried, I felt like I was failing every day.

We were playing with blocks on the living room carpet for the eightieth time that day when my phone rang. I jumped, knocking down our epic tower, and braced myself for Riley to start crying. Instead, he burst into a deep belly laugh. Laughing with him, I looked at my phone and debated whether to answer or let it go.

I knew I had to pick up. She would just keep phoning if I didn't.

"Hi, Mom."

"Breanna, how *are* you? How are you feeling?"

"I'm fine, really. I gave my statement to the RCMP, case closed. Jake's inspector even bought us a new stroller. Isn't that nice?" My voice sounded chirpy and fake even to me.

"Aren't they supposed to do that when things get ruined at a crime scene?"

"No, Mom, that's not how it works."

"I think Jake should ask for a transfer. Don't they relocate Mounties all the time?" Her voice was already getting louder.

"It's not that simple. We're looking into future transfers. I have no idea how long that will take, but we're on a list."

"How about you just move somewhere safer?"

I clenched my teeth. "We've gone over this before. We can only move within the city. We'd just be trading one set of problems for another."

"Well, why don't *you* come here? Jake can join you later."

I sighed—again. "We're a family. We need to be together."

My mom softened her tone. "I'm just worried about you and afraid of what you might be exposing Riley to. What sorts of things you'll both become desensitized to."

Me too. "The incident was random. Isolated. It could have happened anywhere." Not necessarily true, but whatever. As I switched the hot phone from one ear to the other, I glanced at the time. Riley had a block in each hand. If I didn't get off the phone soon, he'd start chucking them across the room.

"Jake isn't doing enough to protect the two of you from all that filth. Anyway, you could just come for a visit and forget your problems for a little while."

I pictured the view out her front-room window overlooking the yacht club, waves crashing at the shore anytime the sky got angry. I'd grown up with that sound; the louder and wilder it had gotten, the calmer and more grounded I'd felt. I closed my eyes and tasted salt.

"Breanna. Are you still there?"

The ocean disappeared, and I was snapped back to the present by the sound of my annoying neighbours walking around upstairs in heels and my mom judging my life over the phone. "We can't come to visit right now. Riley has a check-up next week. I'll look at the schedule and see when we can."

"Please do. And where is Jake right now anyway? At the gym again? He sure spends a lot of time there." She snorted.

"He's at work making money to support his family," I said. "And he goes to the gym to stay fit so he can fight off that filth you referred to and stay alive."

Silence. "I'm sorry. Just seems a little vain. For the hands-on dad he said he wanted to be, he doesn't spend much time at home." She had to throw in one more dig.

"I have to go now, Mom. I'm waiting for the realtor to call, and Riley needs a nap."

"Your realtor? Let me know how that goes. And Bree, please think about what I said. You need to be in a safe place to raise a family. I have the spare room ready for you whenever you need it."

"I know." I hung up the phone before she could say anything else. I believed her when she said she had a spare room open for *me* anytime I wanted. Just me and Riley though—not Jake.

Riley didn't need a nap, but I couldn't be on the phone with her anymore. I was feeling nauseous waiting for the realtor to call me back. I was pretty sure I knew what she would say.

Our next block tower was very tall. This time I knocked it over on purpose so Riley would deliver one of his contagious laughs. Lottie perked up and started barking. It made us laugh even harder. Then I noticed her staring at the door.

I heard a creak, and then the closed door hit the jamb and rattled in place. My heart rate sped up, and I held my breath as I watched. A minute or so passed, and nothing else happened. Maybe I had imagined it. I exhaled and turned back to Riley to build another tower. But out of the corner of my eye, I could see the doorknob slowly turning. I had forgotten to lock the knob, but the deadbolt was in place. This time, there was no doubt: someone was on the other side of the door. They abruptly twisted the handle back and forth, shaking the door. I scooped up Riley and tiptoed toward the door with Lottie barking wildly.

"Who's there?"

Silence. No more knob turning or door shaking. I glided in my sock feet until I reached the peephole. Riley must have sensed something was off. He was completely quiet.

Two grimy, youngish men stood on the other side of the door, smiling.

"Can I help you with something?" I asked, steadying my voice as best as I could while I twisted the doorknob into a locked position.

"Is this Cherry's place?"

"No, it's not." This totally stank. I'd never seen these guys in the building before, and I knew many of the residents. I doubted there was anyone here named Cherry.

"Sorry, ma'am. Wrong apartment."

I watched out the peephole as they laughed and turned away. From the elevator, I heard another voice prompting them to go.

I texted Jake: *Call me ASAP.*

5

JAKE

For the first time in ages, I took a short break. It was a week after I'd arrested Vince Scaggs and it was raining hard, which in Burner meant some of the rats would head in off the street temporarily. I'd have a small window of time before motor vehicle incidents stacked up. I set my status to "file writing," thinking I'd actually be able to chew my lunch today.

The closed toy store parking lot I chose was isolated and empty. Ever since four officers had been ambushed in a restaurant, I ate alone whenever I got the chance. It was safer.

As I took a big bite of my toasted sandwich, my phone buzzed with an urgent text from Bree, so I called her right away.

"Everything okay, hon?"

"No. I mean, yes. I don't know."

When she told me about the door being tested, I sat up and dropped my lunch into my lap.

"There were two men—" she said.

"What did they look like? Are they still there?"

"Early to mid-thirties or a hard late twenties. They were both wearing those bedazzled-looking jeans. One had a gross mustache and the other was wearing a ball cap with *Eat a Dick* written on it. They just left a minute ago."

I grew cold. The blood left my face and congealed in my stomach. "I'm on my way." The sandwich fell into the footwell as I slammed the cruiser door shut and sped off, calling the detachment and then Matthews on the radio.

"The Scaggs just tried to get into my condo." I gripped the steering wheel and pulled at it.

"Fuck. I'm right next door. On my way."

"Don't say anything to Bree."

"You didn't tell her?"

"No, I didn't want to worry her."

By the time I arrived, Matthews was already sitting in the living room with Lottie hovering at his feet. Toys were scattered across the floor, and laundry was piled beside him on the couch. Yesterday's dishes still sat on the kitchen counter. Bree looked as frazzled as her surroundings. I knew being a mom was hard, but I couldn't help being a little embarrassed at the mess.

"Did the men say anything to you?" Matthews used his professional voice even though he and his husband were friends of ours.

"They asked if someone named Cherry lived here," she said.

Matthews shot me a questioning glance as he took notes. The name was familiar, but I couldn't remember why.

"Did anything else unusual happen?"

"Someone with a weird voice called to them from the elevator," she said. "I couldn't see him, but he spoke with what sounded like an Eastern European accent mixed with a speech impediment."

I grew cold as Matthews and I exchanged a look. That was an accurate description of Ivan Bychkov, a convict with a violent history who was a well-known, new associate of the Scaggs. I had to sit down.

I knew the courts would turn those shits loose. I'd been threatened by shit rats before, with zero follow-through, but these guys had already found my wife, and they'd brought along a very dangerous friend.

"Thanks Bree, we'll take care of this," Matthews said. "See you next week at the potluck. Stone, I need to write this up in my car. I'll see you outside?" He gave Bree a pat on the shoulder as he left.

I ruffled Riley's hair.

"You okay, Bree?" I asked. She'd been on edge lately. "I'm worried about you."

Shortly after Riley was born, Bree had become depressed. She'd stopped cleaning up, stopped leaving the house, and for a while, she'd even stopped bathing. Today may have just been a rough day, but this was how it had started last time.

"Yeah, I'm fine. Just a couple of grubby guys, right?" She smiled weakly.

I gave her a hug and remembered to be gentle. The last time I'd given her a bear hug in uniform, I had bruised her. Kevlar hurt when you were on the receiving end.

"Yes, of course, it was a mistake," I said, "but an aggressive one. No one should rattle our door like that. Try not to worry. Matthews and I will handle it. Lock everything and call me or 911 if anything else happens."

"911? That seems dramatic?" She side-eyed me. "This *was* random, right?"

"Yes. I just mean if you can't reach me, okay?"

I stood outside our door and waited until I heard all the locks engage before heading to the car.

The rain had slowed down. Matthews was still parked out front, sitting in the driver's seat of his cruiser with the door open and looking at his laptop. "I pulled up the file report from the Scaggs arrest you were involved in."

"Find anything?"

"The victim of the assault and registered owner of the house is named Cherry Lee." He made a cringe face.

"Right." That was why I'd recognized the name. We'd put her into protection until the trial. "Anything else?"

"Her boyfriend is Bychkov."

"God dammit!" I punched my car. "Those punks wanted me to know it was them at the door and that they're looking for Cherry. Bychkov must have been in the elevator."

"Yep, and we don't have enough to go after them."

"I know." The drizzle cooled my face.

"It's also too dangerous."

"I know. We'd better get back to the detachment and figure out what we *can* do."

More importantly, I knew what I had to do: Get my family out of here, and fast.

6

JAKE

MAY 26, 2012

After the doorknob incident, we put a couple of cars on Scaggs and Bychkov, but that was about all we could do. We didn't have enough information yet to go after them or put sections on any of them, but we would watch them until we had something. I knew I had to talk to the inspector about a transfer now, before something really bad happened.

That morning I made sure I was meticulous with my uniform compliance. I pulled out a crisp new shirt and confirmed that my name badge was perfectly straight and my tie was clipped in just the right place. I'd shaved my stubble so that I'd pass the "card" test if needed and sewed the rip in the seat of my pants tighter. They were my last ones until payday. I made a mental note to order a few new pairs to be safe, hopefully with some overtime pay.

As I approached the inspector's office, my hands felt clammy, so I wiped them on my pants. I didn't normally ask to speak to him about anything, and the two times I'd been summoned to his office had not been pleasant. But this was important, and if I pleaded my case well enough, he should do the right thing.

In truth, I was relieved Bree had brought up moving. I was exhausted from taking file after file in the busiest, highest-volume-of-calls city in our province and possibly all of Canada. I'd wanted a change for a while. The door was open, so I did a firm knuckle wrap and pasted on a smile.

"Inspector, you have a minute?"

"Erm, yeah. Constable ... Stone, right?" He had to search for my name longer than I would have liked.

"Yes, sir." I stood in the doorway awkwardly.

He put down the report he'd been frowning at and removed his glasses. He was a big man in his late fifties—probably a beast back in the day. His muscular frame now housed some hard fat from years of adrenaline and alcohol abuse.

"Sit down." He seemed irritated that he had to give that instruction. "What is it?"

I considered running out but then remembered my son's bloody clothing. I dropped into the chair across from him and cleared my throat. "Sir, I need to ask for a favour."

"No favours, Stone. Don't do favours. What's the problem?"

"Sorry, I don't mean a favour." What did I mean? "I need help with something. You know about the incident at my house yesterday."

He nodded.

"A couple weeks ago, my wife was walking with my son to the grocery store and they were involved in a bloody altercation."

"Oh. Was she at the knife-in-neck incident?" He made a throat-slitting gesture.

"Yes, sir. That's right."

"Good, thanks. We have one more question for her. Can you have her phone in?" He wrote a file number on his business card and handed it to me. "Close the door on your way out."

I wasn't impressed by his quick brush-off, but I also wasn't surprised. "That isn't it. She was pretty messed up about everything and wants me to inquire about a transfer. Would that be a possibility?"

He sighed and shook his head. "You can move to West Bernheim, or north or south of Bernheim, as long as you don't go more than twenty kilometres away from the detachment. You don't need approval for that."

I knew that already. "Those neighbourhoods are bad too, sir. Any chance I could get transferred out of Bernheim altogether? Maybe a rural post?"

"How long have you been here, Stone?"

"Five years. I know, I was told it has to be seven minimum, but I just thought under these circumstances that you could make an exception. Maybe I could take a transfer that no one wants?"

The inspector laughed. "There are lots of postings no one wants, Constable Stone. You're in one of them. And you were misinformed about the seven-year minimum."

"Oh?"

"It's actually ten. This is nonnegotiable."

Ten years was a sentence, not a term. *I'm fucked. I wonder which gang Riley will join.*

"Stone, some advice? On your next days off, take a mini-vacation. Leave the city. Spend some time with your wife and kid and come back refreshed."

I couldn't wait to get out of his office and away from his fruity-smelling breath, but I couldn't leave without having something positive to tell Bree. "With all due respect, sir, that won't solve anything. We can't live here for another five years. My wife and kid can't get covered in blood while walking down the street. Those rats knocked on our door—"

"Stone, we have men watching the Scaggs. You could always move to another building or another part of town. You aren't the only family who's made sacrifices in this job. If you don't like it, there's the door. Close it on your way out. And put some more polish on your boots. That is all." He dismissed me with a shooing motion.

I walked out with a flushed face and a lump in my throat. When I flipped open my phone, there was Bree's text: *Hey baby, did you talk to him?* with a semicolon and closing parenthesis to make a winky face emoji.

I texted back:

He was too busy, I didn't get a chance. Will try tomorrow. Gotta go, luv u.

What were the buttons to make a liar emoji?

If Bree found out how long we had to stay in Burner, she'd leave, I knew it. But worse, what would happen if the Scaggs came back?

7

BREE

JUNE 2, 2012

I had to get out of the house. I'd been a nervous shut-in for the past few weeks, and I was looking forward to my visit with Daphne. Even the twenty-minute drive was refreshing. Riley slept the whole way, as I'd timed the drive to coincide with his nap time. I brought coffee from home and got to sip it while it was hot—a rare occurrence for a mom of a ten-month-old.

For a brief moment, I felt like myself again. The air, the music, the change of scenery—it reminded me of a time when I'd been freer. Not that I regretted having Riley, but if I had to do it again, I wouldn't have moved to become a parent so quickly. I used to have so much confidence; now I was a shaky wreck, afraid of everything. What I would have given for a night out dancing with friends.

Daphne had been part of my core friend group that I used to party with. Before meeting Jake, I'd had a busy social life. We were always out: good restaurants, fancy parties, hanging out at nightclubs until closing time. We spent money like it was nothing, travelled all the time, and drank way too much. I didn't miss the hangovers, but I longed for the carefree bits. Anyway, Daphne had gotten pregnant shortly after I did, so we still got together while the rest of our friends kept partying and forgot about us. The highlight of our lives was gossiping over coffee while juggling Cheerios and soothers.

As I pulled into the driveway, Daphne was already waiting at her front door, barefoot in joggers and holding her baby. She was adorable with her round baby face and giant brown eyes, and youthful looking with her hair in a high ponytail. The only sign that she was close to my age was those dark circles under her eyes.

I put a finger to my lips to indicate Riley was still asleep.

"Leave him in the car, Breanna. There's no need to wake him. It's safer here than at your place." She laughed, but it wasn't funny.

I looked around at the manicured gardens and freshly painted homes in the neighbourhood. It was still Burner, but not the concrete condo jungle of the east side of the city. The only noise out here was a lawn-mower in the distance and birds chirping in Daphne's yard. No one was yelling. There was no crazy traffic, no need to be on high alert.

Still, I couldn't leave Riley in the car. I reached over him and grabbed the diaper bag, willing him to wake up, and I saw his little eyes peel open.

"Never mind, he's awake. Aren't you, sweet pea?" He did the same thing every time he woke up: His lower lip pushed way out, and his eyes moved slowly, fighting the urge to shut, and then he stretched his entire tiny body, thrusting his hands in the air like he was at a rock concert. I loved these moments. When his eyes opened fully, he looked around, trying to get his bearings until he saw me. That mostly toothless, million-dollar smile made me forget everything else.

I stepped inside Daphne's massive, Cape-Cod-style house. It was the kind I fantasized about having one day. Matching couches. Matching lamps. Built-in bookshelves.

"What did the realtor say?" Daphne knew we were exploring our options.

"Nothing good." I pointed at her fussing baby in an attempt to change the subject. "Is she sleeping through the night?" She probably was.

"No, of course not. So, are you listing your place or what?"

Sigh. Hint not taken. "Not right now. We're going to ride it out where we are for a while. We'd lose forty to fifty K if we sold right now."

"If Jake can't transfer, why doesn't he just quit?" She hung onto the *t* in "quit."

If it was that simple, didn't she think he would have already done it? My sweet but naive friend had money and options and didn't understand how trapped we were.

"If he quits, he could lose his pension. We're on a list to transfer, but we don't know how long that could take." Half-truth. It could be months, maybe years. "I'm just going with the flow. Nothing too weird has happened in the neighbourhood lately." Outright lie. "Jake has been working a ton of overtime to try to save for a future move. We have a plan." Biggest load of crap of all. Our original plan of having a couple of kids and a family home with a large yard and white picket fence seemed like a sick joke. With our dire financial situation and shitty living circumstances, there was no point making plans or expanding our family anytime soon.

"You do seem happier. What else is new with you?" Daphne took a gulp of her coffee and spat it back into the mug. "Ugh. Cold. Refill time."

As much as I loved her, I couldn't take the questions anymore. No, I wasn't happy, and no, things weren't good, and yes, I felt powerless and sad. I also felt nauseous.

"How about we refill our coffees and take the babies for a walk?" I suggested. "Get some fresh air?" *And not be trapped into more Q&A.*

"Yes, perfect." Daphne popped off the couch with the enthusiasm I lacked.

Daphne didn't think I noticed her slip some whiskey into her mug, but I did. Her coffee was divine, fancy beans that were straight from Kona. I considered stashing some in my purse while she was in the bathroom, but I didn't know where she kept her plastic bags.

I pulled my new stroller out of the trunk. It was a darker colour, though I often thought I saw the blood-soaked yellow vinyl if I looked down at it too quickly. The stroller wasn't as fancy as the last one we'd had, but it had been free, and I was grateful.

We walked briskly, as it was windy outside. The breeze and sweat from the mild exertion chased my queasiness away.

"Did you hear Becky and Noah hooked up?"

I leaned in. "Oooh no, I didn't. Are they together now?" Our old gang. It was nice to hear about them again.

"Hell no. Noah doesn't even like her. I always thought he had a thing for you. The two of you and your inside jokes all the time."

Now I was laughing. Daphne didn't know I'd actually slept with both of them. Becky happened one drunken night and we swore to never tell anyone, and with Noah it hadn't meant anything. I was so lonely at the time, and it was long before Jake came into my life. Noah was hilarious, and we'd had a blast together, but we were incompatible in every way.

Still, we'd been friends for much longer than the hookups, and I missed him.

"Well, he dodged a bullet, didn't he?" I asked.

"Who dodged which bullet?" We both laughed.

We talked about our friends and the empty fun they were having and how glad we were that we'd chosen to settle down. It was just lip service for me, though, and the booze in Daphne's coffee suggested things weren't perfect for her either. Those old days had been so much easier.

"Is Jake still the prince charming you thought he was when you met?"

I laughed uneasily. "Yes, of course."

There were cars in some of the driveways we passed: BMWs, a few Mercedes. No lawns with overgrown grass. No graffiti.

"How did you manage to lose all that baby weight, by the way? I mean, you were huge. Jake must have been scared."

I was tempted to trip her. "Wow, I don't know. Walking? Breastfeeding? A healthy dose of stress in a new marriage, in a rough town, with no money, and hope running out?"

She looked hurt.

"Sorry. I'm not feeling great, and I really have to pee. Is there a washroom at this park?"

"No."

We turned our strollers around in unison. I decided I'd use her washroom and then make some excuse to go home. Today was not as fun as I'd expected. Maybe I'd drive around for a while with Riley and dream myself into some of the fancy houses on this side of town.

As we turned onto her street, someone ran out of her driveway and up the road.

"Who the hell was that?" she asked. We looked at each other and picked up the pace.

By the time we reached the driveway, the guy was long gone. The driver-side window of my car had been smashed, and the car was covered in dents. Daphne gasped, and my heart and mind were racing.

"I thought your neighbourhood was safer than mine." God, what if I had left Riley in there? Then I noticed that Daphne's car hadn't been touched.

Daphne pointed to the spray paint that read *Mrs. Piggy*. "I don't think the person who did this is from my neighbourhood."

I was fishing around in my bag for my phone when a powerful wave of nausea hit me. I tried to contain it, but then another wave hit, and I threw up on Daphne's driveway.

Jake didn't answer, so I called 911 as he'd instructed. *This* was not random.

The police arrived at Daphne's house within minutes. I gave them a detailed timeline of our movements during the last hour, and Daphne provided a rough description of the man we'd seen running out of her driveway. She kept saying, "There's no way that vandal was from around here" while looking at me. I wasn't sure if she was upset that I'd brought this into her life, or if she was sad that this *was* my life.

The police were taking pictures of the car when my phone rang.

"Bree. Are you okay? I heard the call over dispatch. I'm on my way." Jake's voice went up an octave, uncharacteristically.

"Don't bother. Daphne will take us home. You can meet me there." It all came out in a rush. "We need to talk. And no, I am not okay. Whoever smashed my car knows I'm your wife and must have followed me here. I almost left Riley asleep in the car. Who did this? I want them locked up!" By the end of it, I was shouting.

"You almost did *what*? I'll handle it, Bree. Don't worry. Why do you think someone followed you? It sounds like a ran—"

"Before you say the word 'random' one more time, I'm sending you a picture to answer your question."

I'm not going to let him minimize this incident too. No bloody way. I sent him the photograph of Mrs. Piggy, trying to ignore Daphne's Bambi eyes and wishing I'd stayed home.

8

JAKE

When I got home, Daphne was there, and Bree was sitting on the couch with her arms crossed next to a couple of suitcases. "Are you okay?"

Bree ushered Daphne to the door, ignoring me. "Thanks for everything. I'll call you later."

"Of course." Daphne shot her a weird look, kissed her on the cheek, and left. I'd never liked any of Bree's party friends, but I was glad she wasn't home alone waiting for me.

She secured all the locks on the door, then turned around, her arms still crossed. "I'm done."

"Wait, what?" I knew she was mad, but I hadn't expected this.

She came back to the couch and sat down. "I can't do this anymore. You're lying to me, or at the very least keeping secrets. It isn't safe here." She passed me her phone. On the screen was a picture of a note that read *You're dead, cunt*. "They found this under the windshield wiper. This is it for me. We can't move, and we can't transfer. I'll go stay with my mom." Her voice shook, and her face had turned bright red.

I crouched beside her and put one hand on her knee.

"No, please. You can't do that. We're a family. We need to be together. We'll figure something out." I was threatened all the time in this miserable city—if she left for that reason alone, she would never come back. Plus, she didn't really want to go to her mom's. She'd already be gone if she was actually serious about— *Oh, wait.* She didn't have a vehicle anymore.

I stood up with my fists clenched. "I'm going to kill those little pricks. Bree, I'll fix this. I'll—"

"Fix what? What pricks?" Her eyes were wide.

Shit. Now I'd done it. "I'm not supposed to tell you anything confidential."

She looked like she was ready to stab me. "You tell me what's going on, right now."

I let out a long breath. "Do you remember the day those two greaseballs came to the door, trying to get in?"

"You thought I might have forgotten?" Bree shifted her butt to the end of the couch, sitting more erect.

"They were looking for me. For us." I hung my head, feeling small.

"What?" She jumped up. "Are you kidding me? What did they want? Why didn't you tell me?"

I stood up and reached for her, but she flung my arm away. "You tell me everything, right now, or I'll wake up Riley and walk out that door."

"Sit down." I motioned to the couch, and she complied. "I've arrested those two idiots many times. They're local dealers."

She remained silent.

"The most recent arrest was a few weeks ago. One of them threatened me. He said he knew where we lived, and he was going to 'get us.'"

Her mouth fell open, but she still didn't say a word.

"You have to understand: I'm threatened every day. It's the first thing a lot of these guys do when they're busted. The vast majority of these threats go nowhere. It's usually desperation on their part, and I ignore it and carry on with my day. If I'd thought you were in actual danger, I would have told you." But I should have known. The Scaggs knew what street I lived on. They'd seen me with Bree and Riley.

"But I *was* in danger. They came here. You *knew* this and still didn't tell me. Why?" Bree's voice shook even more as it got louder.

I felt like garbage. "I made the wrong call. I thought I could get it under control and resolved before anything got out of hand. I really did. You can ask Matthews. The two of us have been working day and night on hooking these guys back up. We got approval to have a car outside at all times here at the building—which you may or may not have noticed. We also have tabs on both brothers. We just have to get more information lined up, and then we can lock them up for good."

Bree's face softened. "I did notice a ghost car outside, but I thought they were just writing files. I'm glad you did that. I just wish you would have told me everything right away." She looked around the apartment quietly for a moment and then back at me. "If you were watching them, how did they follow me to Daphne's?"

"It must have been someone who works for them. I got a no-go order approved for our building but couldn't get personal security because the incident at our door didn't fit the criteria for a direct threat against us." Our legal system exasperated me. "When they came to the door pretending to look for Cherry, they actually ..." I paused. I was really breaking my oath here.

Bree's eyes narrowed. "Tell me."

"They wanted me to know they'd found you. Cherry was the assault victim from the last arrest and a key witness in our case against the brothers and their boss. She's also the boss's main girlfriend. They're looking for her too, but we have her in protective custody." I clenched my jaw. "I'm so sorry. I really thought you guys were safe. But now—" With the car, and this note? "We have to get out of here. There's no other way."

"But how?" Bree stared at her packed suitcases. Lottie sat beside her, looking back and forth between us, her tail uncurling. "Did they give you the okay to move?"

"Not exactly." I had hoped to avoid telling her, but now I had no choice. "What did the realtor say?" If we made some money on the deal, maybe we could move somewhere decent that would still be close enough to the detachment.

Bree avoided my eyes. "We'll lose a pile of money if we sell now."

"How much?" Heat spread throughout my chest.

She picked at her fingernails. "Too much."

I struggled to control my temper. We'd fought countless times about her poor choice of buying this place and saddling us with debt.

"I can just go to my mom's or Daphne's for a while until it's safer," she said.

I took a deep breath. "Please don't go. We can work this out. I don't give a shit about the RCMP's rules. They certainly aren't going to any extra lengths to protect us, and this situation is out of control. We just need to figure out how to afford this place *and* rent."

I must have said some magic word, because Bree jumped off the couch, knocking the suitcases out of the way, and grabbed the laptop off the counter. "I know exactly what we can do. We can rent this place out.

That's how we'll afford it. We should get enough to cover the mortgage, and then we'll only have to pay rent at a new place." She turned the laptop screen toward me and showed me what a small condo like this one would rent for.

"If you're serious about breaking the rules, we can move somewhere safer as long as you can commute to work. We'll find a tenant for this place and use this address for mail." She flashed a huge grin.

"You beautiful genius!" I picked her up and twirled her off the ground, kissing her.

"Are you serious?" she asked as I put her back down. "You aren't worried you'll lose your job?"

"Fuck my job. That's what got us into this mess. I have an immaculate record. The worst they can do is write me up. And fuck the distance. How will they find out anyway?"

I had to keep my family safe. Though it occurred to me, if the Scaggs had found Bree at Daphne's, they could find us anywhere. The only real way to keep us safe was to get those scumbags locked up for good.

9

BREE

JUNE 19, 2012

There wasn't much available in terms of affordable rentals just outside of Burner. I looked every day, many times per day. By the time I saw an ad and phoned, it was already snapped up. Everything was so expensive. We were really hoping for a house but would have taken a condo if needed. Basement suites were a hard no—another caveat of Jake's. Besides the convenient ground floor break-ins, Jake had dealt with so many landlord-tenant disputes that living directly beneath a landlord was out of the question. I understood, but it made the search much harder.

As usual, I did all the right things in the wrong order and found a tenant right away. He seemed great and compliant with our ludicrous amount of background checks and requests for references. He wanted to move in as fast as possible, so the pressure was on.

Riley and I had ventured out to look at a few places, and though it kept us busy and away from the building, it was disheartening. We found a nice unit only thirty minutes' drive for Jake, almost within the limits, and though it was small, it was bright and on the top floor. I called Jake to come to look, but when I gave him the address, it was just "Nope." A murder had taken place there.

Then there was another condo that would have worked but for the pit bull growling at us from the upstairs balcony. But I wasn't giving up; instead, I dropped my standards and begged Jake to do the same. Maybe a suite wouldn't be so bad. It was better than waiting around for another visit from those creepy criminal brothers.

During one of Riley's naps, I conducted a routine internet deep-dive with Lottie on my lap and stumbled across a promising ad. I tried not to get too excited when I saw it, but my heart skipped.

3 bd/2 bth Heritage home in south Roxford. Big yard. Close to hwy for commuting. Would suit a professional couple or small family. $1800/month. Lease required. Call to view.

"Jake," I whispered loudly. "Come in here."

He popped up from his nap quicker than usual. "You found something?"

Roxford, though. Roxford was an hour from Jake's detachment. That meant an hour's commute each way, and it was definitely outside the RCMP's boundaries.

I handed him my archaic laptop. "I know it's far, but it's big, and cute, and old, and it has a yard." Lottie would love that. "Look at the pics. Can you imagine?" *So much for holding back.*

Jake stared for a minute. "It's more than we wanted to pay."

"I know, but I think we could make it work—for a house. What do you think?"

His eyes twinkled, and a grin curled the corners of his mouth. "Let's go check it out."

When I peeked over his shoulder, he was still looking at the picture of the yard. I called to set up a viewing, hoping the listing wasn't too good to be true.

10

BREE

JUNE 21, 2012

As we pulled up to the house, I double-checked the address. So much for curbside appeal. This wasn't Daphne's neighbourhood. Everything was overgrown. The reality was so much different from the photos in the ad, it reminded me of my online dating days. The exterior of the house was dirty and rundown, but the unruly shrubbery that concealed the front of the home would be good for privacy.

"Look at all the parking." I tried to keep the mood high and light. I wanted this. I could see us being happier here, the way we'd once been. We could sit in our yard without worrying about seeing the scumbags Jake arrested every two seconds. He'd have so much less stress out here.

The house had a semicircle gravel driveway, with more parking at the side. We only had one car—we wouldn't be able to afford a second one—so I wasn't sure why I was getting so excited about the parking. But still.

"Yeah, there's a lot of space." Jake's eyes darted as though he was scoping out a potential scene. He always did that, but today it really bugged me. "The road is pretty busy," he grumbled. Then he pointed to the neighbour's house. "That driveway has a lot of cars in it."

"Yes, but the house is set back from the road. That's good, right?"

Jake nodded as we rolled into the driveway. He took off his seatbelt and opened the car door before putting the car into park and turning off the engine. Work habit. As he unbuckled Riley, I grabbed the ad and a notepad and looked around the exterior. It was a big house. The roof looked old and rough, and there was a window high up in the shape of an octagon. A tired-looking woman with tangled hair looked out at us—she must have been the landlady. I waved, but she didn't wave back.

We'd both dressed up today. No hole-ridden Lululemon tights for me—instead, a nice pair of jeans and a clean blouse with a blazer that had gotten a ton more use in my working days. I was even wearing makeup.

I'd almost forgotten what Jake looked like out of his uniform and his gym clothes. He was only a smidge taller than me at six feet, but broad and muscular. He had dark hair, dark eyes, and a super-sharp jawline. His smile still made my heart flip, as did his big booming laugh when he would throw his head back, clapping his hands. Whenever he did that, his dimples and eyes would crinkle in unison. It always reminded me of why I'd fallen in love with him. I didn't see that smile or hear that laugh very often anymore.

He handed me Riley. "You take him."

In return, I gave him all the papers I'd been holding, and he crumpled them into the diaper bag that was weighing down my other shoulder as he blew past me toward the entrance. *Sure Jake, I'll carry everything.* I bit it back. Bickering wouldn't get us this house.

A jovial blond-haired woman in her fifties stood on the front stairs—not the one I'd spotted in the octagonal window. This one held a clipboard. *Crap, there must be a lot of people coming to see the place.*

"Jake and Breanna, ma'am." He stuck his hand out for a shake, and I shrugged with my hands full.

"Welcome. I'm Denise."

We followed her up the rickety wooden stairs into the front entrance. It definitely looked and felt like an addition to the home: The plastic siding was newer and a slightly different colour than the rest of the exterior. And there was the lack of heat. It was spacious, though. There was room for a bench so we could sit while putting on our shoes, and there was a huge walk-in closet. I tried to catch Jake's eye with my approving smile, but he was six steps ahead of me and in business mode. Meanwhile, I tried to take off my shoes without using my hands or losing my balance.

When I walked through the narrow door into the home, I was in awe. I'd always admired older homes and their architecture. It wasn't the open-concept home that most people wanted—that is, people without children and shift-working spouses. From where I stood, I spotted several rooms separated by doorways—and in most cases doors, too. This would be great for when Jake worked nights and needed to sleep when Riley was awake. I was admiring the hardwood when Denise piped in.

"We just refinished the floors."

"They're beautiful."

We were in the living room area, and it was massive. The curved crown moldings on the ceiling must have been original. The chandelier was dated but pretty in its own way.

"What happened there?" Jake pointed to a repair in progress on the ceiling.

I held my breath. *Please don't be a dealbreaker.*

"Oh, that. We're just patching it up. The previous tenants left the bathtub running, and the water soaked through the floor." She rolled her eyes. "We were lucky enough to catch it before the whole damn tub came crashing through." She was clearly irritated but tried to smile. "The insurance claim is nearly finished. They're coming back for one more coat of paint."

"Ah." Jake nodded.

Phew.

He and I stood there staring up until Denise motioned for us to follow her. At the end of the living room was a doorway to a kitchen so big I could have almost fit my entire apartment inside.

Denise pointed. "One of the bathrooms is there, a powder room, and behind that is the laundry room."

"An entire room just for laundry?" I whispered to Jake.

A smile crept up the side of his face.

"We'll go through the formal dining room on our way upstairs, but perhaps we should go outside first?" Denise opened the door off the back of the kitchen, and we stepped onto a large wooden deck that spanned the width of the house. That was when we saw the yard. It was huge, the kind people had in the eighties, not the stamp-sized ones that came with new houses in the city.

As if reading Jake's mind, she said, "I don't mind if you plant veggies or flowers out here. Just replace the grass when you move out."

"A garden?" he whispered in disbelief.

Denise smiled and glanced at her watch, reminding me again that we weren't the only people looking at this house. We went back inside and exited the kitchen through yet another door. "It's meant to be a formal dining room," she said, "but you can use it as a bedroom."

"Or maybe even a gym?" I asked.

"Sure, anything," Denise said.

But I wasn't talking to her. Jake squinted, probably already imagining a squat rack.

I shifted Riley to another hip as we reached the stairs. They were narrow and tall.

"Dangerous for an overtired adult," Jake said quietly, "or a child learning to walk."

"I think it's fine."

He waved me away and followed Denise. "How old is the home?"

"Everyone asks that." Her laugh had a funny click to it. "We estimate around a hundred years. We don't actually know for sure. We bought the house a few years ago, and there weren't many records with the city."

"Fair enough. How many rooms did you say it had?"

I had already told Jake all of this, so either he hadn't listened to me or was just making conversation.

At the top of the narrow stairs, a dingy velvet curtain covered the entrance to an odd little passageway. It was long and narrow and didn't seem to go anywhere. Jake and Denise had gone ahead, so I explored with Riley in my arms. There was a tiny room to the left of the stairs with a funky shape to it, and a window that was large for the house's era. I walked over to it and looked down. The street *was* busy, but I didn't care. The window had been painted shut. Probably another reno.

"Breanna, where are you?" Jake sounded irritated, so I hurried over. Along the way, I peeked into the other rooms. A sizable bathroom to the left and another big bedroom to the right. I joined them in the gigantic main bedroom.

"There used to be five small bedrooms up here, but Jerome and I converted them into three decent-sized ones, which seemed more practical.

We left the original iron fixtures on the doors though to honour the heritage."

Several windows overlooked the backyard.

"What's out there?" I pointed to a door.

She shuffled over and opened it to reveal a square-shaped Juliet-type balcony that looked right down onto the neighbours' house. "The deck needs redoing, so I wouldn't have too many of you out here at once." She let out a small fake laugh as her eyes darted left and right.

The railings were short and didn't look secure. I was happy to go back inside.

"I'm gonna leave you two up here to talk. I have another couple due to arrive soon. If you like the place, you can fill out an application, and we'll get back to you. Make sure to include employment, credit check, and criminal records."

"That'll be easy. I'm an RCMP officer in Burner." Jake smiled his killer smile, flashing the eyeteeth that I rarely saw. That was when I knew he wanted this place as badly as I did.

"That's why you want to move out here." She tapped her clipboard. "You'll do fine. If you're interested, grab the form on the way out—and don't worry about the criminal record checks unless she's shady." She motioned to me.

"No, I'm pretty harmless."

We all laughed.

With that, she left, the breeze from her movement pulling the door closed behind her. I glimpsed triple locks on the back of the door: a doorknob lock, a deadbolt, and a chain. *Seems like overkill.* I looked away.

"Well?" He smiled.

"Yes. A hundred times yes. Let's fill it out right away and get it back to her with letters of reference, everything."

"She likes us, I can tell," Jake said. "But yes, let's not waste time. We'll skip the coffee and neighbourhood recon and fill out the forms before my shift tonight."

I hesitated. Research was my jam. "You sure you don't want to drive around a bit?" It seemed okay, but I was suddenly getting cold feet. The narrow stairs and sketchy deck made me uneasy.

"No, it's fine. It's better than Burner, and I don't arrest guys out here. Let's go."

As we walked down the hallway, I noticed locks on the outside of another bedroom, and that the doors were installed backward, opening into the hallway instead of the room. *How odd.*

Denise waited at the bottom of the stairs with paperwork in hand. "I had a feeling you two would be interested. The other couple just cancelled, and I'm so tired of showing this place. I don't normally do this, but I like you guys. Do you want it?"

We stood there silent for a second.

"Yes, definitely!" Jake said.

Denise smiled. "Fill these out so I have the info, but it's just a formality. The place is yours. You can't move in until the insurance claim is done, but I'll confirm everything over the phone in the next couple of days."

I felt like an excited teenager. We wouldn't go out on the rickety deck anyway, and we'd be careful on the stairs. *We're getting out of Burner!*

I sat in the passenger seat of the car holding all the paperwork, still surprised by how fast everything was happening. "Are you sure the drive is okay? Are the stairs safe? The house needs some work. Are we sure the neighbourhood is okay?"

"Yes, yes, and yes." He was happy, but his tone carried an undercurrent of irritation. "I thought this was what you wanted, Bree. You were the one who brought us out here."

"I do. I mean, I think I do. It seems great; it's better than where we are. It's more money, but it's a house. It has extra rooms for guests." I rambled as I looked at the paperwork and tried to read his thoughts.

"Yep, it's great, and we're doing it. It's just a long drive home, and I need to squeeze in a nap before work." He stared straight ahead.

"Oh no!" I gasped.

"What?" Jake looked around frantically to see if we were in danger.

"Sorry, I didn't mean to scare you. I just noticed the lease says no pets. We can't bring Lottie with us."

"Yeah, so? We can't be choosy Bree. I'll see if Matthews will take her."

"Give up Lottie?" Give away my ten-year-old dog, who had been with me her entire life? The dog who loved me when no one else did?

"Yes, Bree, Jesus. I'm sorry, but this has to happen. We both have to make sacrifices for the safety of our family. I don't see the big deal. You'll be able to see Lottie whenever you want."

I opened my mouth to object, but he held up one hand. "I don't want to talk about this anymore. We're getting out of Burner and away from the Scaggs. Isn't that the most important thing?"

"Yes." I didn't even know if the word had come out. I looked out the window, holding back tears. I was so devastated, I felt physically unwell.

11

JAKE

That night at work, I wanted to ask around to learn more about the neighbourhood in Roxford, but I had to be sly about it. Matthews was the only person I could tell what we were doing.

As soon as we had a lull in files, we met at the closed toy store and parked beside one another facing in opposite directions. That made it easy to chat and easy to peel away when a call came.

"I can't believe she just accepted us on the spot," I said, sipping a coffee. "After all the failed attempts with other rentals, this was so easy." Too easy? I didn't want to think it, but a tiny voice inside me worried that something was wrong. I pushed it away. "The Scaggs won't find us out there, and I won't feel like I'm being watched by every punk I've ever arrested."

"That's great, man. I'm happy for you both." Matthews gave his winning former-actor smile, but then he hesitated. "Are you sure Bree's okay with giving up Lottie?"

"I mean, no, she's not, but we asked the landlord for an exception, and they said no, and we desperately need to move; this place is great, and she trusts you guys." I shrugged. "Are you sure you're okay with taking the dog? I mean, she's getting old. It'll probably only be for a year or two."

"Of course. Brody loves pugs. I won't have to twist his arm at all. You and Bree deserve a break. It's been a rough year for everyone. How has she been doing anyway?"

"Still struggling, and she's been sick off and on, but she's cheerful with the possibility of getting the hell out of here."

Our laughter was interrupted by the sound of aggressive coughing. A young man was leaning against the side of the toy store, retching.

"To leaving Burner." Matthews raised his coffee, and we clinked cups.

"We finally booked our vacation to the Galapagos Islands for next year," he said. "We've been saving for a long time, and we're just going to bite the bullet and do it. Brody is so excited, I think he has our itinerary memorized already."

I read his tone. "And you're not?"

"No, no, I'm pumped too, but it's still a long way off, you know?"

I took a big swig of my coffee, wondering where the hell the Galapagos Islands were. "I'm not a big traveler. The only item on my bucket list is to raise a happy family with my wife." Considering my demented childhood, that would be no simple task. "Oh, and maybe early retirement." We toasted again.

"You want to run the address of your new rental and see if we get any hits?" Matthews smirked.

"You know I do." I got out of my cruiser and hopped into the passenger seat of his, leaving the door open in case we got a priority call.

Matthews fed our soon-to-be address into his laptop. Nothing dramatic showed up, but it seemed like they went through tenants frequently. Most of the people listed with this as a prior address had only lived there for a year or less. Weird, but not abnormal.

"Now let's check the neighbours' addresses." Matthews wiggled his eyebrows.

"Serial domestic violence," I murmured as Matthews scrolled. "That's not ideal. When was the last call?"

"Last year." He pointed to the date; no one had been charged.

"I can live with that. Run the house on the other side. There were a lot of vehicles in the driveway." I bit my knuckle joint as he put the house number in.

"Feck." Matthews highlighted a portion of the screen. "It's some kind of rooming house. You could end up with a shit ton of calls there."

I sighed. "I'll have to call Bree before she sends in the application. No wonder they have a high turnover of tenants." I wasn't looking forward to telling her.

"Look at it this way. You'll be saving yourselves some grief, and Bree will be happy she can keep Lottie. This could be a good thing, right?" Matthews always had a way of finding a bright side.

I returned to my car and dialed her number.

"Jake? What's up?" Bree sounded strange. Her words were concerned, but her tone was flat.

"Yes, I'm fine. You?"

"Yep. Just sent in the paperwork. Did Matthews agree to ... what we talked about?" Emotion returned to her voice.

I hesitated. "Can you cancel the application? I don't think we should do this. It seems like the neighbourhood isn't so great, and the Lottie thing sucks, and it might not be much better than here after all."

Silence. "It's too late."

"I'm sure it's not. We haven't paid anything yet, and her ad is still up."

"No, Jake. We have no other choice. We need a bigger place."

Need? "Why?"

"I'm pregnant."

"You're what?" I wasn't sure I'd heard her correctly.

"I'm pregnant. *Again.*" The monotone was back.

"That's great. You could have led with that. Aren't you happy?"

So—that was the reason for her tone. She'd had a rough pregnancy and terrible birth with Riley, but the doctor had assured her the likelihood of it happening again was slim.

"Of course, I'm happy. Riley needs a sibling. I just didn't think it would happen so soon. I'm still getting used to being a mother of one child. I don't know if I'm ..." Bree trailed off.

"Are you crying?"

"It's a lot to take in. Riley is so physically dependent on me. I was looking forward to some reprieve when he stops breastfeeding and starts walking."

"You'll get a break while you're pregnant though, right?"

"Sure. I guess."

We had talked about trying next year; this was just a little sooner than we'd expected. "They'll be so close in age, it will be so great for them growing up. Just like we hoped."

"I also have to say goodbye to Lot—" She stopped midsentence.

"Maybe I should come home quickly. It's quiet right now."

She took a deep breath. "No, it's fine. It's just the hormones. Everything will be great. It's done; I sent in the paperwork. We're moving to Roxford and having another baby."

At least she sounded less dreadful in the last comment.

"When did you find out you were pregnant?"

59

"I went out and got a test after you left for work. I was sick again today, and when I looked at the calendar, I realized I hadn't had a period in quite some time. I'm definitely more than three months along."

I had been at work for a few hours. Why would she sit there with this information for so long without texting me?

I knew why. Either because she was unhappy about it, or she didn't know what she wanted to do. "You should have called or texted me. If I'm busy, I'll always get back to you, you know that. Are you sure you're okay?"

"Sorry. It's been a really emotional day. Riley is finally asleep. I'm just exhausted and overwhelmed. Let's talk tomorrow."

"Yes, of course. Love you," I said, but she'd already hung up.

Things hadn't been great between us lately, but this was huge. I guess she *was* tired, and it *had* been a long day, and she was pissed about the dog. It made sense. Most of it. But something about the way she said she was definitely more than three months along bothered me. Like maybe if she hadn't been, she might have considered ending the pregnancy.

I looked up and was surprised to see Matthews still sitting in a car beside me, drinking his coffee. I'd forgotten he was there. I opened my window.

"So?" he said. "How'd she take it? Back to the drawing board?"

"Not exactly. We're still moving there. Bree is pregnant." I half smiled with my eyes open wide.

"What? Whoa! Congrats?" Because of my facial expression, he made it a question.

"Yeah man, I'm excited. Just in shock, I guess. Gonna raise me some kids in between a wife beater and a halfway house," I said in a hillbilly accent.

"Maybe it's not as bad as it looks," he said in his usual glass-half-full way.

"Well, it's certainly better than living in Scaggs territory."

I hoped so. Sometimes it was better to deal with the devil you knew. At least that way you knew what to expect. I had no idea what we were getting ourselves into.

12

BREE

SEPTEMBER 1, 2012

After the initial shock of my second pregnancy had worn off, I started to get excited for the baby. I was still disappointed not to get a break from the physical demands of breastfeeding, and to miss out on enjoying a glass of wine or two. But when the ultrasound showed we were having a girl, I was over the moon to have one of each. So, instead of wallowing in sadness, I embraced the fact that I would have a long-distance relationship with Lottie and concentrated on preparing for the big changes ahead.

The Scaggs had been arrested on drug trafficking charges and were locked up in pretrial. By the time they got released, we'd be long gone.

Moving day came quickly. I was excited to leave Burner, but a tiny bit sad as I carried the final box out of the first and only place I'd owned by myself. It was the end of an era and of my past life.

When I'd moved into this condo, I had been focused on my career and social life. I'd spent three years living here, commuting to work every day and going out with clients and friends several times a week. But now that carefree time in my life was over.

As I rested a small box of Riley's last-to-pack items on my growing belly, I said goodbye to the old me and looked ahead to suburban life with my growing family. The sound of the door closing made an unforgettable imprint on my mind.

Let's go, baby. We're taking you somewhere safe with lots of room to grow.

"What took you so long? Riley and I have something to show you." Jake seemed happy as he called to us from our new front door. How I loved the idea of opening a door into a house. I hadn't lived in a house since my childhood home.

It took a second for me to hoist myself out of our sedan. At just over six months along, it was getting harder to move around, and if this baby was anything like Riley, she wouldn't be small. Jake disappeared back into the house. I grabbed my purse and my one little box. It was such a beautiful day—warm, and the air smelled clean. The road that had seemed busy when we'd first looked at the house was quiet except for a few women laughing and smoking on the deck at the home beside us. They were engrossed in conversation and didn't notice their new neighbors.

I walked up the three front stairs and Jake held his arms out to carry me over the threshold. "Hell no, honey. Thanks, but no thanks."

"Follow me." He grabbed my hand and dragged me around the corner to where Riley sat, clapping. The living room was set up and unpacked.

"Wow." I looked around. He'd even hung up the paintings. "You guys are quick." I'd had a doctor's appointment in the city, met with our new tenant to give him a set of keys, and picked up my last box before driving out to our new home. I'd been gone for maybe four hours.

"Matthews and Brody came and helped. You just missed them. I have the living room done, most of the kitchen, and the beds set up. Should be good enough for tonight, and I can work on the rest tomorrow. Shall we have dinner in the *yard* tonight?" His smile widened.

Riley waddled quickly toward the back door, waving his chubby hand for me to follow him. Outside sat three lawn chairs, a TV table with pizza on it, and a kiddie pool filled with cold water for my feet.

"Sit down." Jake pointed to the most stable lawn chair for me. I lowered myself into it, and we both pretended we didn't hear the flimsy chair squeak with the strain. I had gained a lot of weight with this pregnancy too. It was nice to take a load off but even nicer to put my hot, tired feet in the cold water.

"Thank you." I squinted through the sunshine. "Can you believe we live here now?"

"Can you believe I still have nine days off work?" He'd taken one block off as vacation so work wouldn't know he'd moved, which gave him twelve whole days off.

He handed me a bottle of lemonade. When I'd been pregnant with Riley, I had craved lemonade like it was water in the desert. With this pregnancy, I only craved peaches.

I was surprised when Jake cracked a beer open for himself. He rarely drank. "To celebrate!" He held up the bottle. "To our growing nugget, our new home, and a new chapter in a safe place."

We clinked our bottles together, and Riley came over to smash his sippy cup into ours, almost sending everything flying.

13

BREE

SEPTEMBER 10, 2012

Today would be our first day on our own, and the house already felt empty.

"Say goodbye to Daddy," I said. Riley and I waved at the window as Jake pulled out of the driveway for his first day back to work. We'd had a lovely week in our new place. Nearly everything was unpacked, and it was starting to feel like home. We'd fallen into a routine every morning of eggs and coffee and a walk around the neighbourhood, where we'd discovered a school, an indoor park, and a corner store all within walking distance. I planned to keep up the walking even with Jake back to work.

"Let's get dressed, okay?"

Riley couldn't dress himself but understood what I meant. I held up his Spider-Man costume and he smiled. "Okay buddy, let's do it."

I loaded him into the stroller and discovered the first difficult thing to do on my own: negotiate the stairs to get out the front door. Three little impossible stairs. This far along, I knew I shouldn't lift the heavy stroller on my own.

"Let's try this another way, kiddo." I closed the front door and took him to the back of the house. "Two stairs, much better." I knew I couldn't make it without something going awry, so I unbuckled Riley, pushed the stroller down the two stairs, and buckled him back in.

One of the women next door was smoking on her deck. "He's so cute. What's his name?" She was thin and tall, I noticed, as she leaned over the railing. How long had she been watching me struggle and talk to myself?

"Thank you. His name is Riley."

Riley looked up and waved obediently.

"You new here? When are you due?" She let out a violent cough.

"Yes, and November 13." I rubbed my tummy.

"Good. I didn't like the last people. Mother and teenager. Seemed like there were always people coming and going. A new boyfriend every week."

Two other women, wearing pajama bottoms and robes, came out on the deck and lit up.

"Well, we're pretty quiet people, except for crying babies, so my apologies in advance." I shrugged.

"No worries, hon, we've all had them."

"People don't stay long in that house," one of the women said. "Rumor has it someone died there years ago."

"Is that so?" *Walk away.* But I didn't move.

The first woman cut her off. "Hush now. Those are just tall tales."

"Do you *all* live there?" I asked.

"Something like that," the first woman said. "We're all staying here." She looked around her yard, mine, and the one behind us, then rubbernecked to look out at the street. "It's a women's shelter."

"Oh. Okay. It was nice to meet all of you." I waved goodbye to them as I closed the gate.

"If you want to hear stories about the house, let me know!" the stubborn woman shouted as she erupted into another laugh-coughing fit. "Weird shit happens there every fall."

I pretended not to hear the last part as I walked away. The women seemed harmless enough, though I was surprised the landlord hadn't mentioned anyone having died in the house—or that there was a shelter next door.

I got to the end of the driveway before I realized I'd forgotten my phone. If something happened and Jake needed to get hold of me, I needed to have it. I pulled the stroller up to the front of the house and ran inside. I couldn't have been longer than ten seconds.

When I came out, I noticed a car pulled up perpendicular to my driveway but closer to the shelter. As I rushed down the stairs, it pulled away.

I hurried to the end of the driveway to get a better look. It was a dark SUV and too far away now for me to read the plates. The man in the car hadn't been doing anything sketchy. He could have been checking a map or his phone. I was probably being paranoid, but I was terrified.

I fumbled with the bulky stroller, getting us back inside as quickly as I could. I locked the doors and closed the blinds but sat beside them, peeking out once in a while to see if anyone came back. The driver had looked older than the Scaggs, but I couldn't be sure.

When Riley started to fuss, I realized I'd forgotten to take him out of the stroller. He pointed out the window while arching his back.

"No, honey. No walk today." *Or ever.*

I called Jake, but there was no answer. I texted Matthews, hoping I wasn't annoying him.

Are those criminal guys that came to our old condo still locked up?

My hands shook as I hit send.

He responded immediately.

They're in pretrial for several more weeks at least, maybe months. I checked this morning when my shift ended. Why?

My phone rang. Matthews didn't even say hello. "Everything okay? Why are you asking about the Scaggs?" Never alarm a cop, on duty or off.

"It's nothing. I'm not used to being on my own. A vehicle parked out front for a sec and drove away. I guess I'm still on high alert."

"I don't blame you one bit. But yes, they're still behind bars. Jake and I are on it."

I heard Lottie bark in the background and was hit with sharp pangs of jealousy and sadness. Matthews reassured me I could call him anytime, but by the time I hung up, I still felt lonely—and now I missed Lottie.

I couldn't shake the awful feeling I'd had when I saw that car outside. If it hadn't been one of the Scaggs, who was it?

14

JAKE

It was my first day back to work after the move. The drive wasn't so bad. My first file, on the other hand, was.

A neighbor had called 911 saying that a man had been yelling in a foreign language, then a woman had screamed, and then ... no noise whatsoever. According to the caller, it had all happened quickly. As I walked up the steps to the front door, the smell of food wafted out the window, something with hints of coconut and onion. My adrenaline was high, but I was also hungry. Nothing looked out of place in the yard or my limited line of sight through the front window. I did notice a large semi-freight truck parked improperly out front.

I knocked firmly. On the third knock a man opened the door enough to give me a full visual of his body except for one hand that presumably remained on the doorknob behind the door. He was slim and shorter than me by a couple of inches. He looked like he might be high, but I wasn't certain. Severe stress and intoxication could look the same.

"Sir, I'm Constable Stone. We received a call about some yelling in your home. We just want to make sure everything's okay. Are you alone here?" I tried to look over his shoulder but couldn't see much.

He shrugged, looking left and right with huge pupils. "Yes. Alone." Either he didn't speak English well or was pretending he didn't.

"I'd like to come in and take a look around." I didn't have a warrant to search the home. It would have taken forever to get, and timing was paramount in a potential domestic. His eyes darted around erratically. He seemed high, and he was definitely hiding something.

"Sure, okay." He stayed behind the door, all the while watching a room down the hall.

I stepped into the house and did a quick scan for potential threats. There was no one else in the immediate vicinity, and I saw no potential weapons save for a handful of umbrellas and some lion statues. The living room contained ornate, oversized furniture. I glanced down the hallway in the direction he was focused on. At the end was a bedroom with an open door.

I heard rustling, so I checked my radio to see how far away the backup was. I also asked for an ambulance—all in code so the man wouldn't understand.

In the bedroom, a woman, her swollen face splotched with blood, tried to crawl out from under the bed but seemed to be stuck. I tried not to look at her, as the man's eyes were watching mine, but I wanted to assess how dire her wounds were. *Will he run? Will he attack me?* Was it this man's violence or that woman's life that needed my critical attention?

Backup was still several long minutes away, and I couldn't get a read on this guy yet. I needed him to believe I didn't suspect him of anything so he would remain calm and cooperative. He had the potential to turn on me at any moment.

"Sir, I need you to keep your hands where I can see them." I pointed to the hand that remained behind his back.

He winced as though he wasn't sure what was being asked of him, so I pointed more firmly. As he moved his arm, my hand reflexed to my gun, ready for anything. He revealed an empty but bloodied hand.

"Did you hurt yourself?" I tried to appear impartial. "Did someone hurt you?"

He shook his head. "Did someone break in and attack you?" I willed the seconds to pass until backup arrived.

He shook his head again. "I chop." He motioned for me to follow him.

I kept him in front of me, certain he wouldn't think twice about attacking me. A knife sat on the counter next to some freshly chopped onions.

He gesticulated with one hand and tucked the bloody one in his pocket.

"Please keep your hands where I can see them."

I moved the knife farther away from him to another counter with my gloved hand and made note of its original location in case forensics needed that information later. "I need to see the other rooms in the house."

As I followed him, my radio went off and he jumped. Backup would be here soon, but the ambulance was still five minutes away.

Steps from the bedroom, I heard a gurgling cry, "Help me."

I knew he'd heard it too. I hurried to the woman, keeping the man in my line of sight the entire time. Her teeth had been smashed in, and her face was pulpy and distorted from being struck repeatedly.

I kept an eye on him as I bent down to touch her neck beneath the bed. "Ma'am, you can come out from there. I'm here to help. Are you okay? What's your name?"

I saw a blur and felt pressure on my back as the man jumped on me. I hit the panic button on my radio as I sprang backwards, throwing the man into the wall behind me. He let out a low, feral growl as I spun around to face him, and he lunged at me. When I got a close-up look at his heavily dilated pupils, it confirmed my suspicion that he was high, likely on some type of amphetamine. He was much smaller than me but full of energy and strength as he tried to grab my neck with both hands. I wrapped my arms around him in a bear hug and squeezed as I dragged him toward the door. *Where is the goddam backup?*

We were nearing the front door when I noticed two elderly men hovering over a coffee table in the living room, casually eating their dinner. They'd been there the whole time? *What the actual fuck?*

The man started to squirm out of my grip, so I let him and then tackled him with enthusiasm. We both went crashing through the front glass door and landed on the lawn a few feet away from Constable Souza, who was exiting his vehicle.

"About fucking time!" I shouted. "Cuff him, but photograph and bag his hand before you throw him in the wagon."

I bolted back into the house. By the time I got to the woman, her eyes were closed. I pulled her wrist out from under the bed, but there was no pulse. I was too late.

Help me. Those had been her last words. I'd heard them. I could have helped; I'd been so close. I'd thought I was stopping him from killing her, but he already had. *Oh God, I could have saved her.*

The ambulance arrived and went to work on her anyway, though she was already growing pale. The way she was positioned under the bed, they couldn't fit the equipment over her mouth. I lifted the end of the bed while the others pulled her out, and we discovered why she'd been stuck: she was pregnant. Probably seven or eight months along. Her stomach had been hit, too; it was caved in on one side. Even if she survived somehow, the baby was long gone.

She looked like a squashed spider. One of the paramedics used a gloved hand to clear her mouth of teeth, blood, and flesh so they could begin CPR. Each time they compressed the resuscitator over her face, it filled with blood. The room swirled, my face got hot, and I saw white.

I barely made it out of the house before I threw up. My empty stomach had nothing in it besides the acidic black coffee I had downed just before this file. The coffee tasted like burnt crayons going in and the same coming out.

I had never been sick at a file before. I yacked until the well was dry, wiped my mouth, and went back inside to finish my job.

"Are you okay?" A petite, blond ambulance attendant smiled sympathetically at me.

"Must be the flu."

I had to look at the victim lying on the floor in front of me. She was at the same stage of pregnancy as Bree, give or take. Her face was swollen from the blows and obvious strangulation. Her stomach had been struck many times. It looked as though she'd been hit with his fists and a blunt object. From what I could tell, she didn't have any visible stab wounds. The clean knife was still where I'd left it. I had to take photos and write up a report and burn it all into my brain so I could recall it for the courtroom months from now. All I wanted to do was run.

She was officially declared dead. The fetus was nonviable. But the man who'd done this? That stupid fucking prick was alive.

If only I'd arrived a few minutes earlier, I could have saved them.

When I was done cataloguing the room where the woman had died, I discovered there had been four more people inside the house while the murder was taking place. Souza and I separated the family and organized multiple translators. They were South Asian, but I couldn't pinpoint exactly from where. We called for forensics and serious crimes to take over. I spent the rest of my shift and several hours of overtime in that house doing scene security, reliving the story as I told it to every new officer who walked in.

I was repeatedly congratulated for taking down the man on my own and ensuring he didn't run. I was usually the first man on the scene—the heavy, the muscle. By the time I was driving home, I just felt heavy and weak.

The scenes from that file plagued me the entire way. I couldn't get the image of the squashed spider out of my head. I was afraid to see my family. As I pulled into the driveway, I realized I didn't remember any part of the drive home. I needed a minute.

Eventually, I got out of the car and took the long way around, entering through the back door. As I feared, Bree was there to greet me. Her eyes were tired. Her face was swollen too, almost like that woman's. I gave her a big hug so I could feel her warmth and reaffirm that she was real and alive.

"You smell amazing. It's so good to be home." I pulled away, but when I looked at her, all I could see was the lady's face. All I could hear was her voice. *Help me.*

"No!" I jumped back and squeezed my eyes shut. I opened them again to see my very pregnant, very startled wife looking at me with a jar in her hands. Riley was hiding behind her legs.

"You don't have to help me open it if you don't want to. I thought I'd make you a quick meal, and then I would go out for a while with Riley and let you sleep in peace."

I could see Bree properly now. She looked so beautiful, intact, and clean. Despite her puffy eyes, her smile and warmth and thoughtfulness made my stomach hurt. I loved it that she was so sheltered. She had no clue of the dangers that lurked outside our walls. No clue of what I'd seen only hours ago. My mind replayed images of the macabre scene over and over. I couldn't tell if my eyes were open or closed, but if I blinked hard enough, I could see Bree again.

She touched my arm and came in for another hug, but I flinched. I could tell this wounded her, but I was frozen. I thought I might throw up again. Maybe I was hyperventilating.

"Jake?" she repeated, rubbing my arm faster. Her eyes were wide. "Are you okay?"

My mind was still playing tricks with my sight, and the ringing in my ears was increasing by the second. I stumbled over to the couch. *I'm going mental.* I couldn't, though. I had a wife, a child, and another on the way. *Seinfeld* was on the TV. I cranked it up—loud, familiar background noise from a safer time in my life. It always grounded me.

Bree waddled over with a glass of water and bottle of melatonin. The sight of her bright white cankles, the sound of her voice, and the familiar scents brought me back to reality.

"Sorry, I had a bad night. Also, I may have caught the flu. I might be contagious," I said. I couldn't tell her the truth.

She let out a sigh. "Would you like me to make you something to eat?"

My stomach would have appreciated the food, but it was a hard no. "I think I just need some sleep." I reached for the bottle of melatonin and popped a few quick-dissolve tabs.

"Can I do anything else to help before I go shopping?"

"No, hon, you really can't." That couldn't have been truer. "Just be careful out there, okay?"

She smiled. "I will."

I closed my eyes and let exhaustion and the sleep aids carry me away.

Help me.

Help me, Jake.

Bree lay underneath our bed. What I could see of her face was unrecognizable, though I knew her voice. She was so swollen. She tried to wiggle out, but her belly was stuck. She had eight black hairy legs. As she broke free, her bump ripped open. There was blood everywhere. All I could hear was gurgling. When she turned to face me, she had no teeth or eyes.

I bolted upright. I was covered in sweat but ice cold and ready to fight. My fist was cocked and aimed at Bree. She was awake and had her hand on my arm, her eyes searching mine.

My throat closed. I couldn't draw in enough breath. The air whistled through a tiny hole.

"Jake?"

I tried to remember the combat breathing from my training. Focus on an object, breathe in for two, hold for two, and breathe out for two. Air started to pass through my throat properly.

"I'm sorry I woke you. You were yelling in your sleep, and you sounded distressed." She got up and grabbed a glass of water, placing it on the bedside table and retreating a few steps as though she was afraid of me.

"I was having a nightmare. It's the melatonin." I paused. "Maybe we should sleep separately for a while."

"Why? What do you mean?"

For your protection. But I couldn't say that. I just looked at her, unable to think of the right thing to say.

"If you think it's necessary, then yes, of course—"

"Just for a while. Sleep aids can do funky things." Vivid dreams, sleep-walking. "We'll be back to normal in no time." *Whatever that means.*

"If you think that's best." She paused, looking down at her hands and then back at me. "I guess I can sleep in the guest room."

I could tell she wanted to talk more about it, but I needed to black out. I watched her walk away and pulled two more melatonin out of the bedside-table stash. I needed sleep but was terrified of what awaited me in my dreams.

15

BREE

SEPTEMBER 21, 2012

I was scared to be alone in the house. It was my first night there without Jake. I hadn't lived in a house for years, and I missed the added layers of security you got from an apartment building such as needing to be buzzed in, the elevator, being physically on a higher floor. The only thing that stood between me and the outside world were some old, single-pane windows.

With *Dragon's Den* on in the background to drown out the creepy house-settling noises, I sat in the living room and texted friends and family to stir up some human interaction. Sure enough, my mother called.

Yes, Riley was fine.

Yes, I was fine (ha, not exactly).

Yes, I was getting huge (ugh, yes).

"I wish I could see you before the baby arrives," she said. She'd had my sister and I less than two years apart, so she knew how chaotic things were about to become.

"That would have been nice." I meant it. "I could use the company. Jake has been so busy trying to work as much overtime as possible before the baby arrives, and those two hours of commuting add to the time he's away." I sighed. "I've been lonely." *Especially since I sleep alone even when he's home.*

My mom just listened.

"Roxford is far enough away from Burner to avoid the criminals Jake arrests, but it's also just far enough that my friends don't want to drive all the way out here. Jake takes the car to work, and I stay home with Riley every day, doing the same thing over and over." It felt good to vent.

"Aw honey, I could cancel my trip to Hawaii. It's nonrefundable, but I'd do it."

"No, it's fine."

"How's Jake?" She asked because it was expected, not because she cared. "Does he like living there?"

"He's okay. He's had some really stressful files at work. It will be great when the baby comes, and he can take some time off."

"He's taking some of *your* maternity leave again, is he?" Mom's tone was critical.

"It's called paternity leave when he takes it, Mom, and yes." Sure, it shortened my paid leave, but I'd just look for work when it was up. "I'm on my own out here and will need help in the beginning. He'll be able to bond with the kids and help Riley adjust to being a big brother. It's common for couples to do this nowadays." I held my breath, waiting for the "in my day" comments to roll in.

"Well, your father and I ..." She stopped when she heard me sigh. "Anyway, you have to do what's right for you and your sweet family ... whom I cannot wait to squish and hold when I get back from my holiday. Which I could still cancel if that's what you want me to do."

Prior to meeting Jake, I used to travel several times a year and loved having some sunshine to look forward to. Rain spattered the windows.

"Don't cancel. We'll be fine."

A thump came from upstairs. We had just transitioned Riley from a crib to a lowered bed in anticipation of his little sister's arrival. Had he rolled off?

"Mom, hang on." I made my way up the narrow, winding staircase. Riley's bedroom door creaked when I opened it. He was sound asleep in the middle of his bed where I'd left him.

"Everything okay?" Mom asked.

"Yes. I'm still getting used to the acoustics of this old house."

"I still don't know why you moved so far away. You could have just come here."

"You know why. I'm not going over this again." I walked downstairs and sat back down on the couch, slightly out of breath. I flipped through some more crap programming and settled on another reality TV show.

"Anyway, I'll bring the baby back one of those cute sundresses from Hawaii and—"

Another noise from upstairs. This time, instead of running up to check, I hung back and listened. I didn't want to be one of those hovering mothers that I already suspected I was.

"Yeah, those dresses are adorable." I tried to stay in the conversation while keeping an eye on the baby monitor. The light blip was going up, but I didn't hear anything. Then came the rhythmic sound of soft footsteps. The light moved up and down in time to the footsteps, though they sounded like they were coming from the upstairs bathroom across from Riley's room.

I held the phone away from my ear so I could hear better, though I was frozen in place on the couch. I wanted to go up and investigate, but I was too afraid. I'd just been up there. No one was in the house. Riley was sound asleep.

And yet ... those were definitely footsteps, moving carefully, like someone who was trying not to be heard. As soon as I sat up, poised to run upstairs, they stopped. It happened at least three times.

"Bree? Are you listening?" I'd forgotten she was still on the line. "You okay? It sounds like you're breathing funny."

"I'm fine, Mom. Just tired. What were we talking about again?"

Now there was no noise. No footsteps, no light on the monitor. I forced myself to take a few slow, deep breaths. The doctor I'd seen after Riley's traumatic birth had shared some breathing techniques with me—the only useful thing I'd gotten out of the sessions.

As my breathing calmed, I got brave and decided to make sure everything was locked.

"You were saying I should go see the surfers and something else on the north shore ..." my mom said.

I did a full circle of the downstairs, checking every window and door. When I got to the kitchen, I heard the footsteps again. This time, the noise was coming from the back deck. A shadow passed by the opaque window that made up half the door. Were those criminal brothers out of jail?

"Mom," I whispered. "Someone's outside on my deck. Don't hang up."

I stood still, not breathing—watching to see if the shadow moved again. Nothing. I spent one long, painful minute just trying to breathe. When I looked out the window, nothing was there. I reached for the door lock, convinced it was important to check and make sure. For me, and for Riley. I slid the deadbolt to the left. I figured if I did it slowly, it wouldn't make that loud *ka-chunk* sound. I was wrong. Just as it clicked over, the baby monitor wailed at full volume.

"Bree, what's happening?"

The red lights were lit up to the max as a bloodcurdling scream filled the old house. I dropped the phone and ran as hard as I could up the stairs. The scream was nonstop, steady at the same pitch. Riley's cries, whether he was hungry or just wanted me, came in rhythmic waves. I'd never heard this one before.

My chest pounded so hard I felt sick. Bile filled my throat, and no air expanded my lungs as I tore down the hall into my son's room. I kicked the door open ... and he was sound asleep. No screaming, no lights on his monitor. Nothing. I put my hand on his chest to feel his breathing, and everything was fine. I checked all the windows upstairs and went into the rooms where I'd heard footsteps. In the bathroom, I threw open the shower curtain, fully expecting something dreadful to jump out, only to discover a tub still half full with cold water and the toys from Riley's bath early that night.

I was so confused. Lately, I hadn't been sleeping well. So many strange dreams occupied my mind. Was it possible I was hearing things? I remembered the pamphlet on postpartum depression Riley's doctor had given me after his birth. It mentioned delusions as a possible symptom.

Once I was satisfied with the security of the upper floor, I grabbed Riley and headed back downstairs to turn off all the lights and get ready for bed. I'd had enough of this night. Riley looked at me, dopey and confused, but tucked his face deep into the crook of my neck and became dead weight in my arms.

As I rounded the corner at the bottom of the stairs, I could see through to the kitchen. The door to the patio was wide open. I ran toward the kitchen and slammed it shut, locking it tight. I recalled unlocking the deadbolt before the scream happened but not opening the door.

I turned around to lean on the now closed and locked door and was stunned by the state of my kitchen. The bureau was open, paperwork scattered across the floor. Some of the kitchen cupboards were open, their contents in disarray. The kitchen looked ransacked.

I'd only been upstairs for a few minutes and hadn't heard any commotion downstairs. This level of damage should have caused some serious noise. I was gobsmacked. I ran to each window to look outside but didn't dare undo another deadbolt or open any doors. There were no cars, no people on foot. The street was quiet.

My mind was all over the place. Had I been upstairs longer than I'd thought? Had the screaming been loud enough to cover up whatever had happened downstairs? What the hell could have caused such a disturbance—other than a person? *In my house.*

I was winded. The baby was kicking so hard, there was no way I'd be able to sleep. I realized my phone was vibrating on the floor, so I bent to pick it up. When a loud bang came from outside, I nearly wet myself. I looked out the window. The wind had kicked up again and was tossing stuff around the yard. *That's what it was.* I must have opened the door when I'd unlocked it and run upstairs. The wind had blown it open and tossed stuff all around the kitchen.

My mom was on the phone, her voice shrill.

"It's just a storm," I said. "Everything's fine."

After we hung up, I looked at the screen and saw she had called over a dozen times before I'd picked up.

I put my sleepy Riley down on the couch and went to clean up the kitchen. That was when I noticed the counter. All of the baby bottles had been lined up neatly by a pot of water sitting on the stove. *The wind can't explain this one.* Creeped out and overtired, I carried a dozing Riley upstairs to sleep with me. I took advantage of the weird door locks on the main bedroom and locked all of the interior ones, then lay there for what seemed like hours, replaying the events of the night in my head. I wanted to call Jake just to hear his voice, but when it went straight to voicemail, I hung up. What could he do about any of this when he was an hour's drive away?

What had happened, and when? Had there been enough time for someone to come in and quietly destroy my kitchen? Could the wind really have done those things? Why would anyone line up baby bottles?

I went back and forth between extremes. *I am insane, I've had no sleep, I could have done those things myself and simply forgotten about them*—couldn't I have? There was a logical explanation for it. It was the wind. An intruder. An animal. Could it have been an animal?

Eventually, my mind must have shut off as I listened to the clock and waited for Jake to come home.

A pregnant woman sat in my glider, touching her belly and staring at me. She wore a long white nightgown and looked miserable. Her plain face had been weathered with worry and time, and it was framed by long, tangled hair. She was silent but kept tilting her head from my belly to hers with a quizzical look on her face as she glided back and forth. It looked like she was holding some of my baby bottles. I closed my eyes and rubbed them so I could see her clearer. She was so blurry.

When I opened my eyes again, I gasped. She was only two feet away from my face. My heart raced, but I was unable to move. She wasn't smiling, but she didn't look angry either. Her expression was blank as she touched her bump with one hand and mine with the other. The bottles were gone. Her touch felt cold. My bump felt cold. The baby wasn't moving. I wasn't moving. I couldn't breathe.

The woman lifted her hand off my stomach and brought it to my face. Her slender fingers came to rest on my cheek. She was touching my face! I opened my eyes, panicked, and saw that it was just Riley. His beautiful blue eyes were an inch from mine as he giggled while clumsily touching my hair.

That vision had been so vivid and disgusting. But it was just a dream. Maybe it all was. Still panting, I shook the sleep off as I pulled Riley in for a hug and a neck full of raspberries.

I scooped him up, and he giggled all the way down the stairs. As we walked past the living room, I noticed our empty driveway. Jake wasn't home yet? Poor guy. He worked so hard. It was eight o'clock in the morning; he should be back soon. Riley and I walked into the kitchen to put on some coffee and make some breakfast. The baby bottles and pot were gone. Had I put them away? Had they ever been left out? I was seriously doubting my mental health and decided to just move on with the day.

But what if someone had been here?

16

JAKE

OCTOBER 4, 2012

After a rough week of nonstop nightmares, I marched down the hallway to Harvey's office, determined to get some time off before I started my nightshift, and ran smack into Constable Doyle.

"Jesus, Stone, where's the fire?" She rubbed her shoulder where I'd smoked her, but she was smiling.

"Sorry. Shit. Did I hurt you?"

"No, I'm a tough girl." She winked and punched my shoulder in fake retaliation. "Looks like we're working together tonight. How do you like your coffee? You look rough."

"Two and two, extra strong."

"Just like you." She laughed. "I'll bring it to the briefing."

As soon as I was sure she was out of sight, I hurried to catch Harvey before he left for the day. Doyle was right; I was in rough shape. I was running out of steam to handle the stress that came at me night after night. I was afraid of getting pulled off the job or being ostracized, but I was even more afraid of losing my mind and my entire career.

I looked to see who was in the hallway before stepping into the office and closing the door. Harvey sat at his desk, surrounded by paper, frowning at the disturbance.

"What is it, Stone?"

"Sarge, I need some time off." I fiddled with my duty belt while staring at a spot on the wall just past his head so I could avoid looking him in the eye. "I had a bad file a few weeks ago, and I can't stop the images from running through my mind. I'm even seeing these things with my eyes open. Is that normal?"

I felt silly saying it out loud, but I didn't know what else to do. When I'd looked at Breanna the other day, I'd seen the woman's smashed face sputtering "Help me" through a bloodied and broken mouth.

Sergeant Harvey looked at me with the corners of his mouth turned up. Harvey was the one who'd trained me when I was a recruit. He was tough as shit and had been in Burner his entire career. He was old school and took guff from no one. I think he'd died on the inside a good twenty years ago. His swarthy exterior was preserved by alcohol and nicotine, the latter of which permeated his office. He must have just gone out for a smoke.

"This happens to all of us, Stone. Totally normal for some files to affect you more. It'll pass. Your baby is almost here, right? You'll be taking some time off. Hang in until then. You'll be fine." His tone was firm.

"But I'm not sleeping, the nightmares are so bad." For a moment I thought I might cry. That would have been a death sentence.

"I have a whiskey or two before bed. Does the trick. Sounds like your commute might be too much for you. Do you go to sleep as soon as you get home?"

He knew about my move. Shit.

"Yep, I go down right away. It's fine, I'll try the whiskey. Sorry to bother you." I had to stop making noise before I got myself in trouble. Generally, I avoided alcohol if I could. My parents were drunks, and I'd be damned if I was going to turn into them—especially my father.

I scurried out of the office, though I could feel Harvey judging me for acting like the pussy he thought I was.

After the long shift and hour-long drive, I didn't get home until 10 a.m. I was bagged.

I put my hand on Bree's belly. "Come on, little one, any day now would be great." The sooner the better.

Bree saw me grab the vodka but didn't say anything.

"Just to help me sleep." Sarge's orders.

Her eyes darted around the kitchen. "Can I fix you some breakfast?" Her smile was pinched.

"No, I'm good." I held up the bottle and took a swig. I laughed and hoped she would join in, but she didn't. I knew she hadn't been sleeping much. None of us had. As I rounded the corner to go upstairs, Bree was watching me, making the same face Harvey had made.

She probably thinks I'm a pussy too.

17

BREE

OCTOBER 30, 2012

The creepy lady was in the rocking chair again, the one where I planned to feed my baby. There were dark hollows under her eyes much like my own. Her hair was long and unwashed; she looked like a tired mom dying for a shower. She wore an old-fashioned nightdress that looked worn with time and hung down to her ankles.

The chair had been a gift when Riley was born. I had many memories of dozing with him in my arms, desperate for sleep. The paranoia of something bad happening to him in my care had often been calmed by swaying in that chair.

But now the haggard pregnant woman was tainting these memories for me. My focus faded in and out. She was on the chair, rocking and holding a baby while she stared out the window. It was a newborn, a preemie, making cooing baby noises.

I blinked again, and the baby was on the floor screaming. And then it was gone. Not even the blanket remained. I didn't hear the baby anymore, and I didn't hear her.

Thank God.

I gasped as the woman reappeared. This time, she stood near the glider, looking down at her belly and then at the floor. She was crying, whispering, "My baby, my baby."

Each time I blinked, she drew three or four feet closer. She wasn't speaking anymore. Three more blinks and she was beside my bed. She looked down at me and reached for my tummy.

I was paralyzed. I couldn't move, and I couldn't scream. *Where was Jake?* She touched my belly with one hand and bent toward me, touching her lips to my ear so gently I could barely feel them. "Wake up," she whispered slowly.

I bolted upright at the same time as liquid trickled between my legs. Every hair on my body stood on end as I sat there frozen from the waist down, peeing myself with fear. Was it a dream? I couldn't bear the alternative—that it had been real.

My legs were stuck to the bed. I was still urinating, but it was trickling out. I reached down; it wasn't blood, but it certainly didn't smell like urine. As I started to panic, the cramping began. It felt like I'd been frozen in this position forever. Finally, I reached for my phone.

The contractions came faster than I'd expected. I had read the books, attended the classes, and watched the videos, but with Riley I'd been induced and had no experience with natural childbirth—these could be more Braxton Hicks. Everything that could have gone wrong last time had. I was excited to meet my baby but also terrified.

Anxiety was taking over. I couldn't catch my breath or yell for Jake who was asleep in the next room. I fumbled out a quick text.

In labour come here now.

Jake burst into the room. I could always count on his disordered sleep to make him easy to stir.

"Are you okay? Should we go to the hospital? Is that pee?"

"Call the midwife." I handed him my phone as I winced in pain. She said she'd come by for a checkup.

"You're early." He looked relieved and stressed at the same time. "I'll have to call into work. I can't work. The baby is coming, right? I'll phone your sister to look after Riley. Did you say she was in town? I'm hungry. Are you?"

His rising anxiety was actually calming me down.

"Yes." Paige was in town visiting friends. And yes, I was hungry. "Food." With Riley, I'd been high risk and was in labour for so long they wouldn't let me eat in case I needed a C-section. Afterwards, I'd been ravenous. "And coffee."

And then, just like that, the cramps stopped, and I was able to get up. I waddled to the bathroom with excitement and fear, and then I heard the voice again say, "Wake up."

Now I was sure I was hearing things. I waited for the liquid to stop tinkling out and made my way downstairs to see about that food.

Half an hour later, Paige flew through the barely open door, wrapping her arms around me as best she could. Paige was definitely the prettier sister: tall and slim, with lightly freckled skin and bright red hair down to her waist. It wasn't as thick as mine, but every time she put it up in a bun, I wondered how she didn't get a headache from the weight of it.

"You got here fast," I said.

She must have broken some laws on the way.

"Well, you *are* in labour, aren't you?" She laughed, but she also must have noticed I wasn't hunched over in pain or screaming.

"Annie!" Riley still had sleep in his eyes and pillow creases on his cheek. He and Paige had a special relationship that warmed my heart. Annie, instead of Auntie, had recently been one of his first words, looking at her photograph. She used to live close to us and had only moved away this past spring. It had been an adjustment for us all.

"Riley, my man." Paige threw her arms open, picked him up, and whirled him around.

"Is that my favourite sister-in-law?" Jake came out from the kitchen to greet her.

At that moment, the midwife arrived with her gear and stood in the open doorway. Carolyn was in her early sixties and barely five feet tall, but she was a force to be reckoned with. I motioned for her to follow me upstairs. Surely, if anything could get this labour back on track it would be all the up and downing of the stairs.

I lay down in bed while she confirmed that my water had broken, checked my progress, and listened to the baby's heartbeat.

"I swear I was having contractions." I felt a little silly at all the commotion I'd caused.

"It isn't uncommon for labour to stop and start again," she explained. "I brought all the ingredients for a midwife's brew. We have time, Breanna, but given how anxious you are, I see no reason to wait."

A brew. I felt like I was entering a secret world.

Downstairs, Jake located the blender while Carolyn explained the potion. It contained apricot juice, almond butter, another secret ingredient that she brought with her in a vile, and a few other items I didn't catch.

"Now, Bree, you have one hour to finish it, and from the time you're done it could take up to an hour for anything to start, so don't panic if—" She looked up from her clipboard as I slammed the smoothie like a shooter at a Cancun nightclub. My years of drinking had finally paid off.

"Well. Okay." She giggled and wrote another note. "That's done."

She rubbed my back for a moment, then looked at Jake. "Call me when the contractions get going—this can progress a lot faster than a regular induction." With that, she disappeared out the door.

"I think I need more coffee." I was chipper again now that I'd drunk the potion; it would be go-time soon. The coffee wasn't even half-brewed when I felt a contraction. By the time it was ready to pour, I felt a second, stronger one.

"I'm going to go"—I had to pause to breathe—"run a bath." I walked slowly up the stairs, pausing every few steps.

About fifteen minutes later, the contractions were consistent, so Jake called the midwife and filled her in. He put her on speakerphone just in time for me to hear, "Get her out of the tub and go to the hospital now. I'll meet you there."

As I said goodbye to Riley, I felt a pang of guilt and sadness knowing this would be our last moment as a family of three.

18

JAKE

When I came back from the hospital, the house was clean, and Riley was asleep. *Maybe I chose the wrong sister.* I chuckled to myself.

"What's so funny?" Paige came around the corner with her coat on.

"Nothing." I pointed to her jacket. "What's the hurry? Stay for a drink." Bree was right. This old house and its noises could be pretty creepy. I also hadn't been alone in a very long time.

"Normally I would, but visiting hours at the hospital are over soon, and I want to swing by and meet my new niece. Oh, and see my sister, I guess." She laughed. "I told Bree I'd bring her some Halloween chocolate."

"You're coming back tomorrow for trick-or-treating, right?"

"I wouldn't miss it. Congrats again, bro." She gave me a quick hug and left.

I closed the door and turned back to my empty house. It felt a little cold, but that was probably because it wasn't full of the rambunctious energy it normally contained. I cranked up the thermostat and poured myself a celebratory glass of brandy. It wasn't every day you became a dad again.

"Cheers." I downed the glass, poured another, and took it back to the living room. I sat down and flipped through the channels. There was nothing good to watch on TV, and it was really quite cold in the house. I went upstairs to check on Riley. His room was even colder. No wonder—the window was open. Why would Paige have done that? I closed it and leaned in to see if Riley was breathing. At what age did parents stop checking? I got close to Riley's face but must have breathed out too heavily. He winced at the smell of my brandy breath. He was fine. I tucked him in and kissed his forehead. Then I wiped it off, thinking of the alcohol on my lips. *I can't believe I'm a dad. Of two now.* It was wild.

I turned on the baby monitor and brought the receiver downstairs with me.

In the living room, I could now see my breath. It wasn't just me; it was freaking cold in here. The thermostat agreed. The furnace must have gone out. I didn't know anything about a damn furnace, but how hard could it be? I grabbed Bree's computer and refilled my glass as I began to Google. There were instructions on how to relight a pilot light; I just had to find the furnace.

I stood up, swaying a bit, and checked in every closet and utility area—no luck. I did, however, find our landlord's phone number.

"Hey Denise, it's Jake Stone, your"—I blanked for a sec—"tenant."

"Is everything all right? It's a bit late to be calling."

Late? It wasn't even nine o'clock. I explained the situation.

"Right, okay," she said. "The furnace is under the house."

Jesus Christ.

"I can send Jerome out in the morning to do it, but you'll be mighty cold by then."

"Yeah, it's already too cold for my son. I'll go down. Where is it?"

"One sec." She muffled the receiver. "Jerome! It's the tenant for the Roxford house. The furnace is fritzing again."

Again? Cool.

"Heya, Jerome here. The furnace is in the crawl space near the front of the house directly below the living room. But the entryway is through a trapdoor on the patio at the back of the house, kay?"

Delightful.

"You'll need to go out to the deck in the backyard and pull open the hatch. Bring a flashlight, a headlamp preferably, as you'll want both hands to find your way. It's a bit of a maze down there. It gets narrower and shorter as you approach the front of the house."

Of course it fucking does. "Is there any other access point?" *You know, where people can hear my screams?*

"No, sorry. If the pilot light is off, you'll need to light it. If the light is still on, you'll probably need to change the filter. There should be some extra down there. If you have any trouble, I'll whip out there in the morning."

I hung up without waiting for a reply. This was unbelievable. To have to go down there, on my own, in the dark. *Thanks a lot, Jerome.*

I checked on Riley again and had another snifter of brandy. There was no way out of this. Riley would be too cold, and Bree and the baby couldn't come home to this. *Don't wuss out because of a few rats and spiders.* When I loaded my police flashlight, phone, and baby monitor onto my duty belt, I couldn't help but laugh. I looked ridiculous.

I walked out onto the back deck and followed Jerome's instructions to get down to the trap door. After reefing on it a half dozen times, I forced it open. But the damn thing wouldn't stay open, so I grabbed a nearby hunk of wood and jammed it tight in the corner.

The stairs down were dark and unpleasant and ended at a dirt floor. The air smelled of rust, must, and history. Another smell, too, that I couldn't quite place. It was acidic, like a chemical or spoiled perfume. Gag city. I took my flashlight out of the holster and turned it on. The light flickered. Not surprising, as I used it daily. It probably needed new batteries, though I swore I'd just replaced them.

It flickered off, so I smacked it. That did the trick for about one second, and then when I was about halfway down the length of the house, it went completely off. I had a backup flashlight with me, of course, but it was dollar-store quality and small.

Holding the mini-light high, I said, "Hello," out of both habit and nerves. I heard rustling in the corner and felt ill. Probably a rat. It was creepy as fuck down there, and rats loved creepy. As I moved closer, the scuttling stopped. I hated rats.

The furnace was small and ancient, just like this disgusting crawl space. It was clear that the pilot light was still lit. *For fuck's sake.* I was getting pissed off when I remembered the landlord's gomer husband had said there might be some filters nearby. By this point, I was having trouble seeing. I'd had more brandy than I should have. I reached around the stupid furnace and found a new filter tucked in behind it. Fumbling around, I eventually figured out where to put it. The old filter was disgusting. It was so full I had no clue when it would have last been changed. Gomer had really dropped the ball here.

I tossed the dirty filter aside and dusted off my hands on my pants. When I stood back up, the flashlight caught something black and furry moving in the corner. It was moving fast, and I did too. The light bounced around as I ran. I tripped over something and landed face down in the dirt, a bunch of it getting in my mouth. I had dropped the mini-light an arm's length away but somehow it stayed on. I spat out the dirt and turned over to see what I'd tripped on. It looked like a wooden tool. I put it in my duty belt and picked up the flashlight.

It revealed a frightening pair of eyes looking right at me. I let out a yelp as I jumped back up.

Someone tapped me on the shoulder.

I spun around, fists swinging. Nobody was there. I sprinted up the steps and knocked into the hatch door, jostling the wooden block out of its position and down onto my head. The hatch slammed shut.

I reached up and pushed. It was pretty solid. I tried again, banging on it and yelling. *Shit.* I was stuck down here? *Calm down.* It was just a dingy basement. I banged and banged on the hatch, but it wouldn't give.

For a second, I thought I heard a baby crying. I looked down and saw Riley's monitor light up. A small cry was followed by screaming. *Shit, that's him.* I picked up the monitor and said, "Daddy's coming," forgetting that it wasn't my work radio. I holstered the wailing monitor and threw my shoulder into the hatch from one of the upper steps. Riley sounded inconsolable. Not like his usual self, though he often got attended to much sooner. *Oh man, what is happening up there, and why the fuck won't this hatch open?*

"I'm coming, son!" I yelled out into the universe as I thumped away on the hatch. Finally, it gave way and I bolted up through the door. I ran through the house with my gear dangling from the belt, losing a few items along the way. I couldn't tell if Riley was still crying, as I'd dropped the monitor receiver as well. I bounded up the stairs two or three at a time and burst through his bedroom doorway, breathless.

Riley lay there, perfectly still. I was moving closer to check on him when he did a little stretch. How could he go from wailing to sleeping in such a short space of time? I could hear the furnace humming now through the vent, which was a huge relief, but Riley's room still felt cool. The stupid window was open again. I thought I'd closed it. I walked over, shut it, and locked it, checking it twice.

My hands were filthy, so I crossed the hall to the bathroom to get cleaned up. When I saw my reflection in the mirror, I nearly jumped back in fright. I was so dirty I looked like a fucking coal miner. A trail of blood ran down from my scalp. I must have hit my head harder than I'd thought.

After washing my hands, I headed downstairs to tidy my mess and fix another drink. So much for all the cleaning Paige had done. I'd left a path of dirty footprints on the floor, along with all the crap that had spilled out of my belt when I'd run upstairs.

I went outside to secure the hatch. When I looked up, I noticed a car idling in the alley, parked behind the neighbor's house. *Oh God.* Had the Scaggs found us? I barreled towards it, but the driver must have seen me and peeled away. The only thing I could see was that it had been a woman. I tried to calm down. It must have been connected with that revolving door of women who lived beside us.

I went back inside, locked up, and cleaned up after myself. As I gathered my things, I saw the item I'd tripped over in the crawlspace. It wasn't a tool at all. It was a toy. I tossed it onto the counter and poured another small glass of brandy to help me sleep.

The car in the alley was still on my mind. But the driver had been female. That meant it wasn't Bychkov, nor any of the usual scumbags I put behind bars. It wasn't anyone I knew. But no matter how many reasons I came up with, habit wouldn't allow me to let it go.

19

BREE

OCTOBER 31, 2012

I didn't want to leave the hospital. The birth had been painful and intense but a beautiful contrast to the trauma of birthing my son. When it was over, Jake went home, and the baby and I ate and went to sleep. I would never admit it out loud, but those six hours were the best night's sleep I'd had in almost two years, free of toddler antics and a shift-working husband waking me up.

Any law enforcement officer's spouse would attest that hearing the sound of your significant other ripping the Velcro of their Kevlar vest was both a sweet relief and a rude interruption to your sleep. But there was no quiet way to do it.

Last night in the hospital, I hadn't had a single nightmare of a scary woman touching my tummy. I did wake up in a panic looking for Riley—until I realized where I was. Then I spent some time staring at Ivy, at first to make sure she was breathing and then to marvel at her. She was so relaxed and at home in this world already. She fed right away, just latched on, had a few sufficient swigs, and passed back out. The entire process had been so opposite of my first one.

The sun was rising. I was sure my little man was already watching *Thomas the Tank Engine* with his breakfast. I texted Jake.

Hey hon, how did you do on your first night without me?

I realized this had actually been my first night sleeping alone since Jake and I moved in together. I was always flanked by him—though not anymore—or Riley. Or I would end up in Riley's bed as that little booger still woke up so often through the night. I missed them, but I hadn't minded the peaceful sleep one bit.

Ugh, it was something, he texted back. *Can you come home yet? And where is the new car seat?*

He still hadn't installed the car seat? Oh well.

The nurse said I can go home at noon. Only sixteen hours at the hospital; way better than the five days of last time. *See you at noon? Kiss Riley for me.*

I hit send and closed my eyes.

I must have dozed off again, as I woke up to the sweetest cry beside me. Milk had soaked my hospital gown, so I picked up my squirmy newborn and latched her on.

"Good morning, beautiful. I'm so happy you're finally here. You get to meet your brother today. He's going to love you so much." I teared up, touching her tiny cheek.

"Knock-knock." A cheerful pair of nurses appeared at the door. "It's almost time for the baby's first bath. Would you like to do it, or would it be okay if we did? We have a nurse in training here." The one who was speaking grinned and pointed to his cohort, who shrugged sweetly.

"You can do it. This isn't my first rodeo." I was happy to have help for the first and probably last time in a while.

They took Ivy away to bathe her and brought me an early lunch. By the time Jake and Riley arrived, Ivy and I were both dressed and ready to go.

Riley rushed over to me. "Mama!" He gave me a huge hug and then pointed to Ivy. "Baby." It was perfect.

We loaded up and headed home, a happy family of four.

I nearly forgot that it was Halloween. Well not entirely, as I had purposely tried to make Ivy arrive before midnight, but in all the excitement of her birth, I'd forgotten that today was a big day for Riley. It was his first year trick-or-treating, and though I was sad I wouldn't be able to go out with them, I was excited to hand out candy.

"I've got dinner under control!" Jake shouted from the kitchen.

What a nice surprise. I could get used to that. I wasn't the best at cooking, probably because I hated doing it. Jake was an amazing cook.

He popped into the living room and thrust a smoothie into my hand. "Supposed to help with milk production." He must have remembered how much we'd struggled to feed Riley the first few months.

"It's going well so far." I pointed at a fast asleep, dream-feeding baby. "But I'll take it." I sipped it cautiously. My last smoothie had been the midwife's hellfire mix just the day before.

Jake didn't wait to see if it was any good, and it wasn't, but I drank it anyway. It was nice to have him home and happy again. I guess if I was on a long break from a hellish job, I'd be whistling and cooking dinner too.

Paige came downstairs carrying Riley, who was dressed in a fuzzy Cookie Monster costume. We figured with his favourite auntie here to trick-or-treat, he wouldn't notice Mommy was missing. Jake slapped on some devil horns and was finishing up in the kitchen when I wandered in.

"Do I need to do anything with dinner?" I asked, mostly because I was still hungry.

He walked over and kissed me. That was when I spotted a weird object on the counter.

"What the heck is this?" It looked like a toy that a high schooler had made in woodworking class: a dozen wooden balls strung together to resemble a doll, with a long string on top. The paint was chipped and it was covered in dirt, but I could tell it was meant for a baby or a small child.

"I found it under the house when I was changing the furnace's air filter last night," Jake said. "Long story." He waved the topic away and pointed to the oven. "Dinner is cooked. I just have it covered on the stove to stay warm. You don't have to do anything except hand out candy."

The doorbell had already rung twice. It was so awesome to be able to do this. Having lived in an apartment for the last decade or so, I had missed giving out candy and seeing all the dressed-up kids.

With that, Jake, Paige, and Riley set off, and I propped myself on the end of the couch closest to the door. I still couldn't believe I'd had a baby only yesterday. I felt amazing compared to the last time. It just felt like someone had kicked me square in the ass.

We got quite a few kids—more than I was expecting, anyway.

"Oh, you're so scary," I said to a pair of goblins. I was wearing a witch's hat, and I held Ivy in one arm as I opened the door. "Take two chocolates and bring one back to your mom."

I spied groups of parents standing on the road as their kids went house to house, and I felt a pang of guilt over missing Riley's first real Halloween. *Next year.* I shut the door to await another bunch of ghouls and was tidying up when there was a booming knock at the door.

"That doesn't sound like a kid," I said to Ivy.

When I got to the door, there was no one there.

I pulled the door closed and locked it in one move. The bad guys were locked up, and Jake was likely only a few houses away, but my heart pounded all the same.

"I see Nicky Nicky Nine Doors is alive and well in Roxford." I spoke to Ivy as confidently as I could, convincing myself this was normal Halloween antics.

As I sat down on the couch and wolfed a couple of chocolates, there was another big, booming knock at the door. This one was consistent, four times in quick succession. When I rounded the corner to where I'd left my costume hat, the door was ajar.

"That's weird," I said to Ivy in a sweet-but-actually-scared voice. "I know I closed and locked it." No doubt in my mind. I opened the door and leaned out, sheltering her behind it.

"Hello?" It had gotten dark outside since the last trick-or-treaters had rung the bell. I looked left and right. No one was there. I flinched and peed my pants a little when I noticed a petite lady, likely in her early seventies, standing at the end of the driveway and staring up into the house. She wasn't dressed warmly enough for the weather, wearing only a blouse and pants and no jacket. Was it a costume? An old-lady mask? The person was short enough to be a child.

She looked right at me.

"Hello?" I called. "Are you trick-or-treating? Have you lost your parents?" I was frozen in place, trying to decide if I should bolt the door or go out and see if it was a lost child.

The person never broke her gaze as she pointed up to our second-floor window. At that moment, a loud bang came from upstairs. I slammed the door and ran up the stairs as quickly as I could, noticing my sore butt all over again.

"Hello? Hello?" *Please, let no one answer.* The light was on in the guest room where the woman had been pointing, and it was extremely cold, but the room was empty. Paige had complained about the temperature in that room, but the windows were thin and the insulation in the house was bad. There wasn't much we could do. It was always cold in there. I didn't remember turning on the light or fiddling with the heat, but perhaps Jake had done it when he was getting ready to go out.

I went room to room to see what could have caused the noise and found nothing out of the ordinary. In the main bedroom, another noise came from the decrepit balcony the landlord had warned us about. My breath sped up as I crept toward the door that led outside. There was no window or peephole to look out of. What if someone really was there?

I set Ivy down on the bed, picked up Jake's heavy work flashlight from the floor near his duty belt, and quietly, slowly, unlocked the door. As I tugged it open, I held my breath, the flashlight poised for attack. A pair of eyes stared at me, and I let out a small shriek. It was a goddamn raccoon.

"Shoo!"

After closing the door securely, I tossed the flashlight onto a pile of dirty laundry.

Ivy began to fuss, so I picked her up and went back downstairs. The old lady, or the trick-or-treater dressed as an old lady, was gone. She'd probably wanted to point out the raccoon. *Thanks, I guess.* I grabbed another chocolate.

No sooner had I sat down to feed Ivy than another knock came at the door. I stood up again, wincing at my soreness, and peeked out the window before answering.

"Trick-or-treat!" Two adorable toddlers stood on my doorstep, dressed as Thing One and Thing Two, and their dad was the Cat in the Hat. I loved that he'd come to the door with them.

I tossed him a candy. "You didn't see an elderly lady standing over there by herself, did you?"

He turned to look where I was pointing. "Nope."

I closed the door, locked it, and set Ivy in her pack and play so I could use the washroom. Just as I was washing my hands, a gigantic crash came from the kitchen. I ran to see what had happened. Mashed sweet potato, along with the shattered bowl it had been in, was spread from one end of the floor to the other, and the gas element on the stove was on.

"Hello?"

I jumped as I heard voices in the house. But it was just Jake, Paige, and Riley coming in the front door.

"Stay back!" I shouted. "There's broken glass on the floor."

Jake walked into the kitchen still wearing his shoes and carrying Riley.

"What happened here?" he asked with a pinched expression. "And why was the front door unlocked?"

I felt the blood drain from my face for the second time that day. I knew I'd locked the door that time. "I have no idea." I was officially losing my mind.

He leaned in closer to me, placing his hand on my shoulder. "Are you okay?"

I smelled alcohol on his breath. "I'm fine." Strange, I hadn't seen him drink anything, but it was a holiday after all. "This happened seconds before you walked in the door." I looked down at all the wasted food and started to cry.

"It's fine, Bree, don't stress." He rubbed my shoulder. "We still have the chicken wings. I cooked too much as usual, so there's still some in the oven."

Riley leaned down and patted my shoulder, too.

I couldn't help but laugh.

"What happened here?" Paige asked as she surveyed the damage.

"We have no idea." Jake started laughing.

Paige took Riley, and we went back into the living room while Jake cleaned up the mess. She studied my face as if looking for clues. All I could do was shrug.

"It looks like the element was left on the whole time, so the bowl exploded," Jake said from the kitchen. "My fault. I thought I turned it off. At least no one got hurt."

Jake came around the corner, mashed sweet potato on his fingers. He put some on his nose, and Riley laughed. "I'm going to wash up and serve us some spooky dinner." He stretched out the word "spooky" for effect. Riley loved it.

From where I was sitting, I could see out the living room window. That woman was back. She stood straighter this time and pointed upstairs again. When I opened the curtain, she was gone.

"What are you doing?" Paige sounded bewildered.

I spun around. "Nothing. Thought I saw something."

I was seeing things. *Great.* None of it was real. It was all me.

20

BREE

NOVEMBER 10, 2012

Shortly after Halloween, Paige made the long trek home to Hazelmere, a nearly eight-hour drive. I missed her already, though Ivy was such a calm and chill baby, our lives were pretty easy. She would sleep for four or five hours, nurse, and then drift off again.

"Baby," Riley would say while pointing to her crib when he wanted time with me, but he didn't have to say it often.

I felt quite spoiled. Jake was so happy with his newfound time off work. A lot of people, my mother especially, judged him for taking *my* maternity leave, but it was the best decision. I didn't have a job to return to—I had only been working a part-time contract from home—so I'd be looking for work regardless of when my time was up. The time off couldn't have come soon enough. He'd been so agitated before Ivy was born; now he was returning to me—to us.

We settled into a routine. I stayed up with Ivy at night when she fed, and Jake let me sleep in, waking me with breakfast and coffee. I was getting proper sleep now. I wasn't seeing things anymore. I was happier and felt more supported.

"Don't forget, the Matthews are coming over to meet Ivy on Wednesday," Jake said from the kitchen that morning. "They would have come sooner, but apparently I've been keeping him too busy at work with my early departure."

"Oh?" I set Ivy down in the pack and play. "I thought they were dividing up your files among the whole watch?"

Jake popped around the corner with breakfast and fresh coffee. "Most of them, yes, but they gave a few crucial ones to Matthews. The ones we were working on together." We clinked coffee cups. "He didn't mind. He asked for them."

"I'm looking forward to seeing them—and Lottie." I thought we were being a bit rebellious by having her here, although the truth was, I couldn't have cared less. I was tempted to take Lottie back. The landlord would never know.

"Matthews loves having her around. Apparently, she sleeps with them." Jake made a face. He hated dogs in the bed, so I used to sneak Lottie up onto my side.

"He's still sore about Ivy's name," Jake said. "He said in return for him taking Lottie, we had to name our child after him." He winked.

"Name a baby girl after him?" I laughed, realizing I didn't even know his first name. If I'd been told it, I didn't remember.

Riley ran in a tight figure-eight around us, yelling, "Choo-choo."

"I'll take him to the indoor park after a shower," Jake said.

"Sounds good to me," I mumbled with a mouth full of eggs. I had forgotten how ravenous one could be while breastfeeding.

Jake threw a towel over his arm, pretending to be a waiter. "Would you like anything else, Miss?"

I was giggling and shaking my head no when his phone rang. How I'd missed this playfulness. The phone kept ringing, but we couldn't find it in the messy kitchen. We looked under papers, dishes, on the floor—and then the ringing stopped.

When the ringing started again, Riley found it and ran into the room with a grin. "Da!" He handed the phone to Jake.

"Unknown caller." He motioned to the phone as he set it down. "I'm not answering it."

As soon as his personal phone stopped ringing, his work phone started. I grabbed it for him, glimpsing the text on the screen:

911 Stone, call in immediately.

21

JAKE

I thought work was being a bit dramatic calling both of my phones to reach me—and so early in the morning. I was about to call back when the phone rang again.

"Hello, go for Stone."

"He's dead," Sergeant Harvey blurted, out of breath but matter of fact. "They're still taking him to the hospital, but I know he's dead. I'm calling the whole crew, but I wanted you to hear it from me first."

"Wait—what?" I had shivers. If he was calling the whole crew, that meant it was one of us.

"It was his last call of the shift. It happened so quickly I couldn't get there fast enough. He was already gone. They'll work on him until he gets to the hospital and then call it. But I'm looking right at him. He's dead."

I felt like I was going to explode. "Who?"

"Matthews." With that, Harvey hung up.

This isn't possible. It's not real. The buzz in my ears grew louder, and the world around me slowed down. I couldn't see anything because my head was in my hands. *I must be dreaming. Please be a dream.*

"Jake, what happened?" Bree knelt before me, bringing me back to the cruel reality that my best friend had passed away in the line of duty, working *my* shift.

"Matthews is dead." I left her there and went into another room to make some calls. None of this made any sense. He should have been off shift by now, or almost off. Shit, Harvey did say it was his last file.

Everyone's phone was either busy or went straight to voicemail. Finally, Abbott called me back.

"Yeah, Stone, it's true. I was on the other side of Burner when the call came in. No details yet. Just come down to the detachment, they promised to debrief us as soon as they had the intel from the videos."

I hung up the phone. "Fuck!" I yelled and put my fist through the wall.

I grabbed the car keys and left the house. I could see Bree crying in the living room, but I couldn't deal with her right now. I drove straight to the detachment. I couldn't be anywhere else.

***

There was chaos at the detachment—as chaotic as a group of trained, paramilitary individuals could be. It was shift change, so some distraught and some stoic members were suiting up while fully uniformed members coming off duty were hunched over on benches in the change room, sitting near Matthews' locker.

"What happened?" I barked. "Does anyone know?"

"I heard fentanyl exposure was involved," someone said. "That's all we were told."

Harvey walked into the room. He wasn't wearing his duty belt. Half his shirt was untucked, and his pants and shoes were caked with blood. I'd never seen his uniform look less than perfect.

"Matthews was one hell of an officer, and an even better man," he said. "This is going to be hard. All of the procedures are in play, and next of kin has been notified."

Brody. I hadn't even thought about him.

"A full regimental funeral will be planned in the coming days. I've called other districts to come help out today. If any of you can't work, we have you covered. I've also called the force psychologist to be here for a debrief this afternoon after the media release for anyone who *needs* it."

I could hear a few sniffles, but no one dared to make eye contact. This crew wasn't going to cry, they weren't going to take the day off, and they certainly weren't going to attend any shrink debrief.

"I'm off to review the footage," Harvey said. "We'll notify you all when we can." With that, he left.

I felt sick. Matthews was a good man. So young, and things had been falling into place for him and Brody. They'd been on their way to a dream vacation later that year. He was coming over on Wednesday. He wasn't supposed to die. It was supposed to be me. *It should have been me.* How the hell could I go on after this? He was the one person I could trust, the one person I could ask for help. The one person who truly understood me.

I could feel everyone looking at me. I knew they were thinking the same thing. No one liked me anyway. Why would they? I was a jerk. I was crude and rude and selfish. Willing my baby to be born early and needing to take the time off, stretching the crew thin, putting Matthews into this position.

I marched out of the detachment and hit my car with my fist. I quickly realized how stupid that was, but it felt good. I needed to feel pain. I needed to feel *something*. I slumped down hard onto the curb.

"Hey." A quiet female voice came from behind me. It took me a moment to realize it was Constable Doyle. We had partnered together a few more times before I'd gone off work, but that morning she was in her civvies, which consisted of dark skinny jeans and a tight, plain white T-shirt. Her hair was always up and under a hat at work, so I hadn't known it was blond and shoulder length until now.

"You okay?" She came closer.

"Fuck, no. You?"

"Absolutely not." She squatted down beside me, resting her hand gently on my shoulder. I felt a small spark of something. Comfort? Connection?

"You can't stay out here alone waiting. It's going to be a while before we find out anything. We're all going for drinks until they're ready to debrief us." She stood up and held a hand out to pull me up off the curb.

When our hands connected, I felt another flicker of heat between us. I stood up beside her, and she looked me in the eye with a small smile. It was like she could see directly into my broken heart. She smelled incredible, and I felt instantly guilty for noticing. I wiped my hand on my pants as I walked beside her, careful not to stand too close.

22

JAKE

Harvey stood at the podium of the media conference room, shifting his girth from one foot to the other, seemingly unable to stand still. He had changed into a fresh uniform, polished his shoes, and shaved. The room was packed full of familiar faces, and they were as pale as the walls, as hard as the shining floor.

"Thank you all for your patience, and for being here today. Before we send a press release out and make a statement to the media, we wanted to tell you, his brothers and sisters, what happened first. We've used body and dash cam footage to piece together the events. This won't be easy to watch, and you certainly don't have to."

No one moved.

"Corporal Matthews was finishing his night shift on C-watch and was driving back to the detachment in car two Charlie seven."

That's my car. Sweat beaded up on my face as the room tilted.

"We received a call of an unattended vehicle down in the flats near the industrial area."

Everyone nodded. Dead-End Fen was a well-known drug trafficking area not far from the detachment.

"We had a vehicle description of a forest-green station wagon. Matthews would have recognized this vehicle as one often driven by the Scaggs brothers, who were local dealers for the largest drug trafficker in the area, Ivan Bychkov. They often did small drug drops in it. The Scaggs had been released from pretrial earlier yesterday, and Matthews was actively looking for them."

I felt physically ill. I'd had no clue those guys were even close to being released. Why were they sitting in a recognizable vehicle in a known drug area? Were they trying to get caught?

I steadied my breathing as Harvey turned on the TV. The video was from Matthews' dashcam. We could see the road as he was driving. Then I heard his voice.

"I got this one; it's the Scaggs. Sorry, I mean this is car two-Charlie-seven. I'm en route. Send backup."

Harvey paused the screen. "Our records indicate that he got there in under a minute—no lights, no sirens. When he arrived on the scene, he set the timer on his dash cam as per proper protocol. He then checked in on backup, and I—they—were at least fifteen minutes out."

"Matthews ran the plate, confirming that it belonged to Cherry, Bychkov's main girl. He radioed that visibility was low because of the fog, but that it looked like there was only one suspect in the vehicle."

Harvey resumed the video. Matthews parked partially on the road as per protocol, many feet behind the suspect's vehicle. This was at the base of the hill, on the flat part of the road, flanked by a ditch that led down into the muddy flats. He exited the cruiser and walked toward the driver's side of the vehicle. The car was running.

Jesus Christ, Matthews, why didn't you wait for backup?

The spliced video shifted to a view from his body cam. These weren't standard issue, but both Matthews and I had bought them to cover our butts after we'd been falsely accused of assaulting a suspect in custody. The car windows were rolled up, so Matthews used his mag light to knock on them. There were actually two suspects in the vehicle. The suspect in the passenger seat was difficult to see as the seat was reclined and he was hunched over a box on his lap. More clearly, I saw that Vincent Scaggs was in the driver's seat. He looked high as fuck.

"Open up, Vince," Matthews said calmly and clearly. "And keep your hands where I can see them. You too, Willy."

After a moment of confusion, Vince managed to roll down the window. "I didn't do nothin' wrong," he said, slowly lifting his hands to the steering wheel.

Matthews used his flashlight to look inside the car. "Get out of the vehicle, Vince. Willy, put that box down on the floor and get your hands up."

The image of the camera was blurry, but I could see Vince reaching toward the passenger seat. Matthews dropped his flashlight to free up his hands as he reached for the car door, knocking his body cam loose. Visibility went fuzzy, and the video cut to the dash camera.

"Hey. Stop. You're—" Matthews yanked the door open while Vince and Willy scrambled with something in the passenger side, maybe with the glove box. The car rolled slowly sideways into the shallow ditch. Matthews leaned in and fell into the car, and then the ignition shut off.

Matthews and Vince struggled, physically shaking the vehicle. It looked like punches were being thrown and some of them were landing, but the visual was too far away. A loud grunt came suddenly, followed by an explosion of white dust. Willy was trying hard to get out, but his door was pinned by the ditch. There was more fighting between Vince and Matthews. As the powder settled, Vince yelled, "Willy!"

Vince let go of his grip on Matthews and leaned over to his brother. Willy slumped over, his head hitting the passenger window in the tilted vehicle. Shortly afterwards, Vince also stopped moving.

Matthews had slipped backwards out of the vehicle. By his face in the dashcam, he was figuring it out as he slurred his words into the radio. "Need a couple buses, and Narcan. The Scaggs are unconscious and I'm going down. Suspected fentanyl inhalation. A box of it blew up everywhere. I've also been stabbed pretty good. Tell my husband I—"

Matthews sank to the ground, lying face down. His gun skittered a few feet away and did not discharge. The video was shortened from the moment he fell to the moment backup arrived. None of us could have watched the nine painful minutes of him lying alone on the ground. At fourteen minutes and thirty-two seconds, Harvey arrived. He quickly secured the scene, looking for immediate threats, and then attended to Matthews.

The chopped footage switched perspectives to one clearer and closer up. This must have been Harvey's body cam. Matthews wasn't breathing. We watched Harvey check his airway and pulse. He did a quick scan to see if anything was broken, and then turned him on his side, and then slowly onto his back. This was when Harvey, and the audience sitting quietly in this room, saw how severe the stab wound was. It looked like it had hit an artery by the amount of blood. Harvey put his fingers in the wound and leaned down to stop any remaining blood from coming out.

Matthews was so pale he already looked dead. But he opened his eyes slightly and asked, "I'm not going to make it, am I, Sarge? Tell Brody how much I love him."

Matthews closed his eyes again. Harvey began slapping his face. "Come on, Matthews, don't go. Tell him yourself. Stay awake, for fuck's sake." He used his free hand to start compressions, not moving his other hand off the wound. "Where the fuck is the ambulance with that Narcan?"

As the ambulance pulled up, Harvey yelled, "Breathe, Matthews, breathe!" He waited until they were able to trade pressure on the stab wound, then said, "No pulse, not breathing." He reverted to his typically untouchable personality as he walked away and picked up his phone, and the video stopped.

One of the media liaisons, a petite woman around thirty, turned off the TV and walked over to the podium. Harvey stepped back toward the wall with his head down and his fingers laced in front of him, looking small.

The young woman straightened her papers and stood tall before clearing her throat. "The attendants from the first ambulance continued to work on Matthews, who officially had no pulse. They worked on him all the way to the hospital, where he was pronounced dead. We're waiting on an autopsy, which will prove definitively if it was the wound or the substance that killed him.

"The second ambulance arrived to work on the suspects. There was a delay in getting to them as they needed help extracting them from the vehicle and had to suit up first due to the contaminate in the enclosed space. William Kenneth Scaggs was declared deceased on first examination. Vincent Joseph Scaggs was taken to hospital, but it doesn't look good. We're still waiting for an update on his status and blood work.

"Early results indicate that the drug in the vehicle was heroin mixed with carfentanil, not fentanyl as we initially thought. The drug squad recovered several large cardboard boxes of it from the trunk. We'll be able to identify where they're from by the large red characters on them. This is a significant seizure." She shuffled papers again and looked into the crowd. "Any questions?"

I looked around at the sea of faces. Some were crying, some were statuesque, and others were angry. Then I saw faces bloated from drowning, blue from lack of oxygen, bloodied from gang violence. I saw Matthews' pale face, and Harvey's blood-soaked pants. Even after rubbing my eyes, I still saw so much death. There was no oxygen in the room, no air in my lungs, and no feeling left in my face. My already heavy heart was desperately trying to pump blood to the rest of my body.

Matthews had been my best friend. I loved him. Not a very dude thing to admit, but that guy always had my back, made me laugh, and cared enough about my family to spend his last few minutes going after the Scaggs to keep us safe, as we had both done together many times before. It had cost him his life. *I* had cost him his life. "How do I fix this?"

"Can you repeat the question?" The media liaison was looking at me. I must have said that out loud.

"No, nothing." I stood up, nearly falling backwards. The room was swirling, as though I'd had too much to drink. I focused on the door, about twenty impossible feet away, and made it through the frame and around the corner before everything went dark.

"Stone? You okay? Sit up. Do it slowly, though." It was Constable Doyle. I must have passed out. *How embarrassing.*

"What happened?" I asked.

"Matthews died."

"I know. I mean, why am I on the floor?"

"Because Matthews died." Tears ran down her face. "And please call me Amber."

I swallowed the tennis-ball-sized lump in my throat so I wouldn't react emotionally.

"I got you some water." She helped me lean up against the wall and sat beside me. "No one else saw you fall. We'll sit here as long as you need. And then we'll stand up again."

From where we sat, we could still hear what was going on in the media room.

Harvey wrapped up the session. "If anyone wants to speak at the funeral, you'll have to submit a form, and it will be in a queue depending on the time allotted. We'll hold a wake a few days after the funeral for members and spouses, so if you don't get to speak at the formal processional, you'll get a chance to say your piece there. You'd better dust off your serges and be in good shape for it."

He paused. "This is one of the worst parts of our job. For some of you, it's the first time; for all of you, it won't be the last. Lean on one another and find an outlet. We're in this together. That being said, as per policy, we have brought in the force psychologist. Dr. Steinman is in the meeting room for the next two hours *if* needed. I am obligated to remind you that all notes from his sessions are made available for the record. You're free to go." He left the room, walking right past Doyle and me.

As friends and colleagues filtered out, I just sat there on the ground. I hated the thought of bringing this stuff home. I felt like the bad guy here, but I didn't see a way forward. All I could manage was to stare at Matthews' locker a few feet away. It had been decorated with photos and kind words. I mustered the strength to stand up and walk over to it.

One photo in the front was of the two of us, with our arms on each other's shoulders, bent over laughing. It was in the early days. We'd already seen some stuff, but not enough to strip our souls yet. *He's a very funny guy.* Then I reminded myself: *was.* He was also so down to earth. Everyone gave him a hard time about his sexuality and his past as an actor, but I loved that about him. He'd wanted something more real, wanted to make a difference. And this was how it had ended.

My head was bent forward, touching the locker, when I heard Amber say, "Hey, let's go next door, okay?"

She meant go see Dr. Steinman. "No way." I wasn't about to get caught talking about my pussy feelings.

"Come on, Jake. Do it for me. I need it too."

I wasn't convinced it was really for her, though it could look that way, which would get my pride off the hook. I wiped at the corner of my eye gruffly and followed Amber to the debrief room to do something I'd never thought I would do, for fear of ridicule and punishment: talk to a mandated shrink.

It was fine. I just had to be really careful about what I said. Any of it—all of it—could come back to haunt me.

23

BREE

NOVEMBER 14, 2012

I was in the kitchen with the kids. Paige had called after seeing the report on TV. "The news is devastating," I said. "Matthews was such an amazing person and a good friend to Jake. I can't believe he's gone."

"How is Jake coping?"

I airplaned a spoonful of oatmeal into Riley's mouth to keep him quiet. Ivy was fast asleep in her swing. "I don't know. The last few days have been a blur." I lowered my voice, listening to hear if she had woken up yet. "He left for the detachment right after he found out and has been going in every day since. He got dropped off by some of the guys very late last night. His phone has been ringing all morning, but I haven't heard any movement."

"You haven't talked to him?"

"No. He was in a bad way when he left yesterday." I looked at the hole he had left in the wall. I kept meaning to cover it up until I figured out how to fix it.

Footsteps sounded from upstairs.

"Gotta go." I hung up. I wanted to be off the phone so I could talk to him. I'd gotten up early and had made breakfast and coffee. I'd even cleaned the house. I didn't want him to have to worry about anything today. As I heard him come down the stairs, I took a deep breath.

"Good morning." I kept my tone carefully neutral. "Would you like breakfast?"

"Nope." He poured coffee in a to-go mug and looked at me in a way I had never seen before. His eyes were hard and narrow, his lips tensed and pursed tightly together. He softened for a millisecond when he saw Riley but hardened again when he looked back at me and Ivy.

"Where are you going?" I tried to sound casual.

"Work." With that he grabbed his keys, put on his shoes, and headed out to the car. I noticed he had forgotten his phone and went to reach for it when he popped back inside out of nowhere, snatching it out of my hand.

"What are you doing? Why are you checking my phone?" He demanded. The look on his face matched the expression of disgust he made whenever he talked about his alcoholic father.

"I was just going to bring it to you, that's all." My lip was quivering now, as much as I begged it not to.

"Sure." He turned to go.

"Where are you going? What happened? When are you coming back?" It was the shrill-wife voice I'd always tried to avoid. But I couldn't control myself; I needed to know what was going on. I had learned more about Matthews' death on TV, but that hadn't given the full details.

He spun around and was up in my face, looking at me and Ivy in a way that made me regret my string of questions. "I'm going to the detachment. There's a lot to do for a regimental funeral. I'll be home when I'm home. Any more questions?"

"No." My voice was barely audible.

He left, slamming the door, startling the kids, and leaving me more alone than ever.

I let out a quick cry in the bathroom. I knew I had to keep it together even if I felt like I was falling apart. Jake was a mess. Grief was confusing. I'd have to figure this out on my own. Just like yesterday, when he took the car and our only debit card. He had lost his and had been using mine ever since. No point in my even considering the credit cards. They were all maxed out, and we were running out of groceries. I'd have to take two kids on foot to the store today with no money.

I raided the children's piggy banks, something I'd sworn I'd never do, but if we were out of milk for much longer, Riley would definitely have a tantrum. Either that, or I'd have to feed him breast milk, which I wasn't above trying if needed.

Ivy was strapped into the front carrier, and Riley was in his stroller. He was not happy about that. This kid needed to run for at least an hour a day to keep the household sane. Normally, Jake took him to the park every day. I'd have to let him loose in the backyard when we got back.

It was nice to get out, and we made it to the corner store without much trouble.

"Good morning." The clerk was always so darn cheerful. "The milk is $5.25, please."

Crap, I only had five dollars. He saw me cringing and looking at the money in my hand.

"It's okay, Miss." He shook the contents of the "take a penny, leave a penny" jar to show me it was covered. The tiny act of kindness made me well up.

"Thank you." I took the milk and assessed my situation. There was nowhere to put it except in Riley's lap, so there it went. He laughed and started tapping the side of the four-liter jug like it was a drum. Well played.

Our walk home was less carefree. We'd made it to about four houses away from ours when one of the women from the shelter spotted us. Normally it would have been a welcome conversation, but this woman had left the shelter, imbibed some substances, and had to dry out before returning, as per the rules.

"Your house is creepy." She slurred her words.

"Okay." I sped up.

"Weird shit happens there in the fall." She tripped and almost fell.

"Do you need me to call someone for you?"

"No. I'm almost Shober. I'm halfway there." When she began singing "Living on a Prayer," I tried to walk away, but no such luck. She lurched beside the stroller, lunging too close to Riley and the baby. "Ah-ah, shagging on the stairs."

Riley kept drumming. In other circumstances, it would have been funny, but all it did was egg her on. She hunched over for some air guitar, following us halfway down the driveway. I tried to get Riley unbuckled and into the house as quickly as I could, and to fold down the stroller without bumping Ivy's head. The entire time, the woman belted out the song in the driveway. I was about to heave the stroller up the stairs when Riley knocked the milk from the top step. It landed sideways, causing the lid to pop off and milk to flood out. I picked it up quickly enough to save about half of it.

By the time I noticed the dark SUV slowly driving by and peering into the house, I was too late to catch a look at the driver.

24

JAKE

NOVEMBER 20, 2012

I 'd been hungover before, but this was a doozy. My head throbbed. The regimental funeral was today. Somehow, I had to squeeze myself into my serge. I hustled into the laundry room to look for a pair of socks.

"Breanna, where are my formal boots?" I yelled, hurting my own head.

"Um, I don't know," she called from the living room. "I'll check the front closet."

I could hear her flapping around looking for them, crashing and making the house messier than it already was. She was such a disaster lately. I didn't even know why I'd asked her to help find something.

"I found the hat!" she shouted. "Oh, and the boots."

Thank goodness. I was fumbling, trying to do up the buttons on the red jacket and realizing I should have had it altered. I hadn't realized how much smaller I'd been as a shiny new recruit straight out of Depot. In fact, the last time I'd worn my formals had been during my graduation.

Breanna came running in with her newfound treasure, looking proud with a huge smile pasted on her face.

"What the fuck are you smiling about? I'm going to a goddamn funeral."

She set down the boots and left the room. Jesus Christ, now she was upset. Was I supposed to go comfort her on the day of my best friend's funeral? *Fuck that.*

I was looking for the last couple of belt pieces and my brown leather gloves when I heard her whimpering in the other room.

"I don't have time for this!" I marched over to her and got right in her face. "I don't have time for your shit today. Matthews was *my* friend, not yours, and he'd still be here today if—"

Breanna had stopped crying. She shrank down into her chair, eyes wide, looking up near me. Not at me, not in the eye—like I was some fucking animal she couldn't make eye contact with.

"You're afraid of me? What have I ever done to you? I can't believe this. Today of all days. I'm out of here." I noticed Riley watching me from underneath the table. He was tucked back against the wall, crouched down and holding on to the table leg.

Fuck, now Riley is scared of me? I grabbed my shit and left.

I was driving way over the speed limit. Bree had pissed me off so badly. I had to perform at a televised funeral and be there to honour my best friend and his family. Couldn't she see how horrible this was? Instead, she'd smiled at me in my formal uniform as though this were a special occasion. Earlier she had even asked me to take photos with Riley, and where she could watch the funeral like it was some sick reality TV show.

If only she had been born on time. I couldn't stand to be in that house or anywhere near her or that baby. I slowed down as it dawned on me that if I'd gone to work that day, Matthews would be alive, and I would be dead. Bree and the kids would be alone. Riley and the baby would grow up without a father. My dad had been a piece of shit, but at least I'd had one, and he paid the bills—just like me.

My head hurt so much from all the booze and from trying to sort out what had happened in the last twenty-four hours. I didn't even remember how I'd gotten home the night before. The car was there, too. Had I driven? I shook my head and drank my coffee.

My phone buzzed with a text from Abbott:

The whole crew is here. Where are you?

Fuck, I was late. I didn't bother texting back as I ripped into the parking lot and joined the crew. They stopped talking when I walked up. I knew I wasn't imagining it; they hated me too. Everyone did—except Amber, who waved gently from her place in the lineup. I nodded at her and took my place as the funeral procession commenced.

25

BREE

"**M**ore!" This kid wanted breakfast for every meal of the day. He was eating like crazy all of a sudden. It was such a relief after the struggles we'd had in his earlier days with breastfeeding.

I had set Riley up in his highchair in front of the TV to watch cartoons while I tried to find the livestream of the funeral procession on my dumpy laptop. Only parts of the funeral would be aired on television, but the entire thing would be livestreamed online, if only I could figure it out.

Some of the spouses had invited me over to watch it with them, which I thought was a bit dark, but kind. But Jake would have been angry if I tried to insert myself into the day, and figuring out a ride would have been a huge headache, so I'd declined. All the spouses watched the funerals, even if they didn't know the member personally. It was a way to honour the officer, the spouse, the family, and it was a sad reminder that it could be your person one day. I didn't understand this ritual yet. But I had known and cared about Matthews. I wanted to be there more than anything.

Riley banged on his tray, and I put another slice of banana on it for him. He was almost too big for the highchair, but he liked sitting in it to watch TV because it put him eye-level with the screen. As long as I kept feeding him, he'd stay happy.

I was a relatively new police wife. Jake and I had been married for less than two years, and I was still learning about the culture, the limitations, and now the end. *What happens if your spouse dies on the job?* There was a massive celebration to honour their life, but really it lacked the intimacy needed for those close to them to heal.

Matthews' death had crushed me. He'd been the only one of Jake's crew who had tried to get to know me, introduce me to his partner, or ask how I was doing when he saw me. He looked me in the eye when we talked, asked Jake about me, and had visited us in the hospital when Riley was born. He'd helped us move and helped Jake survive the day at work. And he made Jake laugh. The sporadic lightness in Jake that had existed when Matthews was still alive was gone now.

"There's no point in you coming, Bree," he had snapped at me. "You don't have anyone to watch the kids, the place will be chaotic and packed, and you'll be sitting there for hours."

As usual, there was no room for me in his police life. No room for me to grieve or be sad or matter. I understood, sort of, but I wasn't okay with it.

"Here you go, sweet pea." Riley was really into bacon. It was actually his first word: "Bakie." We couldn't always afford it, but I'd found some end bits in the freezer that morning. Eggs, bacon, and fruit.

By some small miracle I got both babies fed and down for a nap while the procession was still happening. I snuck away from a sleeping Riley and sat back down to watch. Members from all over the country and the world were attending this event. They marched in two lines along the highway from the detachment to the conference centre, which held thousands of people. It was amazing to see all the different forces come together for this.

I arrived just in time to see Jake's crew walk past. It must have been nearing the end of the march. He looked so handsome. I liked his general duty uniform better than the serge, but there was something so beautiful about watching him and his colleagues walk together in unison to honor their friend. It was clear even with the poor quality of my screen that his group of men and women were more directly affected than the rest.

The exhaustion and devastation were clear on their faces. Jake's pain resonated through the camera. He'd put on the face and the outfit, but his mask wasn't fooling me.

Everyone stood as the commissioner spoke, and then they sat down. A few other high-ranking officers made speeches, and then Matthews' sister was up. Brody sat onstage beside her, clearly in no shape to speak.

She looked so small at the podium, all alone with a lineup of big men behind her. "My brother, Corporal Arlen Matthews, was an incredible man. He—" Her voice cracked, and her lip quivered. She looked devastated and panicked at the same time. A man in a red serge approached her from behind and placed his arm around her. It took me two seconds to realize it was Jake. My heart swelled and blew up.

He held her, and she put her face into his shirt and began to cry. Jake took the notes from her hand and read them calmly and flatly, devoid of all emotion. It was the strangest sight to witness the tenderness with which he'd held and supported her against the robotic tone of his voice as he read her beautiful words. I guess this was what they'd trained for. *Be strong, don't feel, just be there.*

At the end of her speech, he led her back to her seat and got her some tissues before returning to the stands.

I watched the rest of the ceremony, the speeches, the tributes, and the songs. But there was not one mention of Matthews' crew, Jake's name, or their friends. Two or three family members spoke, half a dozen people from Ottawa who had likely never met Matthews, and the local detachment sergeant who had found him and worked on him. Thank God he had the tact not to discuss that. Harvey was known for a lack of social awareness.

When the camera panned the audience during one of the musical tributes, Jake was comforting another woman. My stomach lurched. This looked far more intimate than a casual friendship. Both of his arms were around her, and he looked upset too. The only thing keeping them apart was the size of their Stetson hats.

The event ended with everyone walking back out in procession. That was it. Matthews was dead, gone, and buried, and it was over. They would all go back to work like it had never happened and hope that one of them wasn't next. I didn't know how Jake did this. I wasn't sure if I could do it.

My phone buzzed: *I won't be home until late.*

Are you okay? I texted back.

No. Need to be with the crew.

Okay.

His crew. That woman he'd been holding had been wearing a serge too. She must have been a member of his crew. I couldn't help but wonder if the crew he needed to be with that night was her.

26

JAKE

NOVEMBER 24, 2012

It was the usual daily bullshit: try to sleep, give up, get up, caffeinate. Bree got to sleep in. She looked rested, and of course she wanted breakfast made for her and wanted me to take Riley out to run around while she did ... what? Shower? Relax? I was getting tired of this crap. Didn't she know what I was going through?

"Maybe you should take Riley to Darke Lake for a walk today instead of that indoor gymnasium. It looks like it's going to be such a nice day," she mumbled with her mouth full of scrambled eggs. "We need to tire him out so that he'll behave tonight at the wake."

Whatever. I just wanted to get out of the house.

Riley and I left for the playground.

"Push," he begged from the swings. Then he ran over to a horse-like piece of equipment on a spring and proceeded to rock back and forth as hard as he could, laughing and making animal noises the entire time. Fresh air and time alone with Riley made me feel marginally human again. *This kid cracks me up.*

When he got bored, he took off running past me to the trail we often walked on. I hurried after him. The park had a lake in the middle of it, surrounded by forest, along with a walking path and the playground. Riley loved to play in nature, even more than the playground itself. When I caught up to him, he was squatting near a puddle, poking at the dirt with a stick.

"Look, Da." He held a leaf with his arm fully extended. A black beetle clung to it. He was obsessed with bugs.

I loved him so much, but I couldn't help but second-guess the choices that had gotten me there. I'd wanted a family so badly to replace my own, but I shouldn't have jumped in so fast with someone I hardly knew, and I definitely should have thought twice about bringing children into this wretched world.

My phone went off with a text, snapping me out of my stupor. It had better not be Bree asking me to stop somewhere to pick something up on the way home.

Hey you.

It was Amber. I couldn't help but smile.

Amber got me and what I was going through more than Bree ever would. We had been talking to each other more lately, since Matthews died. She definitely had a thing for me, or maybe she was just super flirtatious. Police culture could get pretty risqué whether you were married or not. I probably wasn't the only person she teased. I was careful not to let it get out of hand, but I was having fun and enjoying the attention.

You're still coming tonight, right? she texted.

Yeah.

You aren't bringing your wife are you?

The whole family actually, I replied, surprised at her directness.

Can you imagine what trouble we could get into if they weren't there?

Could I ever. Amber had spared no detail telling me all about her sex life and preferences, such like how she used to swing with her ex and loved to give BJ's. *One little BJ isn't cheating, is it?*

I looked up from my last flirty text and realized I couldn't spot Riley.

"Riley?" I yelled, likely overreacting. I took a deep breath; he was probably just playing hide-and-seek. I didn't want to scare him. "Helloooo Riley, where are you?" I popped my phone back in my pocket, ashamed of myself. "Come out, come out, wherever you are."

He couldn't have gone far. I hadn't been looking at my phone for that long, had I?

I jumped up from the bench I'd been sitting on. "Riley, come here, now! This isn't funny." All the moms were staring. I was one of the few fathers at the park.

Shit! What have I done?

I glanced at the roadways and parking lots to see if anyone was acting suspiciously or trying to get away with a small child. I was yelling the whole time, using the police holler that terrified Bree. All of Roxford could hear me. But Riley wasn't in the parking lot, and he wasn't near the roadway that I could see.

As I noticed the shoreline, another sickening thought crossed my mind. I ran fast and hard, barely breathing, not certain if my feet were even touching the ground. The combat breathing they taught at Depot for situations like this couldn't help me now.

My brain was projecting macabre memories of the dead child I'd found face down in his mom's pool after only being missing for ten minutes—about the length of time since I'd last seen my son. The pallor of the kid's skin and the weight of his limp body were still fresh in my mind. Flashes of the drowned boy, flashes of a pedo holding Riley's hand

and my trusting sweet son not saying anything. Another video clip of him toddling onto the highway, hearing my voice, and turning around to wave and say, "I okay" as a car annihilated him.

During my frantic search, I ripped a blanket off a passing stroller to ensure someone wasn't taking off with my kid.

"What the hell?" The woman hit me with her purse. I couldn't even feel it. I wished she'd hit me harder.

"My son is missing!"

Her look changed, and she asked his name. I must have said it, because other people started yelling for him with me.

I jogged back to the spot where I'd lost him to begin the procedural police work of tracing my child. First, I had to set up a perimeter and declare him missing. I flipped open my phone to call the local police department and saw another suggestive text from Amber. My stomach sank. This was all my fault. I could never go home. I wished I had my gun with me.

I dialed the back number for the radio room—911 for cops.

As it rang, I mentally noted a timeline. What was he wearing? I couldn't believe I had forgotten. My breathing slowed enough to hear a rustle in the bush behind where I had initially been sitting.

"Riley?" I said in a hoarse whisper.

No reply, but more movement. I snapped my phone shut and went closer to investigate.

"Riley, is that you?"

What looked like a small statue stood a few feet into the vegetation, behind an outbuilding not far from where we'd started.

As I approached, a small porcelain face peered out from behind the bush. It was Riley. He must have been standing there the entire time.

He'd blended perfectly into the background with his forest-green sweater and the hood pulled tightly around his face.

He wasn't talking, and he stood stone still. When I got close enough to grab him, he cowered and stepped farther back into the brush.

"Come out from there, honey. Please. You had me so worried." My sweetness and fear were turning to anger and embarrassment. Why had he done this?

He shook his head.

People were gathering around.

"It's okay, I found him." However, he wasn't behaving like my son at all. Just a few minutes ago, he'd been so happy and carefree, playing with bugs.

After a round of applause, the crowd dissipated, and my phone rang; it was the detachment calling me back.

"Sorry about that. We had an emergency at Darke Lake—a missing child. But we found him." I didn't dare admit the child had been mine.

Riley moved closer to the front of the bush and looked up at me. I wished he were more verbal so he could tell me what the heck had happened. I snapped a quick photo with my phone. There was no way Bree would believe me ... *if* I even told her what had happened. I wasn't sure I would. What would I say I'd been doing while he'd disappeared?

"C'mon buddy, come out."

The front of his pants were soaked. I must not have fastened the diaper tight enough again. Had this hiding been all about embarrassment? Or had he gotten scared and peed himself? After all, I'd been yelling his name at the top of my lungs.

I took off my sweater and wrapped it around his waist. But when I picked him up, he recoiled and didn't hold on to me the way he usually did. He just hung there, limp, cold, and wet, not saying a word.

What had happened in those ten minutes? Why did he seem like he was afraid of me? I thanked all the powers that be for the miracle of finding my son and swore I'd never get distracted by my phone again when I was looking after him. It would be the indoor park from now on.

Why had I been so careless? A few minutes of ego fluffing and flirting on my phone, and I could have lost him forever. *Smarten up, Jake, before you fuck up beyond repair.*

27

BREE

NOVEMBER 24, 2012

We were pulling out of our driveway and arguing, which was the new normal for us. It was either yelling or not talking at all, no in-between.

"I know you don't want me to go," I said. "What I don't understand is why." I was upset but treading carefully, partly out of empathy for Jake's grief and partly for fear of his mood swings. The last couple of weeks had been very silent and rough in our household. I didn't want to go back to that.

"I already told you, I don't think it's appropriate to bring the kids to a wake. Informal or otherwise." He stared straight ahead. "It will be mostly adults, and there will be drinking and swearing and unpredictable emotions."

I threw up my hands. "Well, we're already on our way, so I don't know what you want me to do."

Riley was singing his favourite cartoon theme song and Ivy was sound asleep. She loved a good car ride.

"You can just drop me off," he said. "I'll catch a ride with one of the crew later."

One of the crew. I wondered if he meant that woman he'd been so friendly with during the funeral.

"No, Jake. I cared about Matthews too. And Brody. It's bad enough I couldn't go to the funeral or help with anything. I need to be at this wake—for me and for his family." How could he not see that this affected me, too?

"Fine. But if the kids start acting up, you have to go." He looked at me and then away. "Oh, and stay away from Paskins' wife. She's a hot mess."

"No problem." I put my hand on top of his. He pulled it away.

The wake was being held at Matthews' condo. I was surprised Brody was up to hosting it. I desperately wanted to help out, so I'd brought a veggie platter and some homemade cupcakes. Jake seemed embarrassed by this, but I couldn't arrive empty-handed. Neither of us had known it would be fully catered until we arrived, so I left the items discreetly in Brody's kitchen. But it was hard to sneak around with a baby in my front carrier and Riley at my side. Though to be fair, he was being uncharacteristically quiet. We rarely went out, especially in the evening. He looked around, taking it all in, probably still exhausted from a busy day with Dad at the park.

A few of Jake's colleagues recognized me from the potluck and were polite enough to come over and say hello.

"Hey, little guy." Abbott bent down and booped Riley on the nose. When he stood up, I smelled the alcohol on his breath, so strong it made my eyes water. Jake wasn't kidding; these guys were going to tie it on tonight.

"Hi, Abbott." I felt weird calling them by their last names, but that was what they all did. I wasn't sure if any of them even knew each other's first names.

I really wanted to talk to Matthews' husband, Brody, but he seemed to be always talking with someone. I was also still trying to figure out what to say. Ivy was beginning to root, so I grabbed Riley and headed through the crowd to wait in line for the washroom. The hallway was covered with photos of Brody and Matthews, both of them laughing and posing at Christmases and various vacations. My heart caught when I saw the ones of Matthews with Jake. In the first, they were both in uniform, back-to-back with serious faces. The photo beside it must have been taken seconds later—they were doubled over, laughing at the ridiculous pose. They both looked so young, so this must have been at graduation or shortly afterward.

"Breanna Stone?" A woman with the roundest, happiest cherub face I'd ever seen was barreling towards us. She wore glasses with a cat's-eye shape and looked a bit like a grown-up Cabbage Patch doll. "I'm Tammy. We haven't met yet."

She extended her hand and then noticed my hands were full. She did an awkward air wave with a businesslike expression and then cracked into a full belly laugh. Not appropriate for an event like this, though she wasn't alone in the not-right-for-the-moment behaviour at this gathering.

"I know all the wives," she said. "We get together for brunch with the kids, and some of them go to yoga together. Not me, obviously."

She grabbed her whole frontal area and shook it up and down. She was almost a cartoon. "You should join us sometime."

"Sure, that sounds nice."

My turn came up for the washroom, so I pointed and went inside. As soon as we were in the bathroom, I could clearly smell Riley's loaded diaper and then realized I had to go and couldn't hold it. Having two babies so close together made toileting an urgent and dangerous sport.

Once relieved, I wrestled Riley into a fresh diaper and cleaned up. I had one foot out the door when I realized I hadn't even done what we'd gone in there for.

"Thank Christ!" A guy I didn't recognize pushed past me and began peeing while the door was still open.

I must have looked horrified, because Tammy ran over to me. "It's okay, you get used to the chaos." She scooped Riley up and dragged me down the hall by one arm and into the bedroom. "There's a bathroom in there." She winked like she owned the place. "Don't worry, I know Brody won't mind. I helped plan this party and ordered the catering. I like to take over and help out when this happens."

Even though it felt like I was taking huge liberties, I was getting tired of standing and sank onto the bed to feed Ivy. I didn't much like the way Tammy had said *when* this happens, and I also didn't appreciate her calling this a party.

"Anyway, it's crazy out there, but you get used to it," she said. "These boys know how to drink. They're harmless, but as a spouse, how long can you sit around and listen to them yammer on about files? This dead body, and that drug bust. 'I fought a big guy today, and eww did you hear what so-and-so saw?' They're regular Chatty Cathys but about dark stuff." She was talking so fast. "We have a rule at my dinner table: no death talk."

Riley's eyes were wide as Tammy talked. She was so animated when she spoke. Ivy relaxed in my arms and drank up a storm. Jake never spoke to me about the things he saw at work. I wondered if this was a good thing or not.

"This life is not for the faint of heart. All dark, all the time. Even the jokes are dark. That's why we ladies gotta stick together, right? You really should come hang out. When things are bad or if you need anything, those of us who have been spouses for a long time know all the tricks for dealing with—" She paused midsentence. Brody stood at the open doorway with his arms at his side, looking ahead at no one in particular. The circles under his eyes were darker than mine. It was hard to see him like that. Brody was normally so charismatic his personality entered the room before he did. I felt instantly foolish for being there. Tammy moved over to him, wrapped an arm around him, and squeezed.

"How are you holding up? I told Bree she could feed the baby in here."

Brody nodded and smiled meekly. He looked as though he couldn't decide on his next move. He wasn't coming into the room, but he wasn't leaving it either.

"I was looking for you earlier," I said. "I just wanted to say how sorry I am and ..." I trailed off with nothing intelligent to add.

"I know, thank you." His voice was monotone. "I just need a break from ... out there." His eyes drifted over to an empty dog crate I hadn't noticed until now.

"Lottie is with my mom tonight because of this." He gestured limply to the noise behind him. "Sorry. You probably wanted to see her."

"No, I came to see you. If you need anything, I'm here. Just ask."

"Thanks. What I need is to be alone."

With that, I packed Ivy back up in the carrier, and we gave him side hugs before leaving. As I closed the door, he stood in the middle of the room, likely about to dissolve into a pile of sobs, while his deceased husband's workmates medicated themselves loudly in his home.

Tammy and I took the kids back to the living room, where Jake was standing with a woman I didn't know. He was smiling—and laughing. My stomach twisted and my heart did a quick double thump in my chest. I would have said something if it weren't for the lump in my throat, but Tammy beat me to it. "That's Doyle. She isn't a spouse; she's a member. Pretty new to this watch, I think."

Jake looked up, and the smile left his face almost immediately. He waved me over. "Where were you?"

"I had to feed Ivy." I grabbed a cocktail wiener off a nearby tray and gave it to Riley to stop him from whining.

"This is Amber."

We nodded at each other, smiling the same pensive smile. Something wasn't right here. He had called her by her first name. My eyes widened slightly. She was the woman Jake had been comforting at the funeral. This was all shades of fucked up. I took a closer look at her. She had a sharp jawline and wide-set eyes, though she also had beautiful blond hair and a confidence that I'd had long ago but had lost somewhere during the past few years.

She put her hand on my arm. "Congrats on the new baby. Jake has told me so much about you all. I'm off to get a refill. Would you like anything?"

I felt like an ass—she seemed sincere. I was reading an awful lot into nothing. She wasn't even that attractive. I wasn't at my best after two babies and so little sleep, but I could clean up nicely if required. "No thanks, we're leaving soon." I would have liked to stay longer, but the kids were on borrowed time, and I felt uncomfortable at Brody having found me in his bedroom.

Amber walked away but turned around halfway to look back at Jake. That, I did not like; it made me second-guess her sincerity.

"We *are* leaving soon, right?" I looked at Jake, trying not to beg.

"You go. I need to stay here. I promised Brody we'd clean up after, and we still have some arrangements to make."

I couldn't place his tone. Likely grief or sadness. "How will you get home?" I didn't want to leave him there.

"Someone will drive me. And hey, did I see you hanging out with Paskins' bat-shit-crazy wife?" He pointed his beer bottle at me. "I told you to stay away from her. She's a rumor-spreading trainwreck."

"Oh crap, I didn't know that's who it was. She just told me her first name was Tammy. Sorry."

"It's okay, you didn't know." He put his hand stiffly on my shoulder. "Text me when you and the kids get home safe." He bent down and kissed and high-fived Riley, then gave Ivy an awkward little wave. He hadn't held her since the day Matthews had died.

On our way out the door, Tammy popped outside to say goodbye. "Here's my number. I'm serious about us gals sticking together." She did jazz hands and stuck her tongue out to make Riley giggle.

"Thank you, Tammy. It was nice to meet you."

I wondered what Jake had meant. She didn't seem crazy at all.

That night I brought both kids into the bedroom with me. It was a new bad habit that had formed during Jake's nightshifts or when he wasn't home. I knew he wouldn't be back anytime soon. Still, I lay there checking my phone every few minutes. I had texted him to say I was home safe and ask if he could check in. Would he be coming home tonight? Was Brody okay?

No reply. To any of them.

Each time I fell asleep, noise on the street or creaks in the house woke me up with the hope that it was him. I checked my damn phone each time. When a light came on in the hallway, figuring he must finally be home, I opened the locks on the door and tiptoed out. The light was on in the guest room that we rarely used—the one in the corner that was always too cold. From where I was standing, I could see the entryway, but I didn't see Jake or his shoes, or any other sign of him.

"Jake," I said in a loud whisper, scared that someone would answer and also scared that someone wouldn't. All was silent except for one creak in the floor directly behind me. I didn't dare move. "Jake?" This time it was a creak and a small gust of air on my bare shoulder. I spun around and ran the ten steps back into my bedroom. I slammed and locked the door, startling the kids.

They passed back out within seconds, but not me. I was done. My heart was pounding so hard. What the heck had made those sounds? It was an old house, I knew, but still. And the light?

I picked up the phone and dialed Jake. It was the excuse I needed. I was shocked when he picked up on the first ring.

I heard a few voices and giggles, and then, "Oops, Bree is that you?"

I'd never heard him slur like that. Who the hell else would it be? He would have seen my name when it rang. "Yes, it's me. Are you coming home?" I sounded freaked but I didn't care.

I heard some laughing and some muffling from the receiver. "Home soon, almost there." He hung up.

I was so relieved I wouldn't be alone for much longer that I tried not to let the phone call get to me. His best friend had died, and he was stupid drunk—they all were. As long as this didn't become a habit, I could let it go.

I heard a noise outside in the driveway. Crap. I didn't want to leave this room again, but I had to go out there. I held my breath, unlatched all the locks, and tiptoed back out into the hallway with the phone in one hand. I went into the guestroom to peek at the driveway from the window. It sounded like someone was shuffling around in the gravel outside of the house.

It was just Jake. *Phew.* He was having a hard time getting out of the car and was laughing at each failed attempt, his boots dragging around in the gravel as he tried to stand up again. I was about to go down to greet him when I heard female laughter. *Great.* He'd gotten a ride home from Amber. I made sure I wasn't visible to them and kept watching.

He finally got out of the car and made his way toward the house.

"Will you be okay in there?" she asked.

He mumbled something, and she drove away. Why the hell wouldn't he be okay? This was his home.

I stayed where I was as he stumbled his way into the house and straight to the bathroom. His vomiting was loud and harsh. Then I went downstairs. Outside the bathroom door, I said, "Jake, you all right?"

I heard him puke again. "Yeah, just go back to bed."

"I left some aspirin and a glass of water out here for you. I'm glad you're home safe. I was worried."

"Yeah, Paskins drove me home. He wasn't drinking."

Paskins? My stomach lurched. He had lied to me. *Why?*

28

JAKE

NOVEMBER 25, 2012

Shit. I sat upright, covered in sweat. What a dream—if it was a dream. I must have fallen asleep on the couch again.

I rubbed my eyes and tried to focus on the clock. All I could see was the empty bottle of brandy in front of me. I didn't remember drinking the whole thing. Jesus, that was a lot—on top of whatever I'd drunk at the wake. No wonder my head felt awful. I lay back down and closed my eyes.

Something brushed across my face. It felt as though a lot of time had passed. When I opened my eyes again, there was a face looking right back at me from about six inches away. Looking, but not saying a word.

Jumping up in a fight stance, ready to go, I readjusted my eyes. There was nothing there. To my right I heard a flapping noise, and I turned in time to see a dark blur scuttle off to the ceiling. I stomped around, flipping on all the lights in the house and looking in every corner. Had a bird or a bat gotten inside? Something was definitely there. I had felt it and seen it.

Looking again at the bottle, I wondered if I was losing my mind.

Later, when we were sitting around the table eating breakfast, I debated telling Bree about the weird bat dream. She handed me a glass of water and an aspirin and sat down across from me to breastfeed the baby.

"We should go for a drive today," she said. "It's supposed to clear up. The kids can nap, and we can spend some time together. What do you think?" She liked to go on meandering drives through the valley and imagine we would live there one day.

I felt like vomiting and closing my eyes forever. "Sure, we could do that. I just need to shower first." I reeked of night sweats and booze. I felt guilty over having lied to Bree about the ride home. It wasn't necessary. Nothing had happened between me and Amber other than some playful flirting. She'd suggested stopping at her place for a quickie on the way home, but I'd laughed it off. Still, I couldn't shake the image of how Bree had looked at me when she saw me and Amber standing together.

Almost as though she had read my mind, Bree asked, "So, was it Paskins who drove you home?"

Why is she asking me this? "Yes. I said so last night."

"It's just that I heard a woman's voice when we spoke on the phone."

"I wasn't the only one in the car." I raised my voice. "He drove a few of us home. We were all drunk, so we couldn't drive!" The yelling hurt my head and eyes.

"Okay, okay. Sorry. Go take that shower and I'll get the kids ready. Riley!" she shouted. "Wanna go for a drive and see the cows?"

Riley loved seeing all the farm animals, and if he was awake at the beginning of the drive, we would stop at the petting zoo.

"Riley?" I called as well. Normally he'd come pitter-pattering from anywhere if he thought he was going to the zoo. He'd just been watching TV a few minutes ago.

We were both up and out of our chairs in an instant.

"Riley, come on out," I said. "We're not playing hide-and-seek." I felt nauseous, remembering the episode at Darke Lake. Riley never strayed far from us. In fact, he usually played with his toys at our feet. The TV was blaring, though, so maybe he hadn't heard us.

"I'll look upstairs." Bree placed Ivy in her pack and play. I went the other way toward the front of the house.

"Jake!" she shrieked, and we both saw it at the same time.

The front door was open.

I ran out into the pouring rain in nothing but socks and boxers. If Riley made it to the road, he was as good as dead. I sprinted down the driveway.

"Riley!" I employed my best police officer yell. I ran up the road to the left, looking in the water-filled ditch and the neighbours' yards, yelling his name constantly. There was no sign of him. I ran up the other side of the road in such a state of panic I felt nothing. Not the rain or the cold. He wasn't out here. If he'd been snatched and put in a car, I might never see him again.

As I ran back toward the house, I saw Bree in the upstairs octagon window, waving frantically at me.

"I found him!" she called.

Thank Christ. I took the stairs up two at a time. Bree sat on the floor of Riley's room and pointed under the bed. "But I can't reach him."

"Riley. What are you doing under there? Come out right now." I'd gone from relieved to mad.

"You're scaring him." Bree looked pretty scared herself.

I felt like a monster. I softened my voice. "Buddy? Riley? We love you. Come out here, please."

The base of the frame was solid wood all the way to the floor, leaving only the end of the bed open. Riley had crawled all the way to the farthest corner. There was no way I'd fit underneath to get him out.

I turned to Bree. "If you crawl in, I can pull you out."

Bree flattened herself on the carpet. She fit, but just barely. She slithered in up to her waist and extended her arms so Riley could reach for her. I pulled on her ankles and got them both out. We all sat in a piled hug, me in my soaking wet boxers and socks, and Bree and Riley covered in dust and kid crumbs from being under the bed.

I checked Riley over. He was unharmed. "We looked everywhere for you. Didn't you hear us calling your name?"

He just sat there looking at us with wide eyes.

"Were you hiding?" I asked.

He nodded. This was the second time he had hidden. What the heck was going on with him?

"Who were you hiding from?" Bree asked.

He looked at his mom and then pointed at me.

We went back downstairs to check on an unattended Ivy. Had a stranger been in the house? There were no signs of forced entry; nothing was missing that I could tell. Hard to say, though, if anything was out of place, since the house was such a shit-sty of a mess.

Bree followed me into the kitchen, where I sat at the table, moving dirty dishes aside.

"Why has he been acting so strange lately?" I asked. "Why would he hide from me?"

"There's been a lot of fighting and tension in the house." She stood near the stove and looked down at her hands. "And yelling."

She was right. But that couldn't be it. Something else had to be going on. "Do you think someone was here? Has anyone been lurking around the house? Have you seen anything strange?"

"Well ..." She seemed to hesitate. "The neighbour lady followed us home drunk the other day, and when she was singing, a car drove by slowly and the driver stared at us. But I don't think it's anything to do with us. She was causing a scene."

A terrible stillness settled inside me. "What kind of car?"

"A dark SUV? I didn't think much of it, but the driver was looking right into the house."

"Was the driver male or female?" Amber had a dark SUV. But she hadn't known where I lived until last night.

"I couldn't be sure. There was a lot going on. Why?" Her voice cracked.

Could it be Bychkov? My heart rate quickened. Bree was staring at me. I had to say something. My head ached despite the aspirin. I took a deep breath. "I have something to tell you. Sit down." Now was not the time for me to withhold information, confidential or not. If it was Bychkov, Bree and the kids were in real danger.

We all were.

29

BREE

I pulled out a chair at the kitchen table. It still smelled like coffee despite there being none left. Riley was acting clingy, squirming around on my lap, drooling in my hair. Jake had asked me to sit down and then had promptly left the room. I was irritated until I heard him on the phone asking about someone named Bychkov.

He returned to the kitchen, flipping his phone shut. He opened his mouth to say something, then closed it again. "Remember at the condo in Burner when those brothers who came to the house?"

"Like I could forget?"

"They were involved in Matthews' death."

"What?" I'd heard about it on the news, but I hadn't realized those were the people that had been after us. "Wait, you knew who was threatening us this whole time?" My voice rose. "You knew we were in danger and said nothing to me about it?" I felt betrayed. not being in the loop on this.

Jake looked away. "Well, one of them is dead, and the other is in a coma, and their boss is out of the country. I figured they'd never find us out here anyway, and now that they're out of the picture entirely, I didn't think there was any danger at all."

I just sat there, processing. How could my husband keep such a big secret from me, and why? What else was he hiding?

"Bree, I'm really sorry I didn't share this with you. If you were in my shoes, you would understand." Jake sat down beside us.

Riley was quiet again, looking from me to Jake and back again. I was livid, but also relieved that he was actually talking to me for the first time since Matthews had died.

"There's a lot I can't tell you. When the Scaggs came to the house, it was obvious they wanted me to know they were there, but I didn't feel like you were in actual danger." Jake's voice was soft like it used to be.

"And then the incident happened at Daphne's house," I said, calmer.

"At that point, I knew we'd have to move. If they were following you outside of our area, and wanting the messages to hit both of us, they were ramping up. They were angry we'd arrested them, pissed that we had Cherry, and they were looking for vengeance on the money they'd lost as a result of their operation being shut down. There's more, but I've already told you more than I'm supposed to. You have to trust me that I'm on it. We'd been working hard to shut them down behind the scenes. Matthews and I." His eyes grew watery, and he looked down at the floor. "We also suspect Matthews' death wasn't entirely an accident." His voice cracked.

"You think it was on purpose? Matthews was targeted?"

"The investigation is still ongoing, but we do think he was lured there on purpose. The carfentanil part was an accident. They found a gun in the car. We suspect that when Vince couldn't get it, he grabbed the knife. The serious crimes department recreated the scene, and it looked as though they were using the knife to cut the drugs or open the box. When Vince went to grab it, the car went in the ditch and Matthews jumped in at the same time. The tussle caused the box to burst. You know the rest from the news."

The kitchen was so quiet I could hear a crow squawking in the yard.

"It's not one hundred percent confirmed, but it's a theory," Jake said. "They were sitting in his zone, at the end of his shift, waiting to take him out. But it wasn't Matthews they were looking for." He put his head in his hands.

I was stunned. "They were looking for you?"

He snapped his head up out of his hands. "Yes, Bree, they were looking for me. Matthews was working my shift. He was working my shift and driving my car because I was off on paternity leave."

When I saw how angry he was, it all clicked. This was why he hated me. This was why he couldn't hold Ivy. My heart emptied, and my mind began to whirl. How could he possibly think this was our fault?

Jake's phone rang, cutting into the painful silence. He stepped out of the room again to take the call. When he returned, he said, "I called into work earlier to double-check that Bychkov was out of the country. They confirmed it. No one is casing out our house." He put both hands to his cheeks and rubbed them up and down in one swift motion, letting out an aggressive sigh.

I watched his face. "If you had been on shift that night, you'd be dead." I was still trying to process it. Matthews' death was suddenly darker than before. Life could have turned out differently.

"I wish it were me. Matthews didn't deserve this."

"And you did?" My husband wished he was dead?

"I was the one antagonizing them, putting pressure on them. I'm the one with the key piece of evidence that will lock them up for good at their upcoming trial. I dragged Matthews into the investigation and begged him to take my files and shifts when the baby was born. I sat at home praying the baby would come early so I didn't have to work anymore. This was all my fault. I don't deserve to be here."

"It's not your fault, Jake. You don't know if—" I was mad at him, and shocked by his sudden changes of behaviour and attitude towards me, but I hated seeing him suffer.

He cut me off. "You're right. It's not my fault. It's yours."

He stood abruptly and stormed out of the kitchen.

30

JAKE

DECEMBER 8, 2012

My paternity leave was cut short due to a dangerous staffing short-age. I had no idea how I'd go back to work, see Matthews' empty locker, and carry on without him.

Thank goodness there were still a few people in the detachment who seemed to like me. Before I returned to work, Bree had been squawking about not having enough freedom and needing the car sometimes, so I would be carpooling as much as possible. There were a few members who lived out my way, people who'd already been living in Roxford before they were posted in Burner. Today it had been Abbott's turn to drive.

Turned out, Matthews' locker hadn't stayed empty for long. It had been reassigned to a new guy—more proof that we were just numbers. Matthews had given his life for this job. What did he get? A regimental funeral for the white shirts, and a flag for his spouse. By the next day, he'd been forgotten by the public and by headquarters, but not by his family or his crew. Not by me or Brody.

Amber poked her head into the change room, startling me. "You ready?"

"As ready as I'll ever be."

Amber had been part of the carpool that morning but hadn't said much. She seemed to be the only one who cared about anything I did lately. Bree was always so focused on the kids, and it seemed like she hated me most of the time. Either that, or she acted like a scared victim who had to protect the kids from me. I couldn't make sense of her behaviour. We hadn't been intimate in months.

I followed Amber to our cars. I knew I was playing with fire with her, but part of me no longer cared. When we got to my cruiser, she gave me a hug.

"Today will be okay," she said. "Remember, I'm right here if you need me. For *anything*." She whispered the last word into my ear, and as she pulled away from me, her lips brushed my cheek. Surprised by her brazenness, I stood there saying nothing.

She smiled and winked as she turned to her car, swaying her hips more than usual, or more than I had noticed before.

Did she say "anything"?

Harvey gave me the easiest patrol area that day, along with a recruit. He did it likely to occupy me, and to keep me from thinking about how much I missed Matthews. Twice I went to call him, and then remembered. Would this ever get easier?

Newbie and I stood in a ditch tagging some stolen goods that had been stashed there. He looked like a younger, fresher version of me: dark hair and eyes, but less muscle and five o'clock shadow.

"Constable Slater, welcome to East Bernheim, also known as Burner. This is the craziest place you'll ever work. When a call comes in, listen carefully, and then do your own verification on your mobile working station. Nothing is ever what it seems. You'll get called to help someone who is being attacked, and when you arrive, they'll turn on you. Always be aware, and know how far away backup is."

I delivered the speech in the exact way it had been told to me years ago when I'd begun. As Harvey used to say, there was no use sugarcoating it or you'd just get scorched.

He took notes in a little notepad. "Nothing is what it seems? Is that the case every single time?"

"Fact: You never know what you're going to get, no matter how prepared you are."

And right on cue, one of those stranger-than-fiction moments happened. We heard a loud bang and looked up to see a red sports car fly over our heads, rotating end over end before landing on the other side of us.

"Yep. Like that."

Slater's mouth hung open.

The radio went off in our ears in stereo. "Stone, someone is here asking to speak to you."

Probably a witness or assault victim. "We're due back for lunch in fifteen or so."

"She says she'll wait. Says her name's Cherry and that it's 'real impo rtant.'"

"Roger that."

The other day, when I'd called to verify Bychkov was out of the country, I'd also learned that Cherry had checked out of protection. She was safe—what a relief. I couldn't wait to hear what she had to say.

We secured the accident scene until other members arrived to take over the file. Then I ripped us back to the detachment. It was nice to have someone else with me in the car for once, but also strange. I was becoming acutely aware of how much I talked to myself when I was alone.

When we arrived back at the detachment, I stopped by reception. "Where is she? How long has she been here?"

"Interrogation room," the front desk clerk said. "She stopped by a few times last week when you were off on leave."

Why had no one told me about this?

"We offered to have her speak to someone else," the receptionist added, "but she wanted to wait until you were back."

I headed for the interrogation room, turning to the kid. "You can grab lunch, man. Meet me after?" *Ha.* The only time anyone ever grabbed lunch on this job was when we were trying to lull the new recruits into thinking we got breaks at all.

"Can I join you?"

He was young and enthusiastic, but I couldn't have him in the room with me.

"Why don't you wait in the surveillance room? Eat in there and watch the conversation. Just keep in mind it's not a proper interview or inter-rogation."

He took out his notepad. "Is she a victim or a criminal?"

"Both. It's complicated." I opened the door to the room, leaving him in the hallway.

The room was small, ten by ten—no pacing like in the movies, no two-way mirror—and it was stark. A video camera in the top corner recorded live feed, audio and video. I closed the door. There was a panic button next to it. I'd never had to use it, but I was always thankful it was there.

Cherry sat at the table, bouncing a crossed leg rapidly. She wore a bright-pink Juicy Couture tracksuit, the kind that had been popular in the early 2000s.

"I need to talk to you," she said. "It's urgent. But I got questions first."

"Can I get you a drink or anything?"

"No, man. They gave me a coffee out there. Pretty rank stuff."

She wasn't wrong. I pulled up a chair across the table from her. She was facing the camera. I faced her. "Okay, Cherry. Shoot."

"Look. You know I got a sheet and I got some pendings, but I'm not a main player."

"True."

"But I do know one player in particular. And I know things."

"Yes, that's why we were protecting you. We appreciate your intel."

"If I give you recent info on you-know-who, how about you give me some help? Cancel some charges, look at immunity, help me get out of Burner for good."

I sighed. "I want to help you; you know that. It's not simple, but it's not impossible. Your charges of theft under five thousand and possession of stolen property are summary offences, and I could probably get them downplayed. It takes time and Crown approval, but you have my word I'll work on it. What do you know that you haven't already shared with us?"

Sweat was dripping down my back. The light in here threw off so much heat I'd need to find another uniform shirt after this. If she was asking for immunity, something that was not in my power, she must have still been involved in the trafficking in some way.

She looked around the room and stared into the camera as if to see if anyone else was

around. Then she leaned across the table to me. "He's back."

"Bychkov?" *Impossible.* I'd just checked, and he was confirmed to be out of the country. But how long ago had that been?

She shushed me. "Yes. He's been back for about a week. He can't stay away with his dealers gone, and he has too much business in Burner. I think I know where he's staying, and I know where he's pushing goods and who's helping him."

I was officially excited. We needed to catch this guy.

"I'll help you, Cherry. Give me a list of the names and addresses, and I'll get search warrants started. We'll need to get an official witness statement from you so I can get the warrants approved to go after him, and then we'll work on getting you out of here. Can you hang out here while I get the paperwork started? Should take a couple of hours."

"You'll get me somewhere safe? Maybe back east where my kids are at?"

"Absolutely." I hadn't known she had kids. I couldn't guarantee everything she was asking for, but I could promise to get her back there.

"Okay, how about I go pick up my shit from my girlfriend's house and come back to sign the papers? B don't know where I'm at."

She wrote the information down on my notepad and walked out. I followed close behind her, eager to follow up on the lead.

Slater came running down the hall.

"Hi, honey." She looked him up and down. "You're cute." With that she turned down the hall and was gone.

"That was awesome," he said to me. "I know all about this file—Scaggs, Bychkov, and Matt—" His face went bright red.

"Yes, and we don't have time to waste."

I downed my lunch in the detachment for the first time in ages while I worked my butt off getting the paperwork done on time. Because I had a recruit with me, we weren't considered a number on the road. We were extras. I gave Slater a crash course on writing up Crowns for a warrant to search or raid two of the addresses Cherry had given us. And we started on a witness statement based on my conversation with Cherry. We could fill in the blanks when she got back, which would be shortly.

I hadn't heard from Bree all day and was starting to wonder how she and the kids were doing. I had a few minutes to kill before Cherry was due to arrive. I checked the location app on my phone. She was home. *Unbelievable.* She made such a big stink about having the car and then chose to stay at home? *I will never understand that woman.*

My phone buzzed like she had read my mind: *Do you need anything from me? Yet?* Followed by a winky-face emoji. It was from Amber, not Bree.

I was thinking about how to respond when a text came in from Bree, asking how work was going.

I typed back, *I'm still thinking about what I might need*, and hit send.

Bree replied right away. *What do you mean? Is everything okay?*

Oh shit, I'd meant to send that to Amber. I thought fast. *I just meant if you're getting groceries later.*

Bree replied, *Oh okay, just let me know.*

Will do. I put my phone away.

I didn't know why I was surprised, but Cherry didn't show. It was common for a witness to get spooked in this type of situation, but this case was everything to me. I waited until she was exactly thirty minutes late, and then I decided to go look for her. Slater and I were standing outside my car, going over the shift start checklist so he'd be ready when he went solo next shift. I radioed dispatch and told them to holler if she showed.

"Hey kid, want to help me look for Cherry?" I already knew what his answer would be.

"Heck yeah. Where are we going? Bychkov's strip joint? Warehouse?"

"Nope, they can't know we're onto him, and we have to wait for those warrants. Where we're going is even better for your training. Get in."

We headed for the ring, a circular road strip where the sex workers hung out. We drove up to a group of ladies, who stopped talking as soon as they saw us. Sydney was sitting on her own just past the group.

"Hey, Sydney. How goes it?" I tried not to sound as desperate as I felt—sweating again, activating the smells already infused in the shirt that I'd forgotten to change.

She looked around to see who was listening. "Whaddaya want, pig?" She winked.

"What's going on?" Slater asked. "Why are you letting her talk to you like that?"

I laughed and got out of the car, walking toward Sydney. Slater followed behind me.

"I need your help," I said to her, keeping my voice low so none of the ladies nearby would realize the chat was friendly. Most of them had scattered when I'd pulled up anyway.

"With what?" Sydney cackled. "Trouble in the bedroom?" She said this loudly enough that the other ladies laughed, and Slater went crimson again. Kid was going to have to toughen up, and quick.

"Cherry," I said quietly. "Have you seen her?"

"An hour or so ago. Maybe two."

"Where'd she go? Did she say anything to you? Was she alone?"

"Whoa, Nelly. What you got for me in your glove box?"

I walked back to the car to grab her some protein bars. I knew she'd want cigarettes too, but I wasn't so sure my recruit needed to see that on day one. I slid a pack of her favourite brand in between several protein bars in a plastic bag and walked them back to her.

"Your faves are in there." I tried to be coy, but Slater wasn't even paying attention. He had his eye on some of the younger sex workers, who were whistling and making him blush.

"Slater."

He returned his attention to the conversation.

"She left town," Sydney said.

"Really? She was supposed to come in and chat with us."

"That's what she said. Said she was leaving town, and she had to hurry to catch a Greyhound out east."

Fuck, now what? Without her statement, we were screwed.

31

BREE

DECEMBER 9, 2012

The rain beaded up on my living room windows as I sat on the couch, speaking to my sister on the phone. I felt terrible dumping on her during our weekly phone call, but it was rare that I talked to anyone these days. Besides which, I was competing with an inconsolable Ivy and a grumpy Riley. Both kids were miserable and had been fussing nonstop all day. Must have been a full moon.

"I need help. I just don't know what to do anymore."

Paige sighed. "I'm not sure what to tell you. I've never been in this situation before."

Right. No kids, no hubby.

"Are there any resources in your area?" she asked.

I looked around at the disaster of the room. Piles of laundry. Toys scattered everywhere. Errant Cheerios on the carpet. "I really don't know what there is or what I would need. Jake still doesn't talk to me. He seems like he hates me. He's fine when he's talking to his colleagues, but when it comes to me, he's miserable. I'm struggling with the kids. They need so much from me physically I feel like I've completely lost myself." My voice cracked. I was terrified that if I started to cry, I might never stop. "I cared about Matthews too. I still love my husband even though he hates me, and I still want to be a good mother to my kids even though I'm failing them." *Don't cry, don't cry, don't cry.*

There was more. I was having horrible nightmares almost every night. A lot of them involved the scary woman who was way too interested in my kids, but some of these dreams were about me. Doing bad things—to my kids, and to myself. I couldn't tell Paige about that. She would think I was insane. And I was too embarrassed to tell her about Amber.

"You're not failing them," she said. "You're a good mom going through a rough time, and you just need some help. I wish I lived closer. I found a support group in your area while we were talking. I'll email you the information. It's kind of like a Mommy and Me group."

I groaned. "I tried one of those in West Burner and it was horrific. All those judgy moms with their money and support, gliding through parenthood like it was a breeze. I sat there with greasy hair, dark circles under my eyes, and a kid with a loaded diaper." I could *feel* their judgments. It was terrible. "One mom told me I shouldn't use the Jolly Jumper so much as a babysitter because it would ruin Riley's hips. I left after that and didn't go back."

My sister was quiet for a moment. "This group is different. They should be more supportive." I could tell she was hesitating. "It's for people with postpartum depression."

I nearly leapt to my feet. "I don't have that. Why do people keep suggesting I do? Don't tell Jake. He already thinks I'm awful and incapable. He'll use it against me if we ever break up." So much for composure.

"What? Are you guys okay?" Her voice rose an octave.

"No. Well, I don't know. Things haven't been great. He's miserable or angry most of the time and seems suspicious of me all of a sudden.

It might get better. He's going through a lot. But I've heard horror stories about women being deemed incompetent parents after receiving diagnoses like this. Especially in court battles where one spouse knows the law intimately. I don't want him to think I'm unfit or have a diagnosis hanging over my head if we do split up. I'm going crazy with the kids right now, but I would die without them." It felt good to finally say that out loud to someone. Someone who already knew I was crazy, but capable.

"I didn't realize it was that bad. Maybe I can take some more time off work and come help for a bit."

"No, you just took time off not that long ago for Ivy's birth. You don't have to do that." *Please do that.*

"I'll look into it, but in the meantime, I'm serious about this group. We aren't talking about going to a doctor and going on pills or even having this on record. It's a group called 'Help with Baby.' No one would ever know it's for mothers suffering from postpartum. You really should check it out."

"Okay, sis, I will. Maybe Riley can make friends. The last group's judgy bitches brought their kids with them. I just won't mention a Jolly Jumper or any other hot topics." I had to laugh. It was the only way to keep going.

"Promise me. I emailed you the link."

"I promise."

After we hung up, I checked it out. It looked similar to that appalling Mommy and Me session I'd attended in the other municipality, but I had nothing to lose. I had no friends in Roxford. If these women were snooty Lululemon moms, I'd just leave. The next session worked with our schedule, so I sent an email to register.

"You need the car again?" Jake looked both annoyed and surprised. I usually only left the house to get groceries or run errands.

"It's a play group for Riley." That wasn't entirely untrue.

"Do I have to look after the baby?" He still wouldn't call Ivy by her name, and it hurt every time.

"No, I'll bring *Ivy* too. I'll only be gone for a couple of hours. You don't need the car, do you?" My eyes darted around. "You can check the app to see where I am. It's just at the town hall."

Jake had installed find-my-phone apps in both of our phones so we could locate each other. Friends reacted oddly to that information, but they weren't married to cops, so they didn't get it. If I pulled up the app and saw he was at the detachment, I could breathe knowing he wasn't in danger. And if he could see I was at a play group for Riley and not at the scene of a huge car accident, he'd know we were okay.

"Right, yes. I can do that." He wasn't meeting my gaze; his head was down and focused on his phone. "Have fun, see you later." He waved.

We got in the car and drove to city hall.

It looked like any other stale city hall building. It wasn't that old, so I'd expected it to be more modern, but the terse woven gray carpet and boring taupe walls said otherwise. I followed the handwritten signs with directional arrows down a long hallway until we arrived at the room that had *Help with Baby* beside the entrance. The kids and I were two steps in the door when I smelled the horrible yet familiar cheap generic office coffee brewing. One sip of that and I was guaranteed a fresh migraine would wipe me out for the day.

"Coffee?" a chipper blond woman asked.

"No thanks, all coffeed up." I held up the latte I had picked up on the way, hoping Jake hadn't noticed that unscheduled stop. He hated how much money I spent on coffee, though I couldn't remind him how much more he was spending on brandy. I dared not mention how much he was drinking, period. If this was a phase, it was going on too long and spiraling out of control.

"Are you Bree?" she chirped.

"Yes, why?" I had learned to be suspicious from the best of them.

"Because you're the only mama I haven't met yet, and I'm in charge of the registration forms." She didn't stop smiling despite my rudeness.

I'd forgotten this program was covered by a government subsidy. Though Jake barely made enough money to float us, it was likely too much for this to be free. I had used my own information as an unemployed housewife to secure my spot on the pity committee.

"Fill this out when you can." She smiled again and pointed at my full hands. Baby in a backpack, Riley in one arm and coffee in the other. "You can hand it in on your way out if you like."

I started to feel safe in this otherwise sterile, office-like environment that was filling up with women and children. My heart was pounding, bumping into my ribs, but I was ready for the challenge.

As everyone took their place on the carpet in the "circle of trust"—which was a literal circle on the carpet—I glanced at how much information they asked for on the forms. My info was sufficient to be included in the program at no cost, but they took a lot more information for "other purposes." Husband's name and occupation. My doctor. My diagnosis and relevant prescriptions. It went on. I started to panic, but it was too late to leave. I jammed the paperwork in the stroller's pouch and pasted on a grin.

"Let's go around the room and introduce ourselves and say why we're here."

Crap. I'd used my real name. I wasn't the hottest mess of a mom there, but I wasn't the most put together either. I liked where I was disaster-wise—somewhere in the middle.

"Breanna Stone over here." I waved stupidly, trying to get my part out of the way. "Here for help with the baby," I said, pointing too enthusiastically at Ivy.

Everyone said, "Hi Breanna" in unison and carried on. The other seven women either knew each other already or were more comfortable with strangers than I was. After hearing them chat, it was a relief to know I wasn't alone in feeling overwhelmed. Some of the women even admitted to hating their husbands. I would never say that out loud, but I'd had similar feelings when I realized how much of my life and self were gone forever when I'd had the children, whereas his appeared to be almost entirely untouched.

No one mentioned having dreams of harming themselves or their babies, so I felt like an outlier there. One brave mama with her brown hair loosely piled in a bun atop her head said, "Sometimes I wish I could go back to before I had them, just for a day, or a week, or a bit longer." Whenever she nodded, her hair slopped back and forth.

Another mom who looked hollow and too thin said shyly, "Life would be a lot easier if they weren't here."

"Or if we had help. Or a break," a few moms chimed in. That was as dark as it got, so I stayed quiet, grateful for this hour, knowing I would not be coming back. I couldn't risk Jake finding out about this, nor could I submit the kind of information they wanted.

When it was over, I tried to leave ahead of the crowd, but the sweet blond organizer came after me. "We're so glad you came. Did you fill out the paperwork?"

"Uh no, sorry, I didn't get time and now I have to run."

"No worries." She dragged out the consonant. "You can bring it next week, okay? And if you have any trouble in the meantime, there's a confidential 1-800 number on the bottom of the pamphlet, okay?"

I took a mental photograph of her friendly face and left. I wished I could come back, but there was no way I could allow this to go on record anywhere. I had no idea what Jake's and my future looked like, and he was proving to be an unpredictable and sometimes scary man.

32

JAKE

DECEMBER 15, 2012

I t was Slater's first shift solo. I was supposed to ride to all his calls with him, but that was never the way it actually worked. We were always short on members. Harvey had assured me it would be fine.

A call would come in, he'd answer first, then we would convoy there. The kid was showing some real potential. He had passed his training and was top of his class at Depot. Perfect on paper. He was truly a nice guy, and everyone seemed to like him.

A call came in over the radio about suspicious activity down in the Dead-End Fen. Two adults dragging something and leaving it there. There'd been a real problem with trash dumping since the city had begun limiting its collection amount. The caller confirmed that the people who had done the dumping had left.

I was at the detachment working on some paperwork.

"I got it, boss, I'm close," Slater said cheerfully to me over the radio. This was a new nickname he had for me, and I kind of liked it. It wasn't often a road constable got called boss.

"Okay, I'll be two minutes behind you. Accept the call."

Slater recited his car number excitedly and headed toward the scene. I took a quick piss and headed out to my car to join him.

As I crested the top of the hill, Slater's car came into view. His headlights and turn signal were still on. It was starting to get dark, and it was foggy, as it usually was at dusk on the flats. I wondered how the person who had called this in had been able to see two people carrying or dragging anything. My instincts twigged. I pulled up behind Slater's vehicle and noted that he'd parked partially on the road as per safety protocol. What I didn't see anywhere was Slater.

"Hey, kid? Slater? Is anyone out there?" Standing alone in the fog was eerie. I shined my flashlight around, and it caught on bushes and other shapes concealed in the mist, looking like people or animals. Eventually, in the distance, I saw an actual person crouched over, touching the ground.

"Call for an ambulance and backup," I said into my radio, as I ran to investigate.

The ground was muck halfway to my knees. I waded over to the figure I'd seen. It was Slater. "Hey buddy, are you hurt?"

He looked in my general direction but did not look at me. He turned back to where he'd been staring. A few feet away, partially submerged in mud, was a dead body. Female. I crouched down beside him and noticed a puddle of vomit in front of him. His lips were bleeding.

"Oh man, your first dead body. Sorry. It sucks, I know. It gets easier. That sounds sick, but it actually does."

He nodded. "I gave her CPR."

Oh no.

"Her lips were cold. Her whole body is cold. I did chest compressions, but nothing would budge, and then she made a sound like a moan." He stared straight ahead as he spoke, wiping his lips repeatedly.

"Fuck Slater, you did a good thing, buddy. You should have radioed so we knew what was going on, okay? Bodies sometimes make sounds if they have oxygen trapped in their lungs or were just moved." I should have been faster. I could have saved him from doing CPR on a corpse.

"She told me I was cute."

"Huh? That woman is super dead; there's no way she would have been talking."

He shook his head. "The other day. She told me I was cute, back at the detachment."

My neck prickled and I jumped up, almost losing a boot in the muck as I made my way over to the body.

It was Cherry.

Shit, shit, shit! I grabbed my radio. "Have you ordered the bus?"

"Yes, Stone," a crackly voice replied. "They should be pulling up."
Lights appeared in the distance behind our cruisers.

"I don't want them to touch anything. Send them to me first. I'll flash my light so they know where to go. The victim is dead, and I have to hand this over. Can you get serious crimes and forensics over here as fast as possible?" I spoke quickly, still processing the scene in front of me. "Send Harvey down here, too."

I walked back to Slater, who had removed his hat and was unbuttoning his shirt. "I'm hot, and this shirt is so tight I can't breathe."

I put my hand on his shoulder. "It's okay. Just remember your training. Come on, I'll breathe with you—"

"No. It's not okay. She said I was cute. She told me that the other day. She was alive. She was fine. We were going to get the bad guy and save her. This is what we do. This is why I'm here. Not for that." He pointed to her body.

Her eyes were wide open, as if she'd been scared when she died. I wanted to go over there and close them so the kid would stop staring directly at them, but I knew anything I did, and anything Slater had already done, could contaminate the scene. Bychkov or his men had likely been the ones who'd called this in. No one could have seen anything from a distance in this weather.

Slater was rocking and rubbing aggressively at his lips, which were raw. The ambulance attendant made his way over to me. He was massive, well over six feet, and dressed for body retrieval. His name badge read *Smalls*. In other circumstances, I would have laughed.

"Dispatch said there was a body," he said in a deep voice, "but to hang tight."

I walked him a few steps away and whispered, "You aren't here for the body."

I nodded toward Slater who kept repeating, "I'm cute."

The hulking ambulance attendant leaned down toward Slater, holding his arm with tenderness. "Stone told me you're Constable Slater. My name is Jamie Smalls. What's your first name?"

Slater looked up at him, eyes wide. "I'm cute."

"Okay, Slater, we're going to get you out of this wet bog and somewhere more comfortable."

There was no way to maneuver a gurney in and out of that muck, so Smalls and I each grabbed a side of Slater, hoisted him up, and walked him back to the ambulance. I helped him remove his boots and duty belt as he sat on a gurney to have his vitals checked. He was in shock and looked shattered. First real day on the job. *Welcome to your new life.*

Harvey pulled up. I didn't have to tell him what was going on with Slater; he'd seen it before. You could take the training and be as prepared as anyone can be and still not be able to handle this kind of reality. Harvey nodded for us to take a walk.

"I'll be right back," I said to Slater, who didn't respond or acknowledge me in any way.

Harvey didn't even wait until we were out of earshot. "Told you he was a pussy."

"Jesus, Harvey."

"What?"

"Can we talk about the case, please?"

"I'm off soon, so make it quick."

"The body in the field is Cherry. You know, Bychkov's main girl." My voice sounded a bit echoey in the fog.

"Damn." He lit up a cigarette and the smoke wafted into my face.

"She was supposed to come see me, and she didn't show."

"Well, now you know why. Case closed." Harvey laughed and burst into a coughing fit.

I waited until he was done, barely controlling myself. "Someone called this in. Said they saw two men dragging something out there, but that's bullshit." I gestured to the surrounding fog.

Harvey was silent for a minute, smoking and staring out at nothing. "It makes sense to me."

"Does it?" How could it possibly make sense? Raging heat boiled onto my face at his flippant comments, his vile habit, and his urgency to brush me off.

"Yeah. This is where Matthews died. Bychkov is sending us a message. A pretty clear one, too."

Harvey pointed a few feet away, and then it all flashed back to me from the video. I saw Matthews go down over and over, slipping out of the car and hitting the cement face down. Bleeding out all alone for almost ten minutes before this unfeeling sack of shit beside me showed up.

Harvey stubbed out his cigarette. "Close your mouth, Stone. And go back to the detachment to do up the paperwork for Slater's release. He's done." The last bit of smoke leaked out of his nose and mouth while he spoke.

It was all I could do not to punch Harvey's cocky face. I wanted to question him about Slater. He only got one chance? Shouldn't this be his choice? But when I went to speak, I saw Matthews' face where Harvey's should have been. *Tell Brody I love him.*

"I will. I did."

"You already did?" Harvey's bloated boozer face was back where it belonged on its dumpy frame.

"Sorry, no, I mean I will. Anything else?"

"I'm going home for dinner. I'll follow up with serious crimes and forensics to see if they turn anything up. Stay safe though, Stone. These guys are mad. Be grateful that you've been off work for a while, and these guys have no clue you moved to Roxford."

Shit, that's right. He knows I moved. Thank God Bychkov didn't.

"Sir, I—"

Harvey cut me off before I could defend the move. "You should loop in Roxford PD and request some security check-ins. It's not necessary but probably not a bad idea." With that, he lit up another smoke and headed back to his vehicle.

When I turned around, Smalls was behind me. He was so tall I nearly hit his chest with my face. As he handed me a full duty belt, I looked up and saw Matthews' face again. "My watch is over, Stone. You need to find Bychkov, or he'll come for you."

I jumped back a foot or two.

"I'm taking him in for twenty-four hours," Smalls said. "Here's his gear." He was staring at me. "Should I check you out as well?"

I smiled faintly, not looking directly at him. "I'm good, thanks."

I thought about saying goodbye to Slater, but the doors to the ambulance were already closed. I radioed for someone to collect his car and, before heading back to the detachment, paused in the exact place where I'd lost my best friend.

***

"Hey!" a voice called. Amber was walking down the detachment hallway toward me. "You look like shit. I heard about your file and your recruit. I'm sorry." She gave me a hug.

Part of me was jealous of Slater. He'd gotten out. "I don't know how much longer I can do this," I said quietly. "I need help, but Harvey and the guys can't know, or I'll be branded as a pussy or a headcase."

The few guys in the detachment who'd actually gotten help had been quickly chastised by Harvey or ostracized as though they had a contagious disease. Their records were marred with reports from the doctors they'd seen, making them last in line for promotions.

I was smart enough to be careful, but desperate enough to try.

"I don't think of you that way," Amber said. "Lincoln's on tonight, not Harvey. You should try talking to her."

Lincoln was a woman, and I knew she had a young family. *Maybe.*

"After work, everyone's going out for drinks," Amber said. "I'll buy you a round, and I won't take no for an answer."

"Okay." She was my ride home, so I didn't have much of a choice. But anyway, I could seriously use a drink, and I wasn't looking forward to going home.

I managed to finish the paperwork Harvey had asked me to do and spoke with Roxford PD. They assured me that the area around my house was already frequently patrolled, but that out of an abundance of caution, they would send an unmarked vehicle by a few times a day until we got Bychkov.

When I was done, I decided to talk to the sergeant on shift. I knocked cautiously on the door. Amber had been right—it was Lincoln, her salt-and-pepper hair pulled back in a tight bun below her hat as usual. I didn't report to her, but she was known for her kindness and was the only white shirt around at the moment.

"Stone, are you okay?" She set aside her paperwork. "Sit down. You're extremely pale."

She pulled out a chair for me and closed the door. It was a shared space, but she had a photo of her family on the desk. I was surprised to see four children. I must not have been the only one who appreciated the parental leave from work.

I looked her in the eye. She had a round face that looked friendly even when she wasn't smiling. "I think I'm losing my mind." I didn't break, but I knew my lip had trembled. "Ever since Matthews died, I see him everywhere. I'm seeing my wife and kids at files, too."

"Are you sleeping at all?"

"No, ma'am, I don't think so. I never remember falling asleep, and when I do, I wake up many times a night." I looked down at my feet. "The nightmares are brutal—and so realistic."

"We've all been there. There's nothing wrong with you, and you're not losing your mind. We cut back on file debriefs a while ago, and I think we've all suffered as a result. Why don't we book you an appointment with Dr. Steinman? Do you know who he is?" She handed me his business card.

I was terrified. I knew I had to be careful. "I saw him here at the detachment when Matthews died." He'd been here for the whole crew, but only two of us had shown up. I didn't remember much about my interaction with him, as I'd been too busy staring at the door, worrying about who would see me in there. Average middle-aged white guy. He'd seemed nice enough.

She turned to her computer. "Do you have any unused vacation time?"

I still couldn't look at her. "Yes." I hadn't taken much since Bree and I had gotten married.

"Here is what we're going to do. I'm switching you to a short scene security shift tomorrow, nice and easy to finish out this block, and then I'm going to book the next block off for you. You call this number and book an appointment with Dr. Steinman. I'll let him know you're a priority. You'll get almost two weeks off, have a good vent session, and come back as good as new. How does that sound?"

I looked up at her. "It does sound good, thank you."

She patted my hand and told me she would arrange everything.

I left her office with my tail between my legs. I didn't know if this was a good idea or not, but I had to do something.

With its swinging doors, the Plough Pub was designed to look like an old saloon; in reality, it looked more like a cheap road stop bar in a rundown building. But it was close to the detachment and Harvey knew the owners, so we went there often. Plus, we usually got the back room to ourselves.

It felt good to get out and have a few drinks with the crew. We hadn't done this for a while, aside from the wake. Or at least, I hadn't. Everything got better as soon as my face grew warm and fuzzy, and my thoughts slowed down or stopped altogether. I was four whiskeys deep when the stress of the day became funny.

"To Slater!" Abbott shouted. "Poor bastard. End of watch, day two." Everyone erupted into laughter. We were dicks, but it was a coping mechanism.

When a chair freed up beside me, Amber came over and put her arm through mine. I shifted to the other side of my chair but didn't pull away.

"Feeling better?" She smiled and pointed to the empty glasses lined up in front of me.

"Yeah."

She signalled the server to get me another.

"You're a good friend," I said when my drink arrived. I noticed she was drinking pop and remembered she had to drive. I raised my glass anyway.

"Thanks, Stone. Do you want to stay for another or get going?"

"One more."

"Works for me. I don't have anyone to go home to." She laughed but wasn't smiling. "Are you sure you're okay? It's been such a messed-up day and a fucked-up few weeks."

"I'm A-OK. I just wish I could undo everything, you know? Go back in time, save Matthews, or get rid of the Scaggs. I hate everything those shits stood for. They've ruined my life. Or if I could go back, maybe I would never have become a cop. Or I'd stay single forever. This job is so much harder when you have kids to worry about."

"I can only imagine." Amber flinched and looked down. I wondered if I'd said something stupid.

"Anyway, we can't go back. No matter how badly I want to change things, I'm stuck. This is my reality, and I have to deal with it." I slung back my whiskey. "Let's go."

I didn't realize how drunk I was until we were walking to Amber's vehicle.

"Whoa!" I laughed as I stumbled. She helped me get into the car and leaned over me to buckle me in. On her way back out of the car she stopped in front of my face and looked like she might kiss me. My heart rate sped up. She smelled so good, like she was fresh out of the shower, sweet with shampoo.

"Let's get you home."

The ride seemed incredibly long, as it did when you were drunk and exhausted. We were about five minutes from my house when Amber turned off at her exit.

"I'm just going to stop at my place for a minute," she said. "I have to use the washroom."

This wasn't a good idea, but I was in no position to argue.

We pulled into her driveway, and I fumbled out of the car, following her inside. She used the washroom, and so did I. When I walked out, she pushed me up against the wall like a perp and kissed me. I was so drunk I kissed her back. After a few minutes of sloppy hallway make-out, I pulled away and said, "I can't."

She laughed. "But you want to."

"But I can't." My argument was weak. The flirting had been ramping up between us, as had my disdain for Bree with her neediness and problems that didn't matter.

She slid down slowly, unzipping my fly as she went. After she had me in her mouth for a few minutes, I was hard and ready. She pulled off, dragging her teeth along me, then stood up and led me toward her living room.

"No one will ever know, Jake. Your wife is at home sound asleep. You can shower afterwards, and I'll drive you home. I don't need anything from you, but I do want you. Right now."

She said all the right things. No one would know, not even Bree. Amber didn't want anything else from me, just a one-off. My boner looked me in the eye and took over. I didn't stop her.

She didn't even undress. She was wearing a skirt, and either she took her panties off or moved them to the side. The next thing I knew she was sliding down onto me, right there on the couch. It was messy and fast.

I didn't have to do anything. In fact, I'm not sure I did. It was over so quickly it was like it had never even happened.

I staggered toward the bathroom but lacked the coordination to shower, so I just cleaned up. We couldn't have been at her place longer than fifteen minutes.

We didn't say much on the short car ride home. She pulled up to my door and said, "Go sleep it off. I'll see you at change over."

I was wasted but when I walked in the door, Bree was still awake and on the phone. She hung up as soon as she saw me. I could tell she'd been crying.

"I had a bad day," I muttered. "I'm going to shower and go to bed. Goodnight."

Did she somehow know? *What the hell have I done?*

33

BREE

A lone again, I was later than usual for our bedtime routine. Lucky for me, Riley was tired out and fell asleep quickly. Ivy, on the other hand, was full of beans. She had turned a corner and was crabby a lot of the time. She could go from a calm and barely noticeable baby to a purple screaming nightmare in seconds. She was peaceful right now, so I brought her in her car seat upstairs and ran her a bath.

I organized what I needed for the bath, spreading everything out on the floor, grateful for this large bathroom. While I was waiting for the ornate clawfoot tub to fill, my eyes filled with tears and my chest hurt. *My husband hates me.* It wasn't just one fight or even a series of fights. I saw the way he looked at me now. He looked so angry anytime I asked him for help, or to look after the kids. He was not the man I'd married. He'd become a different person entirely.

"Crap!" I had filled the tub too high. Ivy giggled. "You little booger," I teased as I drained the excess water and adjusted the temperature. She was batting away at the toy I'd hung on her car seat. Someone at the first mommy group had warned me it wasn't good to leave a baby in the car seat for too long.

"What does she know, hey, Ivy?" It had been so helpful for us.

I picked her up and undressed her for the bath. In the tub, she had a seat that she lay in that suctioned to the bottom to keep her in place. She was shivering a little, so I swaddled her in a thin, hooded bath towel and placed her in the contraption.

Despite what the judgy moms had thought of me, I took these mommy aids seriously and carefully followed the rules. I kept one hand on her tummy and used the other to clean her.

As expected, she began to fuss like crazy. Her small, grunty complaints soon became full-scale screams.

"Shh, you're going to wake Riley."

Her uncontrolled limbs wagged everywhere, getting in the way of me soaping, rinsing, and wiping her clean. At one point she managed to splash soap in my eye.

"Tear-free shampoo, my butt." I wiped my eyes frantically so I could see again.

I looked at her, poised to rinse her one last time as she squirmed and screamed. I pictured myself pouring the water directly onto her screaming face. I was immediately ashamed at this thought. I put down the cup that I was going to rinse her with. My hands shook, and I began to cry.

As I removed my hand from her wet tummy, I pictured her sliding off the chair under the water and then rolling over face down. I saw it as clearly as if it were on TV. I watched myself sit there and do nothing as her body went from frantically moving to lifeless. For one short second, I felt relieved of the burden of motherhood. I began hyperventilating and shaking at how terrible and dangerous I felt.

My thoughts were interrupted by quick, light footsteps coming down the hallway. The bathroom door slammed shut. I opened my eyes. A woman's face stared out from the mirror on the back of the door. It was the woman from my dreams, looking right at me. She looked more scared than I felt and shook her head wildly.

I gasped and grabbed a naked, wet Ivy, forgetting a towel, and barreled toward the closed door. There was no one in the mirror now. I ran out of the bathroom and into Riley's room. I dried Ivy off with some of his clothes and sat on the edge of the bed. What had I just seen? What was happening to me?

I stayed there until I calmed down enough to put her to bed. Then I went downstairs with a pamphlet in my hand to retrieve my phone.

"Postpartum Depression Help Line, Jolene speaking."

I sat cross-legged on the living room floor with my back up against the wall. "I don't know who to call, but I need help. This is anonymous, right?"

"Absolutely."

"Okay. I think I'm going crazy. I've already gone to some mommy help sessions, but the timing doesn't work for me." I told her about the shared car and Jake's shift work. She asked how old the kids were and how my pregnancies had been. Her voice was so sweet, I felt safe talking to her—until I realized this might be the same person who ran the Roxford sessions. "Do you run any in-person support?"

"No, Miss, I'm a phone volunteer," she said calmly. "Now, tell me more."

As I talked about the dreams, tears slid down my cheeks, warm and salty. My tears and her voice would have made a perfect snack, like salted caramel.

"How was it adjusting to being home with two kids under two?" she asked. "That's no easy feat for any one human being. Was your husband supportive?"

I smiled even though I knew she couldn't see me. "The first two weeks were wondrous. Jake, that's my husband, took care of the house, and our son. He made me coffee and breakfast and made sure I got rest and hot solo showers. We had been struggling for a while with Jake's job stress, but his being off work for a while took our troubles away."

I went into the kitchen and grabbed a glass of water, then took it back into the living room. "Then my husband's best friend was killed on the job, covering Jake's shift. The shift *he* was supposed to be working." All of a sudden, I realized I'd been using Jake's actual name.

"Oh dear, I'm so sorry."

"That's what everyone says. Why are you sorry? Did you kill him?"

"No, I just— No, there's nothing appropriate to say here. Please continue, I'm listening."

"Jesus, sorry about that. You're just trying to help. This is what I mean. I'm losing myself. I'm turning into a person I don't recognize or like at all." Jake's curtness was rubbing off on me. "I rarely talk to adults anymore. I think I've forgotten how." I laughed a little. And then a lot. This candy-sweet volunteer was on the phone with a bona fide crackpot. As if she wanted to hear about my insane life with my husband, bad guys following us home and more. "This isn't being recorded, is it?"

"No, of course not. I'm just here to listen and provide resources if I can."

"And you don't have my number? You don't see it there? I blocked it." I let all my nutty thoughts fly out of my mouth.

"That's right. I know you as an unknown caller. I can share with you, though, that I was an unknown caller before I was a volunteer."

I set my now-empty glass on the coffee table and pulled my knees up to my chest, wrapping a blanket around my legs and cold toes.

"I was in a similar position," she said. "I was alone. I had no one. My husband was awful; I'm not saying that yours is, but mine was. I had twin babies who needed me, and I couldn't handle them. I was so sick of being needed physically twenty-four/seven. I always had a baby on me, either breastfeeding, needing to be held, or screaming in my face for some unknown request I felt incapable of filling. I was drowning and I couldn't get air, but I couldn't leave either. I loved them so much it hurt, but the responsibility paralyzed and frightened me. I had bad dreams. Eventually I got medication and help. But I want to hear *your* story and help you in any way you can accept."

Relief flooded me after hearing her pain. "I have nightmares and daymares. I promise I would never hurt my children, but the images are so visceral, I often leave them in their cribs or beds where they're safe so I can leave the room until the images go away. The only thing I can't make go away are the nightmares. I also see things sometimes. Did this happen to you?" I sounded desperate even to myself.

"What you describe is common. Most new mothers are afraid to admit these things. You're doing the right thing when you walk away from them until you're calm or in a better headspace. When you say you're seeing things, what do you see?"

I told her what had happened in the bath. "My marriage isn't very stable right now. I'm terrified if Jake ever found out, he would take the kids away, or use this against me if we divorced. That's the number one reason I haven't gone for a formal diagnosis or help. If it's on paper, it can be used in court." And he knew the court system intimately.

"My marriage wasn't great either," she said. "I get it."

"Um, also these nightmares and things I see when I'm awake are recurring. Is that normal?"

She wanted me to describe them, so I told her about the woman who watched me. "She looks very off-putting, scary even, but her warnings are for the safety of my children. She seems angry with me, but I don't think she'll harm me."

She was shuffling papers as she asked for an example, so I told her about the times I'd seen the woman while pregnant.

"Vivid dreams in the second and third trimester are some of the most commonly reported side effects of pregnancy," she said.

"But I've also seen her while I'm awake. I would never hurt my kids, but I see flashes of what it might look like if I hurt them." As soon as I said it, I knew I shouldn't have.

"As scary as this is, it's not uncommon. It has to do with hormonal changes in your body. They're called intrusive thoughts. You're not alone." She was clearly reading from a script. "You mentioned that you saw someone?"

I stopped crying, took a few deep breaths, and told her about the woman tonight in the mirror. The sugary-sweet woman was silent.

"Hello? Are you still there?"

She cleared her throat and shuffled some more papers. "Yes. Sorry, I was just listening." Her voice shook. She sounded tense.

"Is what I described normal? Another symptom of PPD?" I asked, hopeful.

"Um. No, that's not common. But I'm not a doctor. You should really consider seeing one for medication or just an overall well-being check. There are things like ..."

She talked for a while, but I didn't hear a word. I wanted to get off the phone but didn't feel right hanging up. She was horrified. I had freaked her out, and I *was* losing my mind.

I stayed on the phone while she finished her monologue, and I pretended to write down the resources she gave. I did notice one was a psychiatrist, and the other was 911.

"Do you have any friends you can reach out to, who may understand your situation? Preferably tonight?" She was sweet again.

"Sort of. I have someone I can call. And hey, thanks for listening. I'm sure just getting more sleep will help. I'll contact the resources and—"

The front door opened with its characteristic creak. Jake.

"I gotta go, my husband's home." I hung up the phone and prepared to act normal, though I had no idea how to do that. Nothing in my life was normal anymore.

34

JAKE

DECEMBER 16, 2012

My alarm went off in a rhythm that matched the pulses of my headache. I managed to open my swollen eyes and shut it off enough times to be officially late. No carpooling for me today. Thank God Bree was in the kitchen as I scrambled out the front door and took the car. I wasn't sure I could look her in the eye after what I'd done last night.

I burst into the hospital corridor, late for my shift. The hospital was new and shiny and smelled sharply of rubbing alcohol and laundry detergent. I approached the first nurse I saw. "I'm looking for room 302? I'm here on scene security—I mean, to guard a prisoner."

"Down the hall and to the right." The square-faced nurse frowned, likely at both my request and my appearance, and possibly my stale whiskey breath too. I hadn't had time to shave and knew I'd be in trouble if a superior saw me.

I tipped my hat, trying to be polite, but probably came across as cheesy. I followed her directions down the hall and took over for one of their security guards.

"Was there an officer here?" I asked. This was definitely not procedu
re. "Yeah. You're thirty minutes late," the beefy man in front of me said.
"We couldn't leave the door unsecured."

Shit. That meant the last guy on shift knew I was late. "I got lost, sorry.
Did you catch the name of the last officer who was here?"

He raised his eyebrows at my horseshit story. "Nope. But I don't think
it's a big deal. Dude's been in a coma for like six weeks. It's not like he's
gonna escape." He laughed as he handed me the watch log and walked
away.

I looked at the paperwork. There, in terrible cursive across the
foolscap, was his name: Vincent Joseph Scaggs.

Sweet Jesus, he was just behind that wall. I peeked through the small,
Gregorian, wired-glass window to get a look, but all I could see were his
feet. *I could go in there and wipe him out right now.* Pull a plug, pump up
his medication. But I could never do that.

I was so sick. I plopped my weak ass down and gagged. I waited a
minute and stood up just enough to reach a nearby garbage can, setting
it right beside me.

In the window across the hall, I caught my reflection. *What a state
you're in, Constable Jake Stone.* My shirt was unbuttoned—no wonder
that nurse had judged me. I looked like a piece of crap. A tired, sick,
unkempt, cheating piece of shit contemplating doing awful things to an
even-more-awful person.

I fastened my buttons, fanning my shirt to cool down. A water machine gurgled nearby, so I walked over. After chugging a couple of cups,
I felt a bit better. I was not allowed to go inside that room, so I put it out
of my mind. Plus, as long as Scaggs was alive, there was a chance Bychkov
or one of his men might turn up here.

Sergeant Lincoln had been trying to help me out by giving me an easy shift, but she obviously hadn't realized that the shit bag in there had killed my best friend. Not that it mattered if it was me on security or someone else. Any police officer in the world would hate that cop- killer.

Â

The shift went by quickly enough. Not many people came down this way, as the room was at the far end of the hall. Besides the medical staff who came in every other hour, it was mostly just me. I broke the rules and read a boring magazine, sent a few texts, and dozed off. I dreamt I saw Bychkov, but when I opened my eyes, I was alone.

I'd only had a couple of hours of sleep the previous night—and a ton of alcohol. I'd probably still been drunk on the morning drive here. I was looking down at my phone when I heard someone walk up. Uniform pants stood before me.

"Hey, you."

I looked up, startled to see Amber standing over me. "What are you doing here?"

She laughed and rubbed my shoulder. "It's shift change, silly. You don't remember me telling you I was working here today?"

"Right. I was wasted." She was acting like nothing had happened. *Good. I can do that.* I stood up beside her. "Do you know who's in there?"

"I sure do. Haven't you done any shifts here?"

I shook my head. It still felt heavy and fuzzy.

"This is my third. It's a good gig. I mean, you can overwhelm yourself thinking about it, or you can read a book and be grateful you aren't being attacked or running code to files." She held up the book in her hand: *The Shining.*

I lowered my voice. "I just want to go in there and give him a piece of my mind. Sitting out here all day knowing he's lying in there and still has a chance, when Matthews is dead, just kills me."

"Then go in."

"What? You know we aren't allowed to do that."

"No one will know. He's in a coma. He'll probably never wake up. Tell him what you think."

I didn't say anything.

"What's the worst that will happen? He wakes up and tells people he dreamt a cop was saying mean things to him?" She laughed.

I looked down the empty hallway and back. "Okay." I wanted to see that shit pump.

"I'll be out here waiting for you. *As always.*" She looked me up and down.

There it is. Last night was supposed to have been a one-off. I hoped she hadn't changed her mind about that.

I entered the room. Apart from the beeping machinery, it was quiet. I approached Scaggs but kept my distance. "You piece of shit," I said softly. "You don't deserve to be alive. All the grief you caused Matthews, his partner, me, my family. I wish you were dead."

In truth, I didn't feel any better for having said it, but my curiosity had been satisfied. He'd lost so much weight, he probably could have slipped out of his restraints. Though, if he woke up, he'd be too weak to run. He was no longer a threat. I walked out of the room feeling sheepish and a bit silly.

I stood outside talking with Amber for another five minutes or so. Then I left. Desperate for sleep, I hoped no one was home. But it wasn't just that. I couldn't face Bree.

35

BREE

"We're here!" Tammy sounded like a kid as we entered the indoor play place. "I love Dinotown, but my kids are both grown now. It's a lot more acceptable when you show up with kids." She let out a laugh so loud I had to step away from her.

"I'm so glad you were free," I said, "and thanks for driving all the way out here." When she'd invited me over, I'd had to explain that I didn't have a vehicle today, but I did have car seats.

"My pleasure. I'm so glad you finally called."

I felt terrible when she said that. I'd tried Daphne first, but ever since the car incident, she'd wanted nothing to do with me. Paige was too far away to hang out with. Plus, I couldn't keep long-distance dumping on her the way I had been.

Riley ran through the front door, ripping off his shoes and coat and blowing past the gate before the woman behind the counter could stamp him. Dinotown was a kids' indoor play park that we used to frequent more often before we'd tightened our budget.

"Sorry," I said to the attendant. "Do you want me to go grab him for the stamp?"

The woman behind the counter smiled. "Happens all the time. Don't worry about it."

Tammy jumped in front of me and paid for our entrance fees, plus coffees for us and juice for Riley.

"You don't have to do that." My face flushed.

"Don't be silly, I'm happy to. I'll let you pay next time."

We poured our coffees from giant carafes, and she enthusiastically filled hers with powdered creamer and sugar. She wore jeans and a fuzzy white sweater and looked well put together. I couldn't remember the last time I'd made an effort with my appearance. I hadn't even put on any makeup.

We sat down and I adjusted Ivy in her carrier. She was squirmy but hopefully would remain in there long enough for me to enjoy coffee.

"Weeee! Ma!" Riley ran past us trying to high-five or wave, I wasn't sure which. He ran up the stairs and down the slide, and up the other stairs and down that slide in a manic figure-eight pattern. It was hilarious and exhausting to watch.

"How are you, Bree?"

I almost teared up on the spot. "I'm good, how about you?"

"Really? Two kids under two, no car, a grumpy shift-working husband, and you're good?" She laughed. "I call bullshit."

I loved her already. "Well, okay, things could be better. But I'm managing."

"Okay, that's more believable." She tipped her head to look over the top of her glasses. "Anyone sleeping in your house?"

"No, not much—besides Ivy. Jake doesn't, and neither does Riley. Which means I don't sleep a ton either. Some days I'm able to sync the kids' naps though, so that helps."

"I'm just going to go ahead and let you know I friggin' love babies. In fact, I'm restraining myself from snatching Ivy out of that carrier and giving her a friendly chomp. If you ever need a sitter so you and Jake can go out or just get some sleep, let me know." She opened her mouth and bit down so her teeth gnashed together while looking at Ivy.

Too bad Jake didn't want me to hang out with her. I could have used the help. Why didn't he like her, anyway? Was it only because he thought she was a gossip?

"Well, the offer's there. No pressure. Tell me more about you and Jake—how you guys met. I love those stories." Tammy's eyes twinkled.

It had been ages since I'd thought about that. "It's kind of cheesy."

As Riley ran past, she lifted her hand to high-five him without even looking. Then she leaned in as though I were divulging sweet secrets and said, "Do tell."

"We met on a file. I lived in a shitty condo building in East Bern-heim—you know the tall concrete building close to the Burner Central Transit Station? The one across from the grass field that homeless folk tend to sleep in?'

"Yes." She slurped her milky coffee.

"I loved living there when I was on my own, sketchy area or not."

The coffee wasn't good, but I got it down without pulling a face. I understood the optics of a sad broke chick who was a coffee snob. "That night, I was coming home from dancing with friends."

"Party girl?" She smiled.

"Yes, I'll admit it. Young, single, carefree. I was having fun, but I was getting tired. I wanted to meet someone.

"I took a taxi home as I knew the walk from the bus was dangerous at that time of night. When he pulled up, there were two police officers standing at the front door, looking kind of bored."

Tammy snorted. "They probably were."

"Yup. I was swiping my way in, and they followed close behind me. I laughed and asked if they lived in the building. We were instructed not to let in anyone we didn't know. They looked at each other like I was nuts. I just laughed and let them in. Jake thought I was wasted. I was *not*. I was wearing sexy, tall heels that I'd been dancing in, and I stumbled a bit, but I wasn't drunk, I swear."

She put up both hands. "No judgment."

"They followed me into the elevator, and it was so awkward. I thought Jake was cute, but he kept his eyes toward the ground. He was smirking though, so I thought maybe he felt the same way. We made eye contact at one point, and my heart felt all bubbly and weird, so I just stood there. And then when I left the elevator, I said, 'Have a nice evening, guys,' like a department store greeter."

I blushed at the memory. Riley had stopped running in circles around us, and I panicked for a millisecond as I looked for him. Tammy pointed to the entryway of the big kid zone. He had walked over to stand directly beneath the robotic dino. When it moved, he squealed and ran back to us, checking behind him several times to make sure the dinosaur hadn't followed him. "Ma!"

I swallowed my giggles. "It's just a toy. Nothing to be afraid of."

He walked over to the slide, looked at us, looked at the dinosaur, and then back at the stairs. Then he resumed his fast figure-eight slide routine.

"Gawd, I wish I had half his energy," Tammy said.

"Heck ya." I downed the rest of the cold, brown liquid gift, my muscles taut.

"That coffee was putrid." She howled. "You're so damn polite. Why do you think I put so much crap in mine?"

We laughed until we had tears in our eyes. It felt so good to laugh.

"You're not off the hook though," she said. "Tell me the rest of the Bree and Jake love story."

I had been embarrassed by my interaction with the cops in the elevator, so I quickly I let myself into my condo feeling defeated and threw some sloppy nachos into the microwave.

I was about five greasy chips in when there was a knock at my door. *Who the hell is here at this time of night?* I went to the door, grease on my fingers, and peeped through the hole. It was him! Giddiness overtook me, but then I grew horrified at my onion nacho situation. I quickly wiped off my fingers and popped a tic-tac in my mouth. I was still wearing my hot top and PJ pants. *Good enough.* I took a deep breath and opened the door.

"Well, hello there," I said, sounding creepier than I'd intended. "Fancy seeing you again." I wished I would shut the hell up.

"Hello again." This time he was looking right at me and wearing a huge, gorgeous smile. "Ma'am, may I ask you a few questions?"

"Only if you don't call me ma'am ever again."

He wanted to come inside. I thought he would ask me out and probably didn't want to do it in the hallway. I wondered if there was there a law against asking someone out while you were in uniform—or someone that you'd met at a call?

"How well do you know your neighbours?" he asked.

My heart sank. He wasn't there for me. "I don't know them well at all, but I often hear noises from up there. It seems like there's always someone awake. They are rather heavy-footed, and I always hear the guy peeing. It's really loud." I had no clue why I'd said that.

He was taking notes. I hoped he didn't write that down.

"I would ask if you heard what happened earlier tonight, but I know you weren't home. Thanks for letting us in, by the way. We'd been waiting outside for quite a while. The woman who called us wasn't in a position to let us in."

That was when I realized the gravity of the situation. "Is she okay?"

"Yes. We are, however, looking for her boyfriend. My partner and I are interviewing folks in the building. Could I grab your info for further questions if they should arise?" He had a massive smile on his face now. This was so confusing.

"Yes, of course, you can ask me anything." That came out desperate. "I mean, to help my neighbour out."

He took down my name and number and turned for the door. "Those look delicious, by the way." He pointed to my nachos.

I giggled as I followed him to the door. When I let him out, he turned around and handed me his card with the file number on it.

"If you have anything else to add, we could always meet up for coffee to discuss it." He flashed that killer smile.

My heart fluttered. "That sounds like a great idea. I'll be in touch."

"I hope so."

I closed the door and did a happy dance. When I popped into the washroom to let out a squeal, I noticed I had nacho grease on my chin.

I debated calling him for days and tried to gather information on my neighbours so I'd have something to say. I had nothing.

I eventually got up the nerve to call him.

"Constable Jake Stone here." His voice was deep and sexy and so official.

"Hello?" I squeaked into the phone. "It's Breanna from condo 311 in the building on Huxley. You were helping someone in the apartment above me the other night. I let you in and then you came downstairs and knocked and then—"

"Whoa, slow down, I remember you." He chuckled. "Do you have information for me? Should we meet for coffee so I can take your statement?"

I took two solid breaths and sucked up all the courage I could find. "I want to meet you for coffee, but I have no information." If he didn't want to or couldn't date civilians, I'd just hang up. *Say something, damnit.*

"Are you free today?" he asked.

"Um, what?"

"For coffee? It's my day off. I only answered the phone because I saw it was your number. I was hoping you'd call."

Oh, thank God.

The sudden appearance of Riley putting his head on my lap interrupted us. He looked up at me and rubbed his eyes.

"It's almost naptime for the little guy." Knowing Jake's feelings about her, I couldn't bring Tammy back to the house. I was paranoid that he'd put recording devices in the house and didn't want him to know we were spending time together, though I was enjoying her company, immensely.

"Do they sleep well in the car?" she asked.

"Is the sky blue?"

We both laughed.

By the time we pulled out of the parking lot, Riley was already asleep, and Ivy was getting there. I felt a bit weird in Tammy's car now. The last setting had been so comfortable; this felt more invasive.

"Now let's get some real coffee and go for a drive so they can sleep."

Feeling at ease again, I nodded enthusiastically, to the coffee and this wonderful person who seemed to read minds. We grabbed a couple of lattes and were on our way.

"Okay. You had just left off when you were planning to meet at the coffee shop."

"So cliché, I know."

"Coffee shop, maybe. Meeting a cop attending a domestic in your building? Hell no."

I arrived early and sat at the back corner of the room so I would spot him looking around for me. I wasn't great at recognizing people and avoided awkwardness wherever I could.

He walked in, saw me, and marched my way with confidence. Now that, I liked.

"Hi, Breanna." He shook my hand. "Sorry. I don't know why I did that." His head cranked back as he let out a booming laugh. The handful of people in the room turned to look at what was so funny. "Habit, I guess?"

I laughed too, feeling instantly comfortable. He felt easy, familiar even.

One coffee became two, and that turned into drinks and dinner. Our first date led to more dates. Dinner, movies, a drive-in. By the fourth date, we knew this was *it*.

"What do you mean, *it*?" Tammy asked.

"Well, we moved quite quickly into something more serious. We both came from the island. We grew up in neighbouring towns, actually. Turns out we crossed paths more than once and even attended the same university at the same time."

"Wow! And you met in the big city of Burner? How random."

"I know. We had similar values and backgrounds. It was comforting. We were also both in our early thirties and ready to leave the dating scene. It all clicked."

"Oh, I know what you mean about the dating scene," Tammy said. "Stone was going through a lot of girls before he met you." She put a hand to her mouth. "Sorry, that was insensitive." She took her focus off the road to look at me.

"I didn't realize you knew Jake that well."

"I don't, but the members talk more than us spouses do." She laughed. "Tony told me about all these young women Stone would date—'badge-bunnies,' as we call them. Nothing lasted long, and he seemed lost. Tony also told me that shortly after he met you, Stone had one of the guys run you in their system, so he must have been serious about you from the start. He was a bit wild and got a few complaints here and there, which he was absolved of."

"Ran me?" I hadn't known that. I hadn't known about the complaints either. *Maybe this is the reason Jake didn't want me hanging out with Tammy.* "I knew Jake's dating history and that his tastes, um, skewed younger. I dated a lot before him too. Same story over and over. People either wanted a cheap hookup or to merge bank accounts—nothing in between." I'd longed for the days where you met someone and let things happen organically.

"Isn't that the truth? Tony and I met in high school. There's a cliché for you."

"Wow, so you knew him before he went to Depot?" I was tempted to ask her if Tony was different before and if work changed him, but I thought twice, letting the moment pass.

"Yes, ma'am." She tapped the steering wheel. "Okay, back to the juicy details. Just how fast did it go? I didn't even know he had a new girlfriend until I heard about your wedding."

I looked out the window. "Yeah, we were nicknamed 'the runaway train.' My friends were shocked when they heard the news. Before my dating spree, I was in a long-term relationship that moved at a snail's pace, so this was a huge surprise.

"Anyway, we knew by the fourth date. We couldn't get enough of each other, spending all of our free time together. After a stunning meal on the pier in the fanciest restaurant in town, we stayed up all night talking."

"I want to level with you," Jake said as we lay together in my bed. Lottie was snuggled at the base of my feet.

"Uh-oh." I had consumed four large vodka crantinis, but I could focus if I needed to.

"I'm falling in love with you."

I did *not* see that coming. "I feel the same way." The words flew out of my mouth, surprising me.

"In my job, I've learned that life is incredibly precious and short, so I don't want to waste any time. I love you, I want to be with you, and I want it all with you."

I sat up.

"Let's put it all on the table," he said. "Secrets, skeletons in the closet, hang-ups, fears, dreams, desires."

We spent the night discussing everything, a never-ending Q&A that didn't turn up any red flags except for my recent diagnosis of Polycystic Ovarian Syndrome (PCOS). This condition made getting pregnant difficult. We both wanted marriage and children, so I expected him to be disappointed or put off by this, but he put his hand under my chin and tilted my face to his. "Well—we better not wait then."

For the first time in my life, I chose to follow my heart. "Okay."

Tammy looked at me while we were at a stoplight. "Your story isn't cheesy at all," she said. "Tony and I had trouble conceiving before we had the boys." She turned down a quiet country road. "I'm glad it worked out for you. Tell me the rest."

"The rest of the story is asleep in your backseat." We both giggled. "I got pregnant right away. It was such a shock to us that I brought Jake with me to my doctor so she could confirm that I indeed did have PCOS. I didn't want him to think I'd trapped him. I was elated but also straight-up terrified. Everything about Jake sounded and looked so good. He said the right things, had a good head on his shoulders, and I was more than ready to settle down."

"I'm sensing a 'but,' here."

I shrugged. "Only three months into our relationship, we were living together, and I was already pregnant. Any reservations I had at that point didn't matter."

"And you had reservations?"

Reservations I should have listened to. "I had no idea what I was getting into marrying a police officer."

Tammy rolled her eyes.

"I had no clue that he had zero control over where he lived, where he was posted, his hours, the demands. And the possibility of death. I was naive and in love. A friend of mine warned me I was moving too fast. She said you should be with someone for at least four seasons before making a commitment. I would never admit this to her, but she was right."

My diatribe was interrupted by the vibration of my phone. I peeked at the screen as Jake's rage radiated through his incoming text:

Bree, where the hell are you!?!?

Thank goodness Tammy was focused on the road.

I collected myself. "I need to get home. Jake's back earlier than I thought. I should have been home a while ago."

Why didn't I get back sooner? Or not go out at all. He didn't want me hanging out with Tammy. I didn't think he would find out.

I sent a quick text back:

On my way. See you in a few.

As if that would help.

Tammy glanced over. "Everything okay?"

"Yeah. Jake's just grumpy."

"Roger that," she said, then laughed as if trying to lighten the mood in the car.

"Thanks for everything. I had a lot of fun today." Understatement. The outing had been essential for my well-being.

"Me too. Looking forward to next time." She smiled as she pulled into my driveway. I hoped it wasn't the last time I'd get to spend with her.

She woke up Riley while I uninstalled the other car seat with Ivy still in it.

"Do you need help getting settled inside?" Tammy's eyes were fixed on the house. Her face had gone so white, it looked as though she'd seen a ghost. But no, it was Jake, standing at the living room window, watching us through the blinds. It was the scariest I'd ever seen him look. This was new territory. He looked so pissed I wasn't sure what he would do.

"No, I'm okay," I chirped. "Just leave Riley's car seat in the driveway and I'll load everything into the house."

She didn't take her eyes off Jake. "You can call me anytime. For anything. I mean it."

I mouthed, *Thank you*, then turned around to face whatever hell awaited me inside my home.

"Hello?" I shouted as cheerily as I could, my voice wavering.

There was no sign of Jake. Riley was settled in his highchair in front of some cartoons with a handful of finger food, and a sleeping Ivy remained in her car seat near the couch. After bringing in the other seat and hanging up my diaper bag, I looked for Jake. There was no way this was going to turn into another five-day silent treatment where I cried myself to sleep every night.

"Jake?" I circled through the living room and kitchen back to the entryway. Riley was engrossed in his cartoons, so I slipped upstairs. Jake stood in the main bedroom with his fists and teeth clenched.

"Who the hell do you think you are?" he barked. "I asked you not to hang out with Paskins' wife. I spend all my time at work, suffering, making money for this family, and you just do whatever the hell you want with no respect for me."

"I'm sorry, I—"

"I don't want to hear that you're sorry, you liar. You've always been a liar and a cheat. I know all about the affair you're having. There's no

point hiding it. I know you're banging my doctor, you fucking bitch."
He shook his finger at me as his voice grew louder.

What the heck was he talking about? "I don't even know your doctor.
I—" I stopped abruptly as he stomped toward me, his finger soon poised
an inch from my nose. I held my breath, afraid to maintain eye contact
for too long. His pupils were dilated.

"Stop lying to me, Lisa. You're such a skank. I should have left you
years ago."

Time stopped as ice pricked my spine. Lisa was his ex-girlfriend's
name. What was happening? *Is he psychotic?* Adrenaline gushed through
my veins to my extremities. I'd been in shock once before, during Riley's
traumatic delivery. I hadn't recognized it then, but I did now. The panic
drained the blood from my face and settled in my stomach. Fear-vomit
rose in my throat as I remained frozen in place.

Jake's chest heaved with each huff of breath.

At that moment a thousand questions flooded me along side the fear.
Should I run away? Will he snap out of it? Would he hurt me? And
inconceivably, could he kill me?

He grabbed my left arm with his free hand and kept his pointed finger
on the tip of my nose. "Don't just stand there, you fucking cunt. Admit
you did it. You. Fucking. Useless. Bitch."

I squirmed, terrified of what he might do next. *Why doesn't he know
it's me?*

"Lisa, say something. Admit it, you whore."

In the short silence that followed, I could hear Ivy crying downstairs
and Riley's little voice going, "Ma, Ma, Ma." I needed to get to the kids,
but I couldn't let Jake go down there like this. I couldn't move, and his
grip on my arm was tight. The adrenaline wasn't helping me anymore.

"Jake?" I whispered, hoping he would recognize my voice and snap out of it.

A loud crash came from downstairs.

"Riley!" I screamed.

Jake's pupils shrank, his focus changing—he seemed dazed. I wriggled away from his grasp and ran toward the stairs. I tripped on my way down and fell, clipping my head on the corner of the wall and landing upright like a beaten-up alley cat. The highchair lay sideways on the floor with Riley still in it. There was a large pillow underneath him and the highchair—a pillow that I hadn't left there.

I ran over and unlatched a crying Riley from the chair, pulling him into my arms. He stopped crying and raised his chubby finger to touch the blood on my cheek.

"Owie?"

A pulsating lump had sprouted on the side of my head.

Footsteps creaked behind me on the stairs. "What happened to Riley's highchair? Is he okay?" Jake asked.

I turned around. When Jake's eyes lit on my head, he gasped.

"Oh my god, Bree, what happened to your face?" His expression was so soft and concerned as he rushed toward me.

I curled my body over Riley, holding him tighter and turning away from Jake, but maintaining eye contact. He reached over to inspect my head. I flinched as he tried to comfort me, though he looked sincere. *Does he not remember the fight we just had?* Maybe it was time to schedule that psych evaluation.

I resettled the kids, grabbed the first aid kit and a hot cloth, and sat at the kitchen table dabbing the blood off my face. Jake looked genuinely worried as he held some ice to my head. This was not the guy from upstairs who'd looked like he wanted me dead.

"Can you please tell me what happened to Riley and to your face?"

I glanced at him and away. *Why doesn't he know?*

"I was having a nap upstairs," he said. "I had a horrible shift."

He doesn't remember texting me? He'd been in the window, glaring at us. "You didn't see us come in?"

"No." He frowned quizzically.

Uneasy with his confusion, I excused myself and went to the washroom to gather my thoughts. When I looked in the mirror, I didn't recognize the woman staring back at me. She was frail, scared, and tired. Not the strong and confident person who had once stood there. Her eyes were bloodshot and surrounded by deep black raccoon circles. Her hair was going prematurely gray. The lump on her head had stopped growing but was surrounded by a purplish hue. For a second, I was convinced it wasn't me. She was familiar, but she wasn't me.

It was the lady from my dream.

I gasped and stumbled backward, my shoulders banging against the wall. Then I looked again: It was me and it was her. I grew brave and leaned forward until I was a few inches from the mirror. I let out a long breath. All I saw this time was a broken, ragged mom, desperate for sleep.

And then my reflection tilted her head to one side, looked into my eyes and mouthed, *Get out.*

36

JAKE

DECEMBER 17, 2012

I was early for the psych appointment, so I sat in the car for a bit. I didn't know if I should plan out what I was going to say. Apparently, it was five sessions per issue. I wondered what my issue was and if I actually needed to attend all five. I'd been warned to be careful, but I wasn't too sure what careful meant. I wished Matthews was here so I could ask him what to do.

When it was time, I went up the stairs. Ironically, the force psychologist's office was in the worst neighbourhood in town. I still didn't want anyone to see me there.

I introduced myself to the receptionist, who was hot: jet-black hair and the shiniest red lips I'd ever seen in the daytime. I felt like an overgrown man-child arriving for a diaper change.

The waiting room was small and contained only two chairs—both a green velour material that would have been better suited to a strip club, and both positioned too close to her desk. The receptionist gestured to them, and I sat down, but now it was awkward to look anywhere other than at her.

Luckily, I didn't have long to wait before a small, rumpled man skittered out of the hallway. He was thin and entirely bald.

"Jake, right?" He extended his hand.

Hearing my first name always surprised me. "Yes, Dr. Steinman. We met at the detachment." I shook his hand.

"Right. Matthews' debrief. Follow me. I haven't had enough coffee." He led me into a dingy lunchroom with fluorescent lighting.

I would have preferred to be concealed in an office with a closed door. I waited while he doctored up a coffee with an obscene amount of sugar, and then we made our way to his office. I'd never been to a shrink before. I expected a chaise lounge or couch to lie down on and was disappointed when I saw how basic his office was. Cheap furniture and bland beige walls with a painting that belonged in an eighties motel room. I plunked myself on the chair he pointed to and watched him fiddle with his computer.

"Sorry about that. Let's begin. Why are you here?" He took a large mouthful of coffee. It must have been too hot because he swallowed it fast while squinting.

I'd thought Harvey or Lincoln might have filled him in. "I've been struggling at work. I'm not sleeping at all, and I'm seeing things." Already I'd said too much.

He didn't flinch but took a couple of notes. "What kinds of things?"

I told him about how hard work had been lately and how I'd started seeing the faces of loved ones at files.

"That's normal." He wrote more notes and drank his coffee, more cautiously this time. "You're overtired. You can hallucinate when you are overtired. And you recently experienced a big loss. I remember now;

Matthews was your friend, and you feel responsible somehow." He sounded like he was reading a textbook out loud.

Silence hung in the air like the thick fog in the Dead-End Fen. I didn't recall telling him I'd felt responsible. Someone at work must have told him it was my fault. I wondered what else it said in that file he kept referring to.

"Survivor's guilt is tough. I'll bet most of your colleagues feel the same way."

Sure they do.

"What else? Anything happening at home?"

I wasn't sure why he asked me about my home life when we were here to talk about my work struggles. "Everything's fine at home. I have a toddler and a baby, so it's a busy household."

He laughed. "That's probably why you aren't sleeping. I have kids too and remember those days well. How about your wife, marriage? Everything good there?"

"Yes, same as ever," I said, my tone curt. *Where is this going?* I tried not to relive the memory of Amber riding me a couple of nights ago.

"No need to be nervous, Jake. I see you've been approved for five sessions here so I'd like to spend some time on your background and then jump into what's affecting you now. We can also have you see a GP to get some sleeping pills. Anything else we should address?"

His explanation pacified me. "I'm also having trouble focusing, and I keep forgetting things. I concentrate so hard at work, staying alert, making the right calls, documenting every detail, that I have nothing left when I get home. I keep losing my phone, my bank card and keys. It's debilitating. Bree gets frustrated with me."

He took some more notes and then left me with a questionnaire while he went to grab another cup of shitty coffee. This guy was worse than I was for coffee consumption.

The questions were all pretty applicable to my state of mind. Do you have trouble concentrating? Do you lose things easily? Are you having trouble sleeping? Yes, yes, yes.

He was back in minutes and reviewed the form while sipping his dirt water. He wrote a few things down and then turned to face me. "Do you know much about ADHD?"

"Isn't that what hyperactive kids have?" Why were we talking about this?

"Sort of. It's a medical condition with differences in brain development. The form I just had you fill out is for ADHD. It's a common condition in general, but specifically for people in your line of work. It can impair your focus, your sleep, your memory, and your frustration tolerance. You were likely born with it."

My initial reaction was relief. A condition could be treated. If I treated it, my problems would go away. "What do I do to get rid of it? Is it permanent? Will it affect my RCMP record?"

"Whoa, you're putting the cart before the horse here. I'm not diagnosing you, not yet, but I think this is something we should explore over the next few sessions. It's not curable, but it's highly manageable with medication. You'll be able to focus, and work will become easier for you. And no, it won't affect your record if diagnosed. A lot of members have this."

He kept looking at the clock as he grabbed what I assumed was a prescription pad. We had started fifteen minutes late, but it looked like we would end right on time. "You'll need to ask your family doctor for a prescription for Adderall and sleeping pills."

"You can't write me a prescription?"

"Only GPs and psychiatrists can. Don't get me started." He rolled his eyes. "Go to the clinic downstairs. Dr. Lee will do it. Just tell him I sent you." He handed me the paper with the information written on it. It wasn't even on letterhead. "Trust me, you'll feel much better once you start sleeping and can focus during the day."

As we shook hands, he said, "I've booked you another appointment for the day after tomorrow. Your sarge wanted me to get as many sessions in as possible during your time off."

I headed out of his office more confused than ever. I hadn't talked much about the things that were bothering me, but I felt good knowing I might have a solution in hand. What I didn't like was that he and the sarge had been chatting about what to do with me and making appointments on my behalf. What else had they talked about?

"See you soon, Jake," the hot receptionist said on my way out. I headed straight to the walk-in clinic downstairs.

The receptionist at Dr. Lee's office was not attractive. Her short hair was disheveled, and she was studying some paperwork with a giant frown on her round face.

"Dr. Lee isn't in today," she said. "You can see his replacement, Dr. Bell." She took down my details and once again I sat down to wait. I was uncomfortable in public to begin with, and doubly so in my coverage area. Plus, I was experiencing a new kind of discomfort asking people for things I knew little about.

Dr. Bell was tall, slim, bald, and looked too old to still be working. The paperwork in his hand trembled a bit. "What can I do you for?" he said as he hustled into the examining room.

I took a deep breath. "I just came from Dr. Steinman's office. He thinks I have ADHD and told me to come down here and ask for Adderall and sleeping pills so I can focus more at work. I'm not sleeping and am struggling to do my job. I'm an RCMP member here in East Burner."

He raised one eyebrow. "Well, that's a lot. Why does he think you have ADHD?"

I don't fucking know. "I filled out a questionnaire and had mostly yeses." I shrugged.

"I mean what are the symptoms that brought you to him?" He set down his paperwork and looked at me with a kind expression.

"I'm having difficulty sleeping for more than an hour or two at a time. When I do fall asleep, I have vivid nightmares. I'm also having trouble with my memory, difficulty focusing at work, and uh—" I wasn't going to say it, but it popped out. "I'm seeing things." I looked at the ground.

There was a long silence.

This was a bad idea.

I got to my feet, ready to run screaming out of there with my hair on fire. "I don't need anything. It's fine, I'll go."

"Sit down, please. What sort of things are you seeing?" His voice was calm.

"I'm not really seeing things like hallucinations or anything. I just see my family's faces on people in the files I attend. You know, if the situation is similar ..." Once again, I'd said too much.

"These are traumatic scenes, I assume? And are the nightmares related to the files you are attending?"

"Yes to both."

"Has anything else major happened at work or in your life recently?"

Which major thing? Being responsible for the death of my best friend? Or betraying my wife? "My partner was killed on the job. He was working my shift, driving my car, handling my files, dealing with my perps. I wasn't there to help him."

"My goodness, that's terrible. Was it the young man on the news a while back?"

These were the kinds of questions I'd expected the psychologist to ask. I nodded, gulping down the hot lump that had risen in my throat.

"I'm thankful for your service and glad you're here today. I'm going to write you a prescription for sleeping pills. When we don't sleep, our bodies and minds are capable of playing tricks on us. It's essential that you start getting some sleep. I'm also going to refer you to a psychiatrist. I suspect something else may be going on here."

When he handed me the paper, my spine went cold. What the fuck was this? *This guy thinks I'm nuts?* Fuck. I made a huge mistake coming here.

"What about the Adderall Dr. Steinman wanted me to get?" My voice was squeakier than I would have liked.

He clasped his shaky hands together. "I think we should dig deeper into your symptoms before we give you a strong medication. It doesn't sound like ADHD to me. How did you find your psychologist?"

"The RCMP has certain psychologists we have to use," I rambled. "This one was booked for me. He attended the debrief of my colleague's passing."

"Right. Force psychologist." He made a face that I couldn't place. Disdain? "What was his name again?"

"Uhhh ... I gotta go, thank you." I ran out of there as fast as I could, stumbling into the parking lot and into my car. As I went to put the car in drive, Dr. Bell appeared at the window. I unwound it.

"You forgot your prescription." He stood with one hand on the car door and one holding the paper. "It's critical that you get some proper sleep, Jake. Things will get progressively worse if you continue to go without. I included the referral too and will book you an appointment. The receptionist will call you in a few days."

His concern seemed genuine, but I was terrified. There was no way I was going to see a psychiatrist or ask anyone else for medications. I'd have to deal with this on my own.

I grabbed the paper from his hand and got the hell out of there.

37

BREE

Riley and I were decorating Christmas cookies at the kitchen table while Ivy had tummy-time on her floor mat beside us. I couldn't let the full-blown chaos of my marriage interrupt family traditions.

I was drinking the cowboy coffee Jake had made that morning. In the early days, we joked about who should make the coffee based on how exhausted we were. If we needed an extra kick, Jake would make it.

He hadn't said much before he'd left. He'd been avoiding speaking to me lately. Better than fighting, at least.

"Hey kiddo, how about you put some icing on the actual cookie?"

Riley had red and green icing all over his mouth. I handed him a jar of sprinkles.

I was so grateful Jake was seeing a psychologist, though I'd only learned of it while eavesdropping when he booked the appointment. But I couldn't stop thinking of that woman in the mirror: *Get out.*

It wasn't like he'd hit me. He'd just yelled. And I had done something he'd asked me not to. But he didn't seem to have any memory of the incident. When he asked for an explanation about my head, I told him I'd gone upstairs to wake him up, and halfway up Riley's chair had fallen, and I'd hurt myself running down the stairs to get to him. It was sort of true.

He'd stunk of stale booze, and I knew he wasn't sleeping. But the old Jake would have been mortified at this new guy's behavior. *Should I leave?* We were so broke, I wasn't sure how I could pull that off. I looked at my beautiful babies. What kind of future would they have without him? *What kind of future will they have with him?*

I had no job, no money, nowhere to land, and I worried that he might paint me as an unfit psycho—which might or might not have been valid. I was seeing things. As much as the argument with Jake replayed in my head, so did the moment in the mirror afterward. Was that just me losing my mind? Or was there a "ghost" in this house sending me messages? I needed answers, and I needed to make some decisions, but I wasn't sure how I would figure it out on my own.

I poured what was left of my coffee down the drain. I looked outside and noticed a couple of the ladies from next door standing on the deck, smoking.

I cleaned off Riley's face and got the kids outfitted for a walk.

With Ivy in her carrier and Riley at my side, I strode over to the shelter next door and rang the bell.

The older woman who answered recognized me immediately. "What a pleasant surprise. Come in." She reintroduced herself as Shelby. Her hair was dyed blond with long roots, and she wore it in a loose ponytail. She was very thin and had a large heart tattoo on her forearm. It looked like there was a name in the middle, but the ink was faded and blurred.

Shelby led me into the kitchen, which was bright and clean, unlike mine. Everything was labeled and orderly, and there was an intense chore chart on the fridge. I wasn't sure what I'd expected, but it sure wasn't this. Ivy was arching her back inside the carrier, and I tried to ignore it, hoping she would stop.

Shelby offered me coffee, but I couldn't bear another drop after Jake's swill. "I run this shelter," she said. "We aren't doing anything to bother you, are we?"

I thought of the woman who'd serenaded me in my driveway. "No, no nothing like that. I—"

Ivy began to wail. No buildup, just straight screaming. Riley had sat himself down on a step stool and was watching his sister cause a scene.

"May I?" Shelby reached over with open arms.

"Be my guest." I unstrapped her and handed her over like a hot potato. I knew Jake would be mad that I was here. He had insinuated that the women here might have rap sheets or sordid pasts.

Shelby held Ivy gently and confidently, swaying back and forth the way women who'd had children did instinctively. "They don't stay this small for long, that's for sure. What were you about to say?"

"Right. The first time I met you all on the deck outside, someone mentioned stories about my house?" As soon as I said it out loud, I felt ridiculous.

"Oh yes. There are some of those."

Two women came down the stairs. One introduced herself as Sandra, and the other was Leslie. The latter beelined it to Ivy, who was calm and quiet, and that was all that mattered. It was nice to have the extra sets of hands.

"Bree wants to hear stories about her house." Shelby wiggled her eyebrows as the other women made spooky sounds.

Sandra pulled up a chair. We were all sitting at the kitchen table now—all except Leslie, who swayed with Ivy, and Riley, who was crouched on the floor playing with some old toys Shelby had kicking around.

"I could tell you a few things," Sandra said. "What would you like to know?"

"One of you mentioned that strange things happened in my home, but only in the fall. Is that right?"

"I don't know about *only* in the fall," Sandra said, "but we sure notice it more come October and November. I've stayed here a few times."

I waited, unsure of what I hoped to hear.

"The lady who lived there before you was a single mom with a teenaged daughter. She used to tell us about hearing footsteps, creaks, and groans." She paused and looked around, likely for dramatic effect. "But one night, she heard screams."

Okay, now I'm listening. "What kind of screams?" Baby screams? Anguished-lady screams?

"I'm not sure," Sandra said. "But she heard them on more than one occasion. She also used to complain about the temperature. Saying it was always too cold in there."

"Well, that's true." So far, they hadn't told me anything I didn't already know, though it came as a relief to discover I hadn't been imagining these things.

"One night in late October —I guess it was last year or the year before, I can't remember—it was late. After midnight for sure. I was up watching late-night TV, when there was this frantic banging at the door."

Shelby nodded in agreement. Leslie was listening intently, still swaying.

"It was the neighbour and her daughter. She was frantic and pushed her way inside. She said she was woken up by the sound of a woman screaming. After she checked on her daughter, she heard the scream again, coming from right behind her. She didn't turn around; she just woke up her daughter and ran over here. Pretty fucked up, eh?"

"Yes, very." I barely moved. "Then what happened?"

"Well, nothing scares me except for my ex, so I went over there with her, and we looked all through her house, checked windows, doors, closets, that creepy closet at the top of the stairs—and there was no one there. Everything looked fine. I stayed for a cup of tea until she calmed down, and then I left."

That's nothing.

"I went over there the next day to see how she was doing, and they were gone. Packed up only some of their stuff and left." Her eyebrows rose. "Why do you ask?"

"I was just curious."

She waited, clearly not believing me.

"All right. It's silly, really, but I've heard some strange sounds and had vivid nightmares. Someone here mentioned that a person had died in the house. Do you know about that?"

Leslie stopped swaying and moved closer as she spoke. "I heard the original owner's wife killed herself there."

"That sounds like a rumor," Shelby said, wrinkling her nose. "I've been running this place for years and haven't heard that."

"No, it's true. I used to hook up with a guy who lived there about ten years ago. Tom something. He was her nephew or great-nephew. Wish I remembered his name." She scratched her head, trying to recall it. "When he found out this was a shelter, he told me that the owner, his great uncle or whatever, was a cheater and a beater, and his aunt coulda used this place. He always hurt her, and she went nuts and offed herself." She shrugged and stopped talking.

I had goosebumps, and they were spreading.

"Anything else?" I asked, smoothing down the hair that stood up on my arms.

Shelby nodded slowly and redirected the conversation. "Anyway, after the mother-daughter duo left, it was a month or so until new tenants came in. But there was still activity over there in the empty house."

"Oh?" The hairs on my arm rose again.

"More than once, we saw a woman in the front window, just standing there, looking out."

That is strange. "A break-in?"

"It didn't look like it," Shelby said. "None of us have met the landlady, so we weren't sure if it was her, but it was pretty late at night. That's about all we've seen before you moved in."

"And since?" I thought of the ransacked kitchen, my and Jake's fights, and me yelling at my kids out of frustration.

"I've seen a car watching your house," Sandra said.

My heart double-pumped. "What kind of car? Who was driving?" I didn't want them to know Jake was a police officer. Most people hated cops, so we tried to keep a low profile.

"I think it was black. An SUV. Sometimes it's a woman and sometimes a man."

Shelby piped in. "I'd know a ghost car anywhere. The tinted back windows and roll bar give it away."

My stress evaporated instantly. Those were the good guys.

A low grunt came from under the table, and then I inhaled a foul yet familiar smell. Riley's face was bright red as he finished filling his drawers. Sandra plugged her nose, and Leslie laughed.

I was mortified by the overpowering smell. "I gotta go, ladies. Ivy needs a nap, and this one, well, you know what he needs." I laughed. "Thank you for your time and the company."

Shelby walked me to the door, and we both stepped outside. It was cold but bright out. "Don't be a stranger. Visits from babies—and you, of course—are good for these gals."

I noticed there weren't any children around. "Can I ask you something else?"

"Absolutely, shoot."

I lowered my voice. "I was wondering, for a friend of mine—how does one go about staying in a place like this?" I didn't know if my face was as red as it felt, but when I looked down at Ivy to avoid looking Shelby in the eye, there were splotches of heat across my chest.

"Simple. They just show up. There's a main hub with a 1-800 number. You can call and they'll direct your friend to the nearest one, or one with room. Sometimes there are interim accommodations. We get donations from the Roxford Women's Society of toiletries, clothes, and such. Most women show up with only what they have on."

"So there's more than one location?"

"Yes, there are many—and not just in Roxford if your friend needs to leave town."

I noticed as she looked from my house back to where we were standing. "Do you want a pamphlet or a number to give her?"

"No thank you, not at this point. Also, she has children. Does that matter?"

"Many of our shelters take children and families. This one doesn't just because of the way it's set up, but most of them do." She fixed me with her dark eyes. "Bree, is your friend in trouble right now?"

"I don't know." My eyes started to fill, but I blinked back the tears as I looked away.

"The number is answered twenty-four seven, and one of us is always working. We are here and available."

She waved at Riley and Ivy as I started to walk away.

"I'll stop by again soon." *I probably won't.* I walked away quickly, dragging Riley. I had a diaper to change and a lot to think about.

As soon as the kids went down for a nap, I grabbed the laptop and began to google. Rumor or not, I was dying to look into this. I googled our address, something I should have done ages ago. It took some trial and error, but with variations of Tom and Thomas, using this address, I found out that his name was Thomas Belsley. And that this house's original owners were Abraham and Rose Belsley. Rose. My heart slowed as I mouthed her name slowly, not daring to say it out loud.

There wasn't much information, except that this house had been built in 1913 and was recently declared a heritage home, and that there were some records at the Roxford Heritage Museum. None of the hyperlinks worked, except one picture of the house from 1924, donated to the museum by a T. A. Belsley. I read on the website that they were very behind in cataloguing artifacts as they were a volunteer-run organization, and that gave me an idea.

A quick search on a phone directory gave me a current phone listing for T. Belsely. I dialed his number before I could talk myself out of it. He answered right away.

"Tom? Thomas Belsely?"

"Yes?" He didn't sound old, but that was always hard to tell over the phone.

"Hi, I'm Jane Smith." I almost said Doe. "I'm with Roxford Museum—I was wondering if I could ask you a few questions. Could you tell me a bit about the house?"

He let out a sigh but replied.

"My great uncle built it himself. Made all kinds of mistakes when he did, too." He stopped to laugh. "Installed a couple of the doorframes and doors backwards. He was an ironworker and used a ton of heavy iron fixtures throughout."

"I noticed that," I said, forgetting who I was pretending to be.

"Huh?"

"In some real estate photos from when you sold it," I recovered.

"Ah, right."

"Why did you sell?"

He sighed again. "We tried to keep it in the family, you know? My Dad had it, and then I did, but I moved away. I rented it out, but the type of tenants we got in that neighbourhood weren't ideal, and it was a lot of work keeping up such an old home. Eventually, I just couldn't do it anymore, so I moved in for a few months while I made any essential repairs myself and sold it."

I paused for a second, trying to think of the right words.

"For our records, we are trying to track down the history of the original owners—how long they lived there, their story, etc. Visitors to the museum love that sort of stuff. I found some information on Abraham. I'm guessing that is your uncle, but I don't have much on Rose." I dragged her name out while trying to think of a question to add, hoping he would jump in, but also scared he would question my motives.

"You won't find any of this in the box I gave you, all I have are just stories my parents told me. My aunt—er, great aunt—lost a baby and became mentally unwell, and there wasn't any help for that sort of thing then. Her husband was a dick. He was abusive and had an affair when she was in the looney bin. When she got out, she was highly medicated, and at the time, those drugs were powerful. She became controlling and repetitive in her behaviour. Obsessing over the temperature in the house and organizing the baby's clothing and accessories. My parents said that she also suffered from insomnia and paced the halls of the house, babbling to herself. One night she saw my uncle with his mistress and snapped, killing herself."

I'd gotten my answer and was sorry I asked. I couldn't believe my ears. "Wow, I'm so sorry."

"Don't be, I didn't know her. Everything else is in that box I do-nated—pictures and paperwork, floorplans, etc. What did you say your name was again?"

I hung up.

My phone and ear were hot, and my hands were sweaty. I rubbed them on my pants until they were dry and banged out an email to the Roxford Museum to find out more.

Rose's story replayed on a loop in my head. Some of the parallels were unreal. Was there really a ghost in my house? Had she been trying to help me?

38

JAKE

I was sitting in a mall parking lot writing files when a familiar cruiser pulled up beside me.

"It almost seems like you've been avoiding me tonight." Amber winked. "Why aren't you answering my texts?"

"I've been off for almost two weeks. I have tons of paperwork to catch up on." I stopped. "You've been texting me?" I shifted my laptop off my lap and looked around for my phone, but it wasn't there. *Odd.* I jumped out of the vehicle and did a thorough search.

"Can you call it?"

She did. Nothing.

"Crap, I must have left it at home." Shit. It was at home with Bree. My mouth went dry. "What did you text me?"

"You mean, what might your wife be seeing on your screen right now?" She waggled her eyebrows. "Who knows?"

I'm dead. "I don't think you understand how bad this is for me." Red-hot anger rose in my chest to my face. "Give me your phone."

"Whoa, yes Constable Grumpy Pants, here's my phone. It's not my fault if your wife is checking up on you. You know you've been a bad boy." She dangled the phone out her window, teasing it away from me every time I went to grab it. I finally got a hold of it and called Bree.

"Hey. Is my phone there?" My voice came out squeaky.

"Not that I've seen. Are you all right? You sound stressed."

"Of course I'm stressed," I barked. "I'm at work."

"Do you want me to check our app?" She seemed unfazed by my snapping at her.

"Yes." *Please don't let it be at the house.* The sound of her shuffling filled the background.

"Sorry, it says location services are turned off."

Crap. "If you find the phone, don't touch it. Just call me back at this number."

"Whose phone are you calling me from? And why wouldn't you want me to touch your phone?" Now she sounded frazzled.

"This is Constable Doyle's phone. We're at a file together and there's confidential work stuff on my phone." I hung up feeling guilty as fuck and handed Amber her phone back. I was no longer thinking about how much Bree had been irritating me lately, but about the possibility of losing her and my children forever.

"I have to get my phone before she finds out." *Or else my marriage is over.*

"Finds out what?" Amber sounded like she was trying to be cute.

"Knock it off, and cover for me, okay?"

"And what will you do for me in return?"

"Are you kidding me right now?"

"Relax. I'm just having fun with you." She pushed her tongue to the inside of her cheek and pumped it in and out. A few months ago, I would have thought this was hot. Now it made me feel sick.

"Look, I gotta go. If she gets into my phone and figures out what's going on, I'm done."

"Fine." She huffed. "Zip home and set your status to lunch break. If they find out how long you've been gone, I'll tell them you have the shits and are powering through instead of going home sick."

Disgusting, but believable.

"You owe me one." She made to drive off but then hung her head out the window. "Hey, did you check my car? I think you had it when we rode in together."

I smiled with relief. She tossed me the keys to her car so I could go back to the detachment to get it, but it took the entire drive for my pulse to calm down.

After searching for the phone, I came back to the same Tim Horton's parking lot. I loved writing files here. Coffee, washrooms, and quiet—what more could a tired officer want?

"Found it!" I pulled up beside Amber and held up my phone to show her. "Did anyone ask about me?"

"No, it's been quiet. I guess we're fully staffed tonight for a change."

We both laughed. We were never fully staffed. Even when we were, we could have used another dozen officers minimum. I handed back her keys.

"I got you a coffee just the way you like it," she said, passing it from her car to mine. "Two and two." She let her fingers linger on mine. "How was your time off? Did Steinman head-shrink you?" She smiled but looked uncomfortable.

"I've had three sessions," I said, sipping the coffee. "I'm supposed to go back for two more, but I keep canceling them." I told her about the ADHD diagnosis and my wild goose chase looking for Adderall like a dirty drug seeker. "And then he asks me how much I drink and about a pile of things completely unrelated to work."

"Like me?" she asked.

"No. Bree and the kids, my childhood. And get this, I forgot my jacket one time, and when I went back into the office, he was talking about me into a recorder. Do you think head office gets a copy of that?"

"No way. They get high-level reports, but not that kind of detail." She paused. "At least I don't think so."

"Either way, I'm just going to push through the last two sessions and then that's it. I'm never going down that road again."

"Sorry Jake, I thought they would help. Maybe if you control the conversation, you might still get something out of it?" She fiddled with her coffee sleeve, hanging her head.

Don't ask her, Jake. Don't open that door. But out it popped. "What's wrong?"

She hesitated. "I just like you more than I should, you know?"

Shit. I knew she was lonely; she'd said as much before. Being a female police officer was a real buzzkill on the dating scene. Guys had to question a suitor's criminality as well, but we did have it easier statistically—which was why a lot of members dated each other. It was simpler, and you understood one another. The relationships didn't last long, though; a whole lot of baggage came along with the territory—along with affairs.

"Listen. I'm sorry if I led you on," I said. "I'm not happy in my marriage, that's true, but I won't leave my wife or kids, and it's not fair to continue whatever this is."

"Whatever this is?" Amber's voice rose. Her eyes were misty, but she spoke through clenched teeth. I couldn't tell whether she might cry or shoot me.

I glanced around the parking lot to see who, if anyone, might be listening to our conversation, but there was no one around.

"Look, I get it." She got quieter. "You didn't lead me on. We did something that we won't do again. If all I can have with you is a flirty friendship, I'll take it."

Our radios went off with a call. One of us needed to answer it.

"Go for two-Charlie-seven," I said, and patted her hand before driving away.

Well, that was easy. At least I'd solved one problem in my life.

39

BREE

DECEMBER 29, 2012

I was curled up on the couch with a cup of tea, the kids already asleep, talking to Paige during our weekly Bree-needs-to-vent phone call. "Something is seriously wrong in this house," I said, tucking the throw blanket over my cold toes. "Jake is not behaving like himself at all. I thought it had something to do with me, but now I'm having doubts. He's mad at me a lot, but I see him smiling whenever he's on his stupid phone. You're the only person I can talk to about this. Do you think I'm crazy?" *She must think I'm shit nuts.* "I don't know how much longer I can live like this."

I glanced at the hole Jake had punched in the wall when he found out Matthews was dead. We still hadn't fixed it.

"No Bree, I don't think you're crazy at all. I think you're desperate for answers, but I don't know if you're going to get them. Jake has always been kind of ..." She was either searching for the word or debating whether to say it.

"Kind of what?"

"He's always been a bit dark. I mean you met him when he was already in the trenches, so you don't even know what he was like before."

241

She had a point. But I knew how he was behaving now. This was not the man I'd married. Especially the day Tammy had dropped me off after Dinotown. For the first time ever, I'd been scared of him.

"I don't know what to do. He seemed marginally better over Christmas with the kids but was still icing me. He's seeing a therapist, though it doesn't seem to be helping. I want for us to be better, but nothing I do seems to help. The more I try to make his life easier, the angrier he gets." I paused. I was too scared to tell her everything. "I'm also hearing things." *And seeing a scary woman all over my damn house. Want to hear about Rose? What would you think about me then, sister?*

"What kind of things are you hearing?" Her voice cracked.

"Noises in the house, screams on the baby monitor, footsteps at night."

"I wouldn't worry about that. You were nervous about moving to a house from a condo, and it's a big old drafty one at that. It's just your imagination." She was trying to reassure me, but I knew she would have been scared if she were here—of the house, and of Jake.

"That's not all." I took a breath. "I've noticed things in the house being moved around. When Jake isn't home."

There was silence on the line. "Do you think it's those criminals? I thought they were dead."

"One of them is dead and the other is in a coma—last I heard." But I didn't think it was the Scaggs at all.

"So, it *could* be one of them? You should find out if he's still alive, just in case."

We talked until her phone buzzed with a call from Mom, who was still wintering in Hawaii.

"If I don't answer it, she'll call you next," Paige said. "And I'm not sure if—"

"Answer it, please, I beg you. Call me tomorrow."

She hung up and took the other call to save me from endless questions that I had zero energy to answer. I grabbed my laptop from the kitchen, along with some chocolate from my Jake's-working-night-shifts stash, and headed back to my warm spot on the couch.

I needed to sort out what was going on, one way or another. Jake was not himself, Riley was acting strange lately, and weird shit was definitely happening in my house. If the Scaggs were still alive, maybe it could explain some things, but would they really break in just to mess around with my stuff? I doubted it. It also wouldn't explain what or whom I'd been seeing.

I did a search for the Scaggs brothers and found a lot of articles about Matthews. The most recent one said the one brother was still in a coma. It didn't sound like he was on the loose and moving baby bottles around my kitchen.

Maybe the problem *was* me. I was exhausted and not sleeping well. I'd also done a lot of reading about postpartum depression since attending that group. I'd definitely had it after Riley's birth, though I'd never been officially diagnosed. It was possible that I had it again, as there was a high chance of it returning with subsequent pregnancies and stressful circumstances. From what I found on WebMD, however, the likelihood was very small that it was causing me to see and hear things. I noted all the suggestions on how to help yourself with PPD: go for walks, get outside, reach out to friends, and find support. I could do that.

As for Jake, I was at a loss. He'd been through unbelievable amounts of grief and lack of sleep. The alcohol and sleep aids he was taking could contribute to his erratic behavior. But if he'd noticed anything strange about the house, he hadn't mentioned it.

In any case, none of it explained the woman I'd been seeing in my dreams—and now, even when I was awake. Was I losing my mind? Or was it the ghost of Rose Belsley? And if so, how do I get rid of her?

As soon as I typed "ghosts" in the browser, I felt stupid. I looked around the room, my heart rate increasing. It just came up with a long list of scary stories and firsthand accounts of encounters. I tried "Poltergeists in Roxford," and "Poltergeists in BC," but nothing matched my house or area or anything close to what I'd been experiencing.

One website intrigued me—the University of Roxford Paranormal Investigator Team. I was blown away that one of the most well-known and sought-after universities in our province had a paranormal investigative team. I popped off an email to them: *Can you tell me about your services? If I wanted to have my house investigated, what would that cost, and when could you come and do it?*

God, if Jake checked my search history, he'd think I was an absolute crackpot.

The only other suggestion I'd found was to sage the house. But I didn't have any sage and would have to time it for when Jake wouldn't be home for a while. Apparently, it had a strong smell. At this point, I was prepared to try anything.

I deleted the history on my laptop, ripped the piece of paper out of the notepad, and threw it away. Satisfied that I'd covered my tracks, I went upstairs to bed.

As I lay there, unable to sleep, the events of the last few weeks replayed in my head. I couldn't imagine having a team of paranormal investigators at my house overnight. I would have to lie to Jake. If I told him the truth, he'd think I was cuckoo.

But it was all a distraction. Jake was either already cheating on me or he was about to. He didn't love me anymore. Where had we gone so wrong? I could handle the silent treatment and his snappy moments, but I couldn't handle a repeat of what had happened a few weeks back. In one instant I'd been afraid for my life, and then in the next I was dealing with calm and reasonable Jake. And poor Riley and Ivy. If I couldn't find a way to fix things, I would have to leave.

But how?

I had no money, no job, no car, and nowhere to go. My mom was on vacation in Hawaii for the foreseeable future, and anyway, I couldn't handle the "I told you so's" and constant penance for not listening to her sooner or making better life choices. Paige lived a province away. Even if I could leave, Jake could use his authority to twist my words around. I'd been told that you never knew how deep the blue line runs until you were on the other side of it. He could take my kids from me. I would rather die than lose them.

I had no idea what the hell I was going to do, but I needed a plan.

Jake was already awake when I came downstairs with the kids in the morning. I usually tried to gauge his mood and make sure the kids were looked after and quiet before approaching him. If he wasn't in a good headspace, he could cause havoc for everyone. He sat at the kitchen table with a cup of coffee, so I poured myself one and sat down like there wasn't pea-soup-thick tension in the air all around us.

"I'm thinking about going back to work, Jake. What do you think?"

"What do I think?" He looked up. "I think we've tried this before and you couldn't get a job."

Ouch.

"True, but maybe I was looking for the wrong type of work. I can find something that works with your schedule, part-time maybe? You could work less overtime if I did that."

He sipped his coffee. "Sure, if you find something, great, but I won't count my chickens. It would have to work with my hours, and we only have one car."

"What about dispatch? I saw they were hiring here in Roxford. We could work opposite blocks." Dispatch paid pretty well. It wouldn't take me long to save up enough to leave.

"Now that isn't a bad idea." He sounded almost friendly. "You should apply. Why not?"

Maybe this was a good time to chat with him. "How have your sessions been going with Dr. Steinman?" The therapist was one of the few reasons I was staying. A hope for change.

"Why do you ask?" he asked loudly, putting down his coffee and leaning forward toward me.

"I was just wondering. I know you've been going through a lot."

"What are you fishing for here?"

Damn it, I should not have started this conversation. "I just noticed you were extra stressed the other day. I wanted to check in." I couldn't help myself. "I miss talking to you."

He either didn't hear me or pretended not to.

I said it louder. "I miss talking to you."

"About what, Bree? Sage?" He laughed.

The colour in my face disappeared. "What do you mean?"

"I found a note you tossed out when I was looking for a receipt I'd misplaced. What do you need sage for?"

"It's nothing." My face was hot. All I wanted was to escape this conversation.

"It must be something. You can tell me."

"I just thought it couldn't hurt. Weird things have been happening around here, and it's an old house. Sage is good for lots of things."

"You think saging the house will get us out of debt? You think it will bring Matthews back? Do you actually think we have ghosts here, Bree?" He shook his head. "My shrink is gonna love this one."

I left the room to set Riley up in his highchair in front of the TV. What was Jake telling his shrink about me? What was going on record that he could use against me?

40

JAKE

JANUARY 2, 2013

D r. Steinman led me into his office. I was surprised he didn't want
to grab a coffee first.

"How goes the battle, Jake?"

"I'm okay."

He raised his eyebrows. "Really?"

"No, obviously not. Things are still tense at home, and rough at work.
Breanna is ridiculous, and I'm seeing myself or my family in every file
I attend. It makes me not want to open my eyes and not want to close
them either. Nightmares." I picked at my fingers.

"What happened?" He pointed to my hand. Dried skin hung off my
thumbs and most of my fingertips, except for the pinkies.

"I don't know. We wear latex gloves and wash our hands a lot, so likely
something to do with that." *Just another gross thing about me.*

"Just the tips, though. Do you do that a lot?" He pointed again. "Rub
them together like that?"

I hadn't noticed I was doing it. "I don't know. Maybe."

"Interesting. Sorry, a bit off topic. You were saying." He leaned back
and fell silent.

"Bree and I had another fight. She has some insane theories, and she's angry with me because I don't hold our daughter enough and apparently never call her by her name. Don't most parents call their youngest 'the baby'?"

"What is her name, Jake?"

The word rose up in my throat. I opened my mouth, but nothing wanted to come out. I drank some water and tried again. I took a deep breath in and exhaled a quick, "Ivy."

For once, my wife was right. I think that was the first time I'd said her name since she'd been born. Since Matthews had been killed.

"Why was that so hard?"

I wiped my shedding hands on my pants until they were dry; I was sure some skin had come off onto Steinman's floor, but I couldn't look. Angry energy crept up inside me, energy that needed to be worked out before it roared out of me. I stood up clumsily and walked toward the window. "Can I open this?" I asked, lifting my shirt at the neck and fanning my hand in front of my face.

"Sure, go for it." He watched my every move, which only made me sweat more.

I yanked the window open hard. Bree always said I didn't know my own strength and that doing heavy weights at the gym had turned me into a bull in a china shop.

"Whoa." The doc got up and moved toward me, eyeing me but saying nothing.

I laughed. "I'm not going to jump." It wasn't a bad idea, though. We were high enough that it was fifty-fifty—I'd be either dead or mangled. I couldn't tolerate being deformed, though. But if I went head-first, and with some purpose, I could probably pull it off.

"You sure?" he asked.

"I'm sure, sorry. I just need to move around." The cold air was helping calm me down. Steinman stood close enough I could see goosebumps on his arms, but if I had to close the window, I might die.

He was eyeballing me, probably deciding whether to call me in. "You want to go for a walk? We have lots of time left. I can get my coat."

I nodded. "How about Devon Park? Fewer rats there." I couldn't deal with Burner's rejects right now.

"Yes, the last thing we need is for you to be triggered." He leaned in front of me and shut the window.

Triggered? I hadn't heard him use that term before when talking about me.

We grabbed our coats, took the elevator down, and exited the building. Steinman's hot receptionist raised her eyebrow at us, but we kept walking.

It was pleasantly cold. The wind made it even colder, and I liked the way it felt when it stung my cheeks. We made it to the park in minutes. It had a nice loop to wander around the perimeter—almost a jogging track but not quite.

"We were talking about Ivy," he said. "Why it's hard to say her name, and why you don't hold her often."

"Right. I guess I'm afraid."

"Were you afraid to hold your son? Babies are so fragile. I know I was nervous when my kids were born too. Floppy necks, and so small."

The words "floppy necks" stabbed me in the spine, making me feel nauseous and light- headed. My ears rang with a high-pitched whine. I could see the doc's lips move, but I couldn't hear what he was saying. Was this a stroke? My scope of vision started to close in, white walls coming at me from all sides until I could only see out of a pinhole. I closed my eyes to make it stop, but all I could see was the image of a dead baby. I blinked and blinked to make it go away.

Steinman escorted me to a nearby bench and encouraged me to put my head between my legs. After he assisted me to sit back up, we did some breathing exercises until my heartrate slowed down. Eventually I could see—and breathe. I looked at him with my eyes wide; I was scared to close them again. "Did I just have a heart attack?"

"I hope not." He smiled. "It seems we triggered a panic attack."

"I'm not a pussy." Blood was returning to all the right areas as I started to boil with rage. "Only sissies have those."

"That's not true, Jake, but you should get yourself checked out either way."

If I go to the hospital, I can't work. If I can't work, I can't support my family. If I can't support my family, I'm done. What if it got out to my crew that I had panic attacks? I'd be sunk.

"I'm okay. Just give me a few minutes."

He'd brought a water bottle with him and handed it to me.

After a couple of minutes of sitting quietly, I said, "Doc, I'm broken. And I'm afraid to break my daughter. I've already wrecked my wife and my son. I want to spare her."

He was silent for a moment. "You won't break her—and you aren't broken. Things will get better."

The wind rushed past me, through me. "Everything I touch turns to shit. I can't save anyone. By the time I get there, they're usually gone: mothers, fathers, children, babies ... all dead and broken. I'm not a good guy anymore; I'm the cleanup crew. A garbage man. As soon as we die, that's all we are—a mess to clean up." I felt like crying. I wanted to cry, but the tears wouldn't come. My heart was too numb. "My family deserves better."

He clasped his hands in his lap. "I think we should book some more sessions and dig a bit deeper here. There are ways to work through this."

I barely heard him. "And I'm mad, too. I'm mad at myself for taking paternity leave when I knew my crew was understaffed. I'm mad at Bree for having the baby early. And I'm mad at the baby for being born. I'm so angry, I'm afraid if I touch it, I'll hurt it."

His mouth dropped open for a second before he regained his composure. I'd shocked him. *Good old crazy Jake, here to scare everyone.* I was fully mental, a useless jerk who ruined everything. The tears finally came.

He dug into his pocket and handed me some tissues. I took them, but I didn't wipe off the tears. I hoped they would freeze to my face.

"Do you think you'll hurt the baby?"

Shit. This guy will definitely have me committed. I wiped my eyes roughly and forced a laugh. "No, of course not. Just a silly fear."

"That's what I thought. Maybe we should head back inside and talk about your medication options."

I straightened. "What do you mean?"

"The Adderall isn't helping, and this may not be just ADHD."

"I'm just having a bad day, and my wife is blowing things out of proportion and—" I was talking fast and skipping over the fact that I never got or took any medication.

"Don't stress, Jake. I'm here to help. Let's do some breathing and planning for our next session, okay?"

I stood up. *What next session? I'm not coming back.*

He must have read my face. "You have at least one more session you need to attend."

I'd forgotten these sessions were not entirely optional, but I didn't like the way he'd said "need." What else would he say I needed? And how much of this would get back to the RCMP?

41

BREE

JANUARY 3, 2013

I had to ask why he was always texting her. I couldn't stand it any longer.

"Amber lives out here," Jake said while looking for pieces of his uniform. "I'm on her way home."

Yes, I knew she was one of the carpooling crew. But the number of times he put his phone face down when her received a text, the way he'd laughed with her and looked at her the two times I'd seen them interact—it unnerved me. I didn't like finding her long blond hair on the passenger side of our family vehicle whenever he did the driving.

"The carpooling was your idea!" he shouted. "Would you rather I take the car every day?" He ran upstairs to look for something else.

It had started off as a group of four taking turns driving. That had allowed me to have the car more often than not. Now it was mostly just the two of them, giving me the car and anxiety half the time. What could I do about it? Nothing.

I could hear Jake upstairs frantically opening drawers, getting ready for work.

"Bree, where did you put my wallet?" he yelled. For once, he wasn't angry, but it was loud enough to wake Ivy from her morning nap.

I took a breath to control my temper as I picked Ivy up out of the pack and play in the living room. "I don't have your wallet." I glanced at the clock on the stove. "What time is your ride supposed to be here? Shouldn't you be on your way by now?"

"You don't think I know that? Doyle is off today, so Kowalski is supposed to pick me up. I'm trying to find my goddamn phone to call him." He banged around nonstop and then yelled as he ran down the stairs with his phone in his hand, "Fuck! He isn't coming. They've done something screwy with the shifts again, and he forgot." A large hangover vein crawled across his temple as his face turned a darker shade of red. "What the hell am I going to do? I can't get a negative 10-04 again."

I didn't know why he'd be in trouble *again*, and I had no idea what a negative 10-04 was, but it sounded bad.

"Do you really need the car today?" he asked.

"Yes, Ivy has a doctor's appointment."

He stomped past me and Ivy to the back patio while on the phone. I wasn't sure how he was going to pull himself out of this, but I wanted him out of the house as soon as possible. His yelling was scaring the children. It was the quietest I'd ever seen them, watching in tandem as Jake stormed back and forth.

"You have to cancel that appointment!" he shouted from the back deck. "I'll try Sangha, but if he's already past Roxford, you're out of luck."

A black Hummer pulled up in the driveway, but Jake was out of earshot. His colleague must have felt bad and circled back. I walked toward the door with Ivy in my arms and had barely unlocked it when a large, nonuniformed man charged up the steps and tried to push the door open. Luckily, I'd kept the chain on. The door made a loud *clang* and then ricocheted backwards. He stood so close his hot breath huffed into my face.

"Can I come in?" The way he was looking around reminded me of the way Jake cased a scene. He had left the door to his Hummer open with the motor running.

"Kowalski? Are you here for Jake?" I had never met this man before. It sounded like English was his second language, but he spoke so quickly and abruptly I couldn't be sure. He was short and wide with muscle, with a full sleeve tattoo on at least one arm and a strong jawline decorated with a deep scar. When I looked down, I noticed he had wedged a foot in the doorjamb. He wore the shiniest, pointiest shoes I'd ever seen. They looked expensive.

"I used to live here. Can I come in and look?" He then pulled the door closed and forced it open in one abrupt and noisy move, breaking the chain. I turned to call for Jake just in time to see him come flying at us from the patio. He was so fast it didn't look like his feet were touching the ground.

"Hey!" he yelled so loudly I thought our rattling single-pane windows might break.

Both Riley and Ivy started crying at the same time, and I caught myself as I stumbled against the wall. The man had turned, bolted, and was back in his car kicking up gravel as he peeled away. Jake almost managed to grab hold of the Hummer's doorhandle but wasn't quick enough. It ripped out of his hand as the guy sped away.

"Call 911. Tell them Bychkov found us!" Jake yelled as he disappeared around the corner outside, towards the car.

My legs were rooted to the spot, and my heart pounded, as I watched him take off in our family car after Bychkov. The man in charge of those two goons who'd shown up at our condo and had killed Matthews.

He had just broken into our house.

42

JAKE

JANUARY 3, 2013

"Constable Jake Stone here!" I shouted into my phone. "I'm a member with Burner PD. I live in Roxford, and a big fish must have followed me home. He just tried to break into my house, and I'm chasing him down the highway as we speak. I have a long eye on him." He was in my sight as we both barreled down the road, and I didn't think he knew I was behind him—he was driving normally, maybe to not draw attention to himself.

"Sir, your wife already called," the dispatcher said. "She gave us the name Bychkov and your direction. Can you give us an update on your location? We've informed your department, and there are teams from each jurisdiction working on a plan."

"Can you also let them know I'll be late for work?" I looked down and took stock of what I had on: uniform pants, a duty belt minus the gun, a white wifebeater under naked Kevlar and sneakers. *Yep, I'm definitely getting in trouble today.* "I just passed exit 59. I have my radio. What channel can I tune into?"

"Channel five, sir. You should be able to communicate with both teams there."

258

"Thanks. Four." I flipped my phone shut and tossed it onto the passenger seat.

After all the grief the Scaggs and Bychkov had caused, I was about to finally get him. Bychkov was a notoriously slippery guy, evading every apprehension attempt and getting away. *Not today.* I turned my radio on and changed it to channel five.

"Stone? Are you there?" It was Sangha. That cheeky bugger must have gone to work early and wouldn't have been able to drive me anyway.

"I got a long eye on Bychkov."

"Be careful. Give him room, but don't let him out of your sight. We're going to wait until the Douglas Street overpass and throw out spikes. Make sure not to follow too closely or you'll get it too."

"Roger."

Nine times out of ten, when someone got spiked, they jumped out and ran. My body was ramping up for a foot pursuit. The Douglas Street overpass wasn't far away, so I had to be ready.

Bychkov looked in the rearview mirror, and his eyes met mine. *Shit.* He knew he was being followed. He cranked a hard right onto the next turnoff. I followed suit, narrowly missing it myself. *Fuckety fuck fuck.*

"Bychkov turned off at exit 65, one before Douglas Street," I said into the radio. "He knows I'm following him. What now?" I ran a stop sign to keep up.

"All good, Stone. We thought of this. It's not ideal, but we have guys and a spike rope half a kilometer up. Pray that he keeps going straight. Back off if you're too close. Turn off if you need to."

"Okay." *No fucking way I was backing off.*

Sure enough, several blocks out I spotted a ghost car under a tree and two nonuniformed guys crouching near the road. It was busy; he wouldn't be the only one to get hit. I backed off a notch. He looked in the rearview and then to the right, where my men were moving from crouching to standing with the heavy rope. Casting their line to catch their trout.

Bychkov punched the brakes a tad too late. The front tires let out loud pops as they hit. The smell of rubber wafted into the air as Bychkov screeched to a halt despite the tattered state of the tires. He didn't wait for the car to come to a complete stop before rolling out from the pavement onto the grass like a fat armadillo bug. He instantly transformed into a sprinting bad guy as he evaded the two plainclothed men that were now after him.

Having lived there years ago, I knew I could run through the tunnel under the street and come out the other side. Bychkov was fast for his size, but I was determined. *I'm getting him today, Matthews. I promise.*

I sprinted as fast as my legs could take me, wondering why sneakers couldn't be uniform issue. Sure, we needed steel toes for door kicks, but damn if I wasn't faster than ever right now. The duty belt was lighter due to the lack of weaponry, and I didn't have to worry about losing my hat as I didn't have that either. The real concern now was that one of my own men might take me down, mistaking me for a civilian or for Bychkov himself. From a distance, we looked somewhat similar. He had shed some clothing before I'd lost sight of him when I entered the tunnel. Now he wore only a tank top, dark pants, and oddly shaped dress shoes. He was muscular like me, but wider and bald, with a five-o'clock shadow. Shorter, too.

As I exited the tunnel, I saw his wide ass slip through the door of a department store. "Bychkov just entered Willow Oaks mall," I said into the radio. "I've lost sight of him. He ditched his ball cap and sweater on the way."

"We have men approaching the mall now, Stone. You can stand down."

"Oh, now I see him again." "Okay, keep your distance though. Don't do anything. Just watch him and keep us informed of his movements."

"Of course." *Fat chance. This guy is mine.*

I could see him, but he was quite far ahead of me, walking slowly and casually as though he wasn't being chased by two neighboring jurisdictions. This guy was slick. Rumor had it he was ex-KGB. He half turned to look behind him, and I didn't think he saw me duck into the lingerie store. A startled red-faced teenage girl did, though.

"Uh, sorry. Carry on." I made a hand motion like I was showing her a rack of lacy bras and quickly got out of there.

I was back on the path just in time to see Bychkov slip into a maintenance hallway. I grabbed my radio and hit the button but quickly let go. I wasn't going to give away his location. He was all mine now. I wasn't technically on duty, was I?

I opened the door to the hallway and tiptoed in my ever-so-helpful sneakers behind him. All was going well until they started to squeak. Maybe runners weren't meant for duty after all. His head snapped up. He looked in my direction and booked it, so I ran after him.

"Bychkov! Stop! I have backup at all the exits. Resisting arrest won't look good in court."

He had rounded a corner and wasn't responding, but I still heard him running. I needed him to stop so I could confront him without witnesses.

"By the way, Cherry already gave us a statement before you killed her."

That should do it. As I rounded the corner, I came face-to-face with this brick wall of a man. He retracted one big arm to punch me but missed when I dodged. I tried to return the favor from the awkward position I was in, but it ended up as more of a slap than a punch.

He laughed as he turned and ran.

He took a sharp left through another doorway back into the mall and scurried onto the escalator going down, which was packed with people. He made it a dozen or so steps before he turned around and smiled. Out of the corner of my eye, I noticed one of the plainclothes officers rubbernecking to look at us.

"Stone, is that you on the escalator?" Plainclothes asked me over the radio.

I didn't look up or answer. I jumped on the divider between the two escalators and tumbled my way down to him. He reached up and grabbed at me. I went down headfirst, landing on the ground in front of the escalator.

I sat up, dazed and nauseous. A large man smirked as he climbed over me toward the parkade. When I ran my hand across my scalp, I discovered a fair amount of blood and a rapidly growing goose egg.

A heavy-set soccer mom stopped and asked me if I was okay. I waved her off as my radio crackled.

"Stone, what are you doing?" Plainclothes said. "Don't let him get away. He's headed for the parkade."

Right. I was chasing Ivan Bychkov through a crowded mall wearing half my uniform. I jumped up as I realized he'd been the jerk smiling at me as he stepped over my stunned body. I must have hit my head hard.

"Move! Police!" I blasted past surprised shoppers. Bychkov was going to jack a car and get out of there undetected.

"Okay, I see him again by the P4 sign in yellow," I whispered into my mic. "Send everyone you have down here and get some cars blocking the exit."

I slunk down low and crouch-walked toward where I'd last seen him. An engine started up a row over, so I ran, not bothering to hide myself anymore. As the car came toward me, I jumped in front of it. "Stop!"

An elderly man braked hard, his eyes wide.

"You looking for sometink?" a voice asked from behind me.

I spun around and caught his sucker punch in the side of my jaw. I was lucky it didn't hit my fresh and growing head bump. I performed a leg-sweep move, trying to get Bychkov on the ground, but ended up kicking him in the shin. It stopped him momentarily and gave me enough time to grab my baton out of my sad holster and crack him on his fat skull.

"Oof," was the last thing that piece of shit said as he went down. I fell with him, landing on top of his gut. He let out a whoosh of air as we connected with the cement. The baton fell out of my hand and rolled away. I wrapped a chunk of my ripped tank top around my wrist.

The first punch landed on his ugly scar. *Crack.*

"This is for Matthews." *Crack.*

"This is for Brody." *Crack, crack.*

"This is for Bree and Riley and the baby." *Crack, crack, crack.*

"This is for—"

Someone yanked my arm from behind before it could connect with his face again. "Cherry" was what I had been going to say.

"Stop—you're going to kill him." Plainclothes let go of my arm. It was covered in blood.

"He killed Matthews, he went after my family, he ..." I stopped and thought more carefully about what I should and should not say. "He hit me too. It was self-defence." I pointed to my own wounds.

Plainclothes, who looked very young, didn't say anything else. He stepped over my baton on the ground and walked toward an approaching officer.

Bychkov was a mess. He was breathing sloppily, and only one of his eyes was open, but the jerk was smiling.

I leaned down. "You won't be smiling when you're someone's prison bitch-kov."

The plainclothed officers were engaged in conversation, so I gave Bychkov one last kick. I couldn't lie; it felt good.

A few moments later, a uniformed officer from Roxford came over and checked Bychkov's vitals. He was fine—or alive, anyway. It was a good thing someone had stopped me when they did. I hadn't wanted to kill him, but I couldn't stop hitting him either.

Uniformed, actually-on-duty officers took care of cuffing and booking Bychkov once he'd been seen by an ambulance attendant. I got the other ambulance all to myself.

Out of the corner of my eye, I saw Amber running over to the ambulance. What the hell was she doing here? In her civilian clothes, on her day off.

Another attendant held her off. "You can't be here, ma'am."

"It's okay. I'm his partner." She smiled seductively at me.

"Is that so?" The ambulance attendant looked at me for verification.

"Work partner," I said, not hiding the irritation in my voice.

Her smile wavered as she held up her badge for proof.

"What are you doing here?" I asked her. She'd crossed a line.

"Abbott texted me about what was going down. I wanted to be here for backup but didn't have time to get into uniform, so I figured I'd just come down and make sure you were okay." There were tears in her eyes. *Oh shit.* This had definitely gone too far.

"I'm fine, right?" I looked at the ambulance attendant.

"That's one hell of a bump, Jake. You're definitely concussed. No drinking tonight, okay? I'm serious." The attendant smiled. Either I was developing a reputation, or they just assumed I was a big drinker because of the job.

"Don't worry," Amber said. "I'll take good care of him."

I didn't care for her flirty tone.

I slid off the gurney and onto the cement landing with the grace of a dump truck, Amber following close on my heels. As I pushed past the open ambulance door, I was greeted by many smiling colleagues. There must have been a dozen cars there between the two detachments. My core crew from C-watch started a slow clap, just like in the movies, and the others followed. Matthews and I used to joke that our dream was to be slow-clapped off a file or into retirement. It was something he would never see, though for the first time since he'd died, I felt him there with me.

I hated that Amber was standing beside me. I stepped away, and she got the message.

My eyelids felt warm, but I coughed away the tears so that I didn't turn this amazing moment into one where I was called a bitch or a pussy. I didn't deserve a single clap, but it felt good to know Bychkov and the Scaggs were finally gone.

I bowed to get a laugh. The crowd parted as I walked toward my vehicle, which I noticed had taken a hit after all. The dent wasn't huge, but I knew we couldn't afford to fix it. Maybe Bree wouldn't notice? *Oh shit. Bree.* I jogged to the passenger door and grabbed my phone. Forty-six missed calls. And then it rang again.

"Jake—what the hell is going on?"

"We got him. It's over."

43

BREE

The young Roxford police officer who sat in our living room was so fresh-faced he didn't look old enough to work at McDonald's, let alone be a police officer, though he wore a wedding ring. I was about to answer his last question when Jake finally walked through the door.

I ran over and threw my arms around him, not caring if he rejected me.

He let out a short laugh and patted my back, looking at the officer. "It's okay, Bree, it's okay."

I wiped my raccoon eyes and introduced Jake to the officer, whose name I completely blanked on. Riley was eating lunch in his highchair beside us, and Ivy was napping again due to wake up soon.

Babyface jumped up from his seat to fist-bump Jake. "I know exactly who you are. I'm Constable Bullock. Way to go catching Bychkov."

"Thanks, man." Jake looked away. "There were a lot of people involved in catching him. I can't take all the credit."

"Oh yes, you can. I heard most of it on the radio on my way here." He gazed at Jake as though he were his favourite celebrity. "I just have a few more questions for Mrs. Stone and I'll be out of your hair."

ANGELA DOUGLAS

"No worries." With that, Jake sauntered to the kitchen and cracked a cold one before returning to the room.

"What was I saying? Right. You mentioned you'd seen that black Hummer out front before?" He pressed the record button on his hand-held once more.

I glanced at Jake before answering. "Yes, I have seen a black Hummer once before, parked in the hedges out front. I didn't think anything about it, as there's a women's shelter next door. The women told me they often get picked up here and they have in-house rules about who can pick them up. The vehicle never sat still for long."

The young officer took notes. "How many times would you estimate seeing it?"

"Just that once, though I have seen dark SUVs around here two or three other times. A couple times were at night, so I couldn't be one hundred percent sure it was the same make of vehicle."

"Have there been any other instances of strange things happening around here? Attempted burglary, stuff around the house?"

The colour drained from Jake's face. I knew he'd had a rough day and was hungover, but based on our most recent chat about weird things happening around the house, I also knew he was worried about what I might say to his colleague.

"Um, yes, well, I don't know. It's a very old house, and I'm not used to living anywhere other than a large secure condo building. One night there were some noises upstairs." I paused and looked for Jake's reaction—he was still pale but listening intently.

"And when I came back downstairs, the back door off the kitchen to the patio was open. It was a windy night. Stuff was blown everywhere, and some things were out of place." I thought of the weirdly organized setup of the baby bottles but didn't mention it. Surely that big thug wouldn't have done that.

"I looked around outside the back and front yards, and there were no vehicles or anyone around, so I just figured it was the storm."

Bullock continued to take diligent notes in addition to his recording. "Any other times where you think someone was breaking in?"

"I've heard footsteps upstairs," Jake said.

I darted my eyes in his direction, blinking hard. He'd never mentioned this to me before.

"I ran up as fast as I could, but when I got there, no one was around—but one of the windows was open."

"Anything else either of you want to add?"

"I can fill in the blanks about the intruder himself," Jake said. "I gave my statement on scene just now and have to go back to write my report, but you probably need this for your records, am I right?"

"Yes sir." He wore a giant grin.

"My partner and I had been heating up the Scaggs brothers in Burner. My partner, Matthews ..." Jake faltered. "He was killed on duty while on a file involving them. Bree, could you get me a drink?"

He just wanted me out of earshot, but I wasn't missing any of this, so I scuttled off as quickly as I could, returning with a glass of water for each of them. Jake looked at his disapprovingly. I was sure he wanted another beer, but he'd said he had to go back to work soon.

"Thanks, Miss." Babyface gulped his water.

Jake drank his straight away. "One of the brothers died, and the other was taken to hospital and lapsed into a coma. Both worked directly for Ivan Bychkov, who was well aware that Matthews and I had been making life rough for his associates and his business."

Babyface nodded enthusiastically, taking notes.

"The first arrest I was involved in included a substantial seizure of crack and fentanyl- laced heroin from his main hub. When the incident with Matthews happened, we were also able to seize all the drugs that were on them and easily get a warrant for their other operation. This effort would have cost Bychkov a buttload of money."

"I bet." Babyface beamed with pride.

"Also, during a previous file, we arrested the Scaggs during an assault and apprehended the victim, who was also Bychkov's main girl. She was more than happy to squeal in exchange for protective custody. So, he wasn't very happy with that either. She turned up dead a couple of weeks ago, after giving us a statement."

Holy crap. Jake had never told me about that.

"I'm not sure how Bychkov found us all the way out here," Jake added.

"Me neither," Babyface said. "We had guys watching your place, driving by frequently. In unmarked cars."

I wondered if those were the dark SUVs that had driven by slowly.

"Thank you for that. We weren't that concerned about him finding us out here as we had just moved, and I was off for a few weeks, so I was home a lot." Jake finally looked my way. He must have realized this was a shock to me.

"I'm not naive though," Jake said. "I'm aware he knew I was the other cop who'd been heating them up. I think I saw him at one of the trials, and I saw someone who looked like him when I went to visit Vincent at the hospital."

"You went to see him at the hospital?" Babyface and I asked in unison.

Jake had a guilty look on his face. "I know I shouldn't have, but I had just finished duty, guarding the room, and needed to see for myself that he was in a coma. There were other people around, and another member guarding the door in case he woke up. It's all above board and on record."

"What do you think Bychkov was here for?" I asked.

He flinched as though he'd forgotten I was sitting there with them. "Revenge."

I got chills looking at my kids and wondering what would have happened if Jake had left for work on time that morning, or if Bychkov had shown up on another day when Jake wasn't home at all. I wouldn't have opened the door if I'd been alone, but he was a tough man, and he found his way in today—it would have been easy, especially if he'd been casing our place for a while.

I started to cry, and Jake handed me a roll of toilet paper. "Sorry," I said.

Babyface got a call and excused himself.

"I'm sorry too, Bree. I thought we were safe out here. Especially with the Scaggs being out of the picture. I'm so glad my ride dumped me this morning." Jake pulled me in for a hug. It had been so long since he'd touched me, and it felt really good. But then I caught a glimpse of us in the reflection of the window and recognized his expression and the one-armed hug. He was comforting me like he'd just delivered bad news on the job. No emotion in his eyes, just using the right voice and the right touch. As if he'd lost the ability to feel. It made me cry even more.

Ivy was fussing, so I broke from Jake and picked her up. She instantly clawed at my shirt. With all the drama, I hadn't noticed I had expressed milk, and it was driving her crazy. I was so caught up in my emotions that I latched her on without thinking about the guest in our house. I sat there relieved but sad, tears on my face, boob out. It took me a moment to register what the heck Jake was getting at when he shot me a look.

I covered up immediately, but to my surprise, Babyface just looked away. "No worries, Miss. My wife and baby are at this stage too."

Babyface had a baby. Wow.

"I'll leave you two to your afternoon. Thank you for your statement. It was a pleasure meeting you, Constable Stone." He was blushing now.

"What do we do now?" I asked him.

"Now you can relax. Your problems have been solved." He tipped his hat at me and shook Jake's hand. They exchanged information for court, statements, maybe a coffee date, and then he left.

"Well?" Jake smiled.

"I'm so relieved." I smiled back stiffly. The Bychkov problem had been solved, but my intuition screamed at me that it was not the only problem we had.

I *was* relieved, but something nagged at me. Jake had to go back to the detachment to do his part of the paperwork and likely celebrate, but he was grabbing a shower first. There was so much going on in my living room that I hadn't noticed the dried blood on his forehead until he pointed it out to me.

As soon as I heard the shower running, I had to call my sister. She'd been calling ever since she'd seen Jake on the news.

I told her what had happened. "So, all the stuff I was worried about when I thought there was some kind of spook in my house? It was just these stupid guys, the Roxford PD checking on us, and my tired mommy brain. Now that they're out of the picture, everything can go back to normal. Jake even seemed a tiny bit like his old self."

Jake hadn't seemed like his old self at all; he just hadn't seemed mad for once.

"There are loads of video clips from the mall security footage," Paige said. "It caught the spike belt and parts of the chase. It's pretty cool. That guy was really scary looking, but Jake is so badass. I can't believe that man was in your house this morning."

We hung up the phone, and I turned on the TV. I was breastfeeding Ivy again. Riley had fallen asleep on the couch beside me after all the drama of the morning.

"Watch the takedown that happened this afternoon on Highway 101, just south of Bernheim city limits," the TV blared.

I watched the spike belt stop Bychkov's car, with ours not far behind it. There was also some security footage in the mall with Jake barreling down an escalator. It was incredible to think my husband did stuff like this for a living. Usually, I pretended he was a janitor and not someone whose life was constantly at risk.

"William Thomas Scaggs overdosed on carfentanil during an altercation in November in which local police officer Corporal Matthews also died," the reporter said. "Willy's brother, Vincent Scaggs, also inhaled the dangerous drug on scene. Vincent was rushed to hospital where he lapsed into a coma, passing away five weeks later under police supervision." She read off the teleprompter like she was discussing the weather.

The other Scaggs brother had died? Hadn't Jake said he'd gone to visit him? I stared at the TV. When had he died? Why hadn't Jake told me? Did he know? He'd said dozens of times how much he wished they were all dead. I wandered into the kitchen with Ivy to look at the calendar and saw the date where Jake had been scheduled for scene security at the hospital.

All of a sudden, I felt dizzy. I went back to the couch, put Ivy down, and put my head between my legs.

"Bree?"

I jumped and turned off the TV. I'd forgotten Jake was home and hadn't heard him come down the stairs.

"Vincent Scaggs is dead too?"

"I just found out myself," he said nonchalantly.

"I guess we don't need to worry about any of them."

"Exactly. No one will mess with us ever again." He inched toward the door. "I'll call if I'm going to be late. I want to celebrate with the guys. We weren't the only people being haunted by Scaggs and Bychkov." With that, he left.

Was it possible? Did he ... Could he have killed Vincent Scaggs?

44

BREE

Despite the relief that had come with the day's events, my mind spun, still afraid to be alone in this house. I felt incredibly unsettled as I put the kids to sleep, closing and locking all the windows and doors, making sure the blinds were drawn. I sat down to watch some "garbage TV," as Jake would call it, but my nerves were still jangled.

Why hadn't Jake known about Vincent Scaggs' death?

He probably didn't have to go to work, but he'd gone in anyway. Was it just to celebrate? And with who? I knew who. It wasn't hard to guess what was going on. I peeked out the window. Based on our last conversation, Jake was due home soon, but who knew if that would happen?

I pulled out the laptop. I was the one who paid our phone bills, so there had to be some information there. I logged on to our phone account and pulled his records up for last month. They didn't show me what the texts said. *Too bad.* But they did show me what numbers he was texting, and when. I went through my phone and found Amber's number. Jake had called me from it the night he'd been panicking about losing his phone.

I stared at my screen, stunned but not surprised.

He's sent her hundreds of texts. Over a thousand in one week. I had suspected he was getting too close to her, but I'd tried hard to respect his grief and give him space. I knew when I'd seen them in person that there was an unforgivable spark. I was riddled with questions, like had he had sex with her? Did he love her? Did he want to leave me? And was this why he hated me?

I was riding another wave of nausea when my inbox pinged with a message from the University of Roxford's Paranormal Team. I'd completely forgotten I had emailed them.

Dear Breanna Stone,

Many thanks for your email. Our team does perform investigations of the sort you requested, free of charge. A previous tenant from the address you inquired about had reached out to us. We had arranged a date and time to come out. Unfortunately, when we arrived, the tenants had already moved out and the landlord declined access to the home.

That is all this information I can legally provide to you now due to our privacy restrictions.

Best of luck and take care,

U of R Paranormal Team

I wondered if that previous tenant was the woman who'd run to the neighbours' house in the middle of the night? Car tires crunched over the driveway, so I slammed my laptop shut and put it away, only then remembering the more hurtful discovery of the night.

Jake called from the front door to the house, "I'm home, just grabbing a shower."

He ran past me and went straight upstairs into the shower. I needed to talk to him about *her*, but he would insist they were just friends and carpooling. If I really wanted to confront him, I would need actual proof. Now was my chance.

I tiptoed past the entryway to see if he'd left his phone on the shelf. Nothing was on it—not even his keys or wallet. I crept up the stairs. I could hear the water running but could tell he wasn't in the shower yet. I hovered by the door, waiting for him to get in and close the curtain, and was surprised by a loud flush and footsteps. I scooted down the hall.

"Bree?" Jake poked his head out.

"Shhh. I'm checking on the kids." I probably sounded too eager.

He looked at me and closed the door. I went into the bedroom. His uniform was on the bed in a pile with his keys, wallet, duty belt, and a bunch of other junk—but no cell phone. He must have taken it into the bathroom with him. *Shit*.

"Kids okay?" He stared at me from the bathroom door.

"Yes, they're fine. I figured I'd wash your uniform while I was up here." I picked up his clothes quickly.

He raised his eyebrows. "Okay, thanks."

I went downstairs, defeated, and threw a load of laundry on. His clothes weren't dirty, but I noticed a blond hair on his shirt. My heart sank, but I was still determined to get into his phone. The only other way I would get access to it was if he passed out. I went into the kitchen to fix him a drink.

There wasn't any brandy or cognac (his new favourite), so I reached into the cupboard with the hodgepodge of liquors. All the bottles were still there, but as I lifted each one, I discovered they were empty. More than a dozen bottles were empty. How much had Jake been drinking?

"Thirsty?"

I spun to find him behind me, smirking. He must have seen the dismay on my face. "It's been a rough few months."

"Yes, it has. For all of us." I tried to make eye contact with him, but he wouldn't look up. "All the bad guys are gone. I was going to pour us a drink to celebrate. All our problems are done, right?"

"I could go for a drink or two." So much for his concussion.

"That settles it. I'll bust out the good stuff." *If you haven't found it yet.* I went into the storage room, rummaged through some boxes, and came back with two bottles of champagne.

"Whoa, where did you get those?"

"We got them for our wedding, but I was pregnant, and you didn't drink then—" I winced. "So I put them away for our anniversary."

"And on our anniversary, you were also pregnant." He laughed.

"Yes, true. Anyway, we have reason to celebrate now, and I am definitely not pregnant. I have enough breast milk in the freezer to feed an orphanage, so I'll join you." I was actually looking forward to a drink.

We cracked open the bottle and had a glass, and then two and then three. When the bottle was done, we cracked another. I wasn't used to drinking this much anymore. So much for my plan. I stopped, but Jake polished off the bottle.

"Do we have any more?"

"No, that's it." I lay down on the couch and watched the room tilt. When it started spinning too fast, I blinked so that it would start over again.

"You okay?" Jake slurred.

"Yeah, fuckin' great. You?" My unfiltered drunk persona had arrived.

"I'm good. You sure we don't have any more booze?"

"Nope, you drank it all." I started laughing wildly. "You thirsty fucking duck. Save some for me next time. My life sucks too."

"Breanna!" He sat up. His serious expression made me laugh even harder. "Are you for real right now?"

"How could I not be? I'm miserable, and you don't notice or care. I sit here at home day after day, cooking, cleaning, looking after the kids, wondering what's happening in this house, and to you. What happened to us? Will you leave or will you keep fucking Amber and pretend nothing is going on?" There it was. All out there, just like that.

"What?" He looked like a kid who'd been caught shoplifting.

"I suppose you've mistaken my patience and empathy over the last few months for stupidity?"

I sat up in the middle of an out-of-control spin. When my eyes came to a focus on his face, I opened my mouth to speak and projectile-vomited everywhere. That was the last thing I remembered.

My head felt like it had swollen to twice its normal size. My mouth was scratchy with thirst, and my stomach felt ill, but the slow and hard palpitations of my tired heart reminded me: *Bree, you are hungover.*

I was on the couch in the downstairs living room. It was dark, so it was still night. No babies were crying. Jake was nowhere to be found, and my breasts were like rocks. Ivy's dream feeding usually prevented this from happening. I was too sick to sit up and too sick to care. *Please just let me die here in my filth.*

I grabbed each nipple and squeezed hard enough to express some milk. As expected, it continued to express as I lay there motionless, my shirt filling up with liquid. It was a relief and didn't bother me until a few minutes later, when my shirt was cold and wet.

I was shivering. I turned on the lamp beside me and noticed a huge puddle of crusted-up vomit in the middle of the living room. *What fresh hell is this?* Did I do that? Did Jake?

I sat up. The spinning was back but not the fun and playful kind. This was the kind that could drag you down the drain into hangover hell. I'd been here before—many times. Just not for a long while. Before Jake, I used to love to drink. So much so that I had phantom hangovers for a good year after I quit.

I stood up and steadied myself on the wall until I made it to the bathroom. I guzzled water straight from the tap to induce vomiting, and right on cue it worked. I spent the next half hour repeating a move I had perfected in my youth. When no more vomit would come, the next stage was coffee—or food, if I was brave.

Two hours, two liters of water, a cup of black coffee, and an orange popsicle, and I was good to go. I thought about toast but remembered what it felt like coming back up and opted for crackers.

I had to scrub the vomit off the floor, which was not enjoyable. I was mad that Jake hadn't cleaned this up, but he'd told me before how he had spent most of his childhood cleaning up his parents' spilled liquor and vomit. A pang of guilt struck me.

Once I was done cleaning, I changed my shirt and went to check on the kids.

Riley was so sound asleep I had to listen for his breath. He was fine. Ivy wasn't in her crib, but the room was freezing and the window was wide open. I panicked and ran over to the main bedroom, where Jake was passed out. It looked like he'd found more booze after all. An empty mickey of whiskey was still in his hand and had spilled all over my side of the bed. Or what had been my side, when we used to sleep together. I ran to the guest room, and it was unusually cold. Ivy was awake and lying on a mattress on the floor. *How the hell did she get over here?* I picked her up and put her back in her crib. I then went to talk to Jake.

"Jake ..." I tapped his shoulder and shook him—nothing. I checked his pulse: he was still alive. I bent down and went to whisper into his ear, and he jumped bolt upright, his face hitting mine. His fists were readied, and he was breathing heavily.

"What the fuck, Bree!" He sat back down on the bed, clutching his heart.

I was holding my head where his face connected with mine.

"Why was Ivy sleeping in the other room on a mattress on the floor?"

"I don't fucking know. You probably did it. You don't remember last night? Haven't you done enough?"

God, what had I done?

45

JAKE

JANUARY 4, 2013

I couldn't fall back asleep after Bree's asinine wake-up call. I realized I needed to talk to someone. Matthews used to be my go-to, Amber was a no-no, and I didn't have any other real friends. So, I called Dr. Steinman's emergency line and nabbed a same-day appointment. I needed to use up my last session anyway.

I went downstairs and gathered my things. Bree was staring at me with a stupid look on her face.

"Where are you going?" she asked.

I kissed Riley on the head and grabbed a coffee in the to-go mug and a piece of bread from the fridge. I felt like shit in every way possible.

"Jake, talk to me, please."

I locked eyes with her and said nothing. How could she think I was capable of something so awful? How could I have married her without really knowing her? What had happened to us, and how could we continue?

As I walked to the front door, she ran after me. "Jake, please, tell me what I did wrong. Where are you going? Please don't leave. Are you leaving me?" Tears streamed down her face.

I got into the car and slammed the door, then ripped away, kicking up gravel behind me.

"I'm so glad you were able to fit me in," I said. "It's kind of an emergency." Though now that I was here, I felt stupid for having made it a priority.

"No problem. I reserve appointments for member crises." Dr. Steinman wore the same outfit he'd had on last time. I wouldn't normally notice another man's clothing unless it was a perp, but his shirt bordered on Hawaiian, which seemed too cheerful for his job. "I was beginning to wonder if I would see you again after those few cancelled appointments," he added. "What's going on?"

"Last night, my wife accused me of killing someone." I shrugged, trying to play it off like it wasn't a huge deal.

He nearly spat out his coffee. He collected himself and turned away from his desk to face me. "Say that again?"

"Last night, Bree and I were having a drink to celebrate the arrest of Ivan Bychkov, a man who'd been following us and had tried to break into our home. After several glasses of champagne, she accused me of killing another criminal who'd been part of the group that was harassing us."

"Whoa. Okay. I remember you talking about them at our last session. I saw some coverage on the news. He was in a coma, correct?"

When I started telling him about taking down Bychkov, he grabbed his recorder. "Do you mind if I record this? That way I don't have to take notes and can just focus on you."

"Fine, sure." It meant I would have to choose my words carefully. "So, after Bychkov was arrested, I went into the detachment and did a pile of work. When I came home, Bree was acting weird. Less so after the first couple of drinks. Initially."

"Does she drink often?"

"She used to be a big partier when we met, but not since the kids, no."

"And you?"

I picked at my fingers. "Occasionally. To help me sleep."

He steepled his hands and waited for me to continue.

"After the third glass of champagne, she was getting quite bitchy. Throwing out little insults and digs. Saying I wasn't there enough, and I didn't help her."

He nodded.

"I tried to laugh it off. She's a tired and frustrated housewife, I get it. But I'm going through an awful lot, and if those were her only complaints, big deal. Like, get over it." I started to shake, and my face felt hot. "Then she accused me of having an affair."

"Are you?"

"No, I am not *having* an affair. I did something in a moment of weakness, but that's it, it's over. It was a lapse in judgment after a night of drinking." *A horrible five-minute mistake.*

He looked at me with his eyebrows raised. "But you don't drink much." It wasn't a question. "Okay, continue."

"She started yelling. I thought the kids were going to wake up or the neighbours would call it in as a domestic file. She eventually burnt herself out when she started throwing up. I got some paper towels to help clean up, and as I stood up to go, she said, 'You killed Vincent Scaggs, didn't you.'" It took a lot to make me speechless, but she'd done it. "She then asked why I hadn't told her, why did I act like he was alive, and why did I go to see him?"

I stopped and took a sip from the water bottle he passed me. "I didn't know Vincent Scaggs had died. I *did* go to visit him in his hospital room. The detachment had us posted to watch the door of his room in case Bychkov showed up, or if he woke up. I was assigned to the post once. When Amber, er, Constable Doyle took over the post, I went inside. Only for a minute, and only to say my piece. I didn't go near the bed, but I did say out loud that he didn't deserve to be alive or something like that." I hung my head for a moment. "It wasn't a threat, but it wasn't professional either. I know that."

Dr. Steinman sat there, waiting for me to continue.

"He was still alive in a coma when I left," I said. "I didn't learn of his death until a few days ago."

"Why would Bree think *you* killed him?" "Well, I had expressed my displeasure more than once with him being the lone survivor, as did many other crew members, so I'm sure that's part of it. Matthews was my best friend. Who wouldn't want revenge?" I paused. "Bree also told me in her drunken stupor that the date he died was actually the same date I'd been there. Apparently, it was several hours after I left." I glanced at the tape recorder. I didn't like that little machine whirring away while I talked about this. "I called the hospital, and they confirmed his death was uneventful. His heart stopped beating, and he passed away. The dates were just a coincidence."

"It doesn't sound like you have anything to worry about except the state of your marriage," Steinman said. "How will you carry on if your wife thinks you're a murderer? Can you prove to her that you didn't do it? Don't they do video surveillance in high-profile cases?"

I laughed. "You'd think so, but I doubt it. That's a very Hollywood idea."

He sat quietly for a moment. "Maybe this was something that was said to hurt you while your wife was drunk and upset?"

"Yeah." Maybe.

"Do you think it would be helpful for me to see Bree?"

I straightened. "What do you mean?"

"Your household seems to be in crisis. Perhaps you could come in together, or maybe she'd want to come on her own. I can apply for it. There's often help for spouses in extenuating circumstances. Given everything you've both been through, I could easily justify it."

I wasn't sure if he was just looking for more money, or if he legitimately thought he could help. It didn't matter. I was terrified of what Bree might say, or what would get back to the detachment, but I knew we needed to do something to move forward. "Can I let you know?"

"Yes, of course. And Jake, I can't tell her anything you've told me in these sessions unless you choose to talk about it together in front of me."

He must have seen the fear in my eyes when he made the suggestion.

"I do want to hear exactly what happened with Amber, but"—he clapped—"that's time for today." He actually sounded sorry. "If things get heated again, you really should call it in."

"Yes, of course. It won't, though." At least, I hoped it didn't.

I headed straight to the detachment. I needed to find something to prove to Bree that I hadn't killed Vincent Scaggs. Maybe Steinman was right and she'd just said something stupid in the moment, but I was already here, and I didn't feel like going home yet.

I sat in the back office with the boxes of evidence and files and opened the laptop, too. They were still processing and filing all of it. I looked through the paperwork and tracked down the time and date he'd died. It was definitely the same day. I checked and cross-checked to see if there was any way the RCMP had put up their own video surveillance in the room and confirmed my suspicions that no, they absolutely had not.

Among the paperwork, I stumbled across Bychkov's police interview. During the interrogation, he said he'd only come to my house once the day before. When asked why he hadn't attempted entry that night, he'd said it was because Bree hadn't been alone. There was another woman in the guest room, looking out the window. *What the actual fuck?* I must have hit this guy harder than I'd thought.

I found no time of death in the media releases. There was nothing else I could do, so I decided to go home and talk to a sober Bree. Earlier, she'd seemed to remember nothing of the night before.

As I passed the hospital on my way home, I wondered if they had surveillance. I did a U-turn and pulled into the parking lot. This hospital was less than a year old. I thought I remembered seeing cameras in the hallway. It was worth a shot.

I walked in through the emergency room up to reception. Most people there only knew me in uniform and didn't recognize me until I flashed my badge. What I was doing wasn't exactly above board, but it wasn't wrong either. I asked where I could find security and was directed to a room the size of a closet.

"Are any of your hospital rooms covered by video surveillance?" I asked the security tech.

He was an older man with a bristly beard and a determined paunch. "Only a few of them. The psych ward has the cameras for safety reasons, and a couple of rooms that we use for prisoners. Which room were you wondering about?"

"Room 302. Would you happen to have any footage from December sixteenth?"

"This is an official police inquiry, right?" He rubbed his face, making a sandpaper sound.

"Yes, of course." I showed him my badge.

"Make a copy and bring it back, okay?" The tech handed me the CD, and I took off out of there like a five-year-old stealing candy.

When I got home, Bree was in the living room waiting for me. The only thing I wanted to do was grab the laptop and go upstairs to review the video. I'd never seen her so pale. I was betting that would be the last time she drank anything for a while.

I put my bag down and knelt beside Riley to give him a high five. He showed me his Spiderman figurine, and how it could shoot webs. He was getting so big. Most days I was scared to touch him. Allowing any type of emotion often brought on a whole lot of unwanted feelings.

"I'll be down in a bit to play Spiderman with you," I said to Riley, then walked up the stairs, refusing to acknowledge Bree's stares.

I set up the laptop in the main bedroom and secured all the weirdo locks. Then I put the CD into the drive. Of course, I had to install a new program to run the slick new software. Once that was all done, I started the video. It really was the entire day.

There were two files on the CD, each with a different camera angle. One was angled at the door to the room, and the other one was inside the room. The RCMP must not have known that the new hospital had this feature, otherwise the footage would have been included as part of the evidence.

To my surprise, there was audio. I skipped through an incredibly boring day. At one point it looked like I was falling asleep. People walked by and said hello. The only people who went in or out of the room were medical personnel, and they did so at regular intervals—every other hour and just before shift change. It was all very boring.

When Amber arrived, we chatted at the door.

I fast-forwarded to where I entered the room. It was exactly as I had remembered: I kept my distance and said my piece. What I hadn't known then, but saw now, was that Amber had opened the door to listen in. As I turned to leave, she backed away.

I stood outside talking with her for another five minutes or so. This was hard to watch. She was way flirtier than I'd realized, and I'd done nothing to stop it. She must have touched me a dozen or more times in that short period.

Then I left. Scaggs was still alive. I had done nothing wrong ... except betray my wife.

I fast-forwarded and watched the medical staff go in to see Scaggs every other hour, right on time. Then Amber entered the room. *Why is she doing that?*

I flipped from the exterior door to the interior room footage. Amber closed the door and then locked it. *What the fuck?*

I wiped my eyes and sat with my face closer to the screen. She walked over to the bedside and put her face close to Vincent's ear. "You think . you can get away with hurting my man?"

Her man? What was she talking about? My heart rate sped up, and my mouth went dry.

"You killed his best friend and made his life hell."

She went to the window and closed the blinds. It was then I noticed she was wearing her work gloves. I watched in disbelief as she turned off the volume on the monitoring machine he was connected to and eased the pillow out from under his head.

No, she wouldn't.

She looked around one final time, placed the pillow square over Scaggs' face, and leaned her full body weight down on him. During an incredibly long five minutes, the numbers and rhythm changed on the monitor until it showed no further sign of life.

Holy shit. What did I just watch?

She lifted his head carefully and placed the pillow beneath it. She even fluffed it. Then she walked back over to the machine and turned up the volume enough so that it was barely audible but didn't look like someone had turned it off. She reopened the blinds, unlocked the door, and removed her gloves. Her walk out was casual, as though nothing was amiss.

I was flooded with adrenaline, and my brain couldn't process this fast enough. I was dumbfounded. The other video file showed her returning to sit on the chair outside the door as though she'd been at her post the entire time.

Over the next forty-seven minutes of footage, she sipped a soda and read her book. She looked at her phone intermittently and said hello to the people who walked by, and to the medical staff who came in on schedule. Then came a flurry of activity when the orderly noticed that Vincent had flatlined.

Amber stood up and approached a nurse. "What's happening in there? Is the prisoner okay?"

"He has no pulse," the nurse said matter-of-factly. "They're doing compressions on him now." She glanced at her watch. "It's been ten minutes. They'll call it soon."

She proceeded to interview the nurse and other medical staff in great detail for the file. No one suspected a damn thing. It was normal, they said. Not unexpected. When asked if anything seemed suspicious, they all said no. She wrote it up and left.

She'd murdered him. For me. I couldn't believe it. I definitely hadn't asked her to do that. This was over two weeks ago. How could I have not known? Had she been acting strangely? Would I have noticed? *Do I even know this woman?*

I took note of the time on the videos, and with shaky hands I opened my phone and scrolled back.

I will always have your back Stone. I would do anything for you. And I do mean anything.

When I'd read the text initially, I thought it was purely sexual. Now it had a whole new meaning.

46

BREE

J ake had been upstairs for a long time. We still hadn't really spoken about whatever I'd done last night. *I'm never going to drink again.* Finally, I heard his footsteps on the stairs.

"There you are," I said evenly.

"Hi." He actually looked at me. It was a start. "I need something to eat."

I jumped up. "What would you like? I can fix you something."

"Actually, never mind, just a coffee would be good. Can we talk?"

"Yes, of course. Are you okay? You look so pale."

We walked toward the kitchen together. It was the most interaction we'd had since the drinking. I was a bit worried about what he might say. I poured two coffees and handed him one, and we sat at the kitchen table. Ivy was asleep, and I could watch Riley wander in and out from where I sat.

"I'm fine," Jake said. "Just really overtired. I didn't get much sleep last night. Bree, I believe you that you don't remember much, if anything, of what happened last night, but you were acting insane."

We both sat down at the kitchen table. He hung his head, avoiding my gaze.

"I know I've been a mess lately, but I can't believe you think I'd be capable of killing Vincent Scaggs."

I almost fell off my chair. "I don't think that. I was just surprised you didn't know. Wow, I'm sorry. Did I say anything else?" I knew I had.

"You kept throwing up and came up and down the stairs opening and closing doors and windows loudly. I left you alone so we wouldn't fight anymore. You must have moved the baby out of the room and put her on that mattress. I didn't do that."

I was so disappointed with myself. "You must have been really upset with me."

"I was blown away. I know we've been fighting a lot, and I haven't been here." He looked down at his hands. They were in rough shape, cracked, peeling and raw in places. He cleared his throat but didn't look up. "You must think I'm a monster."

"I don't. I've just been so lost these last few months, and you never talk to me. You always seem angry or like you hate me. And then the other day, you *were* scaring me." I watched his reaction carefully. "I just wonder what happened to us." I took a deep, shuddering breath. "I'm sorry, I'm trying not to get upset. I'll stop. I do want to talk to you." I got up and went to the washroom to splash some cold water on my face. It was easier to have a conversation with him if I could contain my emotions.

When I returned, he looked close to tears. "You *do* think I am a monster if you think you can't cry while we're talking."

I sat down. "I just don't know who you are anymore. One day I say something one way, and you're okay with it, or might even laugh. The next day I say or do something similar, and you look at me in such a way—"

"What way?" He wasn't mad—yet.

"Like I'm the biggest regret of your life." I forced myself to look at him. "I can't even begin to imagine what life is like for you right now, but I can't help you if you won't talk to me." The mug in my hand shook so much I nearly spilled on myself. "I'm not your enemy." I tried to breathe over top of my pounding heart, hoping my words would be received the way I intended them.

"I know, Bree. I've been seeing Dr. Steinman again."

"The psychologist who diagnosed you with ADHD?"

"Yes, he ... asked about you." He paused and ran his hand through his hair. "He said he'd like to see you—or could see you if you want."

He was still concerned about me. This was a good sign.

"I told him about our fight last night."

My warm, fluttery relief evaporated. He'd told the shrink I'd gotten blackout drunk and had accused him of murder? "Am I in trouble? Will he think I am nuts?"

He laughed. "He sees all kinds of certifiably crazy people. We're normal to him. And I don't know if it will help *us*, but it couldn't hurt."

We were both silent for a minute. "Did I accuse you of anything else?"

"No, that's it."

He was lying. I remembered having accused him of cheating. That busted look on his face seconds before I'd been sick; that was a face I'd never forget. The only thing I didn't know was how far it had gone between them. If he wasn't going to tell the truth, was there any hope left for us?

47

JAKE

JANUARY 4, 2013

I lay down in the main bedroom, hoping to get in a nap before work. Instead, I stared at the ceiling, listening to Bree clatter around downstairs with the kids. My phone buzzed and I picked it up. It was a text from Amber.

How's your head?

"Fuck, this is the last thing I need right now," I muttered to myself.

I'm good.

You ran off so fast the other night. Is something wrong?

Right. Drinks with the crew. I hadn't even said goodbye.

I had no clue what to say to her next. The investigator in me wanted to get her to admit the truth about Scaggs and ask her why the hell she did it. But I already knew why, and the moment that can of worms was opened, I was screwed. I would need to report her, she would say why she did it, and I'd be implicated too. Bree would find out about the affair, our marriage would end, and I'd lose my kids. I had to act like nothing was wrong.

Hello?

Sorry, I just had a fight with Bree, I replied.

The phone started to ring. She was calling now instead of texting. *Can't talk,* I texted quickly. I thought for a few minutes about how to handle this. I decided to try an interrogator trick on her that I'd learned in training.

I called her back. "Hey, I can't talk for long. You called?"

"Yeah, I thought you'd need a friend. What was your fight about?"

Perfect. "Bree thinks I killed Vincent Scaggs." I let it hang there for a reaction.

"What? She's crazy." She was breathing heavily. "What makes her think that?"

What she means is, what do I know? I chose my words carefully. "Well, after we apprehended Bychkov, she saw on the news that Vincent was dead and asked me about it. I told her I hadn't known he was dead, and she didn't believe me. They announced the date, and she checked the calendar and saw I'd done scene security for him that day at the hospital."

"Weird. I didn't realize that was the day he died."

Ha. Bullshit. "Me neither."

"You *are* glad he's dead though, right?"

I paused for a second. I had to tread lightly. "I'm not sad." I forced a chuckle for normalcy. "I have to go."

"Okay, see you at work tonight. You want me to pick you up?"

Fuck, that's right. I have to work with her. "No, don't worry about it. Bree won't need the car. See you then."

"Looking forward to it, as always." She made a smooch sound and hung up.

How could she shift to flirty like that immediately after we'd talked about someone she killed?

I hung up the phone and my head started to spin. What was I going to do? My marriage was a mess, I'd fucked a sociopath, I was in trouble at work and in debt up to my neck with no end in sight. I was also still seeing things—at work, and at home. I had to be losing my mind.

I parked in the overflow parking lot, which was different from my usual spot, so Amber wouldn't find me. I hid in the back of the men's change room until right before my shift started and didn't see her. When I finally went out to my car, she was driving away with a recruit. She'd be busy and distracted the whole night. Finally, something was going my way.

As soon as the shift ended, I planned to slip away and go home. I had no idea what I was going to do, but I was running out of time sitting on this information. I put the last of my stuff in my locker. When I closed it, Amber was right behind it waiting for me.

"Shit, you scared me."

"Very funny. I missed you tonight. Let's go talk in your car." She tried to hold my hand, but I quickly dropped it, astonished at her balls for doing that when there were so many people around.

As we walked to my car, she said, "Why did you park all the way out here?" She got in and said, "Jake, I think I love you." She said it loudly, with the window open.

Jesus H. Christ. I had started the car to warm it up and thought about driving away so no one could hear us, but that might not be a good plan. Instead, I wound up her window and stared straight ahead. "I'm not leaving Bree, ever. Unless she leaves me. I have two kids with her, and they need me as a father and financially. I made a promise. I know that doesn't mean much to you."

"Is that a dig at my failed marriage? Or my inability to have children?" She looked wounded.

"No, sorry, not at all." Shit, I shouldn't have said that. My eyes wandered over to her duffel bag, and I wondered if her gun was in there. "I just mean a lot of people would leave without thinking." I turned to look at her. The damn car was still blowing cold air. "Amber, it was tempting. You're a beautiful and strong woman, and we've had a lot of laughs. You've been a very good friend to me, and I'm obviously attracted to you. But what's the end game? I leave my wife, we get together and end up with the same problems Bree and I have? What's the point? You need to find someone unattached who will treat you better and not keep you a secret."

"You think I'm beautiful?" She was smiling like a teenage girl talking to her idol for the first time.

"Amber, *this* can't happen. It's over."

Her eyes went wide with panic. "I can be patient. You don't have to leave her right away. Or at all. I can keep quiet. I just can't lose you."

"You don't know what you're saying. It was just a fling. We clung to each other when Matthews died, and I'll always appreciate that." That part was true. "But that's all it was."

She ground her teeth together. "It wasn't about Matthews; I barely knew him. I've always admired you. I had a big crush on you. I got transferred to this district hoping to get to know you. That first time we partnered? That was because I asked to work with you."

This was all news to me. "I have to go. I have to get home to Bree. She'll suspect—"

"She already suspects." She smirked.

"Suspicions or not, she's not going to find out," I said firmly.

"Okay, okay. Don't get your knickers in a knot."

"I'm serious." I remembered the image of her holding a pillow over Vincent Scaggs' face.

"What if I told her? You'd be free to be with me, and she could carry on with her life. I know you must feel something about me. I saw it in your eyes when we were making love."

My stomach lurched. I barely remember doing it. I doubted my eyes had even been open. Did she not understand that I didn't want to be with her?

"I could call her right now. I have her phone number." Amber wiggled her eyebrows. "What are you going to do for me so that I don't tell her?"

Heat rushed to my face. Did she think she could blackmail me into fucking her? "You're delusional, Doyle. Who the hell do you think you are?" I couldn't control my rage. I was almost nose to nose with her when her body language shifted. Her smugly raised chin dropped as she clasped the back of her neck with one hand and looked away from me.

"No, I just mean ... I don't know," she said. "This is getting out of hand. Go home and text me later, okay? We can figure this out. I'm not in a rush. I can't lose this. Good things are worth the wait, right?" She put her hand on my shoulder.

I was on fire, but I reined it in to get the fuck out of there.

"Yeah, I'm sorry. I'm under too much stress. I'll text you later." I picked up her hand and got it off my crawling skin. She misunderstood and thought I was trying to hold it. She gave it a squeeze and smiled.

"Okay, Jakey. Bye." She blew me a kiss as she got out of the car.

I left the parking lot as calmly as I could and sped all the way home. What was I going to do?

As I walked through my front door, the smell of bacon and eggs wafted over me. I had been boiling with anger the entire drive home and hadn't realized how hungry I was. Riley came running out to greet me with grease on his face and a gnarled piece of bacon in his fist.

"Bakie!" he yelled proudly as he handed it to me.

I looked over at Bree. She was blushing and fidgeting with her hair. She wasn't wearing her normal house clothes. She wore a dress. A pretty little brown dress that I thought she'd worn on one of our early dates.

"Hi," I said as waves of regret roiled in my stomach thinking about my behaviour over the past few months.

"I made breakfast."

"I see that." I smiled as I ate the bacon slice straight from Riley's fist. We all giggled, and then my phone buzzed. I held my breath. I knew it was her. Her threat to my family required immediate attention.

I rolled my eyes at the phone dramatically for Bree and Riley's benefit. "Just a minute, guys. I'll deal with this and be right back to check out this breakfast. If Riley hasn't eaten it all." I winked and ran upstairs to deal with my phone.

I've been thinking. We should tell Bree about us together. That way you don't have to do it alone.

"Is this chick on drugs?" I said in exasperation. *No, not going to happen. You need to accept this.*

Amber texted back, *I will not. Either you tell her, or I will. I'm around the corner from your house. I can be there in two minutes.*

Fuck. I barreled down the stairs and hollered to Bree, "I'll be right back." I ran until I saw Amber's car.

"Get us away from my house!" I shouted, getting into the car. "Go to the railyard, it's not far. We can talk there." And no one would hear us.

When we pulled into the railyard, there was hardly anyone there. One train was unloading its freight along with a handful of workers, but no one seemed to notice us pull up. As soon as Amber parked, I jumped out of her car. I was creeped out sitting so close to her. She got out and walked over to my side of the car. We stood several feet apart behind a stationary railcar.

I ran my hand through my hair as I took a deep breath, thinking carefully about what to say and how to say it.

"Look Amber, I am *very* sorry I led you on. I should never have let things get this far. That night was a huge mistake. I am staying with Bree, and I'm not telling her. A few minutes of indiscretion should not be allowed to destroy my entire family." My mind drifted to my wife in her brown dress and Riley's bacon offering. "I am truly sorry I hurt you," I said in the most matter-of-fact voice I could muster.

"Drop the act. You're not fooling anyone."

"Huh?"

"I know you want to be with me. I can feel it. The only thing stopping us is her. We can take the kids. I've always wanted to be a mother, you know that. She can go back to wherever she came from, and it will be like she never existed at all."

Holy fuck, this just keeps getting worse. "There's no way in hell I'm removing my children from their mother to be raised by someone like you!" I shouted over the noise of the train pulling forward, its wheels squealing along the tracks.

Her skin reddened as she spoke through clenched teeth. "Someone like me? Wow. You have a lot of nerve. I'm going to call your wife right now." She maintained intense eye contact as she pulled her phone out of her pocket. "This will all be over soon."

Panic swelled inside me like a tidal wave. "If you do that, I'll tell everyone what you did to Vincent Scaggs."

Her brows unfurrowed, and her eyes grew wide as her breathing became ragged. The railyard had suddenly gone quiet. "What do you mean, what I did to Vincent Scaggs?"

"I know you killed him."

"Just because I was on shift when he was in custody and died, you think I did it?" Her voice faltered a bit.

"Amber, I have video evidence. I watched you do it. If you so much as say one word to Bree about anything, I'll take it to the inspector myself."

For a long time, she said nothing. "Okay."

"Okay what?" I needed to know she understood what she was agreeing to.

"Okay, I agree that I won't tell Bree what happened between us if you keep the video to yourself—or better yet, give it to me." She lowered her voice. "Do you actually have a video, or are you full of shit?"

"I watched you smother him with a pillow after fiddling with the machines. Proof enough?"

She looked down and kicked at the gravel. When she lifted her head, a grin spread across her face. "If you show that video to anyone, I'll say I did it for you or that you forced me to do it. Everyone at work already knows we have a thing. You'll lose your job and go to jail. You'll lose everything. What will your precious Bree and kids do then?"

She was right. I was fucked. Especially if she was going around telling people we had a relationship. I'd get pulled off the job without pay, and the trial would drag on for ages. Bree already thought I'd done it. She would learn about the affair and leave me. I would go to jail, which wasn't pleasant for cops. Even if I eventually got off, my reputation would be ruined. I'd also be punished at work—potentially publicly—for fraternizing with Amber. I was sunk no matter what.

"Vincent Scaggs is a piece of shit and deserved to die. No one misses him." She removed her hands from her hips and walked toward me. "We're meant to be together, Jake. We could have such a good life. It would be a fresh start." As she drew closer, her gun peeked out of her waistband.

I was backed into a corner with no way out. In a moment of stillness in the railyard, I heard rushing water in the distance and knew exactly how to end this.

"Okay, Amber, you win. Let me tell Bree, though, and give me a couple of days to do it."

"Oh Jake." She threw her arms around me and hung on so tight I could feel her gun push against my thigh.

48

BREE

JANUARY 5, 2013

J ake startled me when he came back into the house. He hadn't been
gone long, but he'd left so abruptly.

"Everything okay?" I asked. "Where did you go?"

"Yep. It's all good. I had something of Abbott's, so I met him at the
corner store on his way through." He was shaking. "I'm going to grab a
quick shower and then eat some of that bacon you made for me." His
smile was forced and weird.

He took his work duffel bag and went upstairs, making a ton of noise,
banging around up there and running the water.

After quite some time, Jake came back downstairs and put his bag
by the door. There was something different about him. He was calm. I
passed him a plate of bacon and eggs that I had just reheated.

"Thanks." He wasn't smiling, but he didn't look upset either. He took
a couple bites and put the plate down on the coffee table. Then he turned
to face me and reached out, taking my hands into his.

"Bree, I want to tell you how very sorry I am. I have not been a great
husband to you, lately. I wanted so much more for us."

"Things have been rough," I said, unable to hide my relief at this conversation. "I haven't been perfect either, but—what brought this on?"

"I've just been talking with Dr. Steinman a lot, and it made me realize a few things. Everything is going to get better for us soon; I have no doubt about that. I just wanted to apologize. And to tell you I *do* still love you." His eyes filmed.

These were words I hadn't heard earnestly in a long time. We always said it when he left for work—a police family necessity. You had to say it every time no matter what, as it could be the last time. This was different. It was heartfelt and out of the blue. Maybe this therapy was really helping.

"I love you too, Jake. Everything will get better, absolutely. We can get through anything together, if we just talk more," I said, feeling hope return.

He leaned in, put his hand under my chin the way he used to, and gave me a slow and soft kiss, looking into my eyes as he pulled away. "I want you and the kids to be happy and safe. That means the world to me, and I'm sorry if I haven't shown it."

He walked over and gave Riley a kiss, then touched Ivy's cheek. "She looks like you, you know." He smiled.

After wiping his face with his sleeve, he took a big breath and looked around the house. "I won't be able to sleep right now, so I'm going to go for a run." He walked toward the front door and poked his head around the corner again.

"Bye, kiddos. Be good for your Mommy, okay?"

It looked like he was crying again, but I couldn't be sure. I was distracted by words I'd been waiting to hear for months. He had kissed me and told me he loved me, for real. He'd said things would get better. Affair or not, maybe he would finally return to me.

As happy and full as my heart felt in that moment, I couldn't help but think something was wrong. I looked out the window and caught the tail end of the car driving away. Odd that he'd taken his work bag with him if he was going for a run.

I went upstairs. What had he been doing up there for so long? His gym clothes were on our bedroom floor.

I froze as I realized he hadn't been wearing any running gear when he'd left.

49

Jake

January 5, 2013

When Bree and I first moved to Roxford, we spent our early days exploring. We located all the best places for our kids to play. We found parks, playgrounds, walking trails, a petting zoo, a river, and a lake right smack in the middle of town. The lake where I'd almost lost Riley.

We'd only been to the river together that one time. It reminded me too much of the files I'd attended. Seedy things happened down by the river: drug deals, acts of prostitution, and more commonly, body dumps. The river here moved so fast it was hypnotic to watch. When we'd been here, we had held Riley tightly so he wouldn't get anywhere near the edge.

For the first time in months—years, maybe—a weight lifted off my chest. I was light, almost feathery, like when I was a small boy. As a kid, I would skip rocks on the river near my house and dream of growing up to be a cop. I wanted to save people from the bad guys, save boys from being hurt by their families, the way mine had hurt me. I didn't know then that cops couldn't save everyone. I couldn't save everyone.

"I couldn't save them all!" I shouted. The water was so loud down here, no one could hear me, and I didn't care if they did. "Matthews, I couldn't save you." It was my fault. I wasn't a good guy anymore.

I was broken-hearted that I had ruined so much. Many people were hurting because of me. But in that moment, relief overtook me, followed by guilt for that relief, immense guilt. Though I knew my pain was about to end.

I opened my duffle bag and surveyed the contents. First, my police hat, with a picture of my family firmly taped to the underside. It was another superstitious quirk of being in law enforcement: keeping your family with you to keep you safe. Instead, I had kept myself safe while putting my family in danger, over and over again.

I brought the notes with me that I'd written for Riley and the baby for when they grew up. Dr. Steinman was right—I couldn't say her name. I couldn't even write it. I'd written *for the baby*, like the useless coward I was. She deserved a better father. I had written Bree a letter too, but I didn't see it in the bag.

I put on the rest of my uniform and my hat, pulled out my gun and holstered it. I walked toward the river and turned with my back to it. At this angle, when I pulled the trigger, I would fall in, and the river would sweep me far away—hopefully so far that by the time they found me, I'd be not much more than bones and Bree wouldn't have to ID me. The personal effects in my bag and the car parked nearby would be enough to save her from that. I took a deep breath, put the gun in my mouth, and put my finger on the trigger.

50

BREE

W hy would Jake not have worn his jogging clothes? Had he brought another set with him? That didn't make sense either. I picked up the clothes and found an envelope on the floor beneath them.

It was addressed to me, in Jake's handwriting. The ink was still fresh, smudging under my fingertips. I didn't have to open it. I sprinted down the stairs to my phone, mowing Riley down at the bottom.

His behaviour made sense now. He was saying goodbye. I couldn't read the letter; I had to call 911.

As I rummaged through the kitchen for my phone, the day we'd first met ran through my mind. Then the day we'd decided to start our family. Our wedding day. Yes, I had thought about leaving, and things had been rough, but I loved him. I found the phone and quickly dialed.

"My husband is going to harm himself. He has a gun."

"Ma'am, is he with you?" the dispatcher asked. "Are you safe? Can we speak to him?"

"No, I think maybe he's gone down to the river." He told me he liked to jog by the river and sometimes went there just to sit and think. "Please hurry; it may be too late."

"We have someone on the way to the river right now, ma'am."

"His name is Jake Stone. Constable Jake Stone." I cried hard while she asked me questions about Jake, trying to keep me calm.

"What makes you think he would harm himself?"

"His best friend is dead. His marriage is a mess. We fight all the time. I accused him of murder. We're broke. He's having a weird affair. We're trapped. He is trapped in every possible way," I said in between sobs. "Is that enough?"

Riley climbed up on the sofa beside me and put his hand on my leg. Ivy stared at us from her swing that was still going full tilt, music and all.

Minutes felt like hours as the operator asked me useless questions to keep me on the phone. A knock at the door interrupted us.

"No. Nope. No!" I screamed.

"Roxford PD. Mrs. Stone, it's Constable Bullock, can I come in?"

It was Babyface, and he was about to rip my heart out. I looked at Riley, who was silent. Then I looked at Ivy, who actually looked more like Jake, not me. For them, I had to keep going. I stood up, steadied myself, and walked over to the door.

51

JAKE

JANUARY 6, 2013

I opened my eyes and wondered if I would be received in Heaven or Hell. God knew I'd done some kind things over my career and in my life, but I'd also meet judgment for my indiscretions.

Everything was blurry, but it was white and bright. There was a high-pitched ring in my ear. I squeezed my eyes shut, then tried to rub them to refocus, but my arms were strapped down.

"Whoa there buddy, slow it down. How are you feeling?" a man dressed in white asked me.

"Am I allowed here? In Heaven?"

He chuckled. "You're allowed here, but this most certainly isn't Heaven. I'm going to give you another injection so you can relax."

"An injection? Where am I?" Slowly the room came into focus.

"You're at Roxford General Hospital. How's your head? Can you hear me?"

This couldn't be happening. I'd had the gun in my mouth. I'd pulled the trigger. I felt my head and winced. It was definitely sore. A huge bandage covered most of my head, along with my left ear.

"The emergency response team closed in on you fast when they saw you heading into the river. They were able to tackle you before you could fatally wound yourself. The gun went off, but luckily it just grazed you, though it took most of your ear."

I rubbed the bandage on my head, thoroughly confused.

"That's from the takedown. Those guys didn't mess around. They knocked you down hard. Your head hit a rock, and it knocked you out. You've been down for just over twenty-four hours."

"Great." Two seconds sooner and I would have finished the job.

"Are you up for visitors?" He pointed into the hallway. "She's been here all night."

I panicked, remembering my interaction with Amber. When I saw Bree's tear-swollen face watching me as she touched the window, I could breathe properly.

Bree pushed the door open and wrapped her arms around me but backed away when she felt me flinch. She sat down on a chair beside me. What now? Her expression was difficult to read. Would she yell at me? Leave me?

She held my hand and didn't say a word. The nurse noted the awkward silence and made his way out of the room.

"I read your letter," she said.

Jesus Christ, I don't remember writing a letter. "Where are the kids?" I looked around, hoping they weren't out in the hallway witnessing the mess I'd created.

"They're with Tammy, and before you say anything, I don't care what you think about her. She's a great person and has been an amazing friend to me and the kids. You're not calling the shots around here anymore."

"Okay." I vaguely remembered this side of Bree. I hadn't seen it in a long time.

Her voice became gentler. "Why did you think this was your only option? Why did you think you couldn't talk to me? I'm your person. At least I used to be. You know you can tell me anything."

"Anything?" The drugs had kicked in and I was fighting an incredible urge to sleep, but that word reverberated weirdly through my brain.

"I know you have to keep work stuff a secret, but you can vent to me, tell me how you're feeling, share what's going on in your life. We may fight, but I'm your wife and I love you."

I still couldn't focus or speak very well, but I noticed the video camera in the corner of the room, and it reminded me of something urgent that needed attention. "I have some difficult things to tell you—and a very important favor to ask."

She leaned back but didn't let go of my hand. "I'm listening."

"I had an affair."

"I know."

"You knew?"

"A wife always knows. I had a bad feeling for a long time but didn't really suspect until recently." There was silence, and then, "Do you love her?"

"Absolutely not." My eyes were rolling back, begging for sleep.

"Okay. What's the favour? What do you need? I've got your back."

I sat up so I could focus long enough to tell her about Amber and the video.

52

BREE

The kids were full of energy and excited to see me when I got to Tammy's house. We loaded them into their car seats together.

"I'm so grateful you agreed to come with me," I said as she sat in the passenger seat. I still felt shell-shocked by Jake's suicide attempt and his admission of the affair. Sure, I'd suspected it, but hearing him admit it had made it that much more real.

"Are you kidding?" Tammy said. "I wouldn't miss this for the world. It's not every day us wives get to be involved in solving a crime."

"Well, I really appreciate not being alone right now. I didn't know who to call when Jake ..." I stumbled over my words.

"You don't have to explain a darn thing, girl. I was dead serious when I said you could call me for anything. Most of our men have had PTSD at some point in their career, and this is part of it. I'm glad they knocked him down in time, is all." She sat with her arms crossed high above her breasts.

"PTSD?"

She put her hands on her hips and looked at me. "You don't know about Post Traumatic Stress Disorder?"

"No, but now that you've named it, I can piece it together."

"That's right. You met him long after Depot and didn't get the frightening handbook."

I shook my head.

"Well, it's not the normal illness you sign on for when you say 'in sickness and in health.' Nightmares, anxiety, substance abuse, fits of rage—the list is long. I thought you said he was seeing a psychologist."

"They diagnosed him with ADHD, prescribed him Adderall and sent him back to work."

"Good god. Must be Dr. Steinman. You and I have a lot to talk about."

As we neared the detachment, she said, "What's the plan?"

"I don't really have a plan," I said, "but I have the CD in my purse. Apparently, it's the only copy." I was so afraid of flubbing this up. "Jake said I have to go through the public entrance and talk to whomever is working. Do you know who the watch commander is tonight?"

"I sure do." She beamed. "It's Tony Paskins himself, and I told him you were coming in to see him."

I could feel the colour leave my face. "What else did you tell him?" Maybe Jake was right; she did have a big mouth.

"Nothing. He heard about Jake over the radio. He figured you'd just want to know wife stuff, about his paycheque, medical, him being committed and all." She waved her hand dismissively like this was a commonplace occurrence. "I did tell him this was urgent, though. I can ask hubby to come out to the car or meet you at the door. You don't want Doyle to see you, right? Why risk running into *her*?"

Good point. I cringed thinking about it. "Jake assured me she isn't working tonight. He knows her schedule." This stung as I said it. I still hadn't processed how my husband had slept with that psychopath.

"Okay. You go in, and I'll stay in the car with the kids as long as you need." She paused. "I should have said something before you left Roxford, but you and the kids can stay with us tonight—or for as long as you need to. It isn't safe for you to go home until Doyle is apprehended."

"That's so thoughtful." I wasn't scared, but I was too sad and tired to be alone. "Are you sure it's not an imposition?"

"Not at all, and I won't take no for an answer." She turned around to look at the kids. "To be honest, I need more baby snuggles, so I'm being somewhat selfish." She let out another one of her giant laughs I found so comforting.

"I'll need to pick up some stuff from the house." Thinking about the practical things kept me distracted as I made the turn into the detachment parking lot.

"I'll go with you. We'll finish here, pick up whatever you need, and then head to my house. I have a crockpot of chili, and a fridge full of wine. I can tell you everything I know about PTSD, and you can tell me whatever you want. Or we can just get drunk and watch *The Bachelor*." She clapped her hands.

"*The Bachelor* is probably all I can handle tonight." I glanced over at her. "Why are you being so nice to me? I haven't been in touch since our last visit. You hardly even know me."

"Oh, I know you, hon. You're me. This is a uniquely shared life we live, married to first responders. It's lonely, it's isolating, it's a lot of things. But along with the fucked-up package you didn't order comes a group of sisters. You may love 'em or hate 'em, but they'll all do anything for you if you need it. I'm just sad you didn't know this sooner. It sounds like you've needed us for a long time."

I pulled into the parking spot and let out a few more tears. And like the new best friend I'd never thought I'd have, she looked ahead out the window, saying nothing, and put her hand on mine until I was done.

After I wiped my face and blew my nose, I said, "I think I'm ready."

She shook a fist in front of her. "Go get this bitch!"

Commander Paskins met me at the front door of the detachment. He was well over six feet tall and had broad shoulders. He wore glasses with a slight cat's-eye shape that were similar to his wife's, which I thought was cute. I could still see Tammy in the car when I glanced behind me. She held her phone in one hand and gave me a thumbs-up with the other.

A lot of members looked at me when I walked in—some were familiar, some not. The look on their faces wasn't exactly pity, but it was close. They looked collectively haunted. I wondered how many of them had thought of taking their lives. How many had attended the funerals of friends who had pulled the trigger? I couldn't hold their gaze or I might have died right there on the call centre floor.

It felt like a long walk to get to Paskins' office. He closed the door and the blinds and gestured for me to sit down. These offices all looked the same, especially the watch commanders' office, as it was shared by whoever was on shift. Short grey carpet, eggshell-white walls, oversized furniture, and RCMP regalia art on the wall.

"Tammy tells me you have something critical to show me." He leaned over his desk. "She didn't say what it was, but she told me to drop everything I was doing."

The lump in my throat that was preventing me from crying also prevented me from talking.

I handed him the CD.

"Have you seen this?" he asked.

"No sir," I managed, "but I know what's on it."

"Bree, you can call me Tony. We're a family here, and I hear we might be roommates for a while." He winked. "I can't let you see this, but I'll review it right now with the volume off and the screen facing me."

I watched his face change during that seven-minute video from curious and confused to horrified and pissed. When he was finished, he picked up the phone and called someone. It must have gone straight to voicemail, because he hung up the phone hard.

I spoke. "Jake, as you know, will be hospitalized for a few weeks, possibly longer. He tried to—"

He stopped me. "I was briefed on what happened."

"In the hospital, he told me everything," I said. "He admitted he'd had an affair with Constable Amber Doyle, but he didn't know she'd killed this man until a few days ago. He and I had been fighting, and I accused him of killing Vincent Scaggs one night when I was drunk."

I explained how and why Jake had acquired the CD. My voice was shaking, so Paskins brought me a glass of water. I drank the whole thing before clearing my throat. I told him about Doyle's threat to implicate Jake if he turned in the video, and how Jake felt like he'd run out of options. The possibility that I might leave him. The grief of losing Matthews. The files that had been plaguing him—and likely other things I was sure he hadn't shared with me.

He wiped the sweat off his forehead. "This is a lot. I had no clue about him and Doyle, but this video is a slam dunk. We'll apprehend her right away. If she implicates Stone, we'll have to investigate him, but it would be suspension with pay based on what I see here. Regardless, it's possible he'll be in the hospital for the duration and may not have to testify."

I hadn't even thought about how long Jake's road to recovery might be.

He stood up and walked around his desk towards me. "Stone is one of the good guys here, Bree. They fall through the cracks sometimes. He's always been a good cop. Hard worker, long hours, lots of overtime. We'll do our very best for him. In the meantime, take care of yourself. I'll send a car to your house for security, and let you know when we have Doyle in custody."

I left in a hurry so I wouldn't have to make conversation with anyone in the radio room or the parking lot. Even though Jake had reassured me there was no way I'd run into Amber, I still didn't quite believe it. I wanted to get back to Roxford as quickly as possible.

53

AMBER

Amber drove by Jake's house, grateful that the car wasn't there and that it was dark outside. Her phone started to ring. When she saw that it was the detachment calling, she turned it off and chucked it in the back seat. She turned down the next road so she could park in the alleyway behind. This is where she would sit and watch the house sometimes. To make sure Jake was home and that he wasn't intimate with his wife, like he had said.

She would make this look like a typical break-and-enter. It wouldn't be a problem at all. They'd had so much trouble since they moved to the house, and this neighbourhood certainly was not without crime.

As she turned down the alley, she turned off her headlights. No one would see her enter, and no one would raise any alarms. She drove slowly until she was behind a hedge, making her car invisible to the Stone household.

She'd grabbed her gun from her locker when she was at work. Amber wasn't sure if Bree would be home or not and didn't know if this would end with Plan A or Plan B. She opened the gate to the back fence slowly and not too wide, remembering that it squeaked if you opened it all the way, then slowly walked along the fence to their back door. There was a chance that the women on the shelter deck would spot her, but they didn't this time.

She tested the back door, and it opened just like that. Bree had left the door unlocked. *What an idiot*, she thought. Amber would have to make it look like a break-in later. Right now, she could quietly focus on finding the video. He'd never said what format he had it in— likely a CD, maybe a flash drive?

As Amber walked through the kitchen into the dining room, elements on the gas stove whooshed on. The patio door to the kitchen closed—a short, firm close. Amber was so focused on the task at hand, looking on tabletops and opening drawers, she barely noticed these things happening. Though she did feel like she was being watched.

One window slammed shut, and then another one.

"Bree? Are you there? I came by to see how you were doing?" Amber said in an unnaturally sweet voice, moving her right hand to retrieve the gun that was tucked into the waist of her pants.

There was no reply to her questions. She kept walking from room to room with her gun drawn, clearing them as though she were on the job. She stopped every few steps and rifled through papers and looked under things, gun still poised.

This place is a fucking mess. No wonder Jake was ready to leave you. Two more windows slammed shut. "What the hell? Bree, are you hiding? Come on out, I just want to talk to you."

Amber was starting to think Bree wasn't home, though it seemed as though she wasn't alone. Her car wasn't in the driveway, not many of the lights were on, and there were no children screaming in the background. She heard more whooshing and rustling in the kitchen, so she put down the papers that were in her free hand and placed both on the gun, slowly making her way back.

"Jakey? Is that you? They let you out early? I'm here for you, my love. We are going to be together, I promise. You and I were meant to be. I would do anything for you. And you know it."

As she rounded the corner into the kitchen, a woman in a white nightdress with long, tangled hair came gliding at her, mouth open, screaming. Instinctually, Amber fired off three shots in rapid succession, all of them missing. One shot hit the stove, and a fire began to spread.

"What the fuck?!" she yelled, her chest heaving up and down as she tried to breathe. She couldn't spot the woman anywhere. "Now, I'm seeing things? Fuck," she mumbled to herself, more annoyed than afraid, moving quickly away from the fire, knocking over a stand and breaking a vase filled with dried flowers on her way.

I have got to find that video, and fast. Someone might call in that gunfire. Amber rounded the corner to the stairs, satisfied that the video was not downstairs. She could hear footsteps on the second floor.

"Bree, I'm sorry, Jakey and I are in love. He says I am the best thing that has ever happened to him, and we are going to take on the world together. Don't worry about the kids; I will be such a good mother to them. You can take them when Jakey and I go on vacation. They will love me as much as they love you one day," she said, satisfied with herself.

"Let's just sit down for a chat, shall we?" The hall light upstairs turned on. "Okay, I'm coming."

Amber made it to the top of the stairs and looked around. There was clearly no one there. She holstered her gun, then walked into the main bedroom and tore it apart, looking for the video. Next, she walked back down the hall and ransacked the bathroom and Riley's room. Nothing.

As she walked back out into the hallway, a light turned on in the guest room. The door was wide open, and no one was there.

She drew her gun out again and crouched down, moving slowly and carefully into the guest room. "Hello? Who is there? Come out and show me your face." *It better not be whatever was downstairs.*

As Amber walked through the doorframe to the guest room, she looked out the window and noticed Bree pulling into the driveway. *There you are, you entitled little bitch,* Amber thought as she scurried back down the stairs.

54

BREE

As I drove us away from the detachment, the sense of relief was immense. That part was done. I still didn't know what I would do about Jake. I had accepted his behaviour for so long because I didn't think I had a choice; now I realized I'd had a choice the entire time. I had support from Tammy, my sister, even my mom. Putting my foot down with Jake today had felt good. He didn't know the best way to handle every situation. I'd forgotten how to trust myself.

"I don't know how I'll ever repay you for coming with me and doing all of this." I stared straight ahead. It was dark and pouring rain, so I had to focus harder on the road.

"Then don't," Tammy said. "I don't need repayment."

I knew she meant it. I glanced in the rearview mirror. The kids were finally asleep. "Maybe I'll run into the house and grab a few things while you wait in the car."

"Sure, sounds like a plan."

I turned off at the highway exit and drove up my road. As I pulled into the driveway, I parked closer to the road than the house so the car would remain in the dark, hoping the kids would stay asleep. "I'll be as quick as I can, okay?" I whispered.

"Don't forget frozen breast milk if you have any, so you can drink tonight." Tammy smiled.

Closing the car door gently, I made my way to the front entrance. Walking a few steps into the house, I immediately sensed something was wrong. It smelled of smoke, and the vibe was off. I wasn't alone. Someone was in the house. Holding my breath so I could listen, I heard rapid breathing nearby.

"Hello?" I didn't want anyone to answer, but the silence was scaring me.

No one responded.

I walked from the foyer into the living room. No one was there, but I took a quick look around, spotting a stand in the living room that had been knocked over. A vase of dead flowers lay broken on the floor. I bent down to pick up the glass and froze when a familiar creak came from the bottom of the stairs behind me.

A female voice cut the silence, causing me to flinch. "Hello, Bree."

I spun around with a big chunk of glass in my hand that nicked my skin when I squeezed it, startled. "What are you doing here?" I asked, still holding tight to the glass and backing up a step or two.

"You really don't know why I'm here?"

"No, I don't. Jake's not home right now."

"I know. I just found out what he did today. That explains why he wasn't answering my calls." She flipped her hair behind her shoulder. "I'm so glad he's okay."

She took one step forward and stood at an angle, her body coiled. A shiver snaked up my spine. She must have been so close to me when I'd first walked in.

"Jake's not okay," I said. "He tried to kill himself." I moved back another step, calculating the distance between me and the door, and then her and the door. And then from me to the kitchen behind me. It was too far. Could I take her? I had a shitty makeshift weapon in my hand, but I was no match for a trained police officer and killer.

"Did Jake tell you about *us*?"

Gut punch. "Yes." I could either be coy and pretend I knew nothing, or distract her so I could get the hell out of there. "He told me everything."

She stood facing me. "What do you mean? That we fucked? That he loved it? Did he tell you he's planning on leaving you? We were going to tell you together, but he thought he should do it alone."

She's lying … isn't she? Jake had never mentioned this.

"We planned it yesterday when he ran out and met me at my car."

She had to be lying. Though he had left the house to meet her, presumably.

Amber took another step forward. The light glinted off her eyes and gun, exposing her for the dangerous snake she was.

She's going to kill me. "He didn't mention that," I said, trying to keep the quiver from my voice. "But he *did* tell me he didn't love you because he isn't into murderers."

Her face went red, and I kicked the broken glass in her direction, giving me a millisecond to run through the kitchen, which was on fire. What the hell had happened here? She was hot on my heels. She was so fast, I knew if I ran straight to the back patio door she could easily shoot me in the back. Instead, I cornered hard and ran through the formal dining room, grateful I still had my shoes on. Sock feet would have been the end of me. I could hear her behind me, but she had slowed down. I sped up the stairs and hid in the first available place—the skinny closet to nowhere at the top of the stairs. I barely fit inside. We never put anything in there. Jake and I had agreed we wanted nothing of ours stored in that creepy spot. I was tucking the gross velvet curtain into place as I heard her round the second stair landing.

I wondered what Tammy was doing. Had she realized something was wrong? Surely she wouldn't leave the kids to come into the house. *Please don't leave them alone.* Could she see the fire or smell the smoke from the car? Maybe she'd call 911.

"Bree, where do you think you can go? How about you tell me where that video is?"

She stood inches away from me. I was close enough that I could smell her musky perfume ... and gas. There was a definite smell of gas mixed with the smoke. A door creaked open down the hallway, but I saw through the curtain crack that Amber was still right in front of me. She cocked her head to the side, looking in that direction.

"Come on, Bree. I just want to talk."

Right. With her hand on her gun? She headed down the hall. I didn't make a sound.

"If I don't find it, I'm going to burn the whole house down with you inside."

The gas. She had done something to the gas and lit my house on fire. I had to get out of there.

"Just give me the video and I'll leave."

Bullshit. Where the hell was that car Tony was sending?

I waited as I heard her check for me in the bathroom and Riley's room. Finally, I heard her open the main bedroom closets. She was far enough away that she likely wouldn't discern where my voice was coming from.

"I don't have the video."

"I don't believe you," she said from the bedroom. "It's somewhere in the house. Jake would never turn on me. We're meant to be together."

A closet in Riley's room shut loudly. A gasp almost escaped me as I saw a familiar figure float down the hall and tuck out of sight into the bathroom. Amber ran down the hall and into Riley's room, likely thinking it was me. After a moment, she returned to the hallway.

"Where the fuck are you? Your time is running out."

I was getting dizzy from the fumes, and I rested my head on the wall behind me. All I wanted to do was close my eyes and wait for this to be over. I really wanted to close my eyes.

Through the crack of the curtain, I could see her just outside of Riley's bedroom, looking and listening with her head tilted.

A horn honked outside. Three nonrhythmic honks that could only be my sweet Riley. Awake and restless in the car, he was either playing with the horn or had bumped into it while he played in my seat, waiting for his mama to return. My eyes opened, and I sat as upright as I could in my squat.

"Who the hell is that?" she spat.

"Come see for yourself. I'm in the guest room, you dumb whore."

She stomped toward the guest room. I jumped out from behind the curtain, and as I slammed the door behind her, I leaned my full body weight against it. She pounded on the door, shrieking, trying to get out. I bolted all the locks on the outside of the door and ran down the stairs. She was doing door kicks as I fled.

"You bitch! You think you're so smart. This isn't over." She kicked the door again, and it sounded like it crashed open, but I couldn't be sure over her screaming.

I ran outside, leaving the front door wide open. Tammy's face slackened from jovial to terrified as I raced to the car with my bloodied hand. Riley was in the driver's seat, as I'd suspected. I dropped the glass I was still holding and ripped open the car door. Tammy grabbed Riley and hustled him into the back seat as I jumped in.

"It's Amber." I was out of breath, pointing up to the guest room with one hand, searching for the keys in the other. "She's in the house, set it on fire, she's crazy, she said she's gonna—"

"Oh my god, Bree, start the car."

I thought she would follow me down the stairs, but Amber was watching us from the guest room, her silhouette illuminated in the now-open doorframe. I fumbled around in my pants and coat pocket for the keys. When I looked up, there they were, dangling in the door to my house. I looked up higher and made eye contact with Amber.

She smirked as she lifted her gun and took aim.

In half a second, I contemplated running to the door to get the key. Maybe she wouldn't shoot the car if I wasn't in it. Or I could spread myself across the backseat and protect my babies. I saw a flash of a white dress scream down the hallway, slamming the door full force into Amber, whose gun was trained on the car.

"Get down!" I shouted.

Amber's eyes rolled back as a loud bang rang out.

My windshield cracked, and then a whoosh tore through the night, shaking the entire car. It felt like a fast exhale and inhale of pressure squeezing us and then letting us go. Then came a high-pitched whine that stung both my ears. I still felt dizzy from having been inside the house, and now I couldn't hear.

"She shot at us!" I yelled, looking frantically around the car, trying to figure out where a bullet might have gone.

"Riley! Ivy!" I felt the kids' bodies for wounds. Riley was crying, crouched in the footwell of the backseat where Tammy had placed him. Ivy was upset too, but neither of them seemed to be wounded. I kept repeating, "We're okay," as though it would help.

As I turned back around, my arm got wet as it brushed Tammy's shoulder. She stared at the house, not noticing that her arm was covered in blood. For a few seconds, we both stared at Amber who was standing upright, still and unmoving, her expression blank. Then she slumped forward onto the floor, leaving a dark stain on the door behind her, causing me to remember the iron hook that was affixed there. She was no longer visible as the smoke and flames overtook the room.

Tammy turned to face me. "Your house is on fire. Amber tried to kill us. Amber died standing up. What the hell happened?" I pointed as she looked down at her shoulder. "Oh fuck, not again." She clamped her hand on the wound to slow down the bleeding.

"Again?"

She winced. "A story for another time. Kids okay? You okay?"

"I think so, but we have to get out of here, away from the fire. I smelled gas in the house." I helped Tammy and the kids out of the car, holding Ivy in one arm, and Riley in the other. The house was burning up fast. The house I'd brought my baby girl home to, the one I wanted so desperately for us to become a family in, and this chapter of my life were being incinerated right in front of me. I thought about calling 911, but then I heard fire trucks in the distance.

The ladies from the shelter were running towards us with blankets. Shelby yelled, "I called it in when we heard the first round of gunfire. I thought it was fireworks at first. We had no idea you were inside!"

We all walked across the road together, to where it was safer. The guest room was now fully engulfed, so I couldn't see Amber, but I saw the woman in her white gown hovering near the octagon window, watching us.

I wasn't afraid of her specifically, only what she was or might stand for. The things that were beyond my control and were happening in my house and all around me. I was scared that my marriage was ending, and that something bad would happen to my kids. And even more terrified it would be at my hands or due to my negligence. I was also afraid that this woman *was* me. But she had never hurt me. In fact, she'd helped me save myself.

I looked down and saw Riley waving at the window. When I looked back up at the house, she was gone. *Where do ghosts go if they have no home?*

"Who the hell was that?" asked Tammy.

55

BREE

AUGUST 14, 2013 - SIX MONTHS LATER

That night, while we were waiting for the fire trucks to come and to be questioned by the police, I told Tammy everything I had learned about Rose Belsley. I didn't tell her everything that had happened in the house, only hearing a few noises, etc., for fear of being judged, and it was no longer my priority. Getting my kids to safety and settled and unravelling the Scaggs murder and Amber's death took precedence. Though it was clear what Amber's motives were that night, it wasn't clear who'd turned on the gas and how that door had slammed into her head. When asked, I simply said maybe it was an explosion. Even though I knew what I saw.

Now waiting for Tammy at the ferry terminal, it was hard to contain my excitement, but even more so, Riley's.

"Auntie Tammy!" Riley shouted, jumping up and down when he saw her.

She ran over and gave us both hugs. "Holy crap, you look smokin' hot, Bree!" she shouted in the arrivals lounge of the ferry terminal.

I blushed. "Um, thank you? It's amazing what sleep does. How was the trip over?"

"Fabulous, but I'm starving. Can we go to that restaurant you've been raving about?" She rubbed her hands together.

"Absolutely. Hop in." I buckled Riley in and jumped into the driver's seat.

"Remember the last time I was in this car?" She rubbed her shoulder.

"Hard to forget." We both laughed. "How is it healing?"

"Not too bad. I still don't have full mobility, but the scar gives me bragging rights at home, and some street cred." She made gang signs with her hands, and Riley giggled.

I headed towards the restaurant. "Tony is with Roxford PD now, eh? How does he like it?"

"He loves it. When the RCMP and Roxford were working together on the Bychkov and Scaggs file, he got to know them, and they poached him. It's a lot more pay, and he enjoys it. That reminds me—I brought *the envelope* from Tony." She wiggled her eyebrows. Ever since that night, Tammy has been just as interested in the history of that house as I was. I found a few more details on my own, but I'd enlisted Tony's help with finding more. "I'll dig it out at brunch. How are you liking it here?"

"It's amazing. Living with my mom isn't ideal, but it's okay for now. It's been great for the kids." I'd found a part-time job as an assistant for a real estate agent, and the cost of living was way better, as was the quality of life. "Being near the ocean again has been healing," I added.

"Well, I'm happy if you're happy, but I sure do miss having you all around."

I pulled into the parking lot of my favourite breakfast spot, The Owl Café. It wasn't much to look at from the outside, but the food was superb, and they served lattes in mugs the size of my head. We sat ourselves in the back, at the table with the most privacy. Riley loved all the owl figurines. Plus, he and Ivy were becoming local celebrities. This small town was full of older folks who loved to stop and chat with my babies. The cook cut their fruit into different animal shapes every time. Whether they ate it was a different story.

The server brought over two jumbo vanilla lattes, and Tammy and I laughed as we watched each other's faces disappear into the mugs.

"Bree, I'm thrilled for you. I'm sorry how it all went down, but now you're finally where you want to be."

"Me too. I couldn't have done it without you. I wanted to—"

"If you thank me again, I will lose my shit on you. Seriously." She had loads of foam on her upper lip. I gestured for her to wipe it off, but she waited for Riley to look at her and then licked it off with her tongue in a huge, exaggerated circle. He howled and clapped.

She leaned closer to me. "I still can't believe you brought a shard of glass to a gunfight and survived." We both laughed.

"Well, to be fair, I had some help." I winked, dying to talk about it. I grabbed a tablet and headphones out of my purse and gave it to Riley with cartoons playing. "He's over two now," I said to Tammy. "I think he understands more than I give him credit for."

"Good idea."

Riley began dancing to the theme song of *Toy Story*.

I held my coffee in both hands and took a big sip as Tammy eagerly dove in.

"Obliviously, I sat in the car, singing Barney's 'I Love You' song to the kids," Tammy said. "I did smell some smoke but assumed it was a chimney nearby. I had no clue you were embroiled in battle inside a burning house!"

"No one was more surprised to see Amber than me," I said. "The police were actively searching for her—never in a million years did I think she would actually come to my house. I'm just grateful the whole house didn't blow, and my car didn't explode."

"Tony told me they figured she turned the stove on with the intention of destroying the house and any evidence, but there were too many windows and doors open for the whole thing to blow at once. She didn't think that through."

"Nope." I thought back to the white streak racing toward Amber, slamming the door on her head, and Amber just hanging there on the iron hook in a standing position. I put down my coffee and drank some water to clear the unexpected lump in my throat. I was still coping with guilt.

"They don't know exactly how long she was in my house; it couldn't have been very long. The first shot happened minutes before we arrived, though the ladies noticed her car drive past slowly a few minutes before that." Noticed it? *Recognized* it. "Apparently, Amber used to drive past our house frequently."

Tammy's hand flew up to her mouth momentarily. "Ugh, she was a bad person. We don't have to be happy about her death, but there's no point pussyfooting around it." She leaned in and looked around. "Tony said it wasn't the first time she's done something like this."

"She burned down another house?" My voice came out louder than I'd intended.

"Not a house. Another marriage."

My throat felt tight again. "It still doesn't excuse the husbands' behaviour."

"No, it doesn't." Tammy put her hand on mine. "But that's not all I heard."

I leaned forward to listen.

"She failed her psych exam."

I scoffed. "Big surprise."

But Tammy shook her head. "She failed it more than once and was on her last extension before she was going to be suspended."

I let that sink in for a minute. "Jake never failed anything, but he was late on his too. Maybe if they'd gotten it done on time, things would have been different for him—and us."

Tammy nodded sympathetically, and we sat in silence for a minute.

"Have you heard anything else about the house?" I asked. "Is it still standing?"

"Not really. The foundation and rubble are all that's left."

I thought about Rose, wondering where she was now.

Our food arrived. When Riley looked up from his tablet and saw the fruit creation, he squealed. The waitress laughed as she set it down in front of him.

"Can't wait to dig into the envelope from Tony after we eat."

I nodded with a mouth full of eggs Benny.

"It's about the ghost in the window that night, right?"

I nearly choked at her volume. She leaned in and spoke softer.

"I didn't see what happened with Amber as I ducked down, but when we stood on the side of the road afterward, I thought I was seeing things. I'd just been shot after all, but then I saw Riley waving at her, and everything you've told me since. I still think about it."

I finished chewing. Now *I* was the one lowering my voice. This was a small town, and I didn't want anyone to think I was a nutjob. "What I haven't told you was that that wasn't the first time I saw her." I dabbed my mouth with a napkin.

As we ate, I filled Tammy in on all the incidents that had occurred in the house. Some could be excused away, and some must have been due to Amber and Bychkov. But that still left several unexplained events, along with vivid nightmares that couldn't be rationalized.

"Why didn't you say anything to me earlier?" Tammy said.

"I thought I was going crazy, and after that night, we had more important things that needed immediate attention. Before that, Jake and I were on the rocks, and I was worried he might have used this against me if we split up. I also truly didn't know what to do. And then Jake—" I teared up at the memory.

She waited for me to collect myself.

"The day you and I went to Dinotown, when I got home, Jake had a bout of what I now know was PTSD-induced psychosis. But at the time, he almost seemed possessed." I was embarrassed. It did sound crazy. "I had no clue his trauma could cause something so frightening and dangerous."

"I didn't know that either," she said softly, "and I thought I knew a lot about it."

We talked about my contacting the paranormal team and burning sage. "After I spoke with the great nephew, I contacted the museum where he donated photos and such."

"And? Did you find anything?"

"Eventually, yes. I have a couple photos." I dug around in my purse.

"You do?" Tammy waved the waitress over. "It's not too early to switch to wine, is it?"

"It's five o'clock somewhere." The server cackled and held up two fingers to confirm that we were both in.

Tammy nodded enthusiastically.

I presented her with the photographs, one of the house itself and one of the couple in front of it. "Belsley House. Taken in 1924." I pointed to the two people in the photograph. "That's Abraham and Rose."

Tammy took the photo from me and inspected it. "Is that her? It was so far away, it's hard to tell. But the house looks almost exactly the same."

"It's her. A younger, happier, healthier version of her. I'm sure of it. I've seen her close up."

The wine showed up and Tammy took a big sip. "This is terrible," she whispered.

I laughed. "It's a breakfast place. They're known for their coffee." I took a sip, wincing. "Anyway, I found other stuff on my own, too. A birth certificate and two death certificates."

"Two?"

"One woman, and one baby."

"I just got chills."

We both sipped our wine, though it was truly awful.

"The records I found show that a baby boy was born with the name Abe Jr. on October 4, 1929."

"Okay," Tammy said.

"That same baby died on October 30, 1929." I paused. "Ivy's birth-date."

Tammy gasped. "I can't even."

"When I spoke with the nephew, I assumed when he said she lost a baby, that it was a miscarriage, not a three-week-old, who passed away on my daughter's birthday. This story is so coincidental and wild. I think I'll write a book about it one day."

"Holy shit, you should. And the other death certificate, that's the woman, right? Rose?"

"Yes. She died almost exactly one year later: October 29, 1930. But there was no information on the cause of death, which is why I contacted Tony, hoping he could find out more." I glanced at Riley, but he was absorbed in his meal, still listening to his headphones. "Is it morbid that I need to know this?"

"Not at all." She picked up her gigantic aqua Kate Spade purse and rifled through the contents, pulling out an envelope. "It's kind of small." She wrinkled her nose and handed it to me.

"It's sealed? You didn't look?"

Tammy blushed. "I may have tried to peek."

I opened it and pulled out the paperwork. There was a cover letter with a sticky note on it, along with two stapled files.

Hope you are well, Bree. This was all I could find.
All the best,
Tony

```
Contents contained within included:

File #29-1514 - 30-OCT-1929 - Included - File
Report
File #30-2119 - 29-OCT-1930 - Included - File
Report
File #30-2120 - 29-OCT-1930 - Missing - The
Letter
```

File #30-2121 - 29-OCT-1930 - Omitted - Scene Photograph

30-OCT-1929

FILE #29-1514

It was a warm night for fall. Mrs. Rose Belsley had opened the window to the nursery just a crack, so the baby wouldn't overheat. She said she checked on the baby and went back into her room. She only meant to rest for a moment in the rocking chair but ended up sleeping through until morning. She said the instant she woke up she knew something was wrong. The baby typically woke three or four times a night and hadn't woken up once.

She ran quickly to the nursery, falling and injuring herself on the way. Right knee laceration documented. When she entered the room, it was ice cold. The window was still open, but it was windy, and the temperature had dropped significantly overnight. Her three-week-old baby was also ice cold

Her husband, Mr. Abraham Belsley, heard the commotion from his quarters downstairs. He made his way upstairs and saw Mrs. Belsley on the floor, holding the baby, rocking back and forth and saying, "Mama's going to warm you back up." Mr. Belsley tried to remove the baby from her arms. She thrashed and kicked him, knocking him down. He went downstairs to the phone and called us.

We were unsuccessful in retrieving the infant from her arms. We called the doctor and his team to the home. After some struggle, one of the attendants held Mrs. Belsley down and sedated her.

The baby's body was removed by the coroner, who ruled it a cot death.

I put the paper down and wiped my eyes. "Unreal."

"Is there more information?" Tammy asked. "What happened to her?"

"There's only one more police file in here."

She reached forward and grabbed the wine I wasn't drinking. "So that it doesn't go to waste."

I took a sip of water, cleared my throat, and read the form out loud.


```
29-OCTOBER-1930    TIME 0133
FILE #30-2119


We received a request to immediately
attend the Belsley residence. Mr.
Abraham Belsley said he had been
out late. When he got home, he was
surprised to see a light on in the
nursery as it had not been used in
some time.

He ran up the stairs, spotting Mrs.
Belsley on the floor right away. She
was curled into a fetal position. Her
face was discoloured, and her mouth
was outlined with froth. He touched
her neck to check for a pulse, but
there was nothing. She was cold. He
tried to move her onto her back to
```

check her belly, but her body was locked in its position.

Upon asking why he checked her stomach, he explained she was with child and hadn't been coping well.

When we interviewed Mr. Belsley, he didn't show any emotion about his wife's death, initially causing some suspicion. He did, however, have a confirmed alibi: Motel staff had witnessed him with neighbour and mistress Margaret Winslow for the majority of the evening.

"I'm sorry she is gone, but she was hysterical, institutionalized or heavily medicated for the last year of her life. I'm also very sorry the baby is gone. Margaret and I were going to raise the baby, since Rose was poorly."

It was determined that Mrs. Belsley took an excessive amount of laudanum with alcohol and overdosed. We found empty bottles of whiskey and the

```
prescriptions near her body. She was
clutching a Tom Tinker toy and lying
next to a suicide note written in what
was confirmed as her cursive, ruling
out foul play. The photo and letter
are documented and included in file.
```

"He was going to take her baby away," I said, trying to snap back to the present, though it was hard to separate myself from the story of the woman, whose circumstances were so much more like mine than I had imagined.

"I wish there was a copy of the letter," Tammy said.

"As curious as I am, I'm not sure I can handle more." My heart was broken for her. I folded the paperwork back together and tucked it into the envelope.

"What's a Tom Tinker toy, though?"

We both glanced at Riley's device. I removed his headphones.

"Mommy is going to use this for a minute, okay?" I pointed to his half-eaten fruit. "You need to finish your breakfast anyway."

He nodded and shoved an apple slice in his mouth.

We googled Tom Tinker toy, and I stared at the image that popped up. "Jake found that in the basement. It must have belonged to Abe Jr."

We returned to our breakfasts, which had gotten cold.

"Those police files are so fascinating. In some ways I think it would be cool to work for a police department," I said, "like in records or something. Evidence, maybe? Not the high-octane chases."

"Well," Tammy said. "That's my news."

My mouth hung open. "You're going to Depot? Don't do it! Seriously."

She burst out laughing and nearly spilled what was left of my gross wine. "Oh my god, I'm going to pee my pants." She snorted.

Riley started laughing. "Auntie Tammy is so funny."

After Tammy got herself under control, she said, "No, you goofball. I found out Roxford PD was looking for someone in victim services, so I applied—and I got the job. It's a short contract, but it should help me get back into university. I'm going to finish my degree in counseling."

"That's awesome. Congratulations." I got up from my seat and gave her a big hug.

"With Tony working for a municipal PD, we'll never have to transfer again."

"So, my hopes of you ever moving here are dashed?"

She laughed. "Not completely. We'll retire eventually. I think."

"We have so much to celebrate," I said.

"Maybe we should go somewhere else, though. This wine is seriously disgusting. Why does it taste like potatoes?" She polished the rest off in one gulp.

Jake walked into the café with Ivy in his arms. He was smiling warmly, and there was fresh ice cream on Ivy's face. I took Ivy from him, wiping her chin. Jake had ice cream on his face too.

I laughed. "Like father, like daughter."

Jake wiped his face off and kissed me. "Ivy, say hi to Tammy."

Ivy waved at her.

"She's gotten so big." Tammy waved back.

"She'll be one soon," Jake said. "It's good to see you, Tammy."

"You too. Your ear looks like it's healed nicely. How's your hearing?"

"Getting better." He smiled and pointed to a small hearing aid tucked inside the remaining portion of his ear. He'd lost approximately half of the appendage from the shot and subsequent surgery.

He sat down and gave Riley a fist bump—their new thing.

"You ladies all caught up?" He pointed to the wine and envelope. "What's all this?"

Tammy started to speak but was interrupted by the waitress, who arrived to take Jake's order. "Would you like a glass of wine too?"

"No thanks; I don't drink. I'd love an Americano to go."

She smiled and scurried away to fulfill his order.

Jake turned back to us. "We have to get going. Me and the kiddos. I promised your mom I'd cook dinner tonight, and I can't flake out."

"He's trying to get into her good books," I explained to Tammy.

"Yeah, and I still have a long way to go."

"You sure you don't want to stay?" Tammy said. "It would be great to chat."

When I'd decided to stay with Jake, Tammy had been one hundred percent supportive. At first, I stayed to take care of him while he healed, and then it was because of the improvement I saw in his behaviour. We still had a long road ahead, especially where trust was concerned, but I knew I would stay as long as he kept making an effort.

"Tony sent over some interesting information," I said.

Jake poked at the envelope. "What kind of information?"

"The history of our Roxford house. Tony sent along some archived police files I requested." I widened my eyes. "There was a lot going on in there."

He put up both hands in mock surrender. "Thank you, ladies, but I'm going to pass. I'm sure whatever is in there is fascinating, but real ghosts are the least of my problems. I've been haunted enough." He laughed.

"Fair enough," Tammy said.

"Now, I have to go. I have a date with a mother-in-law who doesn't appreciate tardiness, plus Lottie is waiting leashed up outside. I hope you guys have a rip-snorting night of laughter. I'll see you when you get home, Bree. Have a great time. And Tammy, tell Tony I say hi, and please thank him again for his help getting me here after the treatment centre."

Not long after Jake had been discharged from the hospital, he'd spent three months at a rehabilitation centre back east for first responders with complex PTSD. He was put on desk duty at his new detachment for the foreseeable future. It was an office job, but it was a job, and we were happy. Or at least getting there. He and his new psychologist would decide when and if the time was right for him to return to general duty.

I wanted the best for him, but I hoped he never went back. Even though this town was much smaller and safer than Burner, all police officers saw shit no one should ever have to see.

"Okay, hon. Want me to help you get the kids loaded up?" I asked out of habit.

"No, I got this. You guys go have a blast." He grabbed Ivy and held her close as he blew a raspberry in her neck. Then he leaned down and did the same thing to me. We laughed, and he gave me a proper kiss. He unbuckled Riley from his highchair, and Riley walked alongside him as they grabbed his Americano on the way out. They all turned to wave before they untied Lottie and walked away.

I still got scared whenever things seemed too good to be true, but my heart didn't ache as much, and my body wasn't so heavy. Jake wasn't the same man I'd married, but I was starting to love this version of him even more.

If you are struggling with mental health, please reach out; you are loved and worthy of love.

Canada

Suicide Crisis Line ~ 988

Veterans Affairs Canada ~ 1-866-522-2122

Postpartum Support ~ 1-800-944-4773

United States

Suicide Crisis Line ~ 988

Veterans Affairs ~ 1-800-827-1000

Talking Postpartum Depression ~ 1-833-852-6262

Acknowledgments

The story of Bree and Jake has lived inside me much longer than outside; this is pretty surreal. I have had so much encouragement and input along the way. Bear with me.

First, I want to thank my kids for being the best cheering squad, for squealing when I squealed, and for bringing me coffee and a hug when I needed a boost. And to my talented, creative husband for helping me get out of my own way and insisting I just sit my butt down to write. I would not have finished this book without your love and support. Though I know sometimes you *all* want me to stop talking about books, you still listen and help. You three are my reasons and my everything.

Next, I must thank my parents for letting me read books wildly inappropriate for my insatiably curious young mind. I went from reading Sweet Valley Twins to Christopher Pike, Dean Koontz, and Stephen King. Books inspired me from such an early age, providing windows into other worlds. Not only did I love the stories themselves and the way they were told, but how they transported me to other lands, times, and realities. I always knew I wanted to write, too.

The concept for Every Fall came from the idea that being haunted by actual ghosts is far less frightening than the haunting that accompanies PTSD, PPD and other trauma. It inappropriately tickled my funny bone but screamed at my heart to write about it.

Having first-hand experience with inadequately addressed PPD, I wrote about it for the first time right before drafting this book. It turned into an unexpected healing process that I owe in large part to the Doula Support Foundation, the wonderful women who run it, and their birth story contest. It gave me the confidence to write again and a place to begin to heal.

Inspiration also came from my marriage to a police officer and my astonishment at the resilience of these men and women doing what most people won't, time and time again, usually thankless and sometimes even hated for it. The humanity behind the uniform needs more care and kindness. I have been privileged to call many of them friends, and *they* are not *their* job.

While this book is purely fictional, a couple of character traits come from some fantastic folks. Dr. Bell is named after the late Cpl. Chris Bell, who in real life was a good friend to my husband when he needed it, we miss you. The other character, Tammy, my absolute favourite, is made from a compilation of women who came into my life while trying to navigate *the darkness* alone. Tammy was right when she said these spouses may not know each other but would do anything for one another; I've seen it in action. *Janet, Erin, Stephanie, Margaret, Krista, Rachel, and Tricia, you are all Tammy.*

Now, to my incredible early readers and biggest champions: my mom and sisters, Tracy and Kimberly, my life-long friends Morgan and Stephanie, and other keen-eyed beta readers, Katherine, Char, and Brenda. Reading a book in its uglier stages isn't for the faint of heart, and the enthusiasm and comments you added throughout helped shape it.

This writing community is large but tight-knit. As a member of many writing organizations, ITW, CWC, SINC, SINC-CW, WFWA, TWUC, and FBCW, I have had the joy of learning from, talking to and gleaning snippets of valuable advice from so many authors I admire. I want to say a huge thank you to Alex Finlay, Robyn Harding, Jennifer Hillier and Wendy Walker for your advice and kind words along the way, it has meant so much to me. From this community I have also gained encouraging writer friends with whom I love chatting about writing and brunching—Meaghan, Faye, and Katherine.

Somewhere along the way, my freelance editor Michelle Barker became a friend and part of my process. The way you edit and provide feedback is a masterclass in helping without hurting. I am eternally grateful for all the extra advice and for answering my endless questions.

The talented Nat Mack created this striking cover; it jumps off the shelf and encapsulates a book that blends genres.

Alex and Tina! This dynamic duo is also known as Rising Action Publishing. Thank you from the bottom of my black heart for taking a chance on me and putting this book out into the world. Not only have you given me this incredible, childhood-dream-come-true opportunity, but you saw and restored Every Fall to my original vision without even knowing it. I am so proud of it and to be one of your authors. Thank you.

Last but not least, I will always be a reader before a writer, devouring as many books as I can for the rest of my life. Like with any addiction, I have suppliers and some of the best ones are found on the Psychological Thriller Readers FB Page. You have made me laugh, helped me find comparable titles, and assisted in draining my bank account while filling my library.

To everyone who read this book, thank you so much for taking the time to do so; I hope you enjoyed it as much as I enjoyed writing it. Watch for my next book, *The Bone Trail*, will be released in June 2026.

ABOUT THE AUTHOR

Angela Douglas is a Canadian author who lives in the Okanagan region of British Columbia with her husband and kids. She writes thrillers and creative non-fiction. When she isn't working or hanging out with her family, she hides in her studio with her bulldog, Frankie, writing her next book. She is a member of International Thriller Writers, Crime Writers of Canada, and is the VP of Communications of Sisters in Crime—Canada West.

SNEAK PEEK OF THE BONE TRAIL, RELEASING JUNE 23, 2026.

Jolene Chapman travels the world to run from her past. That is, until she receives the call to return to a place that existed only in her memory and worst nightmares: Mudshark Bay, the now defunct logging camp she grew up in.

She reluctantly returned to the camp to collect personal effects and witness the move of a mobile home she inherited from her ailing father, Glenn. However, when the trailer is moved, bones are discovered under her childhood home, untouched for an estimated twenty years. Jolene and the others—her sister, estranged mother, and various unsavory folk from their past—aren't going anywhere while the barge containing the trailer is held until the police arrive.

As the police begin to suspect the bones belong to a missing teenager from the neighbouring village where Jolene attended school, it brings up the unbearable childhood memories she is trying to avoid. Evidence of homicide points to the Chapmans, Glenn in particular, and although Jolene is dying to get out of there, she is forced to look at herself and her past. She is the only one who believes in her father's innocence and can save his name by doing something she swore she would never do: return to Qlakwan.

Chapter 1 - Jolene - Summer 2008

I missed my dad. He would have loved it here. He wasn't dead, but he might as well have been. I couldn't help but think about him as I watched the sunrise over the Andes. I should have been able to enjoy the moment, but I couldn't shake this terrible feeling roiling deep in my gut.

Gut discomfort aside, it had been a while since I had seen anything so beautiful—not for many years, anyway. Watching the sun slowly peek out between the mountains in complete isolation relaxed me in a way I didn't often experience.

I inhaled deeply, closed my eyes, and popped them right back open. I have tried to meditate a billion times during yoga, but as soon as my eyes shut, they dart back and forth with thoughts racing through my mind. Stupid thoughts like, do other people have their eyes open? Can anyone see me? Do I look like a psycho with my shaky breathing and uncontrollable eye movements? Of course, I tried again when alone, but then I laughed at my foolishness. I couldn't accept peace, or maybe I was too afraid to let my thoughts wander.

When nature overwhelmed my idiotic brain in rare places and moments like this, I could finally breathe—inhale deep breaths, drink in the silence. Despite being a popular tourist attraction, not many people hike up to Machu Picchu at dawn in the off-season—one of the many perks of my flight attendant job.

I'm sure my parents weren't impressed that after four years and thousands of dollars of debt, I left university one semester early for this job and never returned. My anthropology and cultural studies education was now only used to enhance my travel and *Jeopardy* skills. I used to have big plans and wanted more from myself, academically, but this job was all I could handle, and it was paying down the loans in the meantime. If they were disappointed, they never said so and didn't have the right to anyway.

The mountain peak to my right felt so familiar that I felt a strong sense of déjà vu, followed by rapid-fire visceral memories and heart palpitations. I squeezed my eyes shut, but they shot back open when I heard my name. "Jolene, are you ready to go?"

Julio was the gorgeous solo guide of this Lares trail trek—well, he and the sweet alpaca that had been carrying our gear for the last few days. We had to head down to the village to catch the train on time. As this was the last day of the trip, I wanted to make it to the Aguas Calientes hot springs before flying home.

"Yes, of course," I said, standing up and brushing the dirt off the seat of my cargo pants.

Everyone thinks hiking down is easy, but it's not. Despite having to chew cocoa leaves constantly to make it up to the peak, going down was rough on my thirty-year-old knees.

We made it to the train on time and went straight to the hotel to clean up. After five days of hiking the Lares trek, I was dirty, smelly, and repulsive. I looked forward to the longest, hottest shower of my life until I remembered that hot water was scarce where I was.

Don't get me wrong—I was grateful for any water, but I looked forward to my Western comforts at home. I plugged in my dead phone and jumped in, using the warmest three minutes to scrub off the first layer of dirt. After that, I was 'as good as I would get' at that temperature. I reached for a towel and noticed my phone going off nonstop. I must have had it on silent.

"I'm coming, I'm coming," I said to no one. I missed the call—and, by the looks of it, at least a dozen more. A text across the screen caught my eye. I hadn't spoken to *her* in years.

Call me. Or Ruby. ASAP.

It was my mom.

###

I dabbed myself off with the thin cloth the hotel passed off as a bath towel and threw on the cleanest item of clothing I could find. I had laundry to do.

I sat there for a few moments, knowing I had to call, but was unable to do so. I hadn't talked to my mother in years. She had called me a couple of times, but only butt dials and messages of odd drunken rambling. We were never that close, but we completely drifted apart a few years after my parents' divorce when I left for university. *Why the hell is she calling?* It couldn't be about my sister Ruby, since she mentioned her in the text, and I doubted it was about my dad. I didn't think they had contact, or I hoped not.

I took a deep, ragged breath and dialled. The phone just crackled and didn't connect, so I pulled out my trusty phone card and used the landline to call through the operator.

"Hello." There it was, that familiar slurred speech.

"Mom? Is everything okay?"

"I can't come to the phone right now; you know what to do." I heard a cough and then the beep tone to leave a voicemail. It was too late to hang up without being charged.

"It's me, er, Jolene. I am in cell range now. Call me back."

I left the receiver on my shoulder as I hung up and dialled Ruby, who answered immediately.

"Jolene—you're alive? I have been trying to reach you for days!"

"Sorry, I was in the mountains, no cell service; I'm in–"

"Yeah, yeah, somewhere awesome, I get it." Her tone lightened slightly, though I could picture her rolling her eyes.

"So what's the problem? Is everything alright? Is it Dad? Why would Cindy call me?"

"Dad's fine. Mom called you?"

"Yep. And texted."

"Weird, maybe she got a letter too. She hasn't called me, not that I would answer." She laughed.

"A letter? About what?"

"Sister, you better sit down for this one."

"Stop being so dramatic and spit it out," I said, standing up out of spite, annoyed that I was paying by the minute.

She paused and cleared her throat, "Mudshark Bay was purchased by another logging company."

"Yeah, so? Big deal. What does this have to do with us?" Just hearing the name made me uncomfortable.

"Well, we received a letter to come and get our things, pack up the trailer, and move it."

I sat down. My heart sped up, and my vision fell in and out of focus. I thought I was done with that place when we left twenty years ago.

"What stuff? And move the trailer? We owned that piece of crap?" Our father went into a home two years ago when dementia took hold. At no time in the last two decades since we left the logging camp had he said we left anything up there, nor did he say we owned the mobile home we lived in for a few years in the late eighties. Some of my worst memories were in and around that trailer and the now-defunct camp that no longer exists outside my mind.

"I know, right? I was floored when I got the letter. I thought it was junk mail. Like, why would this new logging company be sending us anything?"

"Uh huh." I managed.

"So, obviously, I opened it up. It was addressed to Dad and Mom; she must have also gotten a copy of the letter. It plainly states that they had purchased Mudshark Bay logging camp and its equipment from the former Forrester and that anyone who owned something there had 30 days to remove it. I will email you a copy of the letter when we hang up. It lists a mobile home registration number, with a hand-drawn map of the lower camp and a circle around it. Looks like a two-year-old drew it, but it's ours."

"Wow. I don't even know what to say. Why would they have bought it in the first place? And why would they have left it there?"

"I have no clue; I was young when we left and didn't know anything about what they did and why. Well, I still don't." She snickered. "Do you really think there is stuff left inside? And what?"

A knock at the hotel room door jerked me from my fog.

"Miss Jolene, it's time to go. We leave in five minutes," Julio said while peeking through a crack in the curtains, looking damp and hotter than ever.

I gave him a wave and a thumbs up, and he left.

"When did you get the letter, Ruby?"

"A few days ago."

"Oh good, we have some time to figure this out. We can probably get someone else to deal with it."

"Well, the letter sat for a while. We have two weeks left and must do it ourselves, something to do with insurance." She clucked her tongue.

"Why? Jesus. I don't want to go back there. I don't think I can." My throat tightened. "We kind of have to. Obviously, Dad wanted us to have the trailer or its contents. We need to go." She paused and said in a cheerier tone, "It could be fun. When can you be back?"

"I'm due to fly home tomorrow. I will look at my schedule to see where work is sending me next and what I can do about time off; I'm not sure I–"

"This is important. I wasn't going to say anything over the phone, but the last time I saw Dad, I showed him the letter, and he became agitated when I asked him. He kept saying you all have to go; then he rambled on nonsensically. He remembered for a second and then was back to forgetting."

I didn't have time for this. "I'll see you late tomorrow night, and we can discuss what to do then. I have to go." I told her I loved her and hung up.

Fun?! That place almost ruined me as a child; I don't know how I can go back. The mixture of happy memories in the beginning, running wild in nature, and the torture that followed has taken me years to stuff away. Ruby is lucky she doesn't remember much; nothing awful happened *to her.*

I slapped my cold, wet hair into a messy bun and headed for the lobby to meet Julio. A few drinks and a dip in the hot springs with a hunk should take my mind off this mess. For now.

Looking for more chills? Check out Rising Action's upcoming thrillers on the next page!

And don't forget to follow us on our socials for cover reveals, giveaways, and announcements:
X: @RAPubCollective
Instagram: @risingactionpublishingco
TikTok: @risingactionpublishingco
Website: http://www.risingactionpublishingco.com

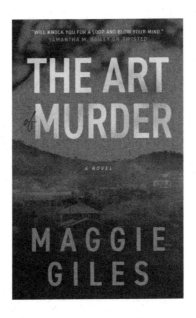

THE ART
of MURDER

A NOVEL

MAGGIE
GILES

In the tranquil town of Cedar Plains, where safety and community are sacred, Courtney Faith's ideal life is upended by a body found on a local farm, shattering her peaceful existence. Her friend, Alexa Huston, intimately familiar with chaos, gets entangled in an accidental murder that escalates her spiraling life into deeper darkness. Alexa wrestles with a disturbing question: Is murder justifiable if it targets the deserving?

As bodies accumulate, the local police scramble for answers. Torn between loyalty and justice, Courtney discovers evidence linking Alexa to the crimes. Their friendship frays as Courtney grapples with a dire choice: expose Alexa and risk her own darkest secret, or protect a friend and possibly destroy everything she cherishes.

In Cedar Plains, some truths are too perilous to unearth. Caught in a deadly dance of secrets and lies, Courtney must decide whether to confront the monster behind a familiar face or let their secrets stay hidden, buried within the town's heart. Their darkest deeds are cloaked in silence, and no one truly knows anything.

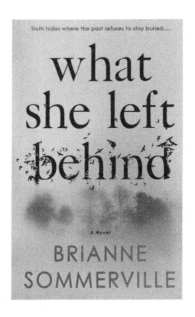

Truth hides where the past refuses to stay buried....

what she left behind

A Novel

BRIANNE
SOMMERVILLE

Recently fired and adrift, Charlotte Boyd agrees to oversee renovations on her parents' small-town summer home that holds a tragic past. After discovering an enthralling diary hidden amidst junk the previous owners left behind, Charlotte connects with the author—a troubled teen named Lark Peters who died by suicide at the house sixteen years ago.

When an unsettling incident forces Charlotte to seek refuge at the local pub, regulars, including the police, warn her of Lark's older brother, Darryl, who has become a recluse since Lark's death, and may know more than he's letting on. But Charlotte sees a side of Darryl others don't, being an outsider herself.

In a search to uncover the truth, Charlotte must question those closest to Lark and reconcile her own past trauma. Because if Lark was actually murdered, then whoever is responsible might be lurking in Charlotte's own backyard.

Releasing Aug 12, 2025

Mae Roberts is certain her new life in the suburbs with her family will be everything she's always wanted. That is, until one of the mothers from her daughters' school goes missing.

Mae never thought she would fit in amongst the beautiful and rich mothers at Riverpark Elementary. Though, when she's accepted into their clique and they ask her to be a part of their unofficial neighborhood watch, Mae finds herself slipping more and more into a world of odd dinner parties, secrets and lies, and even rumors of suicide attempts.

It's only when one of the Riverpark Moms disappears, and then another, that Mae must decide what's more important—fitting in or uncovering the truth.

A fresh take on belonging, obsession and schoolyard politics, Burlington is a domestic suspense that delves into the realities of parenthood and fitting in, and the roles we're sometimes forced to take.